LJ BURKHART

A Blaze in the Shadows

Realm of Queridian: Book 2

Contents

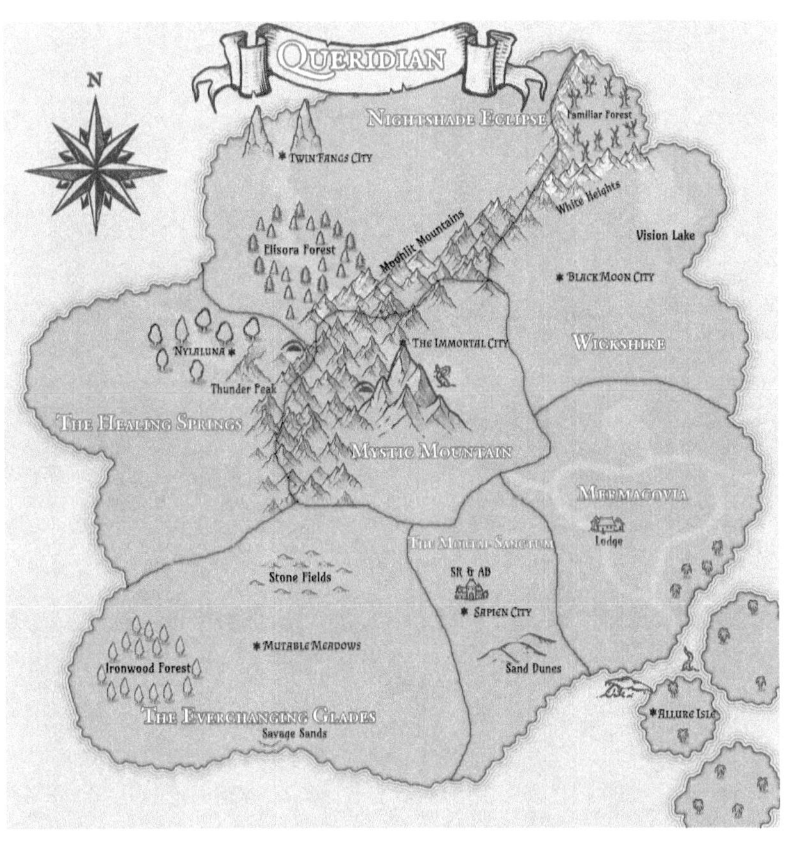

N
QUERIDIAN
NIGHTSHADE ECLIPSE
Familiar Forest
TWIN FANGS CITY
White Heights
Vision Lake
Elisora Forest
Moonlit Mountains
BLACK MOON CITY
NYLALUNA
THE IMMORTAL CITY
WICKSHIRE
Thunder Peak
THE HEALING SPRINGS
MYSTIC MOUNTAIN
MERMACOVIA
Lodge
THE MORTAL SANCTUM
Stone Fields
SR & AB
SAPIEN CITY
MUTABLE MEADOWS
Ironwood Forest
Sand Dunes
ALLURE ISLE
THE EVERCHANGING GLADES
Savage Sands

1

Ember

I fly up to the palace, landing in the gardens where Alexei kidnapped me. The sight is painful, but this is one of the places that I'm fairly certain won't have guests milling about. I should be able to find a servant to fetch my father. I also need to shift back into a human, but I'm not sure how to do it.

I start with closing my eyes and taking a deep breath. I focus on the fact that I want to walk and talk to my father. The urgency behind that need hits me strongly, and a sob escapes me. I open my eyes to see that I'm back in my body, and my knives, crown, and gown are all still in place, although my clothing is not in the best shape.

I walk along the shadows, not wanting to be spotted. I don't see anyone, but I want to be on the safe side. How ridiculous would it be only hours after I was introduced to the kingdom of Queridian, that their beloved new princess was found in this state. I can only imagine how that would go down.

I head up to the library instead of the entrance that leads to the ballroom. As soon as I enter, the smell hits me, and I nearly sag in relief. *I'm safe. I'm alive.* I repeat that to myself like a mantra as I head for the door. I need to find Humphrey, or someone who can find my father. It's too bad there aren't cell phones here. It would be so much easier if I could just text him to come and meet me.

I inch the door open, equally relieved and frustrated when I don't see anyone. I wait a few moments, hoping that a servant will walk by, but when no one does, I sigh, leaving my sanctuary. Looks like I'll need to hunt someone down. I duck and dart around corners. I'm probably being a little silly and over-the-top, but it feels necessary to me.

I get closer to the party, and look for the servants' quarters. I know they have hallways and such, every castle and palace does, even on Earth. Servants have always meant not to be seen. I roll my eyes at the absurdity.

I spot a door that looks like it's exactly what I need. I hear people milling about around the corner, and I hastily duck inside the doorway. I turn around to discover that I was indeed correct.

I'm about to wander farther down the hallway, but just then, Humphrey comes into view, and I almost sob with relief.

"Humphrey!"

He whips his head toward me before his eyes widen in shock. "Princess! Are you all right? What happened?"

"Can you get my father for me? I need to talk to him. It's urgent."

"Yes, of course."

"Will you have him meet me in the library?"

He nods.

"And is there a way that I can get there in these back hallways? I don't want to bump into any guests."

"Wait here, Your Highness. I will have someone retrieve your father, and then I will escort you back."

I nod, but don't speak. I'm extremely grateful he's going to help me. I'm skittish and don't feel like being by myself after everything that's happened. And even though I know I'm going to have trust issues with everyone in the castle except my father after Alexei's betrayal, I know that Humphrey is loyal to him and wouldn't risk me like that. He returns moments later and gestures a hand forward.

"Lead the way, Humphrey. I don't know where I'm going," I remind him, but I also don't want him behind me. I might have a tentative trust for him, but that doesn't mean I'm comfortable not being able to see him.

He nods, seeming to understand, and heads off. I follow closely behind him, and when we arrive at the library from a different door, I collapse into the chair by the fireplace.

"Would you like me to get a fire going?"

"Yes please." Now that the threat has passed, I think I'm in shock. My body is shaking, and I feel cold down to my very bones. I dazedly wonder if I'll ever be warm again.

Soon, a fire roars to life beside me. As I'm extending my hands toward it, the door opens and my father enters. His eyes meet mine, concern already evident in his gaze, but as soon as he spots me it magnifies, followed by rage and confusion.

"Ember, what the hell happened?! Are you okay?" He rushes over and wraps me in his strong arms.

That small touch is enough to send my barely leashed emotions hurtling over the edge. I break down into sobs, burying my face in his chest. In the back of my mind, I know I'm ruining his incredibly expensive and lavish clothing, but when his arms tighten even further around me, I know he doesn't care.

He doesn't press or ask me what happened again, simply lets me fall apart. I don't know how long we stand there like that, it could be minutes or hours for all I know, but eventually my tears slow, and I'm able to breathe normally again.

I pull away, and he does the same, but still keeps his hands on my shoulders as he looks down at me.

"What happened, daughter? Who do I need to kill?" I've never heard anyone sound so lethal and gentle at the same time.

I take a deep breath, steeling myself. I just need to get through this, and then I won't have to talk about it again. I already figured out what I was going to tell him on my flight back here.

"You don't need to kill anyone. I already did that." His brows rise in surprise and pride. "Alexei and I took a walk in the gardens earlier to take a break from the party and get some fresh air, and the next thing I know, we were both drugged. I woke in the forest, tied to a tree with Alexei strapped to the one next to me."

"Who?" The rage in his voice is barely contained.

I swallow nervously. He's not going to take this well. "Mordecai."

Disbelief, anger, and hurt flare in his eyes, but he nods at me to continue.

"When I woke, he had a knife." I break his gaze as the remembered feeling of cold dread once again seeps through my body. "He told me that he needed to kill me. That he heard a prophecy before I was born about how I would be the end of the fae reign. He thought he was doing the realm a kindness."

His jaw keeps clenching with every word out of my mouth, and his hands are forming fists at his sides. If only he knew how much more was going to come out of my mouth.

"Alexei tried to talk sense into him, but he wouldn't listen. Alexei was completely incapacitated and could do nothing to help me." I don't know why I'm defending Alexei so much right now. Probably because of the murderous rage written all over my father's face. I don't want that pointed toward my mate in any way. Even if I hate him. *Not my mate*, I remind myself.

"Mordecai said that you would think I was just one of the disappearances happening around the realm, and that you'd never know it was him, before he stabbed me in the chest."

My father's eyes widen almost comically before they drift down my chest. I swear I see red spark in them at the sight of the evidence of my words. He closes his eyes, and when he speaks, his words are clipped. "How did you survive?"

"I didn't, technically."

His eyes pop open at that, confusion and soul-deep fear swimming in them.

"I died. I saw my mothers. They told me that I was destined for more. That the realm needed me and that I had to go back. My body healed itself."

"How is this possible?"

"Apparently I have elf blood." I sigh and shake my head, still coming to terms with everything that happened. "In fact, I have the blood of every species in the realm. And I contain all of the powers."

A sharp inhale is his only response.

"When I came to, I discovered all this. Each power awakened inside me one by one. I was able to use air and fire to aid me, hindering Mordecai before he was able to kill Alexei, and then my mermaid abilities manifested. I persuaded Mordecai to tell me everything he'd done." I drop my eyes again. This might be the hardest thing to tell him. I have to swallow multiple times to get past the lump in my throat.

"What is it, Ember?"

I meet his eyes, and I know mine are shining with sympathy for him. I wish I could bring Mordecai back just to kill him all over again. "He did some horrible things. He hindered you from having a child. Said he acquired a tonic from someone to prevent you and the late queen from being able to conceive. He couldn't tell me who was helping him, though, believe me, I tried to get it out of him. He also murdered people." I can tell he's holding his breath, tears already swimming in his eyes. "Your parents. And the queen."

His breath leaves him in a whoosh. I relax slightly. That was the worst of what I had to say.

"Finish your story, daughter," he says when he's composed himself.

"I saw a vision of what was going to happen next, and it came true."

"What was it?"

"Me burning Mordecai alive, and then teletraveling behind him so I could slit his throat."

He smiles in vengeful glee. I was a little worried that he would think differently of me, but he's delighted that I killed him in such a gruesome manner.

"And then? You said all the species. Did you shift as well?"

I nod. "Into an owl. A purple one. I flew back to the castle."

"Where's Alexei?"

My heart rate increases. I don't want to talk about him, but I can't be obvious about that. "He brought the horses and wagon back. He might be back by now."

He nods. "Should we go find him?"

I reluctantly nod. I don't want to, but I don't really have a choice. Plus, my room is near his. Hmm. I'll have to change that. I don't want to see him more than absolutely necessary.

"Before we go, I just want to tell you that I'm so immensely sorry that this all happened to you. I feel incredibly guilty that because you came here and are my daughter this happened to you. I trusted Mordecai when I clearly shouldn't have, and you paid the price."

I stop him talking and wrap my arms around him. "It's not your fault. He betrayed your trust. There's no way you could've known. It's okay. I'm just so thankful that we're both here and safe."

His arms tighten around me, and I almost break down again, but I pull away. "Let's go. I'm ready for bed."

He nods before leading me out of the library.

2

Alexei

I watch Ember fly off into the night, and feel like it's the last I'll see of her. I know that's not true, and that she'll be at the castle when I return, but I know she'll never look at me the same way again. I can't believe this got so complicated and, let's face it, absolutely fucked.

I look down at the ashes of my father and can't help but be relieved that he's dead. He's the one who caused all of this from the beginning. He's why I felt so conflicted. He's why I betrayed Ember. My next breath gets stuck in my lungs, causing a sharp pain between my ribs. I betrayed Ember. It wasn't supposed to be like this. We were supposed to go back to Earth, forget about this realm, and finally *be* together. It was the only way it would've worked between us.

But now she can't even look at me. She's my fucking *mate*, and she won't let me near her. Not that I blame her in the slightest. All of this is my own doing, and I have no one to blame but myself. Especially since my father is now dead. I look down at the mark on my wrist, tracing it reverently with my thumb as a tear glides down my cheek. Such a gift, the mate bond, but one that I squandered.

I decide then and there that even if she never lets me near her again, I will make this up to her. I will do whatever it takes, give her whatever she wants, do what's in *her* best interest, even if that means staying away from her when she wants me to. Whatever it takes. I will do it.

I get back in the open wagon we brought Ember in, and I turn around and head back to the palace. I don't know what Ember is going to tell the king, but at least it sounds like she's not going to tell him of my involvement in her capture, which is much more than I deserve.

When I finally make my way through the gates, others are leaving, most likely from the ball. Gods, it seems like days have passed, rather than hours, and I can't believe that the ball is still going on. I leave the horses and wagon with the stable boy and take off in the direction of the ballroom. I have no clue where she'll have gone, but I start here, looking for signs of her, her father, or Pearl.

The king is nowhere in sight when I enter, neither is Ember, and I'm betting they're together. There are still quite a few people dancing and enjoying the night, Pearl included. I see her in a far corner of the room, talking animatedly with the new mimic ambassador. They're tucked in close to one another, drinking, smiling, and flirting. Pearl's skin is lit up in her happiness, and a flare of jealousy ignites in me that they can be together with no problems.

I rush over to her. "Pearl! Have you seen Ember?" I ask, trying to remain calm, even though I'm panicking.

"No, not for an hour or two at least. Is everything okay?"

"Something's happened. I need to find her."

She gives me a worried look, telling her companion that she'll see him later. We take off to Ember's room.

"What happened?"

"A lot. Have you seen the king?"

"He was at the ball, but he disappeared maybe fifteen minutes ago?"

Ember must have had a servant get him so she wouldn't cause a scene with her appearance in front of the kingdom. Smart girl. Well, now we know that Stavros is with her. We check her room, but I was already sure that she wouldn't be here, and am not surprised to find it empty.

"She's with Stavros," I tell Pearl.

"Alexei, what happened?"

I stall, not knowing what to tell her. I don't want my story to conflict with Ember's. I'm going to let her tell everyone whatever she chooses, and I will simply go along with it, but I'm wondering if I won't get that chance here. Just as I'm about to open my mouth, Stavros and Ember come around the corner, clearly heading to Ember's room.

"Oh, Ember! Thank the Gods. Alexei told me that something happened, and we've been looking for you," Pearl says in a rush, running up to give her a hug. It's then that she notices the state of Ember's clothing. "Oh my Gods, what happened?! Are you okay?"

Ember looks at me, and I can see the question in her eyes. Did I tell her anything? I subtly shake my head. She looks relieved for a second before hardening her features and turning away, making my heart ache.

Ember tells Pearl what happened, omitting the fact that I was involved in her capture, instead saying that Mordecai kidnapped both of us, and I woke up tied to the tree, helpless and unable to aid her. When she gestures to the cut in her dress, right in the center of her chest, the absolute helplessness and dread that I felt when he stabbed her all comes rushing back. I clutch my chest as the pain of that moment closes in on me again. The king is a stone beside her, and I know that he's already heard all of this.

"When it was all over, I freed Alexei." I wonder if anyone else can hear the way she says my name with such disdain, or just me? "And then shifted and flew here."

Pearl just stares at her with her mouth hanging open. It takes a lot to stun her silent, but apparently Ember has done it. I can't blame her. It's an incredible story, and if I hadn't been there to witness it all, I would react the same way. The first thing she does is inspect Ember's chest, as if to make sure she's actually okay, even though she's standing right in front of us.

"You almost died?" she asks, her voice breaking as tears build in her eyes.

"Technically, I *did* die. I was just able to heal myself and come back."

Pearl wraps her in her arms, and the two women have a moment. Stavros and I stand there awkwardly, feeling like we're intruding. They break apart, and the dried blood from Ember's dress flakes off and gets all over Pearl's white one, but neither woman seems to care.

Ember looks at the king. "I was thinking that since I'm going to be here permanently, that maybe it's time to move into the royal wing with you?" she asks.

Disappointment shoots through me, making my stomach sink like a stone. I know exactly why she's doing this, and while I'm devastated, I understand. I keep my face a blank mask, and Stavros's eyebrows shoot up in surprise.

"Are you sure that's what you want?" he asks, looking at me and Pearl, no doubt wondering why she doesn't want to be around the only friends she has here.

"I'm sure. I would like to be close to you, and that's where a princess would normally stay, I'm assuming? I think it's time now that we've told the kingdom."

"Of course. I'll let Humphrey know, and we can get you all moved over there in the morning. I think you'll be very happy with the accommodations. While it's comfortable in this part of the castle, the royal wing is extravagant."

She smiles at him, but it doesn't reach her eyes, and I can see how tired she is. It takes everything in me not to go to her and pull her into my arms. It's in our nature to comfort our mate, and the fact that I can't is killing me. It's going to be about a hundred times harder to stay away from her than it was before.

"Can't wait to see it. But on that note, I'm exhausted, and in extreme need of a shower," she says, essentially dismissing us all.

"Let me know if you need anything, okay? I'm right across the hall, and I'll keep an ear out for you," Pearl says. Ember nods before heading into her room, closing the door gently behind her.

"Look out for her, won't you, Alexei?" the king asks me.

"Of course, Your Majesty," I reply, bowing. I can't help but let the guilt eat me up inside. I was supposed to be looking after her this whole time, and instead, I'm the reason she's in this mess. He leaves, and before Pearl can start questioning me, I head to my own room.

I go straight to the bathroom to take a shower. I need to wash this night off me, including the blood of my father. A mixture of emotions comes to life inside me—anger, betrayal, hurt, relief, sadness. Even though he was a horrid man, he was still my father. And even though we weren't close, and he was rarely there for me, there were some good times that we had. Like the story I told Ember the other night.

Memories of that night surface, and I'm unable to push them back. It felt so right to hold her all night, comforting her in the wake of her nightmare. I know that she felt truly safe with me, and the fact that might never be the case again cuts deep.

Then there's my guard position. I've betrayed my sole purpose in this realm, protecting others. Although, before I knew the truth, I thought I *was* acting in the best interest of the kingdom. My father told me that Ember was going to be the end of the fae reign, and the thought made me panic. But what if that's not a bad thing? What if the end of the fae reign brings the change we need to our realm?

As I stand under the hot stream of water, I question my entire life, and the weight of the world crashes down around me. Everything is changing, and I struggle to determine my next course of action.

The panic consumes me, and it's difficult to breathe or even stand upright. I sink down into a squat as I try to stop trembling. I put my head in between my knees and take deep, even breaths. Finally, the shaking stops, and I don't have to focus so hard on getting air in and out. I stand, and with it comes clarity.

One thing is clear to me. I'm no longer comfortable keeping my role as royal guardian. It feels false now, like if I kept it I would be lying to everyone. I'm going to tell the king tomorrow, and hopefully he can direct me on what else I can do here. Mind made up, I turn the water off and collapse into bed.

The next morning, I wake early and try to find the king before he meets Ember for breakfast. I catch him just as he's leaving his wing of the palace.

"Sire, I was hoping to speak with you for a moment?"

"Of course, my boy. What can I help you with?"

I take a deep breath as nerves bubble in my stomach. "I no longer wish to be a royal guard."

His eyes widen in surprise. "Why not?"

I swallow. I can't exactly tell him the main reason, but I can give him a different one that I've also been thinking about. "With what happened with my father, I wasn't able to protect Ember. Or the realm for that matter. It was *she* who did that. She was the one who freed us and killed my father. I wasn't able to do anything. Not to mention that my father was your *advisor.* He should have been doing everything in his power to protect this kingdom, realm, along with you and your family. Instead he did the exact opposite, taking advantage of his position and power. Killing all those who mattered most to you," I say quietly, emotion rising in my chest and throat.

I can't believe he did those things. I can't believe the man who sired me was so horrendous. A murderer. Will I become like him? Will I crave power like he did? Will I do anything to get it? Before I can spiral too deeply, the king lays a comforting hand on my shoulder.

Tears are lining his eyes, but they're kind. "You are nothing like him, my boy. I've known you for your entire life, and you have never acted out of greed for power."

How he's able to cut exactly to my thoughts is beyond me.

"You have always done what you've believed is best for this kingdom and this realm. But if you're no longer comfortable in your current position, we can find you a different one. How would you like to train the new guards?"

I consider that. I would still be helping the realm, but it wouldn't be as active of a duty, not to mention that the oath that prevents me from being with Ember would no longer apply, and I could stay here with her.

"It would be an honor, Your Majesty." I bow to him and turn to leave so he can go to breakfast.

"I'll notify the appropriate parties. Oh, and Alexei?" I stop. "I would like you to start training Ember on her teletraveling abilities now that all of her powers have awakened. I'll be teaching her elemental magic, and now that you're going to be training the guards, I'll take over her combat training as well, but I want someone I can trust to start helping her with her magic."

I'm disappointed that I won't be continuing her combat training, but at least I'll still have an excuse to see her on a daily basis. I nod to him.

"As you wish, Sire."

3

Ember

Everything is different. *I'm* different. And I don't know what to do about it. I have all of this tremendous power inside of me that was sleeping until very recently, and I am picking up on all of these clues that I experienced prior to my power awakening. When my DNA test came back and I freaked out in my house, I felt a wind storm and a blaze of heat. I chalked it up to an open window and my vision going wonky, but now I know that my fae abilities had manifested for a brief moment. I've also always felt like I've had premonitions of things that are going to happen, and now that I think back on it, they've always been right.

I'm tempted to play with my gifts, but after all the drama, I'm unsure of how to access them. When I was with Mordecai, it felt as natural as breathing, but I don't know if that was because they had just awoken, or because I was under attack and my powers took over. Now that I'm not under any sort of threat, it doesn't feel natural in the least.

I strip off my ruined dress from the ball and gently set my tiara on my nightstand. I turn the shower on as hot as I can stand and make my way in when it warms up. I scrub my skin raw, making sure that there's not one fleck of blood on me, or any dirt in my hair or ashes from Mordecai's corpse. I look down at my chest, amazed to see that there's no scar from the blade piercing my heart. Said organ starts beating frantically, the remembered sensation of it being shredded by Mordecai's blade fresh in my mind. I shudder. I don't think I'll ever forget that horrible feeling for as long as I live. Then the experience of my skin and tissue knitting itself back together. Unbelievable. It's too much to wrap my head around. For now, I focus on the fact that I don't have a mark from the blade.

I remember Alexei telling me that elves can heal scars, and I realize my body must've done that on its own. I still see the scars from when I was bitten by the vampires in the caves, and I'm grateful. They're a good reminder.

Alexei. My breath whooshes out of me as I stare at my mate mark, and tears flow freely down my cheeks as I trace it. It's beautiful. And if I could rewind a few hours and still have it, I would be thrilled, but not after everything that's happened. Not after what he's done. A sob works its way free, and I struggle to breathe as I think of the betrayal. I don't know how we can ever move on from this. I don't think I can ever forgive him. Is life really so cruel that it would finally allow us to be together, but because of his actions I can't even stand to look at him?

I don't know what to do now. I don't want to have anything to do with him, even though my heart aches with the thought of him leaving, or not seeing him every day. I curse my heart's stupidity even though it's shattered. I don't know how things are going to work. I won't be able to be obvious in my disdain of him without cause, and with my current story, I don't have a reason to be upset with him. After all, he was captured just like I was.

It's a tomorrow problem, and I pull myself together so I can get to sleep. I'm exhausted, and I'm really hoping I'll be able to sleep after the events of the evening. I don't bother doing anything with my hair, put my robe on with nothing underneath, and collapse into bed. The tears won't stop coming, and I cry myself to sleep.

I head down to breakfast to meet with Stavros the next morning. I haven't seen anyone yet besides Humphrey. He showed up as I was leaving to start moving all of my things to the royal wing. Even though I'm sad I won't be across the hall from Pearl anymore, I'm relieved that I won't risk bumping into Alexei. I walk in to find my father already there. He looks a little worried, but other than that it's like every other day.

"Good morning," I tell him, trying to sound as normal as possible.

"Good morning. How are you?"

"I feel..." I trail off, not knowing exactly what to tell him. "Different," I settle on.

He nods as if he understands, but I don't think there's *anyone* who can actually know how I feel. "That's to be expected."

I resist the urge to snap at him. "Yes. It's strange because I *know* I have all this power inside me, but I don't know how to use it. It's not natural to me. The training I've done with my empath abilities felt easier because I've always noticed them. But these, *all* of these, are so new. I don't know what to do with myself, and I'm nervous to start practicing—I might do damage because I have no clue what the fuck I'm doing." Tears build behind my eyes *again*, and I try to force them back. I'm so sick of crying.

My father grabs my hand, looking at me like he wishes he could help everything make sense. "I know, Ember. That's actually something that I wanted to talk to you about. I'm going to start training you on your elements. I think those will be the most natural for you out of all of your new abilities because you get them directly from me. I will also be taking over your combat training."

With that last sentence, I'm stunned and don't know exactly how to react. I swear to God, why is being a woman so fucking confusing and conflicting sometimes? I want Alexei to stay away from me, truly I do, but at the same time, I'm hurt because it sounds like he asked the king to take over so he wouldn't have to see me anymore. I try to focus more on the relief that washes over me instead.

"Okay."

I'm surprised, because it seems like Stavros picks up on that fact.

"I was the one who told him I wanted to take over your training. He told me this morning that he wanted to give up his guard position."

I almost spit out the tea I just sipped. "He *what*?!"

"I know. I was surprised too, but it seems like he's not feeling the same after the incident last night either. He has a lot of conflicting emotions about his father, and the fact that he wasn't able to protect you."

I have no idea how to process this new development. I think more than anything, it pisses me off. This whole time he wasn't willing to give up his position to be with me, but now that he's screwed me over, he has no problem doing it whatsoever.

"So, what is he going to do now?"

"Well, he's going to be training the new guards that come in, so he'll be fairly busy, which is why I'm taking over."

"Okay."

"He is, however, going to be training you on teletraveling."

My stomach drops, but I nod and force myself to keep a neutral face.

"But we might want to wait to start that for maybe another week or two. Basically until you're more comfortable with your elemental magic. We don't want to overload you with too many things at once," he says.

I fight the urge to sigh in relief that I won't have to spend one-on-one time with Alexei yet. I need to get my shit together first.

"So are we starting my elemental training today?"

"Yes. I still don't have a ton of time though, so what we're going to do is train you on something different every day during our normal time. So today, instead of training you on your mental barriers, we'll focus on this."

I nod, excited at the prospect of learning to control all of this new power I have. I'm nervous about it too, but I know I have the best teacher.

When we finish eating, I assume we're going to head to the training yard, but instead he brings me to a different area.

"Where are we going?"

"We have a separate space to train in magic, specifically elemental magic, but this is where you will be doing your teletraveling lessons with Alexei too."

It has a similar vibe to the other training yard, but it's more open, and instead of weapons, there are metal mannequins, little bits of paper, weights, and candles.

"What is your element?"

"Have I not told you?" I shake my head. "I possess the power of air. We will start with that, since that is what I know best, then once you have a feel for controlling an element, you can give fire a try."

We stand in the center of the space, and I have literally no idea how this is going to go. I've always had a grasp on my other ability, or at least been aware of it. This is brand-new.

"First, I want you to close your eyes." I do. "Now, there's a place inside of you where your magic is housed. It's in your belly, just a tad underneath your belly button. It should feel like a ball of energy. Have you found it yet?"

I nod. So strange. I never noticed it before now.

"Bring it to the surface."

The energy expands outward 'til it's humming right under my skin, waiting to be set free.

"Now, since your magic has many forms, you'll have to focus on shaping it. Think about what you want it to be. Picture the air flowing around you, a gentle breeze blowing at your hair. Guide the magic with your fingers in whatever way is natural to you."

I wiggle my fingers a bit, almost like I'm beckoning the air to me.

"Now open your eyes."

I gasp in amazement as I see my hair has lifted in the wind I've conjured. I giggle as I add a little more power behind it, and am immediately pushed by my own magic. Stavros chuckles beside me as he catches me.

"It's easy to overdo it, especially when you're new. Try to be as subtle as you can at first. We'll work up to more when you're ready for it." He grabs my hand and turns it palm side up. "See if you can start here with just your hand. Start as gently as you can."

I furrow my brow in concentration as I stare at my palm. I try to bring just the smallest amount of air to it. A strong gust comes out instead, and I growl in frustration at my lack of control. I try to lessen the amount, but it remains at the same level.

"Take a deep breath," he instructs.

I do, and the magic seems to pulse with my breathing, ebbing and flowing with each movement of my lungs.

"Good. Now see if you can will it to do something, like make it swirl."

I focus on my breathing again as I imagine a tornado. I move each of my fingers in turn, almost like a wave. I can see the air shift and can feel the motion of it in my hand. Stavros bends down to grab something, and when he straightens, he slowly releases a handful of dirt into the mini storm I've created.

Just when I think I've got it, my control snaps, and the tornado explodes. Stavros has dirt covering his entire face, and I laugh. His expression is similar to mine, and I'm sure I look equally as disheveled.

"That was actually pretty good."

"You mean the part where it literally blew up in my face?"

He laughs. "That's normal. You don't know how your gifts work yet. It's going to take time for you to adjust to them, and to gain control over them. So this time, picture your air as a whisper, letting out the smallest amount that you can."

I concentrate with all my might, and am pleased when the flow is immediately less. It's still stronger than I'm going for, but at least it's not the hurricane level it was at before.

"Good," Stavros praises me. "Now, see those little slips of paper there? As subtly as you can, try to carefully sweep them up in your wind."

I stare at them and will them to lift just slightly for me. Instead, they go flying and are lost to the world within seconds. I huff in frustration as he chuckles.

"That was a good try."

"You don't have to lie."

"Ember, it takes a lot of time to master control. It doesn't happen all at once."

"But I had control when my powers first awoke—with all of them. They did exactly what I wanted them to."

"That was different. You were in a stressful life-threatening situation. Your powers took over and reacted naturally. That doesn't typically happen. Magic takes a lot of training and concentration and control. And it's important to remember that some abilities will come more naturally to you than others. Some will be easier to handle and manipulate, and others you'll have to fight. Just be patient. It'll come to you eventually."

We practice for another hour, and Stavros demonstrates his powers. I'm immediately jealous of the amount of control he has. He creates the perfect mini tornado in his hands and brings in the bits of paper and dirt around the yard with his powers so the windstorm is visible. He widens it so it engulfs us, like we're in the eye of some crazy storm, but the only things it touches are my hair and clothes, leaving me completely steady.

By the end of the lesson, I have a smidgen more control, and am able to manage the flow more easily. I realize after all the discussions I've had with Stavros and Alexei that I need to be more patient. I've always been the type of person who wants to be great at something immediately, and that will not be the case with my newly awakened abilities. And like he reminded me, certain powers won't be as comfortable for me to wield. I know that when the moment comes I'm going to be incredibly frustrated, but hopefully if I can learn now how to give myself a little grace, it'll be easier when I finally get there.

"You did well today, Ember. Tomorrow maybe we can switch it up and see how you do with your fire."

I nod eagerly, giving him a warm smile. I'm so thankful for him. "I would like that." The same urge I've had for a while now rises in me, and I give in to it. "Thanks, Dad."

His eyes widen in surprise before they line with tears, making mine do the same thing. "You're very welcome."

He leans in, and I give him a hug. I breathe in his calming sandalwood scent and take comfort in his warm arms around me. I let a few tears spill over, needing this after last night. I'm grateful we've finally got to have our moment, and when I pull back, he looks equally as affected.

"See you for dinner?"

I nod, and we each go about our days.

Pearl finds me in the hall. "There you are. I've been looking for you."

"What's up?"

"Come on. Let's go to my room so we're not lingering in the hall like a bad smell."

I laugh and follow her, and I give her a questioning look as soon as the door is closed.

"I'm just checking on you. You went through a lot last night, and I thought you might need someone to talk to."

"I'm fine. Thank you for checking though."

"You don't want to talk about it at all?"

"What's there to talk about? I have a shit ton of new powers that I have no clue what to do with, my father's most trusted advisor killed me and I brought myself back to life, I'm apparently going to be the end of the fae reign, and to top it all off, the entire kingdom now knows that I'm the Princess of Queridian, even though I just found that out not long ago myself." I take a deep breath after my rant, trying to rein in my emotions. Emotion clogs my throat, and I know that everything I've gone through is too much.

Instead of responding verbally, Pearl walks over to me and wraps me in her arms. I let the tears go, and it all spills out of me like a tsunami. All of my anxiety, fear, sadness, and devastation. I obviously can't tell her about Alexei, and I think that's what's weighing on me the most. She just holds me through it all, being a support that I deeply need. One without judgment or agenda. Just a friend. Something that I've never had. When my tears finally dry up, I pull back.

"Hungry?" she asks, making me laugh. Pearl and I always seem to eat nonstop when we're with each other.

"Of course."

"I'll go grab us some lunch."

The next day, Stavros and I try my luck with fire. Unfortunately, this skill is more difficult for me since I have only a minuscule amount, an *ember* if you will. I roll my eyes at my own pun. I am able to manifest it, but it's barely anything. However, this is where I got lucky. Since I also have air, I'm able to fan my own fire, causing it to spread. But until I gain control of both of them separately, Stavros doesn't want me using them together as it can be dangerous, especially since I don't know what I'm doing yet. If something does go wrong though, Stavros will be able to put out the fire with his own magic.

Right now, he's having me try to light random candles around the yard. After a few missed attempts, I'm finally able to get one going, only to have Stavros blow it out with his magic.

"What the hell?" I ask, pissed that he ruined my hard work.

"You need to learn how to maintain it. Get it going and *keep* it going."

Why do all the men in my life have to make such fucking sense when I'm training with them? Can't they take it easy on me just for once?

I'm able to get it lit again, but am not able to keep it going no matter how hard I try. I bite back my growl of frustration every time his magic blows mine out, well, like snuffing out a candle. By the end of the hour, I'm frustrated like I almost always am after training with him, but pleased that I was at least able to light the candle in the first place. Stavros tells me that if my fire was stronger, it would be a similar situation to my air where I would probably have a hard time controlling it and do too much, which is obviously something you don't want with fire.

We continue on like that for the next week, alternating between fire and air. I'm not making much progress on my fire, but air is starting to come more naturally to me. I'm able to control the amount that I put forth, and am now starting to work on picking up small things with it, like scraps of paper. Once I get that down I'll be able to start working on heavier things, which excites me. I'll be like Matilda. The thought makes me giggle.

I haven't seen Alexei much, and I know he's giving me the space I asked for. Pearl is starting to notice that we haven't been spending time together. I keep telling her that it's because he hasn't had time with his new position, and that the king has taken over my training. She's been letting me get away with it for now, but I can see the skepticism on her face. I know eventually she'll stop accepting that answer, and I need to be prepared for that day.

I also moved into my new quarters, and let me just tell you, if I thought my other room was beautiful, it has *nothing* on my new rooms. Yes, rooms. Plural. I have an entire suite to myself, complete with an absolutely massive bedroom, including a bed big enough for five people, a luxury bathroom with a huge soaking tub and a shower with multiple showerheads, a closet filled with more and more clothes— thanks to Imelda—that's bigger than my bedroom on Earth, a sitting room with the most beautiful fireplace I've ever seen, and a little breakfast nook. My suite is right across the hall from my father's, and even though it was a little awkward at first, I really enjoy it now. I like seeing him first thing in the morning, and at random times throughout the day when we cross paths.

Because of our training, we've started to get closer and closer, and even though I've tried to temper my attachment to him, it's difficult because he's my father, and he's starting to feel like one. I've realized that he and I have the same sense of humor, and the same way of approaching tough situations. He always tells me I get my stubbornness from my mother, but I've come to learn that he also has a stubborn streak. Every time I notice a similarity between us, it makes me smile. I never knew where I picked up certain personality traits, but then it'll be right there in front of me. Needless to say, it's been very comforting as I transition into this phase where I don't know or trust anyone, including myself.

A week passes, and I've made quite a bit of progress with Stavros. I tell him one day when we're doing our combat training that I want to learn how to shoot my bow and arrow from a horse while riding. Considering that I've improved vastly with my bow skills, he tells me that he thinks I'm ready. He's about to have the stable boy bring me a horse, but I'm insistent on riding Ash. I've missed her, and I've barely seen her since we arrived at the castle. Plus, I know I'll be much more comfortable with her than with a horse I've never met before.

She's brought out not long after and neighs happily upon seeing me. I immediately rush up to greet her. I pet her neck and whisper sweet praises to her. She snorts happily into my hand, and guilt weighs heavily in my stomach; I haven't come to see her in a while.

"I've missed you, pretty girl."

She gives me a look that says that I should've come to see her sooner, then. Stavros wants me to ride around a bit first to get the feel for it again before bringing a bow into the mix. It's a little rough at first since it's been a minute, but Ash and I move faster and faster as we become reacquainted with one another.

An hour later, Stavros hands me a bow and arrow, and I nudge Ash into a steady walk. I take aim at the first target. It's much more difficult trying to aim while in motion. I want to take longer to set up my shot, but I don't have the time. I release the arrow, and it flares wide, hitting the very outer edges of the target. Ash keeps moving along, and I grab my next arrow. This time when I fire, I can immediately tell I've overcompensated. It hits the opposite side of the target, and I bite back a growl of frustration.

Stavros is walking along next to us, watching my progress. "Tighten your core first. It will keep you stable and steady."

I do as he says, and when the next target comes up, it's noticeably easier to take aim. I still don't have nearly as much time as I would like to line up my shot, but my movements don't seem so jarring. I fire, and am pleased to see it hits a little farther in.

We maintain that same slow walk for another hour, and by the end of our session, I've hit the center only once, but am glad when it becomes easier for me.

"Next time, we'll start at this pace, and when you're able to hit the bull's-eye most of the time we will increase your speed."

I nod, dismounting. It's hard for me to even consider going faster than we were today and be able to hit the target, but I know it's possible.

The stable boy comes to take Ash, and I regretfully pat her neck. I missed her and am not quite ready to part with her yet.

Of course Stavros notices my reluctance. "Want to go for a ride outside the castle?"

I look at him in surprise. I figured he would be too busy to spend more time with me today, but am delighted he's able to. I nod excitedly. The stable boy brings Stavros's own horse out minutes later, and I gasp in amazement. He's massive and black as coal. It's immediately clear that this is a king's horse from all the adornments covering him. Stavros mounts him, and I follow suit with Ash.

He turns to me. "Where do you want to go?"

"Can you show me how to get to the library on my own? I would like to be able to go by myself. Plus, I was hoping to do some research."

He nods and nudges his horse forward. "Research on what?"

"Just Queridian. I want to know more about it since I am the princess and everything."

He looks back at me, a surprised but pleased look on his face. "You want to learn more about the kingdom?"

"Of course. Besides, researching cultures and how they used to live is what I thrive on."

He doesn't reply, but there's a small smile gracing his lips. The ride is very pleasant, and I take in the scenery. The last time we came to the Epitome Athenaeum we were in a carriage, and I wasn't able to really see much. It's not far from the palace, but far enough that there isn't anyone else around. We dismount, and I head toward the small waterfall that's the secret entrance.

"Do you have time to come in?"

"Only a little bit, then I'll have to leave you on your own."

We enter, and I marvel once again at how incredible it is here. I've always wanted to go to a library that was not only massive, but also a little magical. I mean, books in general are magical, but this place fits that description to a T.

"I'll show you what section you'll need for your research and then I'll head back."

He leads me to a room that we didn't visit last time we were here, although it's right next to the royalty room, which I will probably visit as well before I leave.

The new room has a huge map of Queridian on the floor, and in each territory, there are books about that resident species. Each section has the vibe of that land, so for instance, there's sand and water in Mermacovia like a little mini beach, and the landscape in the Everchanging Glades keeps shifting. The shelving also has the species symbol on the sides in case you need even more help.

"Have everything you need?"

"I think so."

"And you know how to get back on your own?"

"Yes. I was paying close attention."

"And you have your knives?"

I laugh and roll my eyes fondly. "Yes! Thanks for the concern, Dad, but I'm fine. I am a grown woman, you know."

His eyes twinkle at me calling him Dad and the familiarity with which I tease him. "Okay. Well, make sure to come back before dark. I don't want you to get lost."

"I will."

He takes off, and I am left all on my own to explore, just how I like it. I start in the fae section and learn all about my ancestors, and the different wonderful things that have been done with elemental magic. Apparently earth magic is often used in construction as well as air magic, water and fire are typically used for demolition, and with just a few fae, constructing things that take ages on Earth are completed in mere days or weeks here.

I'm shocked when I discover that the realm used to be ruled by the mermaids thousands of years ago, but there's a strange gap of time between then and when the fae took over. I can't seem to find any information on why or how that happened.

I make my way around the room, reading up on the other species and territories, paying special attention to the mermaids to see if I can find anything about the weird transition in ruling, but still have no luck. I learn about some random interesting events, like the mimic who once impersonated a ruler, giving the entire kingdom instructions to send her gifts in tribute. As far as I can tell, that was when distrust for the mimics really started. Of course the prank was harmless, but the fact that someone else passed as the ruler was terrifying for the kingdom.

I've also found that the witches have always seemed to keep to themselves for the most part, even before the segregation, which didn't happen until the fae took over. Frustrating as it may be, I haven't been able to pinpoint exactly why the separation started. I've combed everything in this room from that time period, all to no avail. It's like an event was erased from their history.

I make my way next door to the royalty room, hoping that I might have some luck there. There's a book detailing the royal line from the very beginning of Queridian, which looks promising. I look for where the rule switched from mermaid to fae, and see something peculiar. One line states that "Yemonja" was the last mermaid queen, but directly underneath, there's a blacked-out name. Try as I might, I can't make anything out. I curse in frustration before moving on. The name directly below says that "Theon" was the first fae king.

Was there a ruler between the last mermaid queen and the first fae king? And if so, what species were they? Why is their name crossed out? Did this potential ruler have anything to do with the switch in leadership, or correlate with the missing event I can't seem to find? So many questions.

I keep looking through the room at the other books and discover that there is a biography on each of the leaders. I locate Yemonja and flip to the back to see if anything happened at the end of her rule. Nothing pops out at me, and I move on to Theon. The only thing I can find out is that he wasn't born royal, but married into the role. However, I'm unable to learn who he married. I do discover that he ruled alone for basically his entire reign, which is a little suspicious.

I call it a day, and put everything back where I found it. When I go out to the main atrium where all the fiction books are stored, I can see with the mirrored sky that the sun's about to set. I promised Stavros I'd return to the castle before dark, so I quickly make my way outside. I climb onto Ash, who's been waiting patiently right where I left her, and we head back the way we came.

On my ride back, I debate on asking Stavros about the information I wasn't able to find and see if he can shed some light on the situation. I dismiss it almost immediately. As much as I love Stavros, and even though we're starting to become closer, I have a feeling he won't tell me what any of this means. I don't know if it's my witch sense, but I am sure he knows what happened and won't tell me. I think it's connected to the segregation issue, and he still has not told me his reasoning behind that.

I'll keep digging on my own to see if I can find anything and keep it to myself. The last thing I want is another fight with him about something that happened a long ass time ago.

Ash and I ride up to the castle just when it becomes dark. The guards let me in, and I head inside after handing Ash over to the stable boy, giving her a grateful pet on the neck and promising to visit her again soon.

I clean up in my room, take a quick shower, and change into some nicer clothes before dinner. When I get to the dining room, Stavros is there waiting and drinking his wine.

"Did you have fun?"

"I did," I reply. "Thank you for showing me. I'm glad I'll be able to get lost there for a while whenever I need some time away."

"When did you get back?"

"I rode in right as it got dark."

His eyes widen. "Wow, you really are my daughter."

I chuckle before taking a grateful sip of my wine and turning my attention to my food. As I look at him, my decision to not mention what I found, or rather didn't find, is affirmed. Not yet.

4

Ember

"So what's going on between you and Alexei?" Pearl asks me. I try not to freak out. I still haven't come up with something to tell her.

"I already told you. There's nothing going on."

"You are so full of shit. You've told me the same thing over and over again, but I can see that something happened. Ever since your powers awakened, you've been distant with him. I mean have you seen him at all?"

"Why are you paying such close attention?"

"Because I'm a nosy bitch. Now tell me. Are you upset with him because he wasn't able to protect you?"

I bite my lip as I think. It would be such a relief to talk to someone about this. Especially another woman. And Pearl is the only one who's noticed that something is off. Stavros is a typical oblivious dad, and hasn't even mentioned it at all, which I'm very thankful for. Although if I were to give him the same answer that I've been giving Pearl, I know he would accept it no questions asked. Men aren't usually very observant.

"Hey, you know by now that whatever is said between us stays between us, right? I will never tell anyone else. That's what best friends are for."

"I'm your best friend?" I ask, shocked. I mean, I know she's *my* best friend—hell, my only friend—but I'm surprised that she says I'm hers.

"Of course. Who else would it be? Well"—she pauses—"I guess *technically* my twin is my best friend, but she's back in Mermacovia, and I don't see her very often, obviously."

"You have a twin?"

"Yes. She's officially older by two minutes. Her name is Opal."

"Is she identical?"

"Yes, we're identical twins. But her hair has more of a bluish tint as opposed to my purple. And both of us have pink tails."

"Wow. Are you a lot alike? How did I not know this about you?"

"No, we're actually pretty opposite. And I don't talk about home much. I miss it, and talking about it usually makes me miss it more. Now enough about me. Will you please tell me what's going on?"

"Okay, but you have to pinky promise that you'll never tell anyone."

"What's a pinky promise?"

I huff in frustration that for the millionth time no one understands me. I hold out my pinky and gesture for her to do the same. "I pinky promise not to breathe a word of this to anybody," she says, and I lock our pinkies together. I lean in and kiss my fist and she does the same. The moment it happens, I swear magic stirs in the air.

"What's going on?" I ask.

"I think our promise was just sealed with magic," she breathes in wonder, smiling down at our hands. My eyebrows shoot up in surprise. I didn't know that was possible. "Okay, tell me, tell me."

I take a deep breath and confide in her. After all, she did just pinky promise she wouldn't tell anyone. "Okay. So the night of the ball, Alexei and I went out to the gardens, and he kissed me." She inhales in surprise, but before she can respond, I plow forward because that is *not* the thing. "When he pulled away, he held up a cloth to my face that had whatever drug knocked me out." Her face scrunches up in confusion. "He's the one who took me to Mordecai."

"No," she breathes, stunned.

"Yes. He didn't know what Mordecai planned to do. He told him that it was necessary since I was going to be the end of the fae reign, and that they were going to take me back to Earth. Alexei told me that he was going to come with me so that we could be together. When he found out that Mordecai was going to harm me, he stepped in and tried to rescue me, but it was too late, and the damage was already done. I died because of his blind trust and stupidity."

Pearl reaches a hand over and squeezes mine.

"Ember, I'm so sorry."

"I told Alexei that I could never forgive him for it, and to stay away from me. He's been following my requests so far, but we won't be able to continue it for long. The king wants him to train me in teletraveling, and I can't tell Stavros. I think he would kill Alexei, and as upset as I am with him, I don't want anything bad to happen."

"That's understandable. I can't believe he *did that*."

"There's something else," I whisper.

"What?"

I take off my bracelet and extend my arm toward her. "He's my mate."

She gasps loudly, grabbing my arm and pulling it closer to examine my mark. "How did this happen?"

"It happened as soon as he touched me after my powers were awakened. I told him that I didn't care, and that I wouldn't accept having a mate who betrayed me like that. He begged me to forgive him, but how can I? Ever since I've covered up the mark because I don't want others seeing it and asking questions."

"So, what are you going to do?"

"I don't think there's anything I can do, except hope that the training isn't too uncomfortable and that he keeps his distance."

"Want me to hit him for you? He would never expect it."

I laugh and appreciate the comic relief.

"I know you don't feel like it right now, but do you think you'll ever be able to forgive him?"

"I don't know, Pearl. I don't see how."

"I know that what he did was absolutely awful, and please understand that I am completely and totally on your side, but the mate mark is significant, Ember. I don't want to see you unhappy, which you will be if you never allow yourself to be with your mate. It affects those who have them so much that you will never want anyone else. Only Alexei."

Here we go with the differences in our cultures. I struggle not to roll my eyes at her, even as a pit sinks in my stomach. I know that I don't understand a lot of what happens here, so maybe I'm just not fully conceptualizing how this is going to affect me, but I don't want to have the choice taken from me. I don't want to be forced to be with Alexei just because it's what mates are supposed to do. Sure, before all the drama went down I would've been thrilled that he was my mate, but that was before he betrayed me. But because I don't exactly know much about mate bonds, there's a small voice in the back of my head that's causing my dread. *What if Pearl is right?*

"I can't think about that right now, Pearl. Maybe he'll earn my trust back some other way, but it's still too fresh, and I'm still too upset about it."

"I understand. I would absolutely be in the same place as you. Just let me know if you need anything. And I'm always here to talk."

I pull her in for a hug, grateful that I told her. It's a relief finally being able to talk to someone about it.

"Thanks, babe. So enough about me. What's going on with you and

Xanto?"

She blushes, and I can't wait for her to spill the tea.

"Well, we really hit it off the night of the ball. Obviously with everything that happened with you, things got cut short, but he's been coming to see me. I'm used to males being so forward with me, and he hasn't made any moves. It's so strange, Ember. I don't know if he likes me or not."

"Oh, believe me, he more than likes you. He could not keep his eyes off you at the ball. And he told me how beautiful you were."

"He did?"

"Yes. He's probably just trying to be a gentleman and get to know you."

"I've never experienced that from anyone before. They've always just been interested in my beauty and charm. They never really wanted to know more about me."

"They didn't deserve you, Pearl. You are such a wonderful person. And of course you're beautiful, but your personality is even more stunning." Her eyes tear up at my words, and she squeezes my hand in thanks. "So he hasn't made a move yet?"

"No. But I really want him to."

"Yeah, but have you ever taken your time with someone?"

"What do you mean?"

"Like taken it slow as opposed to just jumping into bed?"

"No. I've never done that before. Mermaids don't really take their time. Like I said, we're very comfortable with our sexuality and we're obsessed with beauty. That translates to us being promiscuous with no remorse."

"Well, maybe this will be a good thing for you, then. It's actually pretty fun to wait. It builds the tension, and when you finally get together it will be *explosive*."

"Hmm. Explosive, huh?"

I only wink at her in response.

"I think I need a swim. Want to come with me?" she asks, changing the subject.

"Where?"

"There's a lake close by. It's specifically reserved for those of us who need it to shift into our other forms."

"Is there anyone else here who fits that description?"

"A few," she replies. "And that includes Xanto now too."

"It does?" I ask, surprised.

"Yes. His other form is a stingray."

I was totally not expecting that from him at all, but it makes sense as to why he's so drawn to Pearl, besides the obvious. They're both sea creatures, and the more I think about it, the more adorable it is that they can swim and spend time together in their other forms.

"So? Do you want to come?"

I nod eagerly. I've wanted to see Pearl's mermaid form for a while, but I wasn't comfortable asking. We make our way down to the lake, and when we arrive twenty minutes later, I gasp in amazement. It's absolutely breathtaking, and of course we came here at the perfect time, sunset. The river from the palace leads to this pristine lake on the side of the mountain. There are perfect natural lights amid the water, which is the clearest blue, allowing me to see into it. It's deeper than I thought it would be, which makes sense since it's meant for shifting and swimming.

I look over at Pearl, but words fly out of my head when I see her half-naked by the side of the lake. I don't why I'm surprised, but I am. Without another word, she takes off the last of her clothing and dives into the water. I cry out in amazement as the transformation takes over. Her legs fuse together and grow, scales replacing skin, and then her soft pink tail is flipping through the waves. I didn't think it was possible, but she's glowing even more than usual, and I can't help but stare in awe.

She pops her head out of the water. "Are you coming in? It's the perfect temperature." Her hair shines like the moon, and I see a cluster of scales on the blade of her forearms, the same color as her tail and sharp enough to cut. She smiles at me, and I gasp in shock at the razor-sharp teeth that glint from her mouth instead of her normal canines.

I hadn't planned on it, but a skinny-dip with my best friend sounds perfect. I start stripping and make my way into the water. I dunk under, and when I'm fully submerged, I have a strange sensation, like someone is tugging on a thread inside of me. I follow the tug with my mind, and find a bright light. When my mind reaches out to it, it's like ice pouring through my veins, and suddenly I can breathe underwater. I look down at myself, only to discover that while my top half is mostly unchanged, my bottom half is vastly different. Instead of legs, or even a tail, I have tentacles. They're black and purple, the same colors as my bird form.

I am so shocked that for a moment I just stare. I have mermaid blood, so it makes sense that I would be able to shift in the water, but I have *tentacles* instead of a tail. At least they're beautiful. They aren't like octopus's tentacles, they're more slender and sleek. I reach down and touch one, expecting it to be rubbery and unpleasant, but they are smooth as silk and my fingertips glide along them. My nails have sharpened into claws, and I'm extra careful as I touch my new form. I also realize then that my skin is shining like Pearl's, and underwater it glimmers like a diamond in the moonlight. I have some purple scales on my forearms like Pearl does, and my hair looks like oil spilling and floating in the ocean, except for my strip of white, which is so luminous it's like a beacon.

Pearl swims up to me, her eyes as wide as dinner plates in her surprise. I hear her voice in my head, just like she's talking to me out loud, and I startle.

Oh my Gods! Look at you!

I stare at her and try to figure out how she's doing this. I project my thoughts to her and see if that works. It makes sense that mermaids would be able to communicate underwater, but I was not expecting it. *Can you hear me?*

She smiles at me, excitement lighting up her face. *Yes. I'm obsessed with your tentacles. Can I touch one?* I nod to her. The soft touch of her fingers brushes over me, and I shiver in response. They're more sensitive than my legs. Much more sensitive.

Why do you think I have tentacles instead of a tail? I ask.

I'm not sure. We used to have a very strong mermaid queen long ago. She and her descendants were the only ones to have the tentacles, but it was thought that their line died out. No one has had tentacles in centuries. If we're ever in Mermacovia we can figure it out for sure. When a descendant of Surseiha swims in the seas of our territory, glowing runes appear on their skin.

Could I be a descendant from this line? That's the only thing that makes sense to me.

We can talk to the king about it later. Right now, let's swim.

I test out my tentacles, slowly moving them to see how I can power through the water, and am amazed by how much control I have over them already. I can move each individually, or all as a unit. I've always been a decent swimmer, but with this new body, it blows my mind how easy and natural it is.

Pearl waits for me, watching as I adjust to my new form. I twirl this way and that, swirling my tentacles as I go, my glowing skin brightening the more I swim, my joy bubbling over. I want to see what this form can do, and I start pushing myself through the water as fast as I can. Pearl keeps pace with me, and I hear her laugh in my head as we race. She reaches the end of the lake just a hair before I do, and I playfully shove her as we laugh and catch our breath.

Can you jump out of the water? I ask her.

She gives me a cocky look before propelling herself up, up, up. I follow her and pop my head out of the water just as her whole body shoots up and out. For a moment I'm stunned by the beauty and surrealness of this moment. I take a mental picture, wanting to remember this. Her body is silhouetted by the full moon behind her, the surface of the lake glowing under the brilliance of them both. She glides back under with barely a ripple, graceful as can be. She pops up a moment later, a stunning smile illuminating her face.

"That was amazing," I speak out loud now that we're not underwater.

"You want to try it?"

"I wouldn't even know where to begin."

"It's easier than you think. Just go down to the bottom and swim up as fast as you can, come out of the water at an angle, and flip your fin hard right before you come out."

"But I don't have a fin, Pearl."

She rolls her eyes. "You know what I mean. I think it'll work the same way for you. Just try it. What's the worst that could happen?"

"Fine. But if I make an ass out of myself, you can't tell anyone."

"Wouldn't dream of it."

I head back under, going all the way to the bottom of the lake. I take a deep breath and feel the gills on the side of my neck move (such a weird sensation), and start swimming. I go faster and faster, my nerves kicking in the closer I get to the top. When I'm almost out, I change direction slightly and flick my tentacles as one. I shoot out at an angle like she told me to, but instead of gliding across and gracefully down into the water like Pearl did, I belly flop onto the surface. I sputter, and I can hear Pearl losing her shit. I come out of the water and glare at her as she clutches her stomach in a fit of laughter. I splash her, making her laugh harder, not at all the effect I was going for.

"Nice landing," a male voice says from behind me, and I almost scream. I duck down into the water, covering my chest, and turn to see Xanto standing there looking like he wants to laugh as hard as Pearl. I glare at him. Pearl has no problem whatsoever showing off her body, and I imagine that where she's from it's pretty common. "Mind if I join you?" he asks, starting to strip. I guess mimics are the same way in that regard.

"Sure!" Pearl exclaims excitedly next to me.

"I think I'm going to head back up to the castle actually." It'll be good for them to spend some time together.

I swim to the edge of the lake where my clothes are just in time to see Xanto walk fully naked, and unashamed I might add, into the water. I try not to look, but it's difficult. It's not every day that I see a gloriously attractive naked man. When the water is up to his waist, there's a flash, and then he's in his stingray form. While he's swimming toward Pearl, I take advantage that he's not facing me and shift back into my normal form, quickly throwing my clothes on.

"See you later, Ember." Pearl waves at me before diving back under the water.

I smile as they swim around, rubbing against each other like playful kittens.

I'm almost to my wing of the castle when I bump into Alexei. I plan on walking right by him when he grabs my arm, halting me. I try to ignore the heat of his hand, sending sparks through my body.

"Ember, I was looking for you. Stavros let me know that he wants us to start your teletraveling training tomorrow."

I've been dreading this. I have to keep my guard up and harden my heart against him. I can't let him in again, and that will be difficult while we are spending time alone together.

"Okay." I move to continue on my way, but he doesn't remove his hand. I glare back at him.

"I know I've already told you this, Ember, but I am *so* sorry. And even though I regret the part that I played in it, I am glad that you've become stronger because of it."

He's about to add more, but I cut him off, my temper roiling like an angry storm inside me. "Oh, so you take credit for my powers awakening?" My voice is dangerously calm.

His eyebrows lower as if he's confused. "No, I didn't mean it like that, I just—"

I cut him off again. "Because I have news for you, Alexei Dreymonde. You had no part in how strong I became, with the exception of me learning the lesson of not trusting anyone. *I* awakened my powers. No one else. Not you, and not your father. It was *me*."

His cheeks flush, and I can tell he's getting frustrated. "I *know* that. You know I'm not great with words. All I was trying to say is that seeing you now, with your powers awakened, you are a force to be reckoned with. I just wanted you to know that."

"So, when I was just a measly little human I wasn't worth anything, but now that I have powers you admire me?" My voice rises in pitch.

"*No*," he snarls, his own anger matching mine. "Why do you have to twist all of my words? I've always thought you were amazing. Now, though, you are magnificent."

"I don't care what you think of me, Alexei. And I *am* a force to be reckoned with. You'd do well to remember that." I rip my arm out of his grip and stalk off.

I hear him sigh in disappointment behind me. I should be happy that he's suffering, but all I feel is my heart shredding more. The mate mark on my arm burns, and I wonder if me causing him pain hurts me too. I can't bring myself to care as I reach my wing of the castle. His eyes bore into my back, but I pay him no mind as I slam the door behind me.

That night, as much as I don't want to, I dream of him.

It starts out as more of a memory. We're on Ash, riding through Elisora Forest. Alexei is behind me, pressed up tight.

"I've missed this," he says against my ear, nuzzling me.

Because this is a dream, I'm able to respond truthfully. "I have too," I sigh. "Why did things have to be like this?"

"I ask myself that same question every single day. I would've done so many things differently," he admits.

"I would've too." Tears roll down my cheeks at the thought of what we didn't do, and how things can never be now. "At least I still have you here. At least here I don't have to hate you." My voice cracks at the end.

"Don't cry, little doe." Alexei moves my hair off to one side and kisses a trail from my ear down the side of my neck to my shoulder. I moan softly, tilting my head to give him better access. I hate myself a little that I want him so badly after everything, but at least I don't have to admit it to anyone but myself. His hands wander around the front of my body and rest on my stomach. "I'm so sorry. I wish I could do that night over with every fiber of my being."

"I don't think I'll ever be able to forgive you for that, but I still want you, even though I don't want to. And here, I'm at least able to take what I want without anyone knowing." I put my hands over his and move them up to my breasts. He squeezes them softly, plucking my nipples in between his thumbs and pointer fingers.

"I'm sorry." A kiss to my neck. "I'm sorry." Another kiss. "I'm sorry." Kiss after kiss he places along the column of my throat, repeating the words after each one. He's worshiping me, and I let him. I let myself pretend this is real. I let myself pretend that I would actually allow this to happen. "Let me make you feel good."

His right hand drifts down my stomach again and plays with my waistband. I should probably stop this and wake myself up, but I don't want to. I find myself nodding. His left hand is still toying with my nipple as his right hand dips into my pants. I lean back to give him room to work, and he takes his time getting to his destination. I groan in frustration, earning myself a sexy chuckle from him, but he finally gives me what I want. His warm fingers brush over my clit, and I suck in a breath. His fingers dip lower, circling my entrance. He groans low in his throat.

"So wet for me."

"Shut up." My moan takes the sting out of it, and he laughs again behind me. He continues his lazy exploration, and I'm having none of it. This is my dream after all; he should be doing what I want, damn it. I thrust my hips forward, impaling myself on his digits, and we both swear at the contact. I gasp at how hard he is behind me, and I ride his hand and his cock with every movement of my hips. He sucks on my neck as his thumb finds my clit again, circling and circling, each pass driving me higher and higher. By this time he's thrusting against my ass, groaning encouragingly to me, and I revel in finally having this contact with him, even though none of it is real. This might be all I ever get to have with him.

"Are you going to come for me, little doe?" His voice sounds like gravel in my ear. I nod, beyond words at this point. He pinches my nipple hard in his grasp, shoves his fingers deep inside of me while pushing against my clit hard with his thumb, and at the very same moment his fangs pierce my neck. I detonate, screaming my climax to the sky. I'm still spiraling when he thrusts hard against my ass, once, twice, then three times before he stills, growling against my neck. He pulls back before licking up my neck, sealing the bite. "I miss you. Come back to me," he whispers.

I swear I still hear his voice in my head as I wake. My heart is pounding and my pussy is soaked. I reach down to confirm, and sure enough, my panties are ruined. I run a finger over my clit, and find it super sensitive. It's then that I realize that I orgasmed in my sleep. I groan in frustration. I'll never get back to sleep now.

The next morning, I have my normal breakfast with my father, and he mentions teletraveling training.

"Yeah, I know. Alexei told me yesterday."

"Good. I think you've got a strong enough handle on your air and fire that you're ready to start on something new."

"I've been meaning to ask, where does my fire come from? I know that I get my air from you."

"My whole line had fire. I was the first one to possess air. It makes sense that as my daughter you would have both. Especially since it seems you are extremely powerful. And you should get even more powerful the more you practice and come into your magic."

"How did you get air when they all had fire?" I ask.

"Usually it's genetic, but like eye or hair color, it can randomly change throughout the line, and someone will end up with something completely different."

That makes sense, I guess; it's crazy to think about though. Especially since he was the first.

"How did your family react when they found out that you had air and not fire?"

"They weren't pleased at first. They always viewed fire as the strongest of the elements, but I mastered it quickly in my determination to prove them wrong. I showed them all I could accomplish with it, which is a lot more than fire, just to let you know, and they saw how beneficial it could be."

"No offense, but your parents sound like unpleasant people."

He laughs, not looking offended at all. "You would be correct about that. They were very obsessed with image and power, clearly."

"That must've been a hard way to grow up."

He gives me a sad smile. "It was a little bit, but then I met your mother. And now I have you. I'm very blessed."

I reach over and squeeze his hand. "I'm blessed too, Dad."

He beams back at me.

"So, on a completely separate note," I say, deciding to change the subject to something less intense, "I went down to the lake with Pearl last night for her swim and something happened."

His brows knit in confusion. "What?"

"Apparently I not only have mermaid abilities, but I can also shift into their form." His eyes widen in surprise, but before he can respond, I tell him the real kicker. "But the thing is, I don't have a tail. I have tentacles." If I thought his eyes were wide before, they're even bigger now.

"Are you sure?"

I roll my eyes at his question.

"They were kind of hard to miss."

"Yes, of course. I'm sorry, it's just shocking. There hasn't been a mermaid with tentacles in centuries."

"That's what Pearl said. She said the original mermaid to have them was super powerful."

"She was. She was called a sea witch even though she didn't have any witch blood. Her name was Surseiha. She was the most powerful mermaid queen to ever rule. She was feared and adored by many, but her bloodline was thought to have died out thousands of years ago."

"Do you think I'm her descendant?"

"I think you would have to be. Unless you're somehow just a new breed of mermaid."

"Why did they call her a sea witch if she wasn't part witch?" My mind immediately goes to Disney, and I can't help but think of Ursula. Especially with the tentacles.

"She always seemed to know things. She was also very skilled with spells and potions."

Now I'm *really* thinking of Ursula, and I wonder if this is another one of those things that humans picked up on from Earth but we didn't quite get right.

"Has any mermaid been similar to her since? With those abilities, I mean."

"No. Even her descendants looked like her but they didn't have those capabilities."

Interesting. I wonder if she was somehow something *other.* "I want to learn more about her," I decide.

"Well, you could check the Epitome Atheneum, but I don't know if you would find anything on her since she was a different species. We can check though. The other option, which is actually something I wanted to discuss with you, is to have you travel to Mermacovia after you've mastered teletraveling. I know you're friends with Pearl, but it would be really beneficial for you to train with Mermacovia's grand mistress. Honestly, if you're open to it, I would like you to travel to all of the territories. Get training from each grand master or mistress, and you'd be able to experience the realm. There's much you haven't seen," he says, surprising me.

"Really?"

"I think it would be the best option for your training. You could learn from the most skilled of each race. Plus, they all want to get to know you more. They didn't have much of a chance to interact with you at the ball," he says quietly.

I swallow thickly, thinking of that night. "Yes, okay. I would be willing to do that."

"Good. And it will be much easier for you and Alexei this time around because you'll be able to teletravel."

My stomach sinks. "Alexei?"

"Yes. He would need to come with you. He's the only one who is able to teletravel with you who I trust with your safety." I almost snort at that, but refrain. "Is that a problem? I thought the two of you were close."

"Yeah, no, we are. I was just confused. I thought I would be going alone."

"Alone? In a foreign territory? The king's daughter? That is a recipe for a disaster, darling."

I try not to roll my eyes at his tone, but see his point. "Hey, that reminds me. There is something else I've been thinking about and I've made a decision."

"Oh?"

"I've decided I want to officially be your heir."

He drops his fork in surprise before tears line his eyes. "Really?"

I smile at how happy this has made him. "Yes. After the experience that I had, I've realized that I enjoy this life I've been living here with you. And I'm coming to love this kingdom and am excited to be a part of it. I want to make a difference here."

He stands up and wraps me in a tight hug. "Oh, Ember. I'm so pleased. And this trip will also be a good opportunity for you to gain support from the territories then too."

"Support?"

"Yes. Of course you will take over the kingdom regardless, but it's always good to have the realm behind you. It will make your job much easier. But don't worry, they will love you."

I'm not so sure, but I nod along anyway.

After that we stop talking about important things and plans, and just eat and enjoy each other's company.

When it's time for us to train, I start getting excited. This is quickly becoming my favorite part of my day, playing with my magic. But I'm immediately disappointed when he tells me we're going to train on mental shields instead. We haven't done this since my powers awakened, so I get why, it's just my least favorite.

We start out as we always do, with me failing, but then the night with Mordecai pops into my mind. I ripped through his shields without even half a thought. I had finally grasped what my father was telling me. I *knew* I was fucking powerful. It's time for me to start acting like it.

I fill myself with memories of that night, of how it felt for all my abilities to finally manifest, for the anger and pain to come to the surface, for my mind to wrap itself around the fact that I am the *only* being in this realm to have all of these powers. I close my eyes, letting every emotion and sensation and memory arise, and when I *know* I'm the strongest one in this realm, I reach for his barriers. They are as strong as they've always been, but I'm stronger.

I push my will toward them. They hold up, but I push more and more until I know my skin is glowing and I have the wind beating at me. After minutes, but what seems like hours, a crack appears. I lunge for it. It's not much, but I'm able to work with it. I sense my father's pride immediately hit me, followed by an emotion that I'm not ready to acknowledge yet. I change them to pure undiluted joy. I open my eyes to see the biggest smile gracing his face. My voice is a melody as I speak.

"Will you get me some water?" I ask, although my abilities demand it from him. He looks at me with awe, nodding and smiling some more until all of the sudden I'm tossed out of his mind, the connection severing as his face and features return to normal.

"Ember! You did it!" he exclaims.

I blink as I let that knowledge sink in. He was able to recover quickly and shove me out, but I got past his shields.

"I...I did it." I still can't believe it.

"You did it!"

"I did it!" I finally scream. A smile comes to my face, and I bask in the glow of having accomplished something after working on it for over a month. And on someone who I'm fairly certain is the most powerful person in the kingdom.

"Okay, so next time we train on this, I'm going to have Pearl join us. She's going to try to get past your shields while you try to get past mine."

"She's only been able to get past mine once."

"Yes, but with having your attention divided between your own mind and mine, you'll be more distracted, and therefore more open to influence."

"So, what do we do now?"

"We will practice shielding again soon, but since you had success today, we can do combat training instead for a while."

I'm so happy that he's not going to have me continue with the mental shields today. Even the small amount we did has left me mentally exhausted, and it will be refreshing to get my muscles working again. It's been a minute since I trained in combat since we've been working so hard on my new abilities. He picks up his sword and I pick up the one I've worked with in the past.

I'm a little sloppy at first because I haven't done much with swords, but Stavros is patient with me. We train like we did last time, working arms and feet separately. Apparently I'm still not ready to combine them.

By the time we're done, my sword arm is throbbing, but I relish the soreness. I've missed pushing my body like this, and physical activity is good for my mind too.

Stavros heads back in to do more work, but I stay in the training yard. I should be doing this after my time with him anyway. I don't want to lose everything I've worked so hard for and get sloppy. I start with my bow, then move on to hand to hand, and end with my daggers. By the time I'm finished, I'm utterly exhausted, but content. I'm also starving. It's then that I realize I missed lunch.

I head back to my room to find my meal sitting in its usual spot, but it's cold. I'm too hungry to care and snarf it down before taking a long, relaxing soak in my tub, adding some salts to ease my tired muscles. Before I know it, I've drifted off.

A hard knock on my door jolts me awake. My water is tepid, and I realize I must've been out for a *while.* I wrap a towel around myself and run to get the door. I open it to find Alexei on the other side, his face a mixture of concern and agitation.

I steel my features and try not to think about the fact that I'm wet and naked in front of him. I lift my chin higher. "What do you want?" I ask, my voice cold.

"You didn't show up for our training session. I was worried, but clearly you just decided to blow me off instead."

I don't normally do this, but since I don't give a shit anymore, I open my gifts to him. I sense his hurt and frustration, and under it his *lust.* It hits me like a freight train, and I cut off the connection before it backfires on me. Which, by the way my nipples are hardening underneath the thin towel, has already happened. I try to ignore the way Alexei's eyes dip to my chest and clear my throat loudly.

"For your information—" I put as much ice into my voice as I can to cool the heat in my veins. "I had a very grueling training session this morning and fell asleep in the bath when I got back. I was planning on meeting you for ours, even though it's the *last* thing I want to do. So just give me ten minutes to change and I'll meet you down there."

I slam the door in his face before he can respond. I lean against it and take a few deep breaths to try to calm my racing heart. The mixture of anger and lust is a heady combo. One that I do not want to be experiencing with him. It doesn't help that he can hear my heart rate. Hopefully he thinks it's from anger. Then I remember he can smell my arousal, and I groan in frustration.

I stomp away from the door and make my way to the bathroom. I dry off, drain my tub, then braid my hair. I quickly throw on some training clothes and head down to meet him. When I arrive, I'm marginally more composed, and he looks like he feels the same way. His eyes dip to my wrist where I have a bracelet covering my mating mark. Hurt enters his eyes before he locks it down.

I stand in front of him, not speaking. He's teaching me so all I have to do is listen and follow instructions. Simple enough. He doesn't say anything either, apparently waiting for me to talk. All I do is raise my eyebrows at him. He breaks eye contact first and clears his throat like he's uncomfortable. I inwardly smile at my small victory.

"So, teletraveling can be a pretty difficult ability to conceptualize. It's different from other forms of magic. The good thing is that you've already done it, so hopefully it should be a little easier for you to grasp."

He stops to give me an opening, but I don't take it. I have to be here, but that doesn't mean I have to like it. It also doesn't mean that I can't have fun making him squirm.

He takes my hint and continues. "The first step is to visualize where you are trying to go. Sometimes it helps to close your eyes because you can envision yourself there better. The next thing you want to do is to *will* yourself there. You should start to notice a tingle throughout your body, and at that point it's almost like your corporal self turns to mist. Quickly drifting through the air until it settles where you want to be."

I'm sure he can see the confused look on my face, because he gives me one of those infuriatingly knowing smiles. I scowl in response, making him school his expression.

"So, let's start with a small distance. Picture yourself across the yard."

I pick a space on the other side of us. It's next to the water station.

"Close your eyes," he says.

I resist the urge to tell him that I can do what I want, and reluctantly do as he says, but it's harder than I thought it would be. Now that he's lost my trust, doing something as simple as closing my eyes makes me feel vulnerable.

"Now picture the space clearly. Envision yourself standing there."

I do, but nothing is happening. I'm just standing there with my eyes shut looking like an ass.

"It's not enough to just visualize it. You need to wish it. *Demand* it from your body. Force yourself to show up."

I internally tell myself to travel, to move, to show Alexei what I can do. Because I want to master all of my gifts. I want him to fucking *fear* me. I want to become the force to be reckoned with that he said I was.

Tears well in my eyes. This has suddenly become about something so much more. And the fact that I'm here with *him.* It's too much for me to stand. I keep breathing and force my tears back.

His voice becomes soft next to mine, and I can tell he's moved closer. "You have to want it, Ember. Think of it like taking a leap. Jump across the yard."

I am so conflicted. My mind doesn't want him anywhere near me and is trying to teletravel just so I don't need to have him close anymore, but my body and my stupid heart are reaching out to bring him closer. I shut my heart and body down and focus solely on my mind. That is going to be my key to teletraveling.

He comes even closer until his breath tickles the back of my neck. "*Want* it, Ember."

With his proximity, I force every ounce of hate and anger toward him that I feel, my ultimate desire to be as far as I can from him in this stupid yard. My fingers start tingling, and I gasp at the sensation. I don't remember experiencing this the night of the ball. At that point my body took over, and I was too overwhelmed with my emotions that I didn't even notice it.

"That's it. Focus. Will it to happen. You can do it."

The tingling spreads from my fingertips and up my arms. I picture that space I want to be in, and it's suddenly as though I'm a whisper in the wind. I stumble when my feet touch solid ground again. I peek my eyes open, nervous to see what happened. Well, I'm definitely not where I was trying to be. Instead, I'm a few feet in front of where I was originally standing, but now I'm facing Alexei. I'm disappointed, but at least I was able to move. Better than nothing.

"Not bad, Ember. It can be really difficult at first to reach your target, so don't get discouraged. You'll get there."

Something occurs to me then, and as much as I don't want to talk to him, I'm curious about this, and not asking would be like cutting my nose off to spite my face.

"So, can you teletravel somewhere if you've never been there? You need to visualize it to make it work, right?"

He looks surprised and pleased that I'm engaging with him. "It depends on the situation. Sometimes you can do it by looking at a map, but that can be dangerous because you don't want to run into something that you don't know is there. You can also look at drawings or sketches done of the location. We have a lot of those specifically for that reason. Or if you're with another vampire who's been there before, they can guide the travel."

"How does that work?"

"The two individuals just need to hold hands. The one who knows the location guides where they go."

I'm tempted to ask him, but I really don't want to touch him right now. I nod instead. It's then that something that he said hits me. Something stupid and obvious. He said *another* vampire. Meaning that I'm also one. For some reason, it's much stranger than being part mermaid or fae for example. Maybe it's the thought of drinking blood. Something else occurs to me then.

"If I'm part vampire, why don't I have fangs?"

"I'm not sure. There's never been someone like you before. It could be that because the fraction of vampire blood you have in you is so small that you don't have the need to feed, and therefore don't need fangs. But enough stalling, keep practicing."

I roll my eyes at him. Ever the hard-ass. It's almost pleasant to have this normalcy between us, but I make myself cut that shit out quick.

We train for another hour, and by the end, it's like I've gone through a meat grinder. On the plus side, I'm getting closer. I mean, I'm still pretty far away from my target, but at least I'm making progress.

"Same time tomorrow?" he asks as I'm about to leave. I nod. "Try not to fall asleep in the bath this time."

I roll my eyes and walk away. I know he's trying to pretend things are normal between us, but I'm not having it. It feels too good and too painful all at the same time, and I can't stand to have my heart broken again. I wouldn't survive it a second time.

5

Ember

The next couple weeks continue on much the same. I train every day. Almost all day. I work on my air and fire in the mornings with Stavros, do combat training by myself after that. Sometimes Stavros isn't busy and is able to stay and help me with that as well, but those times are few and far between. We've also trained with Pearl a few times on my mental shields. So far she's been able to breach my barriers only one other time, and that was the first time the three of us practiced together. After I felt it, I was able to better prepare.

I've gotten past Stavros's shields multiple times now, each time for a little longer than the last, but I know I'm still not fully penetrating his mind. Hopefully with more practice I'll be able to accomplish that soon, but he always likes to remind me that these things take time. I know I'm an adult and everything, but I literally hate that sentiment. I wish it didn't take time to become proficient in something. I want to be great immediately. Which is probably why I always struggled with instruments when I was younger.

Things are slowly improving with my teletraveling lessons as well. I'm now able to stick the landing, as I like to call it, and end up where I intend to. Well, at least most of the time. If I'm distracted I usually end up a few feet from my goal. Unfortunately, with Alexei always being present, I'm distracted more often than not.

He's started having me travel farther each day, and I find that I'm able to do it, but it still is just as difficult as the day before. He assures me that soon I'll be able to travel long distances, and hopefully within the next month or two we will be able to make our trip around the realm.

As much as I don't want to travel with Alexei, I am excited about seeing more of the kingdom. The kingdom that will eventually be *mine*. Wow. That's crazy to think about. I can't believe I told Stavros I would willingly take over one day. But then I think about all the wonderful things I'll be able to do and all of the much-needed changes I'll be able to make. Yes. It'll be worth it.

Pearl and I have also been swimming every single night, and let me tell you, it is the highlight of my day. The two of us have gotten incredibly close, and I'm so grateful to have her in my life. I imagine my relationship with her is a lot like how sisters are with each other. But, like clockwork, Xanto always comes to meet her an hour and a half in. She tells me nothing's happened between them yet, but I see the way they look at each other. And when they're in their shifted forms they're always rubbing up against each other, like their base animals can't resist the temptation that their human forms can.

She keeps inquiring about Alexei, and I keep telling her the same thing. Nothing has changed. Although, I have been having dreams about him regularly. And of course they're always sexual. I haven't told anyone that though. It is my own little secret. One that I guard, and reluctantly cherish.

"So, you and Pearl seem to be getting along nicely lately," the king remarks over breakfast one morning.

"We are. It's been really wonderful having a close girlfriend here. I've never really had friends, so it's a good change of pace."

"She told me that she wants to come with you when you go to Mermacovia," he adds.

That bitch never mentioned anything to me! But the excitement and relief that comes over me is overwhelming.

"Really?" I ask, my joy evident. "How would that work since Alexei and I will be teletraveling?"

"Yes, really. She can just leave before you do and then she should hopefully be there by the time you both arrive. She's been wanting to go and see her family anyway, and this way you will have a personal guide. Alexei has been to all of the territories, but Mermacovia is her home. She knows it well."

"I will really enjoy that. I'm glad she's coming with us."

We head to training after that, and Stavros informs me that I'm finally ready to see what I can do with both of my elements together. I jump up and down in excitement, giving him a hug before we get started. He looks a little startled, like he doesn't quite know how to react, but he pushes through it. I mean, he has a daughter now. He's going to have to get used to this behavior.

"So, today I'm going to line up all the candles, and you're going to light the first one with your fire, and then with your air try to pull the fire along to the next candle. Make sure to keep all the previous candles lit."

I swallow. That sounds difficult. I light the first one easily with a flick of my hand, but I knew that wouldn't be the hard part. I call on my air, dragging the flame with me. Instead of it lighting the next candle though, I end up extinguishing my own flame. I roll my eyes at myself before lighting it again. This time I try a more subtle breeze, but it once again goes out. I try for about ten minutes with no success, and I growl in frustration, my fae side coming out, and Stavros chuckles.

"Okay, stop for a moment. Remember all our lessons on how to keep your flame going while I try to blow it out? Apply that same lesson here."

"But that was using my fire magic. Not my air."

"And you have both. You can try to do it however it works for you."

That was stupid of me. Why didn't I think of that?

I light the candle again, this time focusing my energy on keeping that one lit. When I'm sure it's going to stay, I drag a subtle breeze through it. It finally catches, bringing the flame to the next candle. I whoop in excitement, glad I was able to manage it. I have sweat beading on my brow from how hard I was concentrating, but I did it.

The next candle is easier since I know what I'm doing, but there's a huge line of candles, and the farther down the line I look, the bigger the space is in between them. I take a deep breath before repeating the same thing. This time, the candle blows out, and I huff. I relight it, making sure to focus more on maintaining it before continuing.

By the time I'm almost to the end, I'm drenched in sweat, almost like my fire gift is igniting me from the inside out. The jumps between candles have been difficult, and I'm struggling to focus on keeping both elements going at once. I take a second to recenter myself, breathing deeply, and when I make that final push between the last two candles, Stavros's air pushes against mine.

I have another fae moment, snarling at him, nothing human in my voice. He chuckles again, making me even more pissed. I push my fire and air against his, and just when I think he's going to push me back, I break through. I light the candle, but the grass beyond the yard catches on fire. I squeal in alarm, cutting the air off from my flames before they can do any damage. When I turn to face Stavros, his smile is enormous. He rushes over to me and wraps me in a hug.

"Well done! I think you earned a very well-deserved break. I know you normally do combat training after this, but after that accomplishment, I think you should rest. Or do something fun. You've been working hard, and there's nothing wrong with taking some time for yourself."

"But…"

"No buts. Go to your room," he orders like a typical dad, making me smile.

"Thank you," I say, leaning over and giving him a kiss on the cheek.

As I head that way, I try to think of how I want to spend the rest of my morning. He's right. I have been training very hard, and I need a break. I think I'd like to take a hike and explore some more of the territory. Since I haven't been using my phone much lately, I bring it and my headphones with me too, wanting to feel a little bit like my old self. As soon as the music starts up, I let out a sigh of relief. It's like coming up for air.

I take a few deep breaths, savoring it, and when I'm centered, I begin walking. I make sure to pick a direction that I've never been in before, wanting to see something new. Since the Immortal City is at the very top of the mountain, I have to travel down first and then hike back up, which is not something I'm used to.

I follow the path of the river so I won't lose my way, and won't have to concentrate on how to get back. I can just enjoy the scenery. Plus, let's face it, I love water. Which now makes sense since I've discovered I'm actually a freaking *mermaid.*

I get lost in the beauty of this world that I'm in. Sometimes I still forget that it's not the same place as where I grew up. It's easy to pretend that I'm still somewhere on Earth I've never been before, like Europe or Asia. But then the lack of electricity or all the magical abilities reminds me that I'm not in Kansas anymore.

As I walk, I take in all the otherworldly plants and flowers along the way. Ones that don't exist back home. *Home.* Why am I still calling it that? I don't belong there. I never have. And now that my mom is no longer alive, there's literally nothing for me there. Although, I would like to go back at some point and get some of my things. It's also too bad that I can't just take electricity back with me. That would be handy. I also promised Pearl and Alexei that I would bring them so they could get the full Earth experience. My mate mark burns when I think of him, and I sigh.

Oh Alexei. I've been dreaming of him almost every night. That's the only time I let myself think of him with anything that doesn't resemble hostility. At least I'm the only one who knows about it. I haven't even told Pearl that little tidbit, and I'm sure she would love to jump at the chance to lecture me again about why I need to forgive him.

I must admit that the dreams make it difficult to resist him. I see what things could be like between us. What things *would've* been like if we had worked out like we were supposed to. Because I'm betting that if we had become mates, then none of the issues that were keeping us apart before would apply. From what Pearl told me, being mates kind of trumps everything. Except having a part in your kidnapping and death, apparently. Pearl still isn't convinced.

The thing that kills me is that if he hadn't betrayed me, there's a good chance my powers wouldn't have awakened, and then we would never have become mates. Ugh. Irony can go fuck itself.

I let myself look at the scenery around me, and try to put all of my troubles and anxieties out of my head. I have somehow come across another waterfall. There is so much water here. Not that I'm complaining, I'm just not used to it.

The waterfall leads right into a lovely little pool. I dip my hand in it, and find it's the absolute perfect temperature. I'm a bit warm after my hike, and I'm so tempted to cool down. I look around, trying to determine if this is a good idea. There is no one around, and I have literally passed by no one this whole time. Fuck it. I start stripping. Once I'm deep enough, I shift into my mermaid form. I take a moment and revel in the beauty of this new ability I have. If someone had told me six months ago that I was a freaking *mermaid* and could shift forms,

I would've called them batshit crazy.

I swim around for a while, cooling down and stretching my tentacles. I don't get the chance to swim on my own much, and I have to admit, I enjoy it. Don't get me wrong, I love swimming with Pearl, but I like the silence. Plus, she's been swimming her whole life, so she makes everything look so easy. It's hard when I have to try to do something that she does so flawlessly, and then inevitably make an ass out of myself. It's too bad this little pool isn't big enough to try that jump. Maybe I should make it a habit to swim on my own more often.

After enjoying myself for a while, I'm about to get out and head back up the mountain when I eye the waterfall. How cliché would it be to rinse off like a true mermaid? I snicker as I head over to it. I push the upper half of my body out of the water with my tentacles as I tip my head back, letting the refreshing water rinse down my hair and back. I sigh in appreciation, but the pounding of the water is so loud that the sound is drowned out. When I'm done, I lower myself back down and open my eyes. I let out a squeal when I discover I'm not alone. Alexei is standing there staring at me with wide eyes. It's then that I sense his overwhelming lust spearing straight for me. I scowl at him.

"What the hell, asshole? Why didn't you tell me you were there?" I ask, covering my chest, even though the water is coverage enough. Not to mention the fact that he just saw everything, and *has* seen it all before anyway. I mentally roll my eyes at myself.

"I was calling your name, but you must not have been able to hear me over the waterfall."

"So, you just thought you'd gawk at me instead?"

I fight a smirk when a blush rises to his cheeks.

"I didn't mean to."

"Sure you didn't," I remark sarcastically.

"I really didn't," he snips back. Clearly my bitchiness is starting to get to him. "I often come down here on my own to get away from everything, and I wasn't expecting to see you."

I find it interesting that we both came to the same spot. I guess that's another reason we're mates. I stop that thought in its tracks before swimming to the edge and shifting into my normal form. I make my way out of the water, despite Alexei sputtering and attempting to give me privacy *now* and turning around. I dry myself off with my air magic before quickly throwing my clothes on. That sure is a handy skill to have.

"You can turn around now."

I'm tempted to take off back toward the castle, but something stops me. He takes a seat on a wide flat rock by the pond. I sigh and sit down next to him. His head whips to me in surprise. I roll my eyes at him, but give him a small, reluctant smile.

"I've never seen you in your mermaid form before. You're breathtaking. But that's nothing new. You've always been stunning."

I blush under the praise, but turn away so he can't see.

"I didn't know you had tentacles," he remarks carefully.

"I was just as surprised as you. We think that I might be descended from Surseiha."

His brows rise. "Wow. There hasn't been someone from her line in ages."

I nod. We sit there in silence for a while. Weirdly, it's not uncomfortable. At times like these, it's hard to remember to stay mad at him. Maybe I should try to start letting some of that go. He has apologized, and hating him so fiercely isn't helping either of us, especially since we have to spend so much time together. I don't think we'll ever be able to go back to the way things were before, but maybe I can let go of some of my hostility.

"Stavros wants us to travel to the different territories together," I tell him after a few minutes.

"He told me. Are you going to be comfortable with that?"

"Well, I don't really have much of a choice."

"You always have a choice, Ember. If you don't want to, I understand, and we can think of something else to tell the king."

I sigh. I hate that he's being so kind and understanding about everything. I take a deep breath and release some of the tension that's been clinging to me since he betrayed me.

"It's okay, Alexei. I've very recently decided not to hate you so much."

His eyes are so big, and there's a hope behind them that I don't want to acknowledge.

"Don't look so excited. I just...I've been thinking about everything lately, and while I can't forgive you for what happened, I'm starting to...*understand* why you did what you did. You didn't know what Mordecai was planning, and he was your father after all."

"Ember—" he starts.

"Don't." I hold my hand up to stop him. "I don't want to talk about it anymore, and I don't want you reading too much into this. I still don't want to be with you, and I still don't trust you." My mate mark burns at the obvious lie on my tongue, but I push past it. "I would just rather start being civil to you. We need to spend a lot of time together, so it would be easier for me not to dislike you so much."

He gives me a self-satisfied smile, like he can tell that I'm going to cave to him.

I glare at him. "Stop looking at me like that!"

"Like what?" he asks me innocently.

"Alexei Dreymonde, stop it!" I scold.

"I have no idea what you're talking about, mate."

Even though I hate it, my heart skips a beat at hearing him call me that. I brush it off, and give him a half-hearted growl before shutting up and looking over the beautiful view in front of me.

"Where are we going to go first?" he asks.

"Well, Pearl needs to go to Mermacovia, and wants to meet us there, so we'll probably go there first. I think she's supposed to leave within the next week. Hopefully that'll be enough time for me to be trained in teletraveling that I'll be ready for the trip."

"That should be plenty of time. Especially since I'll be able to guide you. We probably won't be able to make the whole trip in one go though. We might need to make a few stops along the way."

"How long will we need to stop?" I hope it's not long. I don't want to have to spend the night with him at an inn or something. It will feel too reminiscent of our last trip.

"It all depends on you. We'll be able to leave as soon as your magic is recharged. It's different for everyone. But eating helps to restore it, so we can stop at a tavern in between, and then see if you're ready to continue on. If not, we might have to stay the night."

I try not to let him see how much that thought unnerves me. I nod, looking away from him. Of course, he knows me too well by now.

"If we do have to stay, we'll be in separate rooms. It won't be like last time."

I almost sigh in relief, but I don't. I just nod again.

"Okay, well, I should head back up to the castle. I'll see you for lessons."

Before he can respond, I stand and head back the way I came. I shake my head at myself. I need to be careful. It would be all too easy to get back into how things were before. And while I don't want to be angry all the time, I don't want to just let him off the hook completely for what happened. I need to keep my shit together and resist him as much as I can.

6

Alexei

I smile to myself as Ember walks away. I know she told me that her declaration didn't mean anything or change our current situation, but it's hard not to get my hopes up. She also told me that she never wanted me near her again, and here we are. I told her we could figure something else out for her trips to the territories, and she wants me to go with her. Well, maybe *want* is a strong word, but she didn't take me up on my offer. That's saying something, right?

I know what I really need, though, is to find a solid plan to win her back. I haven't even thought about trying to come up with something until now because I wanted to respect her wishes and stay away from her as much as I could, even when it caused me physical pain to do so. But with her telling me that she wasn't going to hold on to her hate, and that she understood where I was coming from, it made me look at things differently.

I go through all the things that men usually do when they've, well, been men and screwed things up. I could get her a gift, I could do something special for her, I could grovel some more and get her some pretty flowers. But of course, all of those things would never make up for how badly I fucked everything up. I sigh as I look down at my mate mark. It burns as if it knows how much I hurt her. I trace it reverently, this precious gift I was given. Determination fills me. No matter what, I *will* make this up to her.

We're on the road again, only this time we're lying in one of our beds for the night. I immediately know that I'm dreaming of her again. They're always so bittersweet because I'm able to touch her how I want, but my subconscious still knows she's upset with me, so she never truly forgives me. Nonetheless, I cherish them.

She lies on her side and looks at me. Her eyes are full of want, but there's a sadness to them that I wish I could erase.

"Can I ever escape you?" Her words break my heart, but not as much as the way her voice hitches.

"Never, little doe." I scoot closer to her and slowly bring my hand up to her cheek. I brush my thumb under her eye as a tear falls from it. "Don't cry, my love." I lean in and graze my lips over her cheeks, tasting the saltiness of her sorrow. She wraps her arms around my neck, bringing me with her as she lies on her back.

"I hate that I want you so much," she whispers to me, like it's a secret. And if this were real life, I suppose it would be. She would never admit that to me for real. Even after what she told me today.

"I want you too. More than anything," I tell her. "I think about you every moment of every day."

I slowly move my mouth from her cheeks down her body. My hands drift to her shirt, pushing it up. She arches her back to accommodate me. When it's under her collarbones, we sit up so I can remove it fully. She lies back down and I admire the view. Since I've seen her in real life, I know the shape of her body, and I trace her curves with my fingers, my eyes following the movements. In my dreams, I've touched her before, but it was never when she was laid out beneath me like this without her clothes. It's my own brand of torture. But at least I can have her here since I'm unable to in reality.

Her nipples pebble under my touch, and she lets out a soft moan as I graze them. Unable to resist, I lean down and take one in my mouth. I flick my tongue back and forth across it, and it gets harder. When she starts writhing under me, I suck hard, making her gasp. I smile against her skin and switch to her other breast as my fingers toy with her waistband. I don't go any further, enjoying teasing her.

After another minute she pleads with me. "Alexei, please!"

I chuckle, but give her what she wants. I sit up so I can tug her pants off completely until she's utterly bare before me. I growl at the sight of her. I could drink her in all day. My hands graze her legs, and when I reach her knees, I clasp them and force them wide. She flushes, but doesn't stop me or pull her legs closed.

"I've wanted to taste you from the moment you tumbled into my world."

Without waiting for her to respond, I dive in. My groan almost drowns hers out. She tastes like honey. I know in real life she would taste even better, but I can't imagine how. I never want to come up for air, and I can't get enough of her. I feast. There's no other word for it. I'm a starving man, and only she can sate me. She grips my hair in both hands, and before I know it she's grinding against my face. I love that she's using me for her pleasure.

My erection is pinned between my body and the ground, and my hips start moving in time with hers. I moan at the friction, and when I peek up at Ember, she looks completely unhinged and ready to explode. The sight *brings my own orgasm to the brink, and to move her along more quickly, I push two fingers inside her. She pulses around them, and within a matter of moments, she's screaming her pleasure and convulsing around me. It all pushes me over the edge, and I follow her into oblivion moments later.*

I crawl up her body and kiss her senseless, letting her taste herself. "I'm the only one who can make you feel like this," I tell her, my possessiveness making a sudden appearance. There's a fire in her eyes, like she's about to tell me off, but before she can, I blink awake.

I look down to find that just like all the other nights I've dreamt of us, I'm covered in my climax. I roll my eyes at myself. You would think that I'm fourteen years old with how often this has been happening, but I know it's the mate bond. I glance down at my mark again and find a pleasurable tingling coursing through it. I don't know what that means, but usually it burns, as if in retribution for the crimes I committed against my mate.

Knowing I won't be able to get back to sleep, I get up and hop into the shower. I didn't make a mess of my sheets, just myself. Once I'm rinsed off, I look down to find myself still excited. I sigh. I can't get the taste of dream Ember out of my head. I know it wasn't real, but I swear a hint of it still coats my tongue. Before I know what I'm doing, I have my hand wrapped tightly around my length. I groan at the pressure and picture my dream again. The taste of her, the feel of her spasming around my fingers, her scream when she came. All too quickly my release barrels down on me.

Mates are notoriously horny for each other. The obvious problem here is that we aren't sleeping with each other. I have a hard enough time when we're alone and training together. Luckily, or maybe unluckily, it's not like combat training where we're in close contact with each other. That would almost definitely end inappropriately whether she wanted it to or not, and then would inevitably lead to her being even more upset with me.

I groan in frustration as I get out of the shower and dry myself off. With nothing to do, and restlessness building inside me, I head to the training yard. I pound myself into the ground until I can't walk or think anymore.

Ember meets me for teletraveling training in the yard later. I wore myself out so much earlier that while I'm of course still affected, it's not as bad as normal. Although, she usually doesn't pay much attention to me in that sense to even know that I'm uncomfortable.

Today, however, she seems to be sticking to her word from yesterday. While things between us are not like they were on the road, it's been much more pleasant and less tense. It's also affecting her training. She was already improving quite a bit before, but now since she's not as on edge, she's able to focus more. Almost every time she travels to exactly her target, and I think she's ready to start with longer distances.

"Ember, you see that structure on the horizon out there?"

"Yeah."

"I'll meet you there."

Without another word, I vanish. I reappear a moment later right in front of the structure. About ten seconds later, Ember pops up about ten yards in front of me. I smile proudly at her. She wasn't able to make it exactly to her target destination, but for that distance she did really well. "Well done! Now, let's travel back to the yard."

I once again disappear, but this time she's only a few seconds behind me, and lands almost exactly where she was the last time. I knew she would have an easier time coming back because she's more familiar with the space. I grab her some water as she tries to subtly wipe the sweat off her brow. She's been training hard today, and that was her first time traveling that distance, so it took more concentration and effort.

I sit and gesture for her to do the same, and she looks relieved. I push her hard, but I like to think that I'm good about knowing what her limits are. She should be ready to try again in ten minutes or so.

"How is that feeling for you? You're definitely starting to get it down."

"I think it's finally clicking. It makes more sense to me today than it ever has before." I smile at that.

"Give it a few more days and you'll be a pro."

She scoffs at that. "Unlikely. You're just trying to flatter me because you're in the dog house."

"I'm not in a dog house," I tell her, confused.

She shakes her head in frustration, but laughs. "Never mind. So, when do you think I'll be ready to travel across territories?"

"I would guess another week or so. Now that you're starting to drastically improve, we can take bigger and bigger steps in your training, and travel farther distances."

She nods. "Okay, I think I'm ready to keep training." The conversation is clearly motivating her to keep going, especially now that she's getting in the groove.

"Are you sure?" I still ask, because I thought she would've needed more time to rest.

"Positive."

"Okay. Well, this time we are going to travel a bit farther, but instead I'm going to guide you, like we'll be doing on our trip."

She visibly swallows, but she nods all the same. I walk up next to her and hold my hand out. She takes a deep breath before slowly lifting her own hand and settling it in mine. Immediately, the mate mark flares, even letting off a subtle light. Both of us gasp in response. It makes sense since it's the first time she's touched me willingly since we became mates. I grasp on to her hand tighter, the connection between us almost overwhelming me. I struggle not to pull her into my arms, but I know she's not ready for that. Our eyes lock for a moment, and I swear the same struggle is written in her gaze as well. I swallow the huge knot in my throat, and when I speak, my voice is husky.

"Ready?"

She nods.

I close my eyes and try to focus on what I'm supposed to be doing, instead of the sensation of her hand in mine. I picture the field about a mile from where we just were. My body starts to tingle like it does right before I disappear. I clutch Ember's hand harder.

"Concentrate on following me. I'll do the rest."

The point where our hands connect solidifies and melts all at the same time, and then we're gone. A moment later we materialize in the field exactly where I wanted us. I look over to see Ember panting, but grinning.

"Well done," I praise her. "That was about a mile farther than the last time. How do you feel?"

"Tired, but it was manageable. Especially with you guiding me."

"Good. When we go back I'll have you travel on your own to see if you can do that distance without assistance. Then we can be done for the day. I'm sure you're exhausted."

She nods gratefully at me, but doesn't elaborate. I give her a few minutes to rest, and before long, she tells me that she's good. My brows rise in surprise. This has happened multiple times. I marvel at how powerful she must be for her to barely need any time to recover.

We teletravel back to the training yard, and she ends up exactly where I directed her. I'm so impressed with her that I whistle in amazement.

"Ember, you are doing really well."

She blushes slightly under my praise, but turns her head so that I don't see it. It's cute that she thinks that would hide it from me. I am a vampire after all. But I'm a perfect gentleman and don't mention it.

"Thank you. It's getting much easier. I can't believe I've improved so much in just one lesson."

"That's pretty common with magic. As soon as it clicks, you start making drastic improvements. Although, I am also surprised at your progress today, even saying that."

She grins widely, and I return it. What I wouldn't do to put that look on her face as often as possible. At least I'm still able to accomplish it after everything that transpired.

"So, tomorrow?" she asks, and I nod in response. My heart is lighter than it's been in weeks.

7

Ember

I trudge back to my room, more exhausted than I've been in a long time. I went through a lot of magic today. Probably more magic than I have since my powers awakened. I'm dead on my feet.

Pearl comes out of her room as I walk by, and as much as I love her, I almost groan in frustration.

"Hey! Where are you going? I thought you were going to meet me down by the lake?"

"Pearl, I don't have the energy tonight."

"Oh," she says, looking dejected. "Well, want to hang out instead? We could eat copious amounts of food and girl talk?" I almost tell her no, but at the look on her face, I reluctantly agree.

"Come on, then. But don't expect me to be good company."

"Duly noted," she says excitedly, pushing past me to lead the way to my rooms.

I roll my eyes at her back and follow her at a much slower pace. When I arrive, she's already making herself at home, and Humphrey is there. I don't know if she managed to snag him on the way, or if he was already here, but I'm glad we don't have to hunt him down.

"Miss Ember, the king wanted me to tell you that he won't be able to make it to dinner. He has an appointment that he cannot miss. Would you like to come down still, or would you prefer to have dinner brought up?"

Pearl answers for me. "We want our meals to be sent here. Thank you, Humphrey."

He looks to me, and I nod.

"Thank you, Humphrey."

He nods and turns to leave. Something occurs to me then. I realize I don't know his last name.

"Humphrey, wait. What's your last name?"

He looks at me a little strangely, but answers. "Bogart."

My brows rise in surprise, and I let out a disbelieving laugh. His face scrunches up in confusion, and honestly probably a little offense too. Fuck, I'm being so rude.

"I'm sorry, I didn't mean to laugh. You just have the name of someone very famous back on Earth."

"Humphrey Bogart is famous on Earth? What for?"

"He was an actor. He appeared in a lot of very well-known and classic movies."

"Well, okay, then." He nods to himself and gives me another smile before leaving.

"Gods, it's so weird being the only one to get *any* reference from where I'm from."

"Maybe when you take me there I'll get some of them," Pearl chimes in.

"Let's hope so. Hey, speaking of travel, Alexei thinks I'll be ready to teletravel to Mermacovia in about a week or so. Did you still want to meet us there?"

"Yes! That's partly why I wanted to talk to you tonight. I was thinking I would start heading home within the next few days, so

I was hoping you would be ready soon."

"How long will it take you to get there?"

"It's about the same distance as the trip you and Alexei made to come here, but we won't have the mountains to contend with and we won't be training like you two were."

"So, how long?" I ask because she didn't answer me. That's Pearl for you though.

"A little over a week."

"That should be perfect, then. We can leave in like two weeks and that will give you plenty of time to get there and prepare them for our arrival."

Pearl gets a strange look on her face.

"Is that okay with you?"

The next moment the look is gone, and I wonder if I imagined it. "Yes, that will work perfectly."

A knock sounds, and Pearl gets our food. We do like we normally do, devouring everything in sight.

When we're finished, and I'm not quite as drained, we start chatting. "So, how does Xanto feel about you leaving for a while?" I ask.

"I'm not sure. Nothing has even happened with us yet. We spend so much time together, but he hasn't made a move at all."

"Does he even *know* you're leaving?"

She gives me a sheepish look.

"Pearl!" I chastise her. "You need to tell him."

"Do I though? Like I said, we're not technically anything to each other."

"He still deserves to know! You've been talking and hanging out every single day."

She sighs dramatically. "*Fine.* I'll tell him tonight. We're swimming at the lake in a bit."

"I know, Pearl. You do that every night. If he hasn't made a move yet, what are your interactions like? I mean do you guys flirt, or rub against each other while you swim? Does that count as flirting?"

"We do do that, but that's pretty common for our species. Both mermaids and mimics have very tactile natures, especially when we're in our shifted forms. Well, I shouldn't say *all* mimics. It really depends on what animal they are. If they are something like a wolf or an otter, or in Xanto's case, a sting ray, they're usually very affectionate. With more loner type animals like a fox or a honey badger, they aren't usually as touchy. Or interested in being around others for that matter. Mimics are weird in general, but loner mimics tend to be very strange."

When she says "honey badger," all I can think is that those mimics don't give a fuck. I mentally laugh at my own joke, not telling Pearl because once again she won't get my reference.

"Okay, thanks for the lesson, but that didn't answer if you thought that constituted flirting or not. Are you saying you aren't sure if you're both just doing that because of your species' natures or because he likes you?"

"I guess I'm saying that I don't know. And that is driving me absolutely crazy. I like him, but I'm not sure how he feels. And let me tell you, I've never experienced this before, and I am not a fan of it."

"You've *never* experienced liking someone and not knowing if they return the sentiment?"

"No! That's what I'm telling you. I don't know what to do!" she practically screams at me. If she didn't look so frustrated and freaked out I would be pissed that she's never had this problem before.

"Well, there are a few routes you can take. The first is to make the first move. I know he thinks you're gorgeous because he told me so at the ball. So, it could be that he's worried you're out of his league. The second is to ask him about it. The third is to not do anything and see if he eventually grows a pair and does something himself."

"I think I'll take option three. That sounds the safest." I scoff in disbelief and frustration.

"You weren't supposed to pick that option!"

"Well, it's your own fault for throwing that one in there."

"Fine. Do what you want. Maybe when you tell him that you're going back to Mermacovia for a little while it'll push him to finally do something."

"Oh, good idea," she remarks, looking like she wants to leave now that she has that figured out, but instead she grabs some stuff from my bathroom and sits behind me. "Speaking of men, and the trip, what's going on with you and Alexei? Is he really coming with you?"

She puts product in my hair and gently brushes it. She's pampering me after my long day because I'm exhausted, and I couldn't be more grateful. I almost purr like a cat, but somehow refrain.

"Yeah, he's coming with me. We've reached a bit of an understanding."

"An understanding, huh?" she asks with a teasing lilt to her voice.

"Don't read too much into it, Pearl. I just realized that I was sick of putting so much energy into hating him. We have to spend a lot of time together, and now we're going on this trip. It's been exhausting being so mad at him."

"So, you've forgiven him?"

"I didn't say that. Because the answer to that is a definite no."

"Sure it is," she says in that same annoying tone.

"I haven't forgiven him, Pearl. He hasn't fucking earned it," I snap at her. I know she thinks that I should, and that I inevitably will, but just because I don't want to hold a grudge doesn't mean that I've forgotten what happened.

"I'm sorry, Ember. I didn't mean to upset you. I know he doesn't deserve your forgiveness. And I think it's very big of you to let some of that go." She's released a little of her allure, her voice sounding even more soothing than normal. I allow it to wrap around me like a balm, needing to be soothed.

"Thanks."

I finally relax as the movements of her brushing my hair lull me into a serene state. She starts humming under her breath, and it's hauntingly beautiful, pulling me even closer to sleep. When she finishes, she gets up and encourages me to lie down, not that it's difficult to do.

"Good night, Ember," she says softly to me.

She blows out my candle as I crawl under my blanket. Between the events of the day, my training, and all the work Pearl just put into relaxing me, I'm asleep almost instantly. My last thought before I drift off is that it was totally worth it having her join me.

I'm not surprised in the least when Alexei shows up in my dream. What I am surprised about is the excitement that builds in my chest. This time we're in the caves, lounging in the healing springs. Of course under the same circumstances as last time, meaning naked. I resist the urge to cover myself. This is just a dream after all.

"Well, fancy meeting you here," I tell him.

His mouth quirks up in a smirk. "Indeed it is," he replies, drifting closer to me in the water.

I hold my breath as he stops in front of me and reaches a hand out to caress my cheek. I involuntarily lean into his touch. I curse myself for being so weak, but I'm glad I'm the only one who has to know that.

Our bodies glide against one another in the water, and before I can stop myself, I wrap my legs around his hips. He hardens against me, and I shift against him, making both of our breaths catch.

"Gods, I wish this was real. What I wouldn't give to have you against me like this in real life instead of in my dreams." His words turn my blood to ice, even as his voice heats it.

"Alexei?"

"Hmm?"

"Are you real?"

"What do you mean, Ember? This is a dream," he says, making me relax slightly. Just a dream. He moves his hands to cup my backside, bringing me even closer. "It's my own form of twisted pleasure. I know you would never be like this with me in real life, so my mind conjures you at night to please me and torture me all at the same time."

I suck in a shocked breath. He still isn't getting it.

"Alexei, you don't dream of me. I dream of you."

His brows furrow in confusion. He shakes his head. Even throughout this conversation, we're still shifting against each other, and I build higher with every slide of his cock against me.

"If you're saying that you dream of me, and I'm saying I dream of you, I think this is real to a certain extent. I think we're meeting in our dreams," I tell him as the horror slides through me. I've been letting him touch me, lick me, make me come. Speaking of which, we're still moving, and I'm getting to the point of no return. I want to tell him to stop, but can't seem to make myself.

"Is this really you, Ember?" he asks desperately, hope filling his eyes.

I nod, closing my eyes. Irrational tears build behind them. I'm so conflicted right now; I don't know what to do. My body is wound so tight, and only Alexei seems to be the one who can break that tension.

"Do you want me to stop?" he asks softly.

Even though I'm going to hate myself for it later, I shake my head.

"Eyes on me, Ember," he commands, and my eyes snap open.

"This doesn't mean anything, Alexei. I'm still going to pretend this is just a dream, and this is the last time. Okay?"

He has a self-satisfied smile on his face that I have the urge to smack off. "Whatever you say, little doe."

I bring my hands up to rest on his shoulders so I can move against him more easily. He smirks knowingly at me, and I glower in return. He leans forward and slowly brings his mouth to mine, giving me time to change my mind. Once again, I can't seem to control myself, and I let him. This time, however, when he kisses me, it's not some gentle thing. I put all of my anger and feelings of unfairness into it, biting him as I attack his mouth in a fierce battle for dominance. He growls his appreciation against my lips, and the vibrations move through me. I didn't think it was possible, but he hardens even more against me, and our motions become more frenzied.

He breaks the kiss and looks into my eyes. "Are you going to come for me, Ember?"

"Not for you," I respond like a brat.

He smiles cockily. "Come for me, little doe. Come against my dick."

I whimper, my orgasm building quickly with him talking to me like that. One of his hands moves to my breast, and he grasps my nipple tightly, the sensation shooting straight to my core.

"Come," he commands.

My body obeys immediately and I explode, my pussy clenching and unclenching around nothing, and I suddenly wish he was inside of me instead. I shut that shit down quick though. The next moment Alexei groans against me, and I know he's also found his release.

"Mine," Alexei murmurs against my mouth. My mate mark flares in agreement, but I ignore them both, knowing that this can't happen again.

8

Pearl

I head down to the lake, hoping that Xanto won't be there quite yet so I can swim on my own for a while. As much as I love swimming with Ember and Xanto, I realize then that I haven't been able to do it by myself for a long time. I breathe a sigh of relief when I find it empty. I strip quickly, ready to dive under and let out my mermaid. As soon as I do, it's refreshing to be able to stretch and *move*. My other form is handy for getting around on land, but it's not quick or easy in the slightest. Not like this body. And with my enhanced strength and glittering claws, I'm a *predator*. Not a lot of people know that about our species. We're seen as sweet, beautiful, majestic creatures. But therein lies the danger. We lure you close to us, and when you're least suspecting, we can rip out your godsdamn throat. This body is powerful, and I have always loved that.

I don't typically let out my bloodthirsty side, especially here at the palace, but with plans to go back home, uncertainty with Xanto, and a considerable decision to make in front of me (a clandestine one, no less), I'm wound tight and ready to do some damage. I wish I had some prey to chase or maim or *something*. I settle for pushing my body to its limits, swimming as fast as I can and jumping as high as I can.

Half an hour later, my restless energy has somewhat dissipated. I float on my back and look up at the sky, the moon and the stars glittering and shimmering down at me. I feel an odd kinship with them. They are beautiful and glimmer just like me when I'm using my allure. Maybe mermaids are connected to the stars in some way. I mean, we do live in a magical world after all, and stranger things have happened, right?

It's when I'm being all introspective and distracted that something swims underneath me. Something large. Another predator. I don't move, but try to gauge where it is without alerting them that I'm aware of their presence. I take in a deep breath, and the next moment I'm shooting through the water, rounding on them, claws bared and skin flaring brightly. I huff in frustration when I see Xanto swimming in the water beneath me, eyes twinkling mischievously. I roll my eyes at him and give him a filthy gesture. Stingrays can't laugh or smile, but I swear he is.

When he knows I won't attack him, he swims up to me and rubs against me. I usually love when he's like this, but being on edge tonight, I'm not having it. Maybe it's just because I'm sick of all the mixed signals he's giving me. I swim away from him, effectively cutting off contact. I swim around a bit more, but now that my alone time is over, I'm not really enjoying it anymore. I swim to the edge of the lake and shift. I'm out of the water and getting dressed in the next moment. Before I can take off, though, Xanto has shifted as well and is yelling out to me.

"Pearl! What's wrong?"

"What's wrong, Xanto? Seriously? Are you that obtuse?"

He strides out of the water naked as the day he was born, utterly gorgeous and completely comfortable in his own skin. His face is scrunched up in confusion, making him even more adorable and me even more frustrated.

"Apparently I am because I have no clue why you're so upset. Care to fill me in?"

"Put some fucking clothes on! I can't concentrate on this conversation with you looking like a god striding out of the water."

Despite my mood, he smirks to himself as he quickly dons his pants. "Happy?"

"Thrilled."

"Pearl, what is wrong?" he asks gently, coming up and grabbing hold of my arms.

"Do you want me?"

His eyes hold a mixture of surprise and confusion. "Do I want you? *Of course* I fucking want you. I have wanted you since I first saw you at that ball."

Relief melts through my body, but I hold on to my anger. "Then why haven't you done anything about it? We're here alone together every single night. And I'm leaving in the next few days and I have no clue where we stand!"

"Wait, you're leaving? Where? For how long?"

"I'm going to Mermacovia. I'll be gone for about a month."

His face sinks, but he nods all the same. "You are coming back though, right?"

"Why do you even care, Xanto? You still haven't answered my question."

He takes a deep breath, his eyes closed tightly. "Of course I care!" he yells at me, taking me off guard. "How can you even ask me that? I'm in love with you, Pearl!" He's still shouting, but his words take a moment to register.

"You love me?" I ask in astonishment.

"How can you not see it?"

"You've never done anything about it! Obviously we're friends, but I've been waiting and wanting you to make a move. I've never been in this situation, so I'm thoroughly confused. Whenever someone wants me, they act on it right away."

"That's partly why I haven't done anything yet. No one has ever gotten to *know* you before. They just lust after you, and I didn't want to be that guy. I want to be different. I wanted to learn every wonderful thing about you, and become just as taken in by your mind and personality as I did with your beauty."

My emotions rise, because he's right. No one has ever bothered to put that effort in before.

"You said partly. What's the other part?" I ask quietly, willing my tears not to fall.

"The other part is that I thought maybe *you* didn't want *me.* You can have anyone you want. Literally anyone. I'm no one. Why would you be with me when there are so many others better for you to choose from?"

His words break my heart. "Xanto, how can you think that you are no one? You are the most wonderful person I have ever met. I've never wanted *anyone* else like I want you. I've never had anyone else do something as simple and wonderful as get to know my mind before they get to know my body. They've always wanted that first and foremost. The fact that you respect me enough to want my mind too, to want deeper than that, Xanto, it means more than I can ever tell you." So I don't tell him. I *show* him.

I wrap my arms around his neck and pull him to me, melding our mouths together. It's soft and loving at first, but it escalates quickly. He groans, almost as if he's in pain as he pulls me tight to him so there's zero space between our bodies. My hands trace his cut torso, and I marvel at the muscles that jump under my palms. Now it's time for him to find out what actually makes a mermaid so alluring. I shift just my hands so my claws are out. I lightly run them over his skin, not breaking it but enough to ride that line between pleasure and pain.

He growls against my mouth, and the sound is all animal, making me smile against his. My hands run down his chest and stomach, stopping right at the waistline of his pants. My fingers tease along it and his breathing speeds up.

I break the kiss and his eyes instantly meet mine. They are full of heat, and it looks like he's a second away from losing his shit in the best way possible. I give him a tantalizing smile as I back away a step, letting my skin flare as bright as it can, and take off my clothes. To his credit, he maintains eye contact with me until I'm fully naked. At that point, his eyes shoot down my body, like magnets being pulled together. I let him drink his fill, but just when I think he's going to move toward me, I hold up my hand to stop him. He looks at me questioningly, but stays where he is. I kneel in front of him and reach up to tug his trousers down his body.

"Pearl, you don't have to do this," he says, but his voice is telling me he wants this very badly.

"I want to, Xanto. I need to show you how I feel about you," I tell him before I take him into my mouth. He groans low and long, his fingers automatically fisting in my hair, encouraging me along. I swirl my tongue around the head of his cock before sucking hard, making him inhale sharply.

"*Fuck*, Pearl. You're going to be the death of me."

I stop for a moment to remark, "At least you'd die happy." I dive back in before he can respond.

My head bobs along his length, and I can tell he's getting close. His breathing is coming in pants, and his hips shoot forward of their own volition more than once, as if his body can't help but fuck my mouth. I grasp his backside in a firm grip, my claws digging in slightly, once again riding that fine line to bring him to the edge.

Just when I think he's going to topple over, he pulls back. His hands already in my hair pull me up, and as soon as I'm standing, his mouth is back on mine. This kiss is *wild*, just like him, and I know that his animal nature is more in control right now. The thought gives me immense pleasure, and I bask in the knowledge that I can do this to him.

He guides me to lie on the ground, and in the next breath he's on top of me, his hardness pressing against my softness. I moan at the contact, and I grind myself against him. My wetness is soon coating his length, and I am desperate to have him filling me.

He breaks away from my mouth and trails his lips down the side of my neck before landing on my breasts. He lavishes both my nipples with plenty of attention, and soon I'm writhing underneath him. He moves to continue south, but I stop him.

"Need you inside me," I murmur.

"Pearl, I want to taste you."

"No. You inside me, now," I order, past the point of forming full sentences.

He growls in acceptance as he lines himself up with me, and his gaze meets mine as he pushes forward until he's fully seated inside of me. We both groan at the same time.

"So good. Too good," he says as he starts to move.

It's not a gentle coupling. It's rough and feral and oh so good. My claws are still out, and I'm scoring lines down his back with every thrust. The earth underneath me is rubbing my back and ass raw, but I couldn't care less. He brings his mouth back to mine, and there is biting and sucking and teeth knocking, and I just can't get enough.

His thumb reaches down to press against my clit, and I see stars as he swirls it round and round. I feel myself tightening around him and know that I'm a moment away from combustion.

I break the kiss. "More," I demand.

His eyes light at the challenge, and he brings his forearm to rest underneath my upper back, exposing my breasts even more fully to him. He takes full advantage, bringing his mouth to them, nipping and sucking them. It pushes me over the edge and I wail. My body pulses around him over and over, my climax never-ending.

When I finally come down, Xanto pulls out of me. I'm just about to protest, when he flips me onto my stomach and hikes my hips up so I'm on my knees with my chest down. I'm displayed crudely in front of him, and I know his eyes are taking in every inch of me. I revel in the attention, my skin flaring brighter.

Just when I think he's going to enter me, he smacks my ass, hard. I'm about to lay into him for it, when suddenly his tongue is licking right through my slit. My loud moan comes a second later, and he spanks me again in encouragement. I like it too much to be angry with him about it. Usually I'm the aggressor and the one in charge. He's trying to go all alpha on me, and I want to be upset, but he's making it feel way too good.

His tongue spears into me a few times before he moves down and sucks on my clit, hard. He flicks his tongue over me until I'm a writhing mess and begging him to come.

"You taste better than I ever could have imagined," he tells me, his voice rougher than I've ever heard it. "I never want to stop."

"Then get back to it!" I yell in frustration.

He chuckles before diving back in. This time he brings his fingers with him, plunging them into my pussy punishingly. I thrust back against him with every stroke, and when he nips on my clit, I lose it entirely. I'm thrown into a full-body climax, my fingers and toes tingling, my head spinning. Before I can come back to myself, his cock pushes inside of me again. I spiral into another orgasm, and spurts of wetness shoot out of me, coating the ground beneath us. I'm screaming it's so intense, and I never want it to end.

I'm brought back down, and my knees are scraping roughly against the ground. They'll be rubbed raw tomorrow, and I love it. Behind me,

Xanto is quickening his thrusts, and I know he must be close. Hell, he was close when I was sucking him. I have no idea how he's lasted this long, but I am definitely not complaining. He fists my hair a moment later, bringing my head up and bending my spine a little awkwardly. His other hand grasps my nipple firmly, and the pinch shoots all the way down to my clit. I whimper, unable to communicate what I need. It's too much, but I want more all at the same time.

"Touch yourself," he grinds out between clenched teeth.

I do as I'm told, and I'm building again. I thrust back against him desperately, wanting to come again, and wanting to feel him spurt inside of me too. He leans over me, changing the angle slightly, making me gasp at the sensation. The next moment, he bites me where my neck meets my shoulder, not quite hard enough to draw blood, but almost, and it sends me over the edge again. I spasm around his length and hear his deep groan a second later as he pulses inside of me.

We collapse into a heap on the ground, both breathing like we've just run a marathon. I haven't met someone who can keep up with me in a long time, and damn did he keep up.

After a few minutes, he rolls off of me, and I turn on my side to face him. "You really have to leave?" he asks.

"Yes. I've been meaning to go home for a while now. Not to mention that Ember and Alexei are going to meet with Coralia Harbor, and I wanted to get there before them to give her a heads-up. I would also like to show Ember around and introduce her to some people."

He nods. I can tell he's not happy about me leaving for so long, but he understands.

"Xanto, there's one other thing I want to talk to you about." He nods at me to continue. "I don't know how much you know about mermaids, but most of us are polyamorous, and bisexual. I love you, but I want to talk about this now before anything else happens. There's no one else right now, but that might not always be the case, and I wanted to let you know that if there is, I'm not an exclusive type of partner."

"Mimics are typically polyamorous and bisexual too, Pearl. I've personally never been with more than one partner, but I'm not opposed to it. My only request is that we do this together. If we decide to bring another person into our relationship, I want to make that decision with each other, and I want it to be a true relationship between all of us. And no secrets. I am not okay with you sneaking off to be with someone else. Agreed?"

I nod. "Understood. I can definitely do that," I tell him, giving him a sincere smile.

He returns it and leans in to deliver a soft kiss on my lips. "Want to go for a real swim with me this time? Now that you aren't whipping your tail in anger at me?"

"Hey! I didn't whip you with my tail!"

"Only because I dodged out of the way," he teases.

I run into the water, splashing him in punishment for his comment. He laughs, following me in. I shift, and before he has a chance to, I bring my tail up and whack it against the water, effectively dousing him.

"Baby, you forget that I love the water as much as you do. You may as well be kissing me." He shifts, ending our conversation, but making me smile in the process.

This time around, we swim with each other lazily and lovingly, brushing up against each other at every opportunity. I think at that moment that it's the happiest I've ever been.

The next day, I tell Ember all about what happened. Of course, being me, I go into extreme detail, and she's fanning herself before slapping my arm lightly, telling me how jealous she is that I'm getting some and she's not.

"So, you're leaving tomorrow?" she asks.

"Yes. I have an escort coming with me. There are lots of waterways on the trip, so I will probably swim a good portion of it. And my escort will be able to carry my things, so I won't need to worry about that."

"Oh good. I'm glad you have someone traveling with you."

"The king insisted. Plus, it's just smart. There are a lot of creatures and individuals who can cause trouble in this realm."

"Don't I know it," she remarks. "Do you need help packing?"

I nod. I could use the company, and I'm going to miss her for the week or so that we'll be apart. Soon we're picking out outfits, and I of course take my most daring and extravagant articles of clothing. I mean, I know we're in a palace, but mermaids are obsessed with beauty. I explain it to Ember when she remarks on the ridiculousness of the items I'm packing.

"Am I going to be expected to wear things like this?" she asks worriedly.

"Mermaids are more over-the-top than half of the court here. You know this. But if I were you, I would pack a lot of your more elegant things. Especially for your meetings with Coralia."

"She's the Mermacovia grand mistress, right?"

"Yes. And she will be doing your training personally."

"Have you met her?" she asks.

"Yes. She's very beautiful and very cunning. She also takes every advantage she can get, so make sure to keep your mental shields as locked up as possible."

She swallows nervously, but nods all the same.

"You'll be fine. I'll be there with you most of the time anyway."

The next day, I'm sent on my way by Ember and Xanto. I hug Ember, and she squeezes me tightly before she gives me and Xanto space to say goodbye.

"Travel safe," he tells me.

"I will. Don't fall in love with anyone else until after I get back and we can fall together, okay?"

He laughs but nods. I lean in and give him a heated kiss. It's over way too soon, and the next thing I know, we're pulling away and I'm climbing onto my horse. I wave to them, and then begin traveling back home with a mixture of sadness, excitement, and trepidation about my looming decision.

9

Ember

After Pearl leaves, the week passes by in a strange combination of fast and slow. It's boring without her here, and I have more alone time than I've had since arriving at the castle. But with my nerves about going to another territory soon and Pearl's cryptic warning about the grand mistress, it passes more quickly than I'm ready for.

When I see Alexei the day after our dream, I'm mortified to see a mark where I bit him on his lip. At least now I know that I'm not crazy. I also know that Alexei loves having it on display because he could've easily gone to the healer's wing to have them get rid of it, but he doesn't. He gives me a knowing smile when he catches me staring at it and I glare at him.

I keep up my training with both Alexei and my father, now making large strides. I've progressed so well with my air and fire training that we are switching between magic and combat training every other day. I am now very confident in my skills, and know that now it would be difficult for someone to get the better of me in a fight.

My teletraveling training is progressing nicely too, and I'm able to travel farther distances every day. At this point, Alexei and I have traveled to multiple places around the border of Mystic Mountain. It's been incredible being able to see more of the territory, and with the distances we're traveling, I have to rest between jumps for quite a while in order to let my magic refill. That means that we're able to explore. Alexei has been showing me different beautiful spots around the fae's lands, and even though I know we're technically training, it doesn't feel like it. It's like a fun adventure, and I'm reminded of our trip from Twin Fangs on more than one occasion. Usually Alexei brings some food for us so that our magic regenerates more quickly, and we camp out in front of a scenic area while we have our picnic.

Mystic Mountain has some of the most gorgeous landscapes I've ever seen, and I know that places like this don't exist on Earth. I wonder if it's because of magic. Alexei has told me on more than one occasion that the land often contains the magic of whatever species lives there, and I bet that makes the whole realm more breathtaking.

After a week of exploring, I've seen most of the territory. We've had several instances where we've come across others, and I never know what kind of reception we're going to get. We've had people be very welcoming and gracious, but there's also been some who you can tell are used to the segregation and do not enjoy having Alexei and me around with our mixed heritage.

One day, when the two of us are at a tavern, getting plenty of dark looks, I ask him about it.

"How often are you treated like this?"

He looks around, scoffing slightly, as if he finds it funny and inoffensive. "Less than half the time. It doesn't bother me anymore. It used to when I was younger, but I've come to the realization that the people who act like this are just closed-minded. I pity them. I know that I'm a good man, or that I at least try to do the right thing," he adds, looking at me a bit uncomfortably.

"I've helped out the kingdom more than any of them have, and I know that I'm an asset to the king, even if I'm a half breed. It gives me more power than they have as well, and I learned long ago that most of them are jealous of the multiple powers that half breeds have. That makes us stronger than them, not weaker like they like to tell themselves."

I smile at his words, because he is absolutely right. "I'm glad it doesn't bother you, Alexei."

"Don't let it bother you either. Remember what I told you in the next few months. With all the different territories we'll be traveling to, this is going to get more and more common. You are slightly different since you have the blood of all the races, but I have only fae and vampire, so when we travel to any of the other territories, I might not be well received."

I nod in understanding. "I won't let it get to me. I don't know if I told you or not, or if Stavros did, but I've decided to be next in line for the throne," I say quietly, considering we're in public. His brows rise in surprise at my words. "That being said, Stavros wants me to try to gain some support from the other territories while we're there. I don't quite know what that will look like, if that means the grand masters, or if I should be interacting with the general public, but either way, I'll need to be prepared for things not to go well."

"Well, we'll start with the grand masters, and go from there. You don't need to have the support of the entire realm. You technically don't need any support at all since you're the king's daughter, but it will work in your favor if you have at least the leaders of the territories on your side."

When we're done eating and drinking our ales, we head back to the castle. It's exhausting to travel as far as we are, but I'm relieved that it's starting to get easier. I still won't be able to make the entire trip to Allure Isle in one jump, but I should be able to at least get to the halfway point. Alexei said I'll need longer to rest when we do, because it'll be the farthest I've ever teletraveled before. Our plan is to leave in the evening, stay overnight at a lodge, and then travel the rest of the way the next morning.

The night before we leave, I have a private dinner with Stavros. Alexei joins us occasionally, but tonight it's just the two of us, and I'm glad we get to be alone before my tour of the realm.

"So, tomorrow's the big day. Are you ready?"

"I think so." My fidgeting gives away my nervousness about it all.

His eyes home in on me picking at my nails, a small smile gracing his mouth. "They're going to love you, Ember. Everybody does."

I chuckle skeptically. "I don't think that's true. You're just saying that because you're my father."

"No, I'm serious. You should have heard everyone talking about you at the ball. They were enchanted with you."

"That's probably just because they've never met someone who had the blood of every species before. I know Alexei could tell something was different about me before we knew what I was. It makes sense that they would know I was special even before my powers awakened."

He shakes his head. "That might be part of it, but Ember, you're not seeing yourself clearly. You're wonderful. You're caring, brave, feisty. Just like your mother. I can tell you're going to be a wonderful queen. I would never leave my kingdom to someone who wasn't."

Emotion clogs my throat, and I nod and smile. I'm still not used to having a father to tell me these things.

"So, on a separate note, there's something else I wanted to discuss with you."

I pull myself together. "What's up?"

"Well," he starts, looking slightly uncomfortable. "Now that you're going to be the next in line, there's something that we might want to think about. I want you to know that there is absolutely no pressure, and if it's not something you want to do, or aren't comfortable with, I am totally fine with that."

"Just tell me what it is, Dad."

Me calling him "Dad" seems to have made him less nervous. "I wanted to let you know that there has been interest in you."

"Interest in me?" My stomach sinks slightly.

He clears his throat, looking uncomfortable again. "Umm, yes." I don't think I've ever heard Stavros say "umm." "There have been some fae males telling me that they would like to marry you."

My stomach fully drops at this point. "Marry me? They've never even met me."

"Of course, but they did see you at the ball, and there is the allure of you being the king's daughter. You don't have to think about it now, but I was wondering if you would be interested in meeting with any of them when you get back from your travels?"

I take a deep breath and think about it logically. First of all, Stavros said there was no pressure, so it's not a necessary thing. Second of all, there's no harm in meeting them. My mate mark burns at the traitorous thought. Third of all, I told myself I wasn't going to be hung up on Alexei anymore. I told myself, and him for that matter, that things would never happen between us. In order to move on, I need to actually open myself up to the idea of being with someone else, regardless of the mark on my arm. Stavros has been patient, letting me think through this bomb he just dropped on me.

"Sure. I would be willing to *meet* them."

His eyes widen in surprise. "Okay, wonderful. When you return I'll set it up."

I nod and turn back to my food, even though my appetite has vanished. The thought of bringing this up to Alexei has anxiety burning a pit in my stomach. I know he's going to be upset, but I need to stick to my guns, and he needs to accept that things are over romantically between us, despite the shared dreams we were having. As soon as I realized what was happening, they stopped. Well, at least the sexual aspect of them. Occasionally we still meet in our sleep, but there seems to be an understanding between us that things won't cross over into that territory again. I can see the strain from Alexei whenever we're together or sharing dreams. I know that it's painful for him not to be able to touch me anymore, but he respects my boundaries.

As much as I don't want to admit it to myself, I'm equally relieved and upset about that. I know I can't let myself give in when it comes to him, but at the same time, I almost wish that he would disregard the rules I've set and just take me like we both want. Every time I have that thought, I mentally slap myself to get my shit together.

Even though I'm set on not being together, it doesn't make it any less difficult. Especially when the fact that we're mates is thrown in our faces on a regular basis, whether it be the dreams, the mate mark, or just the general sensation of emptiness when we're not together. It's exhausting, and I'm so tempted to give in.

I meet him in my dreams that night, like my subconscious can tell that I want to give in to him. Now that we've stopped the sexy stuff, most of the time we just hang out and talk. Of course, there is always an undercurrent of sexuality behind the dreams, but we push past it.

"How was dinner with your father?" he asks.

Fuck. Now would be the time to tell him. Maybe it'll be better since we're not actually in front of each other. "Well, he told me that there have been a few fae males who are interested in my hand in marriage."

A rumbling is coming from his chest, and I know he's trying with all his might to suppress a snarl. He closes his eyes and takes a few deep breaths.

"What did you tell him?"

"I told him that I would be willing to meet them," I tell him gently.

Devastation is written clearly in his features followed closely by anger. "Wow. I didn't think you would be one to settle for anything that wasn't a love match."

I bristle at his tone. "How do you know that none of them will be a love match, Alexei?" My voice rises as my own anger does.

"Because none of them are me!" he shouts.

"That's presumptuous. You're assuming that I'll never be able to love another just because they aren't you?"

"It's not presumptuous, Ember. That's how it is. We're mated. I know that you still haven't forgiven me for what happened, but you're delusional if you think that you would be happy with someone else. We're fated to be together. That's what this mark means!" He thrusts his arm in front of me, then he grabs my arm gently, stroking his thumb over my own mark. "And this one," he says a bit more softly, the act of touching me seeming to calm him.

I rip my arm out of his grasp, backing up to give myself some space. "Don't call me delusional. I'm not willing to accept that just because we have these doesn't mean that I can never be happy again. That's called being an optimist, jackass, not crazy."

He stalks up to me and wraps me in his arms. "When are you going to acknowledge that we're meant to be?" Before I can reply, he seals our mouths together. His tongue plunges into my mouth punishingly, and I moan, my hands twining around his neck. His hands go to my backside, and as he pulls me firmly against him, his hardness pushes against my belly. I return his kiss for a few moments before sense comes crashing back down. I push him away from me, slapping him across the face for good measure.

"Fuck you, Alexei." Tears are streaming down my face, and I will myself awake.

I'm breathing hard when I wake up. I reach up and touch my cheeks, finding that I'm actually crying. I bury my face in my pillow, allowing myself to wallow for a bit. He can be such an ass, but I fear he's right. What if I never *can* find anyone else? I finally am able to get back to sleep, and thank my lucky stars when I don't dream of Alexei.

I train with Stavros the next morning for the last time before I leave. We work on combat training instead of elemental so I can save up all my magic for the journey. It's bittersweet. I'm excited to go on this trip, but I'll miss him and I wish he could come with me.

When we're finished, I head up to my room to pack. Over the last few days, I've been slowly picking out clothing options, keeping Pearl's advice in mind. Normally vampires can't carry heavy loads with them when they teletravel, but Stavros told me about a handy little spell that shrinks things. This way I'm able to pack a huge trunk for our entire trip, and then I can basically just shrink it down and carry it around in my pocket. It's extremely handy, and I'm grateful that I'll be able to have a wide variety of clothes to choose from.

When that's all set to go, I head down to the entrance hall to meet Alexei. I haven't had any contact with him since our dream the night before, and I'm a ball of nervous and angry energy. Stavros is going to send us off, and I'm glad he'll be there as a buffer, even if he doesn't know it.

One look at Alexei and I can tell he's just as upset as he was last night. He's glaring at me, and surprisingly giving subtle looks to the king as well. Fortunately for him, the king is just as oblivious as most men and doesn't seem to notice.

"Do you have everything you need?" my father asks us.

"I do," I reply, patting my pocket where my trunk is stored. Alexei simply grunts an affirmation. I struggle not to laugh at his mood. I don't know why I always find it hilarious when he's so angry, but it's a welcome reprieve from my previous emotions.

Stavros gives me a tight hug. Unexpected tears gather behind my eyes. I squeeze him back just as firmly, and we share a rare father/daughter moment. I cherish these more than almost anything, and from the look on his face when we pull back, he feels the same way.

"Travel safe. Write to me when you can, and update me on when and where you're going."

"I will," I promise.

"I love you, Ember."

Those pesky tears are back again, but I blink them away. "I love you too, Dad."

He smiles gently at me before turning to Alexei. "Take care of her. You understand me?"

I'm surprised. I've never heard Stavros take that tone with him before.

"Yes, Sire." Alexei takes his hand, shaking firmly before bowing his head over their joined grip. Alexei looks at me. "Ready?"

I nod, coming forward to grab his outstretched hand. My palm tingles pleasantly where it meets his, but I ignore it. I maintain eye contact with my father as Alexei starts pulling me with him. I focus all my energy on following him, and the last thing I see is my dad smiling proudly at me.

A moment later, we materialize in Mermacovia. We're about halfway between the Immortal City and Mermacovia's capital, Allure Isle. Alexei told me that we would be crossing the border before we arrived, and that it would be farther than I've ever teletraveled before. Two things hit me at once. First, my absolute exhaustion. I know I've been traveling farther distances lately, but I barely made that jump. Second, I can definitely tell we're in a different territory. It's muggy from all of the humidity, and it reminds me of how I imagine Costa Rica's climate would feel. There is a massive ancient jungle spread out around us with waterways cutting through it. Since we're basically in the middle of the territory and not near the ocean yet, it makes sense that there would be other forms of water, and as a result lush landscape would be prevalent, but I'm still surprised all the same.

Alexei gives me a few moments to take it all in, and when I'm finally ready, I turn to face him. He has a small smile gracing his lips.

"I always enjoy watching your reactions to seeing new areas of the realm."

"It's just so marvelous," I breathe.

"I forget sometimes. I've been all over this realm, and I've gotten used to it. Being with you always reminds me to appreciate it again."

"I don't know how you could ever get used to this."

"I'll remind you that you said that in a few years. Ready to get some food and rest?"

I nod, exhausted and starving. I'm also curious to see what kind of food this territory will offer.

He leads me to a lodge that's literally *on* the river. It's warmly lit and inviting, beckoning us to walk inside. I gasp in amazement when we enter. There are windows along every side of the building that face the water, sparkling lights dance all through the river, and occasionally a mermaid swims by.

I'm pleasantly surprised that this lodge has a tavern downstairs, so we can eat at an actual table as opposed to in our rooms, much like we did on our trip to the Immortal City. We take a seat right next to a window since I want to be as close to the water as I can get. A server comes by with a bottle of white wine for us, and while I normally don't enjoy white as much as red, I have to admit that it's fitting and refreshing for our climate. Not long after, he brings each of us a plate of the tavern's nightly meal. I found out when we last traveled that the lodges have one meal every night, and that's what you get. They don't cook something specifically for you, you eat whatever they make.

I'm even more pleased with the white wine when the meal is a white fish with lemon, dill, and garlic, and roasted asparagus with a white cream sauce. My mouth waters at the scent, and I dig in, my magic demanding that I eat to replenish. Alexei does the same, eating faster than normal, and I'm glad to discover that his magic is almost as drained as mine is. I hide my smirk behind my glass of wine.

Everything is delicious. The fish literally melts in my mouth, the lemon and dill giving it a fresh summery taste. The wine pairs perfectly with the meal, and I take another greedy sip before starting in on my asparagus, which is crisp and slightly tangy from the sauce.

All too soon my plate is empty. For the first time ever Alexei finishes eating before me. My brows rise in question and surprise. "Wow. You were hungry."

"Well, so were you," he retorts.

"Yes, but I'm *always* hungry. You know this. You, however, are never this hungry."

"I used up a lot of magic getting us here."

"Does the person guiding the jump use more magic? Or are they equal?"

"The one guiding usually has to use a little more. Not a significant amount, but it can sometimes be difficult to pull the other person with you."

"Am I hard to pull?"

"You were a little at first, but not anymore. You've gotten used to the sensation. And you trust me." I narrow my eyes at him. "Well, you at least trust me enough to not teletravel us into something."

I nod concedingly. I see his point. I have to have some level of trust in him in order to let him guide me like that. I don't want to have any trust in him anymore, but apparently I still do. We finish our wine in relative silence, and when our glasses are empty, we head to our separate rooms.

"Well, good night," he tells me awkwardly when we reach my door.

"Good night."

He reluctantly turns and walks to his room, which is right next to mine. Even though we aren't sleeping in the same bed like we were the last time, this is as close as we've slept since before my powers awakened. For some reason, it gets to me. I try to dismiss it, and enter my room. It's just as lovely as downstairs, and I resist the urge to squeal in excitement. Even though I know I'm going to miss Stavros, I have to admit that it's nice to get away from the palace for a little while. Almost like a little vacation. There's an enormous window taking up one side of the room with a cozy seating nook in front of it, and I can picture myself curling up with a good book there.

The bed itself looks like it's covered in seafoam, and I know I'm going to feel like I'm sleeping in the ocean tonight. Everywhere I look there are things either from the sea or modeled after it. The tub is larger than any I've come across before. It's essentially the size of a small pool. I bet I could shift while in it and still have room to move around and be fully underwater. I take advantage and relax after our travels. I spot a few bottles next to the "tub" and discover one of them is bubble bath. I smile as I add a generous amount.

The water is warm and inviting, but cool enough to be refreshing in the hot weather. I dunk under the water and shift. Sure enough, I have room to move around in my other form. It's like I'm a child as I flop around in the bubbles, and I almost wish I had bath toys to play with.

I realize then that I could potentially take advantage of having tentacles instead of a tail. I should probably start practicing using them for something other than swimming. I begin with focusing on just one, lifting it out of the water, waving it at myself, picking up random objects. It's a bit difficult at first, but soon the actions become smooth. I repeat the exercise with all of my tentacles, and when I can use them without knocking stuff over or dropping anything, I call it a night, drain the tub, and head to bed. I sleep like the dead.

10

Pearl

It takes me just over a week to arrive at my destination. It was refreshing being able to alternate between riding my horse and swimming the waterways when I got tired of one. My skin and lungs welcome the humidity as I breathe in the familiarity of home. I'm looking forward to seeing my twin sister, Opal. It's been too long, and I miss having my twin around to understand me like only sisters do.

I need to meet with Coralia soon, but I want to stop at home first to drop my things off, see my family, and freshen up. Our home is on the same island as Allure Isle, which is convenient, because that's where Coralia resides as well. I'm a bit nervous about that conversation. I have some things to reveal to her, and I don't know how they will be received.

I walk into our beach house and relax for the first time in *months*. It smells the same, like ocean and lemon. I breathe in deeply, but am startled when my twin's shriek sounds.

"Pearl! What are you doing here?"

"I thought I would surprise you! I've been wanting to come home for a while, and I need to meet with Coralia. The king's daughter is also going to be here in a day or two, and I thought I would introduce her and show her around."

Jealousy streaks across Opal's features, but it's gone a moment later. She launches into my arms, her white-blue hair flinging me in the face as she squeezes tight. I sigh in relief at being reunited with my sister. I've missed her.

"Well, it's really good to see you. Even though you look like shit."

I shove her, even though I know she's right. More than a week on the road has not done me any favors in the appearance department.

"Want to help me get put back together before I meet with Coralia?"

She nods eagerly. This is what mermaids do, how we spend quality time together. She grabs my hand and leads me to the bathroom. I start undressing as she fills the tub, pouring in oils to make my hair soft and silky. I breathe in the scents of coconut, driftwood, and orange blossom. When it's full I sink into the massive tub, allowing myself to relax fully.

"Dunk your head," Opal orders.

I do as she says, and when I come back up, she pours a generous amount of shampoo in my hair. The next moment, her fingers are working wonders on my scalp, washing my hair and easing the headache I've had from traveling.

"So, what's new?" she asks me after a few minutes.

"Well, I have a new man."

"Ooh, do tell."

"He's the mimic ambassador. His name is Xanto."

"A mimic?" she asks with disdain, and I can practically hear the scowl that I'm sure is plastered on her face.

"Yes, Opal. He's really wonderful. He actually spent time getting to know me before he made love to me."

Her fingers stop moving in my hair. "Why would he do that?"

I've been home less than half an hour and I'm already frustrated. "Because he wanted to get to know my mind, not just my body."

"Huh. I've never had that happen before."

"Neither had I."

She shrugs. "It sounds overrated to me."

I don't know if I've changed after living among the fae for so long, or if I just never noticed the vapidness of the mermaid race, but her comment rubs me the wrong way. Did I used to be like that when I lived here? The thought makes me sad, and I realize that I might be able to have only a superficial relationship with my sister. Now that I think about it, mermaids are surface level creatures, and I despise that.

Mermaids have always been resentful of the fact that we haven't been in power since Yemonja, claiming it's because we're underestimated due to our beauty, but I'm starting to see the real reason is that we lack the depth and sincerity to rule the realm.

I change the subject to steer my mind away from the depressing thoughts. "Do you have anyone new?"

"Oh, you know me. I have multiple someones, but none of them are serious. Dunk," she says when it's time for me to rinse my hair. I do so, and when I come back up she puts a mask in my hair. The ends are so dry from not taking proper care of my locks while traveling.

"Did you want to come with me to meet with Coralia?"

"What are you going to see her about anyway?"

"The king's daughter. Ember."

"What about her?"

I hesitate, not sure if I should divulge it before speaking to Coralia. "She's different, Opal. She's not what we all thought."

"How so? I heard about her after the ball that was at the palace, but I thought she was just a pointless human."

I bristle at the fact that she just called my friend a *pointless human*. "Even if she was just a human, she's still special. If you heard about her, I'm sure you also heard that everyone at the ball was captivated by her."

"What do you mean, if she was just a human?"

I curse myself and my loud mouth. "Okay, I'll tell you, Opal, but you have to swear to keep it to yourself. I don't know how many people are supposed to know."

"Okay, sure, whatever. Just tell me."

"Ember has the blood and powers of every species in Queridian."

Her silence behind me speaks volumes.

"There's more," I tell her. "I went swimming with her, and she has a mermaid form, but not just any form. She has tentacles."

"Tentacles?" she breathes. "Are you sure?"

"They were pretty hard to miss, Opal. I need to make sure Coralia knows. It changes things."

"I don't know if she'll see it that way."

I don't reply, because she's absolutely right. There's a good chance Coralia will think that nothing's changed, and I don't know what I'm going to do if that's the case. If I'm being honest with myself, speaking with her is the *real* reason I came down here. The other things are just extra.

I get out of the bath, and with the help of my sister, make myself presentable enough to see our grand mistress. We've done this routine with each other a million times. She tackles my toenails while I do my makeup, and then she switches to my hair while I paint my fingernails. She twirls little sections of it so that it curls as it dries, and as for makeup I go for a "I can do what I want" look. I pick out my best outfit, complete with my signature little pearls hanging from the fabric, and before I know it, I'm ready to go. It's amazing how much two mermaids can accomplish in such little time.

"Okay, I'll be back soon. Wish me luck."

Opal kisses my cheek and sends me on my way. I try not to get too nervous as I travel to see Coralia. I rehearse the speech that I prepared during my trip from the Immortal City. It's not long, and I wanted to find more to say, but nothing additional comes to mind. I have no idea how she's going to take the news, which means I stall out when trying to anticipate her responses. I just wish there wasn't so much riding on this conversation.

I shake my head to clear it of my anxieties, which doesn't really work, but I've arrived at my destination. I'm let in and taken to Coralia's greeting room, which I've been to many times before.

I look around while I wait for her. It's exactly the same as the last time I was here. There's a grand chair on one end that closely resembles a throne fit for a mermaid. It's covered in the sea—shells, coral, starfish, you name it. On the other end of the room, there's a large pool that connects directly to the ocean. This is where Coralia transitions from her home to the sea. She also has a home in the pool that mirrors this one. Mermaids usually like to switch between living in the water and on land, but most of us don't have the ability to do that, unless they have a significant amount of money.

The pool is where she emerges ten minutes later. Like every other time I've seen her, I'm struck speechless by her beauty, which is exactly how she became grand mistress in the first place. Her head pops up out of the water first, her seaweed-green hair floating around her. Her sharp and striking features are set in a mask of pleased welcome, which is uncommon for her. She's not typically pleased about much, and she's definitely not welcoming.

Her bare torso is exposed moments later, her full, perfect breasts gleaming as water streams down her chest. I see her tail then, flickering under the surface. It's rose gold from her waist down, and then ombres to a gorgeous pale coral pink at the tail. She shifts, and her tail disappears in favor of long tan legs that go on for miles. She shimmers rose gold as she stands next to the pool, looking radiant, and the epitome of mermaid.

A servant appears out of nowhere and hands her a towel. She takes her time drying, as if I haven't been waiting on her. When she's done, she all but throws the towel at the servant, who then hands her a gorgeous rose-gold silk robe. It flows down to her feet and makes her look like she's wearing an evening gown.

Finally she turns her attention to me, and her piercing rose-gold eyes that match her tail perfectly home in on me. "Pearl, darling, how wonderful to see you." She pulls me in close to her—her nails are still shifted into claws and they dig slightly into my arms in what I know is a deliberate move—as she kisses me on each cheek.

"You as well, Coralia. It's been too long."

She takes a seat on her "throne" and gestures for me to sit on what's basically a stool in front of her. It's no secret that Coralia is very big on power plays. "How are things going at the castle, dear?"

"Interesting," I reply, deciding to just dive right in. "There have been some new developments that you need to be aware of."

This seems to pique her interest. "Oh?"

I take a deep breath. "I have become quite close with the king's daughter."

"The human girl?" she asks in disdain.

"I know you met her at the ball. At that time, we all believed her to just be human, but it turns out she's not."

Her brows furrow ever so slightly, the only sign of her confusion.

"She has all of the powers, Coralia. She's all of the species."

She blinks in surprise, but still doesn't respond verbally, letting me continue.

"She shifted in front of me after her powers awakened. She doesn't have a tail."

"I thought you said she shifted?"

"She did. She doesn't have a tail, but she does have tentacles."

Her face scrunches up in first shock, then fury. "That's not possible."

"Coralia, I'm telling you, I saw it with my own two eyes. She's a descendant from Surseiha's line."

She doesn't reply for the longest time. I stay silent and let her absorb the information. Minutes later, a look of determination crosses her face and settles there. "This changes nothing," she finally says.

I'm so shocked that I don't know how to respond. I forget myself for a minute, my anger getting the better of me. "How can you say that? This changes *everything*."

"You forget yourself, Pearl. I have decided. Nothing will change."

I tamp down my anger, knowing that yelling at her will only cause further damage, and might even hinder any changes that I could make without her knowing.

I swallow and take a deep breath. "Forgive me, Coralia. I did not expect that. I also wanted to notify you that Ember will be here in a few days, and per the instructions of the king, you are to train her in her new powers." I take the letter from the king out of my bag and hand it to her.

She reads over it quickly. "Well, this works in our favor, doesn't it?"

Dread works its way through me as a scheming smile manifests on her face. "Yes, Mistress."

11

Ember

I wake well rested. I don't know if it's this bed in particular, or all beds in Mermacovia, but it felt like I was sleeping on the water all night. I make sure to spend extra time getting ready, knowing that I'll be arriving at our destination soon, and more than likely meeting the Mermacovia grand mistress.

Pearl's reminder rings in my head, making sure my appearance meets mermaid standards. I pick out my most daring dress. It's plum and sheer, with bits of material covering only my intimate parts, a plunging neckline, and a slit on both sides, almost up to my hips. It's definitely more slutty than anything I would normally wear, but Pearl specifically told me to put it on for this occasion. You can make a first impression only once, and if there's one thing mermaids respect, it's the ability to captivate everyone around you. To them, sex isn't something to be ashamed of. It's something to be proud of and displayed, and boy am I ever on display in this dress.

I do my makeup just as daring, using bold colors on my eyes and lips, and leave my hair down with big loose curls. Before I can talk myself out of changing, I take a deep breath and walk out of the room. Alexei meets me in the tavern minutes later, and his eyes heat as he takes in my outfit. I can feel them blaze a path across my body, and I squeeze my thighs together as my pussy clenches with need at his look. His nostrils flare, and I know he's scenting my arousal. A blush rises to my cheeks, but I make myself act as if nothing is different.

"Are we getting breakfast before we leave?"

"You can't wear that," he cuts in, skating over my question completely.

"I can and I will. Now answer my question, because I either want to get going or eat."

"Why are you wearing that? It reveals way too much."

"That's the point, Alexei. You know what mermaids are like. This outfit is strategic." Now that I mention it to him, I realize that we now seem to be getting more respect. More people are dipping their heads to me, and letting me pass in front of them or holding doors for me. That definitely was not the case the night before.

Alexei looks around and notices the same thing. He reluctantly nods and gestures me forward into the dining area. "We'll eat here first."

I sit, and they bring us tea, along with a bowl of fruit. Not long after we're served rice, along with some sort of meat patty covered in gravy with a fried egg on top. It looks interesting, but upon trying it, I find it's delicious and devour it.

When we're both done eating, we head outside. Alexei turns to me. "Are you ready? We're going to teletravel right outside Coralia's house."

I take a deep breath, pushing my nerves away. "I'm ready."

He grabs my hand, giving it a reassuring squeeze. I hate the way my heart pounds harder in response. Especially since he can no doubt hear it. He pulls me along, and I focus on following him. This distance is about the same as yesterday's, and it's not quite as difficult this time. I'm pleasantly surprised when Pearl is there to greet us when we arrive. She hugs me as soon as we land.

"I've missed you. How were your travels?" she starts in immediately.

I chuckle. "Give me a moment to breathe."

"Okay, you've had a breath, now how has it been without me?"

"Boring. And our travel was extremely easy compared to yours. Did your trip go smoothly?"

She nods. "I got a lot of swimming in, which felt wonderful. I don't remember the last time I was in the water for that long." She appraises my appearance. "You look perfect."

"Was it your idea for her to wear this?" Alexei chimes in heatedly.

Pearl smiles coyly at me, giving me a subtle wink before turning her attention to him. "It was. I thought the territory of Mermacovia should see from the beginning how fierce and beautiful she is. After all, beauty is the only thing that matters to most of them."

I notice that she doesn't include herself in that statement, and I file that information away for later.

"Well, are you ready to see Coralia? I notified her that I expected you would be here soon."

I nod, thinking I'm mostly ready. Pearl leads the way into what is basically a mansion. It's not as extravagant as the palace in the Immortal City, but it's not too far off. We're taken to what I'm assuming is a receiving room, and I don't fail to notice that Coralia is sitting on a throne. I wonder what she's trying to accomplish here, but I have to play our interactions right. I am the king's daughter after all, and I need her support. I have to appear strong and not let her walk all over me, but also be kind and gracious. It's a hard line I'm walking, and I need to make sure I do it right.

I hold my head high and my back straight, a coy knowing smile on my face. I'm not going to speak first. I don't know if that's a thing here, but it definitely is on Earth. We stop in front of her throne, and I look down on her, letting her see the queen I will be someday. I pull all my powers forward and let them simmer under my skin. The room fills with my magic as my skin brightens like the moon. Her eyes widen ever so slightly. My mind reaches for hers, and I'm unsurprised to find a mental shield in place. Unluckily for her, I've been practicing with Stavros, and hers isn't nearly as strong as his. Within moments I've subtly gotten past them, and am able to identify her emotions.

I sense surprise and reluctant respect first, and I smile to myself that I'm making the impression that I was hoping for. I dig a little deeper and find boredom and a hint of disdain. Not overpowering, but enough to let me know that she either has some vendetta against the humans, fae, or the king, maybe all three. I also feel her sheer determination and loyalty, and I wonder who she is loyal to. I would guess it's not my father.

We stare at each other for endless moments, and her frustration bubbles that I'm not breaking first. I tamp down the smile that wants to come up and raise an eyebrow at her in question.

Finally, she gives in, her voice not giving away any of the emotions I sensed under the surface. "Your Highness. I'm so glad you could make it. What a pleasure it is to see you again." She smiles at me, and though it's more lovely than any I've seen before, it's also lethal.

"Thank you so much for hosting us. I trust you read the letter from my father regarding our training?"

"I did indeed, and I would be thrilled to assist you and your father in this."

"We greatly appreciate it, Coralia." It's so subtle, but I notice she clenches her jaw at my use of her name instead of her title.

"It's an honor." I don't have to be connected to her emotions to hear the lie. I don't know what this bitch's problem is, but I act like I'm unaware that she's trying to play me like a fiddle. "In the meantime, I would love for you both to stay here. I have plenty of room in my home."

I smile back at her. "That's very kind of you. Thank you."

"Well, in that case, Pearl can show you to your rooms, and you can get settled and then meet me in the dining room for lunch." She stands and walks out, effectively dismissing us.

Pearl looks at me and I can tell she wants to comment on the interaction, but I shake my head at her, not wanting to be overheard. She nods in understanding before leading us to our rooms.

This one is even more extravagant and ocean-like than the lodge we stayed at. There's a swimming pool on one end, which I can smell is full of seawater. I wonder if it connects to the ocean like the one in Coralia's receiving room. The bed is at least a king, and the frame is a huge seashell. I know when I sleep in it, I'm going to feel like a pearl. The curtains on the window have the texture and appearance of seaweed, and I can't tell if they actually are. There's also the same lighting all around the room that I've seen in Mermacovia's waterways, and the whole room appears as if it's underwater, as the light reflects subtle patterns on the ceiling.

The three of us walk into the room so we can talk privately. As soon as the door shuts, Pearl chimes in with what she wanted to say earlier. "Bitch, that was fantastic! I have never seen anyone interact with Coralia like that."

"She's going to be a tough one, but I need to play things right if I want to win her over. I can tell she's hiding something, but I don't know what. I sense she doesn't like me, but after our interaction I can tell she respects me, even though she doesn't want to."

"Even though she loves to scheme, you can learn a lot from her. You're literally learning from the best."

"I wish you could just teach me. I think things would go more smoothly."

"I know. Me too, but it's better that you're learning from her. You need the most skilled person for this, and that's Coralia."

"I know, I know."

I resign myself to the fact that there's nothing I can do about this situation. Alexei takes my trunk out of his pocket since my dress doesn't have any. I perform the spell to enlarge it, and Pearl smiles at the magic.

"Should I change now? Have I made my impression, or do I need to make it for the rest of the mermaids who might see me?"

"I would keep it on. Change before dinner."

She tells Alexei his room is across the hall and helps me unpack my Mermacovia clothing so it doesn't get wrinkled. We spend the rest of the morning catching each other up on our week.

Around noon we fetch Alexei and head down to the dining area. No one else is here yet, and I know this is another of Coralia's power plays. I debate taking her place at the head of the table, but think that would be a bit much in her own home, so I settle for the seat next to her.

Ten minutes later she waltzes in as if we haven't been waiting for her, and takes a seat next to me wearing a dress more scandalous than mine. I ignore her, and instead turn my attention to the male behind her.

He's by far the most beautiful man I've ever seen. His features are so striking he's almost painful to look at. His eyes are rose gold, and his hair is green, but so dark that it's almost black, and is slightly shaggy, sweeping across his prominent brow. As I'm staring at him, I realize he shares a lot of features with the woman in front of him, and I have a sneaking suspicion of who he is.

"Ember, this is my son, Proteus," Coralia introduces, her voice haughty as she says, "His name means sea god."

He bows, showing me the respect that she should have, but didn't. "Your Highness, we are honored by your presence."

He comes up to me, captures my hand, and brings it to his lips. He locks eyes with me as he plants a kiss on the back of it, lingering just past what would be acceptable. A blush rises to my cheeks, and I hear Alexei's growl next to me. Proteus releases my hand and takes the seat across the table. Alexei's eyes bore into me, and my mate mark burns traitorously on my arm. I avoid both of their gazes and instead focus on the food that's placed in front of me.

"So, Ember, we will start our training after lunch," Coralia tells me.

I swallow down my nerves and remind myself that I do well with allure. Plus, I've already gotten past her mental shields, which is the hard part. I nod in response.

"I was also hoping to see the underwater community while I'm here."

"I would be happy to give you a tour," Proteus's whiskey-smooth voice cuts in from across the table. "We can go after your training if you'd like."

"Ember, we're doing our training after, so I don't think that will work," Alexei says next to me. My brows rise. I didn't think that we would still be training while we're here. "Stavros told me you need to keep up on your combat training," he clarifies.

I don't know if that's true or not, but it sounds like a good idea all the same.

"Well, tomorrow morning, then," Proteus concedes.

"I would love that," I tell him, genuinely excited about seeing the ocean here.

He smiles warmly at me, and I respond in kind. A blush rises to my cheeks again, my heart beating just a little harder. I don't want to be drawn in by him, especially considering who his mother is, but I can't help it. I don't know if it's his mermaid allure, or just his natural charisma, but I find myself looking forward to our tour tomorrow.

I can suddenly feel everyone's attention on us. Coralia is stewing as well as Alexei, who is glaring daggers at Proteus. Pearl is the only one who looks like she's enjoying herself, a sly smile playing around her lips.

I turn my attention to my food to avoid any awkwardness, but it's heightened because no one is saying anything. I remember to keep my head held high, like I'm not ashamed or embarrassed. The uncomfortable moment eventually passes, and I breathe a sigh of relief when conversation starts back up again.

When lunch is finally over, I'm extremely grateful. Between Proteus's subtle flirting, Coralia's death glares, and Alexei's growling fest next to me, I'm ready to be out of this room.

"Are you ready to start, Ember?" Coralia asks me and I nod. She snaps at Alexei, not addressing him by name. "You there, come with us. She'll need someone to practice on." She takes off before either of us can object, and we reluctantly follow her.

She brings us to the same receiving room as earlier, where she proceeds to gracefully sit herself down on her throne. Alexei and I stand awkwardly in front of her, waiting for her instruction.

"Well, go ahead," she tells me.

I raise my eyebrows in surprise. "You haven't told me what I should do yet."

She huffs in frustration. "Let your shields down so she can accomplish it," she tells Alexei before turning to me. Neither of us correct her on the fact that I can get past his shields just fine. "Ember, look into his eyes and let your mermaid simmer beneath the surface. Your mermaid wants to reel him in, and you need to let her."

I reluctantly lock eyes with Alexei, and we have an unexpectedly intimate moment. So many emotions are flitting behind his gaze, and things he wants. I force myself to focus on the task at hand and bring my mermaid forward. It's quite a bit more difficult while I'm not in the water. My skin lets off a subtle glow, and Alexei's eyes narrow on me. He looks as enamored with me as I know he is, he just usually doesn't show it, especially in front of others.

"What can I do for you, little doe?" His voice is full of the urge to please me.

"What would you do for me?" My voice comes out angelic.

"*Anything and everything.*" I'm struck by the intensity behind his words, and know that it's more than my allure fueling his vehemence.

"Well done, Ember," praises Coralia. "Now make him do something."

I really don't want to make him do anything. It feels wrong. But then I remember all those days training on the road with him. This is really no different, and I know he won't mind. I just have to make sure that I don't make him do something terrible, but also something that he wouldn't normally do.

"Alexei, dance for me." He immediately obeys, and I have to resist the urge to chuckle. He's basically doing the dances he showed me before the ball, but it looks silly without a partner when I'm not trying to learn the steps. "Now dance like I showed you we do on Earth." It instantly backfires when he comes up and starts grinding up against me.

"Well, you sure have interesting ways of dancing on Earth," Coralia comments, making me blush.

"Stop," I command, and he does. "Take a swim," I tell him, gesturing to the pool. He walks over and hops in, fully clothed.

I'm surprised how easy this skill is coming to me, and I wonder if it's partially from who my ancestor was.

"Have him get out and strip," Coralia says, ogling him like a perv next to me.

I don't want to do that at all, but I don't really have a choice. "Alexei, get out and strip."

He doesn't follow my order, and instead stays in the pool and smirks at me. A rush of relief sweeps through me. I don't know if it's because I didn't want him to follow it, but my command didn't work.

"It looks like you're not as skilled as I first thought," Coralia snarks, and I resist the urge to glower at her. She has to be the worst teacher ever.

I urge more allure into my voice, my skin flaring brighter. I want to prove this bitch *wrong.* "Alexei, get out of the pool and come to me."

He does as he's bid as soon as the words are out of my mouth, the expression on his face full of the need to please me. I block out the image of us together in bed with that same look on his gorgeous face. He stops right in front of me, literally as close as he can be without touching me.

Instead of having him strip, I hold out my hands and release a stream of heated air on him. He's thoroughly dry a moment later, and when I smirk at Coralia, she's glaring at me. I have the strong urge to break through her shields and bend her to my will, but I don't want her to know how powerful I am yet. I'm not sure why, but I know that information is better kept close to my chest.

"Alexei, that's all for today. Leave us," Coralia commands, persuasion in her voice.

Alexei turns to me. "Ember?"

I smirk at him. He's still under my persuasion, and it appears that mine is stronger than hers. At least, that's what I'm assuming is happening. I hear Coralia's gasp of outrage, but we both ignore her as we keep our eyes locked.

"I'll be fine here on my own. Thank you for your help, Alexei."

He looks reluctant to leave me with her, but I nod at him subtly. He looks back at me once more before he takes off, not giving Coralia another word or glance. When I finally turn my attention to her, she looks livid, but masks it quickly. "Well done, Ember. I thought we could take a swim. I want to see how well you do in the water."

I push back my trepidation. Something about this woman just screams "Don't trust me!"

I nod and head toward her pool. She stands and starts stripping. I follow suit, albeit more reluctantly. Swimming with Pearl is one thing—she's my best friend, and I don't care if she sees me naked. But this woman, it's like she's one of those girls in high school who starts pointing and laughing at you in the locker room as soon as you take your clothes off. I shrug that feeling off. I am a fucking *princess.* Not to mention, I'm almost thirty now; I'm past high school games, and I'm not ashamed of my curves.

I hold my head high as I take off the last of my clothing. Her eyes skate over my body, but I ignore her as I dive into the pool without waiting for her. I shift a second later and focus on what it's like to swim in my shifted form in mermaid territory. There's something about the water here. I can almost hear it singing to me.

I hear Coralia a moment later and see a bright flash signifying that she's shifted as well. I turn to see her in all her glory behind me. She really is spectacular. Her tail sparkles in the light from above and the surrounding rocks in the water. Her face is shocked as she takes in my form. I wonder if Pearl told her. I assumed that she had, but looking at her, it doesn't seem like she knew.

Did you know? I ask her telepathically.

I did, but hearing it and seeing it are two very different things.

I nod in understanding. I open my senses to her again, wanting to see what else she might be feeling. Shock is the most evident, followed closely by denial. I can also still sense her loyalty and determination, and once again wonder who her loyalty is geared toward—certainly not me.

I look down at myself and gasp in shock at the glowing runes covering my arms and torso. I remember then what Pearl told me when she first saw my tentacles: that we would know for sure if I was Surseiha's descendant if these appeared when I went swimming in Mermacovia's seas. Here's the proof.

I shake off my shock as Coralia swims ahead of me until we're in a fairly open area where we have room to move around.

She cocks her head to the side and gestures in front of her. *Well, let's see what you can do.*

I take a deep breath, forcing down my nerves, and start swimming. This time, I focus more on how each individual tentacle is moving, since I practiced with that last night, and I actually can tell I'm moving faster. Delighted, I try some of the more difficult maneuvers that I've struggled with in the past. While they aren't perfect, I've definitely improved, and I make a mental note to keep practicing.

After a few minutes, I hear Coralia's condescending voice in my head, and I shudder at the intrusion.

Mediocre. We need to get you more adept in the water. Mermaids are swift, graceful, ruthless. You are sloppy. Any prey would be able to sense you coming from a mile away.

I bristle at her tone, but listen to the advice she's giving me. She's likely exaggerating, but I'm sure there's truth to her words. Even though it feels natural to me to swim, I haven't been doing it long at all, and I'm sure that I'm more clumsy than every other mermaid.

Any suggestions? I ask, even though I shouldn't have to.

Tighten your movements. You're putting too much effort forth, and it's drawing far more attention than you want as a predator. You're being too obvious. Try to sneak. You need speed as well, but stealth is just as important.

I close my eyes and take a deep breath to center myself. Of course she pointed out everything I am doing wrong, but not many tips on how to accomplish or improve these deficiencies. That's okay. I don't need her help.

When I open my eyes, I imagine what it's like to be a shark. It isn't hard with my teeth as sharp as theirs, and my claws ready to slice and rip. I picture Mordecai in the water with us since he's the only one I've ever hated enough to want to hunt and maim—well, besides Mosher, I correct myself, but that was child's play compared to Mordecai. My eyes narrow, my blood heats, and before I know it, I'm shooting through the water, faster and swifter than ever before. My arms tuck in to my sides as I maneuver through turns, tight and quick. My heart pounds, and I relish the adrenaline pumping through my body. The only time I've felt like this is after my abilities awakened and I had Mordecai in my grasp. Raw power sings through my veins, and I relish the urge to bend Coralia to my will.

I stop swimming so I can rein myself back. This is a part of myself that is completely new to me. I have to admit that it's addicting. I am unsure if it's the power I have now, or if it's a natural part of being a mermaid, but I can't deny how wonderfully intense it feels to be a weapon.

Good. Better, she reservedly praises. I can tell she doesn't want to even give me that much, although it's clear my performance was a vast improvement. I guess it's as good as I'm going to get from her, and I'm fine with that.

We continue for a while, and she gives me a few more pointers, but not many. I swear getting any useful information out of her is like pulling teeth.

We finish up for the day and head back to her room. I climb out of the pool and quickly dry myself with my air magic, my hair falling around my shoulders in loose curls. I'm completely dry by the time Coralia gets out of the water. Her eyes widen slightly in surprise, and I suppress my smug smile as I get dressed.

"Want me to dry you?" I offer.

She looks at my hair enviously, but she shakes her head. I'm not surprised. Coralia doesn't strike me as the type willing to accept help from anyone, especially people she doesn't like, as much as she would love to have her hair dry and beautiful after a swim.

"Same time tomorrow," she says, effectively dismissing me.

I nod and head back to my room. Alexei is waiting for me there when I arrive.

"How did it go?"

"It was fine."

"You need to be careful with her."

"I know, Alexei." I look around, not trusting having a private conversation like this out in the open. I'm also tempted to call Pearl in here, but I keep in mind that we're in her territory, and she's known Coralia for a hell of a lot longer than me, no matter how close we are.

I gesture for Alexei to come into my room so we can talk. He follows me, and when the door closes behind him, I'm able to talk more freely. "I sensed her emotions. She's loyal to someone, and that loyalty is fueling her determination. I can also tell she really doesn't like me."

His brows shoot up in surprise. "You were able to break through her mental shields?" At my nod, his mouth turns up in delighted pride. "She couldn't tell?" I shake my head. "Did you change any of her emotions?"

"No. There's no reason for me to right now, and I don't want her catching on and knowing that I can get through her shields."

He nods in understanding. "You said her loyalty was fueling her determination. Any idea who she's loyal to or what she's determined to do?"

"Nope. Unfortunately my power doesn't work like that."

"Was she able to teach you anything? Also, thank you for not making me strip in front of her."

I give him a look of disgust. "I would never. And she was able to teach me how to swim more efficiently. I don't think I'm going to learn much about my powers from her. Fortunately, I think I already have a good grasp on the mermaid skills, and my best friend also happens to be one, so she can help me with it, too, if I need it."

He nods. "Well, are you ready for combat training?"

"Were you serious about that? I figured that was just an excuse to keep me away from Proteus," I tell him, a teasing knowing glint in my eyes.

His narrow back. "Hey, this is completely legitimate. You need to keep up with this training, otherwise your skills will slip, and considering Stavros isn't around, you'll have to settle for me. And as for Proteus, I don't like the way he was looking at you. Not to mention, he's Coralia's son. If he's anything like her, you'll want to watch your back."

I smile at having baited him. "I have you to watch my back for me."

"Except when you go on your little *swim* tomorrow. I won't be able to come with you. Not to mention that all mermaids swim naked. He is going to see you, and I don't like that."

I didn't think about that, and even though I don't show it outwardly, I'm freaking out on the inside. He's right. Proteus is going to see my tits when we shift. Not to mention that they'll be *out* the whole time we tour the underwater community.

"He won't even notice. They see that shit all the time, Alexei. I'm sure it won't even faze him." I try to reassure him, but it does nothing to calm my own anxieties.

"Oh, please. There's no way any man could not notice your body," he says, his voice lowering as he steps closer, his eyes traveling the length of me.

Heat builds between my legs, and I struggle not to give in to his obvious want and the tension between us. His nostrils flare and his eyes dilate as he scents my arousal. He growls softly, almost a purr, as he closes his eyes and takes a step back. The action breaks the spell, and I put even more room between us.

"I really wish you could forgive me and accept our bond," he says quietly. I don't respond, and after a few moments, he opens his eyes and looks at me, all business. "Let's train."

Alexei leads the way outside, and it's a good thing he brought many weapons with us, because Coralia doesn't seem to have any, let alone a training yard. Or at least not one that we're allowed to use.

"What do you want to start with today?" he asks.

"Swords," I respond.

His surprise hits me before he hands me my weapon. I take my stance as I realize he hasn't seen me use a sword yet, and I have a moment of nervousness. Before I can think about it too much, he attacks. I meet his sword with mine, and the movement jars my body even more than I'm used to. I know it's because Alexei is stronger—he works with weapons on a regular basis.

I also realize that I have an advantage here with Alexei that I've never had before. He wasn't the one who trained me in the sword, and therefore doesn't know my signature moves. I smile viciously at him, my predator side coming out to play.

"I missed seeing you like this," he tells me, smiling back.

I snarl at him in response, swinging my sword. He deflects easily and parries, smiling even more broadly. We dance around, circling each other, striking and deflecting in turn. I'm not as skilled in this arena, and Alexei quickly bests me.

"You're using your arms too much. Stabilize your core when you swing, and focus on your shoulders and upper back taking a good portion of the weight from the sword, then it won't be as heavy. Again."

It takes a lot of concentration to change the way I've been holding the sword, but Alexei is patient with me. After a solid hour of training, it's starting to become more natural to me, but I know I'm going to need a lot more practice.

"You did well today, Ember."

Training over, we head back to our separate rooms. Pearl is sitting on my bed when I walk in. I missed her so much that I don't even reprimand her for intruding in my space.

"I'm going to go home for dinner to hang out with my twin, and you're coming with me."

I grin at her. I've been wanting to meet Opal, and I really don't want to spend any more time with Coralia than I have to. "Deal. Help me pick out an outfit."

12

Ember

Pearl helps me get ready, making sure I look my best to meet her sister, and in what feels like no time at all, we're heading to her house. It's not far from Coralia's, and we're able to walk. The home is modest but tasteful, and sits right on the beach. I wonder if they have a space in the water for themselves as well. Opal opens the door as we approach, and it's strange to see Pearl's face on someone else's body. There definitely are differences, but the similarities are slightly unnerving.

I focus on the differences so as not to wig myself out. Where Pearl has a purple tint to her hair, Opal's is more blue. They also carry themselves differently. Pearl is generally a bit more relaxed, whereas Opal is stick straight. Her face is also harsher than Pearl's. Not her features, per se, but her expressions are more severe, making her seem much less approachable than my best friend.

"You must be Ember. Welcome!" she greets, smiling, although it doesn't reach her eyes.

"Thank you for having me. It's so great to meet you! Pearl has told me so much about you." I hold out my hand for her to shake, and she grasps my forearm in greeting.

"Come in." She waves me inside, and I survey the subtle, but beautiful home. There's ambient lighting everywhere, along with numerous windows that open up to the ocean. The sun is setting over the water, and I sigh as I relish the sight. I can smell dinner cooking on the stove, and my mouth waters at the scent of butter and garlic.

"What are we having for dinner?" Pearl asks her.

"Lobster, asparagus, and white wine."

She pours us both a glass, and the three of us sit outside next to the water while we wait for dinner to be finished.

"So Ember, you met Coralia today?" Opal asks me. It's an innocent enough question, but I get the sense that she's prodding.

"I did."

"How did it go?"

"Fine," I reply. I know I'm being short with her, but I can't tell her how the encounter truly went.

Pearl saves me. "Are you excited to go on your tour with Proteus tomorrow?"

Her question brings my earlier anxieties roaring back to life. "Oh shit."

"What?" Her brows pull together in concern.

"I was just talking to Alexei earlier, and he brought up the point that I'll be topless in front of Proteus."

Opal looks thoroughly confused. Pearl probably would be if she didn't know me better. "What's the problem with that?"

"Ember wasn't raised the way we were. Things are very different on Earth," Pearl tells her before turning to me. "Ember, it's really not a big deal. We mermaids see each other naked *regularly*. He won't even notice."

"I know all of this, but it's still a big deal for me. Is there anything I can do?"

"I can't think of anything."

"What about a seashell bra? Aren't mermaids supposed to wear those all the time?"

Pearl and Opal look at me in confusion. "What's a bra?"

I sigh in exasperation. "It's something that supports your breasts. It has cups that cover them and then a band that holds the cups in place. Don't you have anything like that?"

"No, but we could probably make you something."

"Yes, I've got the perfect seashells," Opal chimes in. "Although, I don't see this being very comfortable." She leaves the room and comes back with two perfectly matching seashells. They're purple and will accent my tentacles.

I hold them up to my chest, delighted to see that they will work. They're barely big enough, but at least I won't have to be topless in front of Proteus and the entire mermaid community tomorrow.

"Take your top off. I'll get the twine and we can fashion you something. Who knows, you might even start a trend." Opal goes back into the house to grab the twine, and Pearl helps me out of my top. I hold the seashells up to my chest and giggle as I look down, feeling a bit like Ariel.

"I bet Alexei wasn't too keen on Proteus seeing you topless, huh?" Pearl asks now that Opal isn't around to hear.

I huff out a laugh. "No, he most certainly was not, although I'm glad he brought it up so I could figure this out."

"Are you going to tell him you found a solution?"

"Hell no. Let him think that Proteus saw me topless and couldn't keep his eyes off of me."

Pearl's eyes glitter in malicious delight, her smile feral. "I had such fun watching him suffer through your and Proteus's meeting. Maybe I'll tease him a bit while the two of you are gone."

I return her smile. "Oh, would you? That would be fun. I only wish I were there to witness it."

Opal comes out a moment later with the twine. Between the three of us, we make my very own seashell bra, and I'm surprised by how great it looks. Opal might be right about me starting a new trend here, and I'm excited to show it off tomorrow. I put my top back on, and we head inside for dinner.

After a few glasses of wine, Pearl states she wants her own seashell bra, causing Opal to chime in that she does too. A mermaid's house has no shortage of seashells, and by the end of the night, we all have one. Pearl's is white, and Opal's is pale blue. Even later into the night, when we've had even *more* wine, we all put them on. For some reason, I just *knew* I would need to bring my phone with me tonight, and am so grateful at the moment. Maybe my witchy senses knew that this night needed to be documented.

I turn my phone on, cursing as I see I'm finally on low battery. I still haven't used any of the juice from my portable charger yet, so I'll be able to recharge it when I need to. I open my camera app and hold it up in selfie mode.

"Smile!"

"Why?"

"Yeah, what are we smiling for?"

I huff in frustration. "Okay, ladies, pay attention, because this is important. You see this thing I'm holding in my hand?" They both nod.

"It's like a mini mirror," Opal says.

"Only unlike a mirror, this can capture the moment and we can look at it later. So, look at the camera and smile."

They finally obey me, and after that, we get stuck in a selfie black hole. You know what they say. Give three mermaids a camera...

By the time we're going through the pictures and laughing our asses off over our facial expressions, my phone dies.

"What happened?"

"Where did the pictures go?"

They both start freaking out, and I chuckle at their desperation. I may have created a monster. I try to explain that my phone is dead, but that sends them into an even more dramatic spin. I finally am able to explain that it needs to recharge and the pictures will still be there when I turn it back on.

I wince when I realize how late it is. Time passed so quickly with these two, and I groan at the thought of having to get up early the next day for my tour. I wish I could just sleep all day.

"All right, lovelies, I need to get to bed. I'm going to head back to Coralia's."

"You shouldn't go back on your own," Pearl says.

"It's just right across the way, and you're staying here tonight anyway. I'll be fine."

"No. You've never been here before, and I don't want you getting lost or running into any unsavory characters."

"Fine," I relent, knowing she's not going to change her mind. "Opal, it was so wonderful to meet you." I give her a hug.

"You too, Ember."

As soon as we walk out the front door, I see a figure coming out of the ocean just a ways away. I can immediately tell it's a male because he's huge. He shakes off almost like a dog, but somehow makes it look sexy. It's then that I realize he's completely naked. I can't see any details from here, but I see his firm ass as he turns away from us to grab a wrap and tie it around his waist, obscuring my view. He turns around to face us as we get closer, and I realize it's Proteus.

His eyes widen in surprise. "Your Highness," he addresses me, bowing. I appreciate the respect, but it's so strange to have someone call me that.

"Hello, Proteus. What are you doing out here so late?"

"I was just going for a swim. Sometimes I like to go later so I don't run into as many mermaids. It's enjoyable having the ocean to myself.”

"Yeah, I like swimming by myself sometimes too," I comment.

Pearl doesn't engage in the conversation at all, instead just standing back and watching with a sly smile on her face.

"Were you heading back to my mother's house?"

"Yes. Pearl was walking me back, even though I insisted I would be fine."

"I'm going back there as well. I could accompany you, if you'd like. That way you don't need to, Pearl."

I look at my best friend; she has her brows raised at me in question.

"Sure. That would be great. Pearl, I'll see you tomorrow?"

She nods. "Good night, you two." She turns and heads back inside.

Proteus and I start walking. "So, how are you enjoying your time here so far?"

"Oh, it's been very enjoyable. I just met Pearl's twin, Opal. We had a lot of fun. They're quite the pair."

He laughs, and I melt a bit at his smooth as whisky timbre. "They sure are. And my mother? How did training go today?"

I clear my throat and look away. "It was fine."

"Ah. Not great, then. I understand. She's a tough woman, and very particular about who she shows favor to."

"Yeah. I get it. I'm a stranger, not to mention daughter to the king."

"It's an honor to have you here, Your Highness."

"You can call me Ember. And thank you," I tell him, smiling sincerely.

"Well, if you need any help or have any questions, feel free to come to me."

I whip my head toward him in surprise. I did not expect that he would be willing to do that. It also takes me off guard that he's so lovely while his mother so obviously isn't. I wonder if he takes after his father in that regard.

"Thank you. I may take you up on that."

"I hope you do." We've reached the front of the house. He opens the door for me, and a moment later we're ready to part ways for the night. He steps forward and grasps my hand, bringing it to his mouth. His lips skim the back of it, and his eyes lock on to mine. He presses a firm kiss there before pulling back. "Until tomorrow, Ember."

"Good night, Proteus."

A slight heat builds in my body; nothing like with Alexei, but pleasant. Speaking of the devil, he's standing outside his room staring at me with a thoroughly pissed-off expression on his face.

"Where were you?"

"I had dinner with Pearl and Opal."

"Then why were you with Proteus just now?"

"He walked me back so I wouldn't get lost."

He scoffs. "I'm sure. Since it's *so* difficult to teletravel here."

I stop and blink at him. He has a point. I totally could have teletraveled. I didn't even think about it. "I'm still not used to being able to do that."

"Nice excuse, Ember. Why don't you just tell me the truth?"

I storm up to him and shove him. "I *am* telling you the truth, asshole! And if there were something going on between me and Proteus, guess what? It is *none* of your business. Just because things have been better between us lately, that doesn't mean that we're together. I can be with Proteus if I want to. And you know what? I *might* want to, and you have absolutely zero say in it."

He takes me in his arms, somehow being rough and gentle at the same time. "Bullshit," he snarls before melding our mouths together.

I melt into it for about 4.2 seconds before my brain reconnects with my body. I mean, can you blame me? I break the kiss and glare up at him.

"You are *mine*," he whispers gruffly.

I pull fully out of his arms at that comment and slap him across the face for good measure. "I'm not your *anything*, Alexei. And fuck you for calling me a liar." I storm into my room and slam the door in his face before he can follow me.

As much as I don't want to admit it to myself, with the combination of our fight, our kiss, and the fact that he called me *his*, I'm more turned on than I've been since our shared dreams.

The next morning, I get ready for my tour. I braid my hair back so it's out of my way, and while I'm doing that, I come across the waterproof makeup Pearl had told me about. Astounded, I apply it, and am pleased to see that it's also gorgeous, and better than any makeup I've ever worn before. I make a mental note to ask Pearl if I can stock up.

Time to dress, I put on my seashell bra from the night before, laughing as I think of all the fun we had, and throw a wrap dress over it. I appraise myself in the mirror and am pleasantly surprised by what I see. I thoroughly look like a mermaid, and the vain or maybe mermaid part of me is loving it. I wonder if it will be like this in every territory I visit, where I start to become more like that species the longer I spend there.

I hear a knock, and set my musings aside to think about later. I'll find out eventually anyway. I open my door to find Proteus on the other side, looking handsome as ever. He's got on a black wrap around his waist, and nothing else. I wasn't able to see very well last night because it was fairly dark on our walk back, but it's not dark now, and I more than glance at his chiseled body. Before I make too much of an ass out of myself, I meet his eyes. I see male pride along with amusement glimmering there, and know that he enjoyed me looking at him.

"Good morning, Ember. You look lovely today."

"Thank you. So do you," I say awkwardly before I can catch myself. "I mean, you look nice."

The amusement in his eyes grows, but like a gentleman, he doesn't laugh or comment. "Thank you. Are you ready to go?"

I nod and step out of my room. Alexei is standing in his doorway when I come out into the hall, glaring at Proteus. Proteus doesn't seem to notice him, and we walk in the opposite direction. Alexei meets my eyes, and I can sense the jealousy and regret pouring off of him in waves. I break eye contact before I do something stupid, and Proteus and I head out.

I'm surprised when we don't go to Coralia's receiving room. When I ask Proteus about it, he tells me that he doesn't like using that entrance because people expect Coralia to come out of that area, so there's usually more expectations involved, especially if there are questions or concerns. He's told me that he's fairly involved in the community, so it makes sense that the merfolk would come to him when needed. He assures me that he has the perfect spot to enter the underwater community. We walk to the area where I saw him come out of the water last night, and I wonder if this is his favorite spot.

He steps in front of me, and while I'm admiring his gorgeous koi fish back piece, he takes his wrap off and my eyes are drawn straight to his perfect ass. He looks over his shoulder at me, giving me a wink before diving into the water.

I release the breath I didn't realize I was holding. At least this way I don't have to undress in front of him. I take my dress off and drop it next to his wrap and dive in after him, shifting as soon as I have enough room. Proteus is waiting for me ahead, and I quickly swim up to him. My seashell bra is securely in place, and his eyes dip down to it. His brows rise in question.

What is that? he asks.

I laugh. *It's a seashell bra.*

Why do you have seashells on your chest? I don't know him at all, but I can tell he's amused, even without sensing his emotions.

Hey, give me a break. I grew up on Earth. Nudity is not something normal there. I'm not used to strangers seeing me without clothing.

Fair enough. My eyes take in his mermaid form, and I admire the differences between males and females. His tail is thicker, longer, and bulkier than the women's I've seen. It's a gorgeous inky black, but his scales are all tipped in the same rose gold as his eyes. The protruding fins on his outer forearms are larger as well and look sharp enough to cut through anything.

He also seems to be observing my tentacles with awe, almost reverently. His hand reaches out, as if he wants to touch one of them, but he stops himself.

May I?

I nod and then his warm finger softly glides up one of them. I shiver. My tentacles are much more sensitive, and I'm not used to having them touched.

Incredible. His voice is awed. *I'm sorry. I never thought I would see someone with tentacles. It's an honor.*

I'm a little uncomfortable, so I change the subject. *Okay, show me everything. I'm ready.*

Of course. He shakes his head to clear it and then leads the way.

So far it just looks like an ordinary ocean, but the farther in we venture, the more I begin to see signs of civilization. The lights start getting brighter, and there are more mermaids. It's so colorful between all of the merfolk. They all have bright tails and hair, and perfect pairs of tits as far as the eye can see. Everyone we pass stares at me with such intensity that it unnerves me.

No one has seen someone with tentacles here in thousands of years. That's why they're all staring. They're amazed by you. Well, that and they don't know what to make of your seashell breasts. His eyes twinkle at the joke and I laugh, surprised by his humor.

Pearl thought I might start a fashion trend.

You probably will. My mother will love that.

I chuckle again but it turns into a gasp when I see what we've swum up on. It's truly an underwater city. There are modest walkways, or I guess I should say swimways, that lead to enormous lit domes. There are substantial pillars supporting the spherical forms, made completely out of glass, enabling the light from within to illuminate the bottom of the ocean and outward into the surrounding seawater.

There are creatures swimming by everywhere, intermingling with the mermaids, and I can't help but marvel at the unity of it all, prey and predator coexisting peacefully.

This is the main square, and the most popular area in the ocean because of its proximity to the capitol. That's where we live.

This is incredible. It continues on for miles, and I'm astonished that this can all be under the surface of the water. *Do all mermaids live above and below? Or are there some that just live underwater?* I ask.

There are plenty who just live underwater. A good portion of the population can't afford to have multiple residences, so they just live beneath.

Next, Proteus shows me inside one of the domes containing rooms and furniture just like you'd expect above, but everything here is from the sea so it doesn't degrade. Some have brought trinkets from above as well that can be underwater, and I'm reminded again of Ariel. If only she were this kind of mermaid who could travel between the two worlds and shift as she pleased.

Proteus introduces me around to a few mermaids who he's acquainted with, and even though they all seem friendly enough, there's something about most of the mermaids I've met that sets my teeth on edge. It's as if they're all wearing a pretty mask and underneath they're vain and vindictive, waiting for the opportunity to stab one another in the back.

I'm grateful I put the waterproof makeup on this morning when I see how gorgeous everyone appears. It's amazing to me that they've come up with ways to enhance their beauty, even underwater. I receive many appreciative glances from both men and women, and even get some unsolicited pets. Mostly to my hair, but a daring woman approaches and runs her hands over my seashells, marveling at what I've invented. As much as they appear to want to touch my tentacles, they aren't quite bold enough. Apparently that would be more taboo than my tits.

I told you Pearl was right about the fashion trend. I should bring you back down here in a day or two so you can see for yourself.

When I've finally seen enough, Proteus and I head back to where we entered. He lets me leave first so I have time to quickly dry myself with my air magic and put my dress on, and I'm grateful for the gentlemanly thought.

I hear him get out of the water, but make sure that I don't turn around just yet. When I'm sure he's all covered, I face him.

"How are you already dry?" he asks, astonished.

"I'm part fae, remember? I have air magic." I extend my hand toward him in invitation. He nods and I quickly dry him off.

His eyes widen. "Wow, that's amazing."

"Have you never seen fae do elemental magic before?" I ask in surprise.

"I've only seen it once or twice, and I've never had it used on me. Air would be a very handy skill to have as a mermaid."

"Believe me, it is."

"As much as I would like to show you more of the territory, I should probably get you back to train with my mother."

I sigh regretfully. Strangely enough, I enjoy spending time with him, and I'm not looking forward to dealing with his horrid mother. We walk side by side, and a few times his hand brushes mine. I know it's intentional, and I don't mind. I glance at him sideways and give him a shy smile. I'm grateful that he either doesn't seem to have the normal overly sexual mermaid tendency, or is deliberately toning it down for me.

We reach the house, and he gives me the same farewell he did yesterday, although this time he lingers a bit longer. "I really enjoyed today, Ember. Can I see you again tomorrow morning?"

I nod. "I would like that."

"Until tomorrow, then, Ember."

I blush slightly but smile at him.

I head inside and go straight to Coralia's receiving room for another day of training. I try not to think about how much I don't want to be there, and hope that she's able to give me some good advice this time.

Coralia is sitting on her throne when I enter, reading something. I stand there and wait for her to acknowledge me. A minute passes and she still hasn't looked up. I clear my throat.

"Oh, hello, Ember."

I fight an eye roll with everything in me. "Hello, Coralia. I take it we're still training today?"

"I suppose so. Take off your clothes and get into the water," she demands.

I smile sweetly at her, doing as she instructs. I can tell the fact that I'm not letting her outwardly get to me is really pissing her off, which makes it all the more fun. When she sees my seashell bra, her eyes widen in shock and what looks like disgust.

"What is *that*?" I almost laugh at the horrified expression on her face.

"It's a seashell bra. I'm a bit more modest, so I didn't want to meet the mermaid community with my breasts exposed."

She scoffs. "Pathetic."

I don't reply. Instead I just jump right into her pool, hoping I splash her. I shift immediately and swim ahead to where we trained last time.

She takes her damn sweet time getting to me, and I use the time to practice what she taught me yesterday without her watching me. It's even more natural today, and I'm able to use more speed. I sink into my predator nature, and of course that's when Coralia swims past me, coming into my personal space and rubbing against me as she goes. I almost take a swipe at her, but I'm able to curb the instinct before I get myself into trouble.

Looks like you listened to what I told you yesterday. Are you ready to do something a little more fun? There's a malicious glint in her eyes as she smiles at me, all shark teeth.

I swallow down my nerves, refusing to let them show. *What did you have in mind?*

Want how to learn to fight?

I feel like this might be a trick, but I remind myself that I have healing magic (although I don't know how to use it yet), and it would be very beneficial for me to learn.

Sure. Do we use any weapons?

She flexes her claws at me, and opens her mouth before snapping her teeth down, indicating our only weapons are teeth and nails. I know this is going to be a much more primal form of fighting than any I've done before, not to mention much more personal.

I also know that she's not going to give me many tips or tricks. I can tell she's just going to jump in and start attacking. I take a deep breath and once again call on my predator nature, but have enough focus to remember my previous combat training as well. I know it's not the same thing, but if I keep it at the forefront of my mind, maybe I'll be able to remember something that will apply.

I nod to her that I'm ready, and just as I expected, she attacks. I dodge just as her claws swipe where my torso was, but she doesn't miss a beat before whipping her tail at me, throwing me off guard and slamming me into the cavern wall behind me. She takes full advantage and clamps my forearm between her vicious teeth, preventing me from using that hand. The pain finally spurs me into action, and I grip her hair in my right hand, digging my claws into her skull, forcing her to let go and ripping her head back.

She pulls away from me and swims to the other side of the cavern. *Took you long enough to retaliate. First lesson, mermaids fight dirty and we don't wait to act.*

I nod. Before she can come at me again, I try to heal my arm, but don't know what I'm doing, so nothing happens. Sparing all the time I can on that, I attack first. I spring forward, slashing my claws at her, but she anticipates my move and ducks out of the way, once again slapping me with her tail. This time she didn't get a great shot, so I'm able to recover fairly quickly and predict where she's going to be next. I slash out, and am thrilled when four red lines bloom on her chest. I belatedly realize that I almost got her nipple and am horrified. I wouldn't want that for anyone, even her.

She takes advantage of my distraction and gets me on the shoulder, dangerously close to my neck. I'm already sick of this and realize that she's been using her tail while I haven't been taking advantage of having tentacles. I can use them to immobilize her, but only if I can catch her. I fake one way and go the other, and she falls for it. I whip her across the face with a tentacle, stunning her before I pin her against the cavern wall. She starts slashing at me, and makes a horrible screech. I quickly grasp her hands in my tentacles while one snakes around her neck. She tries to whip me with her tail again, but I'm too close for her to be able to do anything. I hold my claws up to her chest and push slightly so she can feel that I could rip out her heart if I wanted to. She bares her teeth at me, but is unable to do anything else.

Submit, I tell her. I can see the pure hatred and refusal on her face. I dig my claws in harder while my free hand grips her hair, tilting her head and opening my mouth, positioning my sharp ass teeth right at her major artery. *Submit.*

Fine. I submit, she finally caves.

I release her and she glares daggers at me. *Are we done for the day?* I ask.

If we keep going it will get deadly. She nods at me, and I turn to swim back to the receiving room. As soon as my back is to her, she slashes with both hands from the tops of my shoulders all the way down to my low back.

Second lesson, never turn your back on your opponent. We fight dirty, remember?

I let out a wail as the pain sets in, but she's already out of sight. I follow more slowly, wary she might be hiding around a corner, waiting to attack, but I don't come across her. When I make my way out of the water, she's not in her receiving room, and I'm grateful that I don't have to interact with her anymore today. I put on my wrap dress, wincing and whimpering as it rubs against my ravaged back. I don't even want to dry myself off right now, and head straight to my rooms.

Alexei is of course waiting for me when I get there. His eyes immediately shoot to the bite on my arm and his face scrunches up in concern.

"Little doe, what the fuck happened?"

"I was training with Coralia."

"Training? I thought she was teaching you how to use your allure?"

"Only yesterday. Today she taught me how to fight in the water."

"Fuck. Well, let's go into your room and I can help you clean it."

"No thanks. I'm fine."

"Ember, that is a vicious bite. I'm coming in there with you."

I huff in annoyance, opening my door and walking into my room.

"What the hell happened to your back?"

Fuck. "Training."

"Take off your dress," he commands.

I don't have the energy to argue with him. I unwrap it, and try with all of my might not to whimper as it slides off my back. I'm not successful.

"*Ember.*" His voice sounds pained as he takes in the damage. I can only imagine how it looks.

"Do you know how the elves heal? I was trying in the water, but I was too distracted by that cunt." My heart pounds with anger. I don't use the C word often, but if there's one person deserving of it, it's Coralia. Coralia the Cunt.

"Well, before you attempt to heal it, let's disinfect it. Gods know what's in that water." He leads me into the bathroom and I'm struck by a moment of déjà vu. This is awfully similar to when I was attacked in the caves. I stand in the empty bathtub, naked, since that bitch shredded my seashell bra off, but I'm not self-conscious. Alexei has already seen me naked plenty of times, not to mention that he's my mate. He rummages around in cupboards until he finds what he needs. My body is already tensing in anticipation of the sting that I know is coming.

He, of course, notices, and gives me an apologetic look. "I'll be as quick as I can."

Before I can respond, he douses the bite on my arm. The pain steals my breath away, and when I finally take a full gulp of air, he pours the antiseptic over my back. I bite down on my lip to stop the whimper that tries to escape.

"Okay, I'm all done now."

I nod, keeping my eyes shut as I wait for the burning to stop. After what feels like forever, it finally starts to recede. When I open my eyes, a tear slips free. Alexei steps closer and wipes it before I can do it myself.

"I'm sorry I had to do that. I'm sure that was miserable, but I didn't want you accidentally sealing the bacteria in those wounds."

"I know. It's smart. Now, how should I go about this?"

"I'm not sure. Try the bite first since you can see it."

I think about when I watched Agatha heal Alexei's nose. She had skimmed her thumb down it. I try to mimic the movement, and hiss in pain as nothing happens. But of course it was stupid of me to think it would be that simple. I picture the bite healing over, skin stitching together. I keep that visual in my mind as I move my thumb over it again, slower this time. I'm amazed to find that it works. Well, *works* is a bit of a stretch, but it closes, even if it's very messy. I press down on it and find it's still tender underneath, which I'm not surprised about. She probably did quite a bit of tissue damage. I focus more on the bite, and picture healing energy, which for some reason is green and as bright as the sun. I imagine it flowing from my hand into my arm. It seems to help even more, but not completely.

This magic is different and more complicated than any I've done so far. I don't know if I would be able to accomplish anything without the motivation of being injured.

"Well done, Ember." I try not to preen at the praise, but it's difficult not to. "Now turn your focus to your back."

I already know this one is going to be much more difficult. First off, I can't see it or touch it like I did with my arm. Second, the wounds are much bigger and more brutal. I take a deep breath to center myself before feeling the burning lines down my back. I try to visualize them in my mind's eye and attempt to do the same thing as I did with my arm, but when a sweat breaks out across my brow and my ravaged back isn't even the slightest bit better minutes later, I know it's not working. I growl in frustration. It would be helpful if I had a teacher here to help me with this.

"Here, let's take you to the mirror. Maybe once you see it, that will help." Alexei gently grabs my arm and steadies me as I get out of the tub. I hiss through my teeth as the movement pulls at the skin on my back. Out of the corner of my eye, I can see Alexei clenching his jaw—his anger bleeds toward me, and I know that he must want to rip Coralia to shreds. He'll have to get in line for that one.

I turn my back to the mirror and gasp. It's so much worse than I thought it would be. I knew she'd broken skin, but my back is absolutely *shredded.* Angry tears build in my eyes, and I promise myself that I will eventually make her pay. It might not be anytime soon, but she will get what's coming to her.

I lock my eyes on to the gashes on my back and use all of my angry energy to force my skin to close. It's a slow process, especially since I don't know what I'm doing, but it works. It's not perfect, but it will do for now. When the pain is mostly gone from my back, I finally let everything go, sagging in exhaustion and relief. Alexei scoops me up before I can protest.

"Bath or bed?"

"Bath, then bed." I think the warm water will feel good on my wounds now that everything is closed.

He nods and sets me gently in the tub, turning the water on hot. As it's filling, he rummages around in the cupboards again, coming back with salts, bubble bath, and oils. He dumps everything in the tub, and I sigh in contentment as my body finally relaxes. Alexei sits on the toilet next to me, and I don't bother to tell him to leave. As much as I hate it, it's satisfying having him take care of me.

"So, what happened?"

I lay my head against the back of the tub and look at him. "She said we were training and she didn't hold back. That wouldn't have pissed me off too much though. What really got me is that I fucking bested her, she submitted, and when I turned away from her, she did this," I tell him, gesturing to my back.

A low growl is emitting from him, and he is vibrating with anger. I reach over and put my hand on his arm. "It's okay. I'm going to fuck her up eventually, but now is not the time for it."

His eyes darken. "I will be first in line to see that show. Until then, I think we need to figure out a better option for your training. She clearly isn't giving you what you need. Maybe Pearl can teach you instead?"

"She probably could, but Stavros wanted me to learn from the best. I bet Proteus would be willing to teach me."

"Oh, I'm sure he'd be *willing*," he spits in disdain.

"Hey," I snap. "The whole reason we're here is so I can get quality training. If Proteus is the best option, then you need to suck it up, or you can leave. Understand?"

Rage lights up his eyes, but instead of snapping back at me, he simply swallows hard before taking a deep breath and nodding.

"Good. I'll talk to him about it tonight. This way, too, it will hopefully take less time, and we will be able to get away from that bitch sooner rather than later."

He brightens at that. "And then we're going to the Everchanging Glades, right?"

"Well, I actually really want to visit the Abandoned Bliss."

His brows rise in surprise. "Why?"

"I want to see where my parents met, and maybe talk to people who knew my mother."

"Oh, of course. That makes sense. We can take a day to do that. Unless you want to stay longer?"

"We'll see. Maybe two days, but I think one should be enough."

"Okay. And we should be able to do that jump in one go. It's about the same distance to Sapien City from here as it was to our midpoint."

"Good. It should be a perfect stopping point, then. And allure has always been one of the easier powers for me, so I don't anticipate us being here much longer. Especially if I have a decent teacher."

He nods, but doesn't say anything. I open my senses to him and feel his anguish. I know it's over Proteus. Guilt sours my stomach, but at this point he needs to get used to it. He needs to accept that things between us are never going to happen, and as harsh as this is, maybe seeing me move on with someone else will help him realize that. I sever the connection and lean back, closing my eyes.

We don't say anything after that, and even though I should ask him to leave, I don't yet. My exhaustion kicks in, and I drift off in the tub. I don't know how long I'm out, but I'm startled awake by Alexei pulling the drain.

"Shh, it's okay. Your water is going cold so I was just going to bring you to bed."

"I'm fine, Alexei. You don't have to coddle me like this." I move to stand but he grabs my hand, helping me up before wrapping me in a towel.

"Yes I do" is all he says, his jaw clenching in anger again, and I understand then that his mate instincts are riding him hard.

I know I shouldn't let him, but I promise myself it'll be a one-time thing, and he'll be calmer after he takes care of me. I nod in permission, and he visibly relaxes, smiling at me as he gathers me in his arms. I try not to focus on how my heart soars as he brings me to my bed.

"Want to just climb right in? Or would you prefer to get dressed?"

My exhaustion is still overwhelming me, and I don't think I have the energy to get dressed. Instead of answering him verbally, I just pull the covers back. I'm asleep almost immediately, and I swear Alexei's fingers skim down my spine before I'm out completely.

13

Ember

Alexei is gone when I wake, and I roll onto my back and suck in a sharp breath. Even though I did okay healing myself, I'm still pretty sore. I get out of bed, and am pleasantly surprised when I find a tray of dinner waiting for me. Appreciative that I don't have to socialize with Coralia, I throw on my robe before plopping down to eat. I inhale my food with my normal gusto—the confrontation followed by using my freshly learned healing magic took up a good portion of my energy.

After I've finished the meal, I throw on one of my fancier outfits before doing my hair and makeup. Maybe if I look pleasant enough it will help convince Proteus to train me. When I go out in search of him, Alexei is not lingering in the halls, and I'm grateful. I don't want him asking why I've gotten all dressed up.

I start with where I suspect his rooms are. I wander around, hoping to come across him, but with every passing minute, I'm getting more uncomfortable. I'm relieved when a servant comes into view.

"Excuse me. I'm looking for Proteus. Do you know where he is?"

The servant basically sneers at me, but answers me all the same. "He's not here. He went for a swim."

"Thank you."

I take off toward where we went into the ocean this morning. I'm pretty sure that's his favorite spot anyway. I don't see him there, but the same wrap he used this morning is sitting in the sand. I park my ass down right next to it, and wait for him to show up. Fifteen minutes later, Pearl walks by.

"Ember, what are you doing out here?"

"Waiting for Proteus."

"Oh, is that right?" she says suggestively, waggling her eyebrows at me.

I scoff. "It's not like that. I'm trying to see if he'd be willing to train me instead of Coralia."

"Why?"

"Have you met her? First off, she's a bitch. Secondly, there was a little incident while we were training today that made me realize that I don't want to have anything to do with her."

"What happened?"

I don't want to get into it with Pearl at the moment, so I brush it off. "Nothing important. It just opened my eyes to how awful she is."

She narrows her eyes at me, as if she can tell that I'm lying, but doesn't call me on it. "How does Alexei feel about Proteus training you?"

"Well, I have to get him to agree first. But he wasn't thrilled. I told him if he didn't like it then he could go home."

"I bet that shut him up quick. That boy would glue himself to your side if you'd let him."

"I know."

She's about to respond, but Proteus chooses that moment to emerge from the water like a Greek god. Water runs down his chest in rivulets and flows down to something much more interesting. I try to prevent my eyes from following, but they drift down anyway. I almost gasp at his impressive length, but stop myself before any noise escapes. I force my gaze up to meet his, and he seems surprised to see me.

"Ember, Pearl, what are you doing here?"

I stand so I'm not looking up at him while he's naked. That would be even more awkward. "I need to talk to you about something. Pearl was just keeping me company while I waited."

Pearl gives him a polite smile and nod before taking off to wherever she'd been going. Proteus turns his full attention to me as he ties the wrap around his waist.

"What can I do for you?"

"I was wondering if you'd be willing to take over my training?"

His brows shoot up in surprise. "Are things not going well with my mother?"

I clear my throat uncomfortably. "Well, we don't exactly connect like I was hoping."

He chuckles at my clearly underexaggerated statement. "I understand. She can be a bit much. Sure, I can train you. When do you want to start?"

"Now? I'd like to be trained as quickly as possible."

He smirks at me. "So ready to leave us?"

"I just have a lot of territories to visit."

"Well, maybe I'll take my time training you so you're forced to stay here and keep me company awhile longer." There's a flirtatious glint in his eyes, and it brings a blush to my cheeks.

"I wouldn't mind getting to know you better," I flirt back.

He brightens at that. "Well, let's get started, then."

"Here?"

"Would you prefer to go back to my mother's house?"

"Erm, no."

"Very well. I'll have you practice on me, then. Allure doesn't work as well on us mermaids, but it can still affect us. Especially if it's powerful enough."

I nod. I had figured as much, but I appreciate the confirmation. He looks at me expectantly, and I shake my head at myself, realizing he wants me to start. I bring my mermaid to the surface, full force, knowing that I'll need more power if it's going to work on him.

I try to think of a command to give him to see if my allure is powerful enough. I don't know him that well, so I don't really know what he would be reluctant to do. I stick with the same one I asked of Alexei. "Dance for me."

His eyes glitter in amusement, but he doesn't move. It's then that I realized my rookie mistake. I didn't get past his mental shields; they're firmly in place. I debate on whether or not I should. I don't want his mother knowing that I'm powerful in this area, but if I'm actually going to learn from him I need to see what I can do.

Fuck it. I don't get the impression that he likes his mother or confides in her anyway. Within moments, I'm through his barriers, which are strong, but not nearly as strong as my father's or mine for that matter. His attraction is strongest, followed by respect. None of the vileness I sensed with Coralia is present, and I'm glad that my instincts seem to be correct about him. I let my allure free again, and this time I see the tell-tale adoration in his eyes, although not as strong as with others. I smile, knowing that I've got him now.

"Dance for me," I command again. This time he resists me for a few moments before reluctantly beginning to dance. I let him continue for a while, seeing how long it will last. A few minutes later he finally stops.

"That was good. A few things though. You lost focus at the end, that's why I was able to stop on my own. Also, your allure will be much more powerful if you *want* it. I could tell you didn't really care about the command you gave because I wasn't as compelled as I should've been. That's why I didn't follow it immediately. Make sure, especially with other mermaids, that you really want them to follow your instruction.

Even if you don't, then make yourself *believe* that you want it. But first, let's have you practice with things that you do truly want me to do, and once you have that down, we can start you on things that you don't really care about, and then finally, things that you don't want me to do."

"Why things that I don't want you to do?"

"It doesn't happen often, but there may be times when you don't *want* someone to do something, but you *need* them to do something. If you don't have the conviction behind your allure, it won't work."

I ponder his advice, and am immediately grateful that I decided to come to him for this training. My instincts told me he would be a good instructor, and every tip he's provided makes complete sense. It also helps that I'm practicing on a powerful mermaid. If I can control him with my allure, I control anyone.

I focus on the task at hand, thinking of what I want him to do. There is something that I think I would like. It's not anything he would be opposed to, but that's not the point right now. I reach out to his mind, finding his barriers still down for me. I let my allure out again. "Kiss my hand."

This time, he doesn't resist, and basically scrambles forward to follow my order. His warm lips are nice on my skin. Not as electrifying as Alexei, not by a long shot, but still nice. He pulls back, and I can see the want in his eyes.

"Tell me what you want from me," I order.

"I want to get to know you."

"Is that all?"

"I also want...you."

"Me?"

"You're beautiful, Your Highness. I would be a fool to not want you. In fact, I think every mermaid here wants you. You're gorgeous and extremely powerful, the two things mermaids covet more than anything else."

"I see," I say, somewhat disappointed. I don't want to be wanted just for my beauty and power.

"But that's not all. You're also extremely smart, funny, and I have to say, I love the sass that comes out of your mouth and lurks behind your eyes."

I smile at the compliment, liking that answer better than his first. I decide to ask him another question—something I want to know, but don't think he'll want to share.

"How do you feel about your mother?" I put my desperation to know the answer into my allure, wanting to see if he'll tell me.

His brows furrow, and I can sense his reluctance. I unleash my power a bit more, and a sweat breaks out across my brow. I use my empath powers as well to push trust and honesty on him. It might be unfair that I'm doubling up my powers on Proteus, and it's also cheating a little bit with my training, but I don't care. Apparently, according to Coralia, mermaids don't fight fair. I want to know this answer. I realize that he will probably be pissed at me when it's over, but at the moment, this question takes precedence.

"Tell me."

"My mother is an ambitious woman. Most of the time, I don't agree with the way she handles things. I try to get her to approach things differently, but she rarely listens to me. She's conceited and does what she wants, no matter the end result."

I turn off my allure, satisfied that I got something I wanted from him that he didn't want to give me. I'm still in his mind, and when he snaps out of it, his anger mounts. I brace myself for the storm.

"What the fuck, Ember?"

"I know you didn't want to tell me any of that, but I needed to know."

"That was not okay. That's private information that you have no right to force out of me. I agreed to train you because you needed help, and you took advantage of that." Before I can apologize, he storms off, leaving me standing there watching him.

Guilt starts to creep in, turning my stomach, and I sigh in regret. I shouldn't have done that. He's right, and I feel like a total ass for abusing my power like that. I guess that was a lesson all in itself. One I wasn't anticipating learning.

I teletravel directly back to my room, not wanting to run into anyone else. Unfortunately, Pearl is waiting on my bed when I return. Not that I don't love her, but I just wanted to wallow in my guilt for a while.

"Hey, girl. I thought I would wait for you here to hang out since we haven't had much time with each other lately. I brought food."

I smile at her, but she can tell it isn't sincere.

"What's wrong?"

I take a deep breath and tell her what just happened with Proteus. A sympathetic, knowing look comes across her face, and even though I wasn't thrilled to see her here originally, it's a relief to talk to her about this.

"I've been in this situation before, Ember. I get it. It's awful, and you'll feel guilty about it for a while, but now you know. You won't make the same mistake anytime soon."

"Anytime soon?"

She grimaces. "I wish I could tell you that you'll never use your powers like that again, but it's not a guarantee. I've made that mistake multiple times, and sometimes it can't be helped. Sometimes it *has* to be done, no matter how much you might not want to, and how guilty you feel afterward."

I groan dramatically. What she's saying makes sense. And honestly, as awful as forcing that information out of Proteus was of me, I do think it was necessary. And now I know that Proteus is different from his mother. Perhaps I can trust him.

"What else did you have him do?"

"Dance, kiss my hand, and tell me what he wants from me."

"Kiss your hand, huh? *Scandalous.*" I roll my eyes and push her playfully. "What did he tell you he wants from you?"

"To get to know me. And, well, he also said he wants *me.*"

She smirks. "Well, that's obvious. I could've told you that. Every mermaid who has seen you wants you. Especially after you toured the underwater community. All the women are wearing seashell bras now. I told you you'd start a trend."

"They really are? Already?"

"Of course. You are the talk of the territory, and as such, everyone wants to emulate the most powerful and beautiful individual they come across. Not to mention you're the king's daughter. They envy you, and they want you. It's basically the highest praise you can receive from mermaids."

"Wow. I didn't expect that. I figured others wouldn't like me much, especially since I have mixed blood."

"Ember, there hasn't been anyone like you here in their lifetime. They're enamored with you." For some reason, her words niggle at something in my brain, but I can't pinpoint what. I let it go for now.

"Well, I hope the other territories like me just as much. I'm trying to get all the support I can."

"They'll all love you when they meet you. You can win over anybody."

"Even the elves?" I think back to Agatha's *friendly* demeanor and shudder at the thought of what awaits me in the Healing Springs.

Pearl laughs loudly. "Yes. Well, maybe *love* is a strong word for them, but you'll sway them to you."

"I'm excited to learn about all of my magic, but it's also overwhelming."

"I can imagine. Is there one in particular you're more worried about? Or just all of them?"

I think about it for a moment. "Well, all of them are overwhelming because there's so much to learn, but there are a few that I'm particularly concerned about."

"Which ones?"

"As weird as it sounds, I think I'm going to struggle with my mimic powers."

"Why do you say that?" she asks. "I figured that one would be easier for you since you have no problem shifting into your mermaid form."

"You would think so, but I've tried on my own before, and my owl is just far away from me, and I haven't been able to manage it. Maybe because with my mermaid form, I also shift in the water. Maybe I would have an easier time if my animal was a water or land animal?"

"Are you worried about any others?"

"Healing, a little bit. I mean, I was able to accomplish it this morning, but I think that was only because I was legitimately injured."

"You were injured?!"

I wince. I had forgotten that Alexei was the only one who knew what happened between me and Coralia. "That was the incident with Coralia this morning."

Her eyes narrow on me. "You told me it was no big deal! What happened?"

I tell her, albeit reluctantly. When I'm finished, she rips my top off to examine my back. I hear her gasp of horror behind me.

"What the *fuck*?!" Her anger is bleeding toward me. "I can't believe she did this to you. You should tell the king about this."

"No. Absolutely not."

"Why not? He would punish her. Potentially remove her from her position."

"I don't want him getting involved. I don't want the kingdom to know me that way."

"What way?"

"Like every time something is wrong I go running to Daddy to fix everything for me. I am a grown-ass woman. A powerful one at that. I will handle Coralia. Eventually. I don't quite know how yet, but I will take care of her."

She reluctantly nods. "Well, all right. But for the record, I still think you should tell him."

"Duly noted. I will take it into consideration."

"Said like a true princess," she teases.

After that we scarf down the food she brought, and we decide to have a slumber party. Pearl falls asleep with me soon after.

The next morning, I seek out Proteus. I don't know if he'll forgive me, but I need to apologize. I look all over the house, and I can't find him anywhere. I have a feeling he's avoiding me, and I don't blame him. I teletravel to the spot he usually chooses to enter the water, and while I don't find him there, I do find his wrap. I could wait for him here, but I'd really like to talk to him sooner rather than later. Deciding not to overthink it, I quickly strip, and dive in, shifting as I go. There's not many people around at first, but the farther I go, the more I see what Pearl was talking about. There are seashell bras everywhere, and I try not to be self-conscious about the fact that I'm topless right now while all the other mermaids aren't. I see a few who don't have them, so I'm not the only boobs in sight, thank the Gods.

I head in the direction we traveled last time, hoping to find him.

When I arrive at the main hub, I finally see him. He's chatting with a small group of mermaids, and seems to be genuinely enjoying himself. It also looks like he's schmoozing a little, like all mermaids do when they're the center of attention. I can't help but wonder if he has some ulterior motive, especially after what he revealed to me yesterday.

I wait until he's finished talking to them, and when he turns to head my way, we lock eyes. His features harden, and I give him the most sincere look I can in the distance separating us. He deflates a bit, and I can physically see when he gives in. I give him a smile before swimming up to him.

Hello, Ember.

Hello, Proteus.

Can I help you, Your Highness? This time, he's not calling me that out of respect, and I flinch.

I just wanted to say I'm so sorry. Everything you said yesterday was right on point. I had no right to do what I did. You offered to help me, and I took advantage of you. I understand if you don't want to train me anymore.

He doesn't respond for several moments, and I fight the urge to fidget. Finally, he gives me a small smile.

I forgive you, Ember. Even though I'm not happy you did it, I understand why. My mother is a...difficult woman, and you wanted to know if you could trust me.

I nod, grateful that he's forgiven me, and that he's able to see my side.

Thank you, Proteus. If you're willing to keep training me, I swear I'll never do anything like that again.

I'll keep training you. And as much as I hate to admit it, I'm impressed that you were able to do what you did. You're powerful. That was probably part of my anger. I'm not used to anyone being able to take advantage of me like that.

I blush at his praise. It's then that his eyes move down my body, and

I fight the urge to cover myself. His brows rise in surprise, his eyes lingering on my breasts.

You're not wearing your seashells today?

I was in a hurry to see you, and your mother shredded the twine holding them together yesterday.

His brows furrow. *She did what?* Without another word, he swims around to my back, and his touch skates along the marks. *What the hell did she do to you?*

I almost lie, but after yesterday, I owe it to him to be honest. I tell him exactly what happened.

Well, no wonder you did what you did. Your Highness, I am so sorry. There is no excuse for her behavior. I hope she didn't make you think that our species is all like her. Of course, some are, it can't be helped, but there are a lot of us who are honorable.

I reach out to touch his arm. *I know. I can see the man you are.*

I swear he blushes in return. *Well, do you want to go up and train?*

I nod eagerly. We return to the surface, get dressed, and stay there to train. After yesterday and the way Proteus explained the tactics, the ability comes much more easily, even though allure was one of my magics that felt more natural to me.

We're training for at least an hour, maybe two, and by the end I'm starting to become more comfortable with him as well. We walk back together, even though I could just teletravel if I wanted to, but I find I enjoy time spent in his company.

He reaches over and grabs my hand in his, butterflies flitting in my stomach. The gesture also causes my mate mark on my wrist to burn, but I ignore it. We arrive at the house, and I find I'm reluctant to end our interaction.

"You did well today, Ember. I don't think you'll need much more training, but I almost didn't tell you that because I don't want you to leave."

"I understand. It's been really interesting getting to know you. I can see us becoming really good friends."

"Just friends?" he fishes, a twinkle in his eye.

"Well, I'm not sure right now, Proteus. My life is a little complicated at the moment, not to mention the fact that we live in separate territories. I also don't know you well enough yet."

"But you find me attractive?" he asks, even though he knows I do. I'm pretty sure everyone does.

I shove him playfully. "I guess," I tease.

"Well, at least I've got that goin' for me. How about going out to dinner tomorrow to get to know me better?"

"You mean on a date?"

His face scrunches up in confusion, making me laugh. "What's a date?"

"That's what we call it on Earth. When you're interested in someone, you go on a date with them to see if you're compatible."

"Oh! Then yes. Ember, would you do me the honor of going on a date with me?"

I smile at him. "Yes. I would like that very much, Proteus."

"Until tomorrow, then." He grabs my hand, giving it a slightly more sensuous kiss than he has in the past. With that, he turns and grabs the door, holding it open for me.

"Until tomorrow," I repeat, heading off to my room.

When I arrive, I attempt to get my emotions under control. I'm excited about our date. I mean, he's gorgeous, kind, and gentlemanly. What woman wouldn't want him? But an image of Alexei flashes in my mind. My stomach sinks, and my heart breaks at the thought of being with someone other than him. Maybe Pearl and Alexei are both right. But I would at least like to try. And who better to try with than Proteus?

I see Alexei later for training, and I'm a little nervous. He, of course, notices immediately.

"What's wrong, Ember? You're distracted today."

"It's nothing."

"You forget that I know you better than that. I can tell something's wrong, and it's affecting your training."

I huff in exasperation. "Well, I'm going out to dinner with Proteus tomorrow."

"Dinner? Just the two of you?" I nod. "Are you...interested in him?"

I bite my lip and avoid his gaze. "Yes. I mean, I might be. I'm going out with him to see if there's the potential for more than friendship between us."

He doesn't say anything for so long that I finally meet his eyes. There's a storm brewing behind them.

Just when I think he's going to go all macho man like he has in the past with me, claiming that I'm his, and all of that nonsense, his eyes shutter, and the anger evaporates from his face. "Okay."

My jaw drops in complete surprise. "Okay?"

"Yes. Okay. Because even though I *hate* that you're going out with him, I know that you won't find him as interesting as you're hoping."

I scoff. "That's mighty presumptuous of you. What makes you say that?"

The look in his eyes is all predator as he prowls toward me. "Because, Ember. Even though you haven't admitted it to yourself, we are meant for each other. We're *made* for each other. You won't find anyone you want like you want me. And I'm betting that when you spend some time with him, you'll see that for yourself. Until then, I'll be here. Waiting for you. Even if it takes the rest of my life."

At this point, there's barely an inch separating our mouths, and just when I think he's going to kiss me senseless and change my mind, he turns and heads back toward his weapon.

"Ready?" he asks, holding his sword up.

I swallow as I fight off the mixture of lust and anger that's burning through my body and raise my sword. I won't let him catch me off guard.

166

14

Ember

Nerves flutter in my stomach the next night as I stand in front of my wardrobe trying to figure out what to wear for dinner. Luckily, I have Pearl to help me narrow down my outfit.

Finally after much debating, we settle on an apricot mermaid-style dress that has a silver art deco–style design. It's a V-neck and sleeveless, showing off some skin and curves without being over-the-top. It's a little fancier than I would normally go for a first date, but Pearl has reassured me that mermaids are always over-the-top, and anything less will make me underdressed. I trust her since she's never steered me wrong before.

She helps me with my hair and makeup, and when it's time to go, I hear a knock at my door, and my heart starts pounding.

"Have fun!" Pearl says. "I expect all the details when you get back."

I shoot her a wink before I open the door. Proteus stands there looking handsome as ever. His hair is slicked back, and he has a suit on. He takes me in, and his eyes flare.

"You look divine, Ember," he compliments as he leans in to give me a lingering kiss on the cheek.

"Thank you. You clean up pretty well yourself, Proteus."

He smiles at me. "Ready?" He offers me his arm.

I take it as I nod. "So, where are we going?"

"There's a restaurant on an island close by. I thought we could swim there and then eat dinner. Sound good to you?"

"What about our clothes?"

He holds up a bag that I didn't notice before. "I brought this. It's waterproof. We can put our clothes in it and I'll carry it over while we swim."

"Good thing I have waterproof makeup on," I tease.

He winks at me, and we make our way to his favorite spot, where we both quickly strip and throw our clothes in the bag. We shift and start swimming, this time in the opposite direction than I've been before. This area isn't as populated, and there's more room to swim. Proteus points me to where we're going and we race, having fun swimming together. He beats me, but I tell him it's only because he knew where we were going and I didn't.

When we come out of the water, I gasp at the sight before me. We're on an extremely small island. The only things on it are a restaurant, a hotel, and a huge cliff. There are beautiful lights everywhere, and the restaurant opens up against the beach.

A few people look at us when we emerge, but look away before my self-consciousness can creep in. The nice thing about being here is that no one cares about the whole nudity thing. I quickly dry us both off with my air magic, and Proteus opens our swim bag. Sure enough, our clothes are completely dry and unwrinkled. We dress and he offers me his arm as we head inside.

"Welcome t—oh, Proteus, how wonderful to see you." The hostess lights up upon seeing him. He must come here often, although now that I think about it, he is very social with the community and frequently interacts with the mermaids (something that Coralia should be doing as well).

"Hello, Cressida. Two for dinner, please."

"Outside or inside?"

Proteus looks at me to answer. "Outside, please."

She smiles warmly at us before escorting us to the patio. Unlike normal restaurants on Earth, there's no flooring outside, just the sand from the beach, and I notice almost all of the patrons have their shoes off. I take mine off as soon as we get to the table, and Proteus holds out the bag for me to throw them in.

"What would you like to drink?"

"I'll take an ice water and a white wine, please." I don't normally drink white wine, but for some reason I've really been craving it here. Maybe because of the tropical vibe.

"I'll have the same," Proteus adds.

When the server walks away, I ask him, "So, what's good here?"

"Everything." I'm about to say he needs to help me out a bit more than that when he continues. "*But*, the seafood and pasta are both exceptional."

Having had quite a bit of seafood since we've been here, I get pasta. Our drinks come out, and Proteus also orders us calamari. I haven't had calamari since I was on Earth, way before I discovered that I had my own tentacles, and I wonder if I should feel a little cannibalistic, but decide I don't care as soon as I take my first bite.

"You did well in training today, Ember. I think a day or two more and there won't be much more I can help with."

"Well, you've been much more helpful than your mother. No offense."

"Believe me, none taken."

There's a bit of an awkward silence for a while, and I think of something to try to fill it. "So, I've noticed that you're really active in the community here. I take it that's something that's important to you?"

"It really is. I've felt since I was young that the grand masters should really be more involved with those they lead. I think I feel so strongly about it since my mother was so *uninvolved.* It always really bothered me. I think the first time I noticed it, I was eight, and I had a friend whose brother was terribly sick and the family didn't have enough money for treatment. I went to my mother, thinking that she should help his family. She laughed at me and told me that it wasn't our job to worry about such things. It really made an impression on me in the opposite way she wanted. I've never wanted to be someone who just ignores their duties and community or those in need. Especially when I have the power to help. So, ever since then, I've been really mindful of seeing what I can do for those under my care."

I'm speechless. I open up my senses to him to see if he's being sincere, even though I'm almost positive he is. Sure enough, his sincerity and honesty are evident as soon as I connect with him.

"Wow, Proteus. It's amazing that you do that for your people. The mermaids are very lucky to have you."

His cheeks shimmer slightly at my praise, and I can tell he appreciates my approval. After that, we talk about more surface-level matters; how it was growing up on Earth, my career, things like that. Although, I notice it's difficult to find common discussion topics since we were raised in different realms.

Normally on a date I ask what kind of music, movies, books he likes, but in this case we have no common ground.

Our food arrives, and we're silent as we eat. Proteus was right, the pasta is phenomenal. We each order another glass of wine, and by that point I'm starting to relax. Conversation flows a little more naturally, and we become more comfortable with each other.

Proteus pays the bill, and I head toward the ocean, thinking we're going straight back. He stops me with a hand on my arm.

"Want to be a little adventurous with me?" he asks.

"What did you have in mind?"

"Come with me." He grabs my hand and starts dragging me up the cliff.

My heart is pounding, but I follow him. It's difficult to hike in my outfit, but I make it work. When we get to the top, I look out over the view. It's breathtaking. I can see the other islands from here, dotting the darkened landscape, as well as the city underneath the water. Everything glows. The only word to describe it is *magical*.

"Let's jump," Proteus says.

When I look over at him, he's already stripping, throwing all his clothes in the bag. My eyes widen as I look down at the drop. It's not Mount Everest or anything, but it is high, and I've always struggled with heights.

"What about rocks?"

"I've made this jump many times. There are hardly any stray rocks down there."

Well, that isn't exactly the reassurance I was looking for. I look at him as he strips off the last piece of clothing. He smirks at me and raises an eyebrow in question. Fuck it. I strip off my dress and throw it in the bag. Proteus's grin lights up his face as he closes the bag.

"Ready?" he asks, holding out his hand.

I grab it tightly and nod. He counts down from three, and we sprint and leap off the cliff, naked as the day we were born. My stomach drops along with my body, and I let out a piercing scream. Proteus's hand tightens in mine as we struggle to hold on to each other midair. Moments later, we crash through the water, and I shift immediately. The fall hurt a bit more than I thought it would, and my heart is pounding right out of my chest, but it's so exhilarating. A huge smile is plastered to my face, and Proteus's expression matches mine.

Enjoy yourself? he asks.

Yes. I've never done anything like that before. Thanks for sharing it with me.

He nods. *Are you ready to head back?*

I nod. As fun as the night has been, I'm ready for it to be over. We swim back to Allure Isle in companionable silence. We shift, and emerge out of the water. I dry us with my magic and we get dressed. When we reach our destination, we linger outside the front door.

"Thank you for tonight, Proteus. I had a lot of fun, and I really enjoyed getting to know you a bit more."

"I had fun too, Ember."

He leans in, and I know he's going to kiss me. I have a split second to make up my mind if I want this or not. I give it a shot. That's why I'm on a date with him after all.

I tip my head back, and his mouth descends on me. It starts out soft, just him gently pressing his lips to my own, but then his mouth opens just a bit, his tongue reaching out to meet mine. I indulge him. I realize then that while he is a fantastic kisser, I don't want to be kissing him. I am not into this in the slightest, and even with how wonderful and attractive he is, there's no heat with him at all. I pull back, breaking the kiss.

"Is something wrong?" he asks.

"I'm sorry, Proteus. I can't do this."

His face falls a bit, but he gives me a sad, understanding smile. "It's Alexei, isn't it?"

I flinch back at the sound of his name, and notice that my mate mark has been screaming in pain at me. I rub along it to try to dissipate the sting, but it doesn't seem to be working. Proteus latches on to the movement, and his hand shoots out to grab my wrist before I can stop him. His eyes widen slightly at the mark.

"Is...is this what I think it is?"

I reluctantly nod, and his face pales.

"Why did you come out with me, then? Why did you let me kiss you when you belong to another?"

"Jesus Christ. I belong to *myself*. No one else. I may have a mate mark, but that doesn't mean that I belong to him. I chose not to be with him." Anger at everyone not understanding what I want and need makes my tone harsh.

His face knits up in confusion. "Why?"

"It's a long story. I like you, and I thought I would see if things could work between us, even though I have this. But it just doesn't feel right. I'm so sorry, Proteus."

"I understand, Ember. It's okay. I like you too, and I would really like to still be friends with you."

I sigh in relief that he's not upset and that he still wants to continue our friendship. I smile at him, putting my hand gently on his arm. "I would like that very much. Thank you for being so kind to me. It's not very common in this realm, I've discovered."

"I unfortunately know what you mean. It's probably better this way with us living in separate territories. We'll keep in touch."

I give him a grateful hug. "Yes, we will. So, are we still training tomorrow?"

"I don't think there's anything more I can teach you, Ember. Your mermaid blood is powerful. I was just trying to keep you here for a few more days for selfish reasons."

I laugh, excited at the thought that Alexei and I will be able to leave tomorrow and get away from the grand bitch, also known as Coralia.

"Well, thank you for everything, Proteus. I really enjoyed getting to know you."

"The honor was all mine, Your Highness." He bows to me, planting another kiss on my hand. This one is much different than any of his previous ones however. There's not an undercurrent of sexual tension like there was from the beginning.

I head inside and change quickly before going across the hall and knocking on Alexei's door. He answers within moments, as if he's been waiting for me.

I don't let him get a word in, and I don't tell him anything about what happened tonight between me and Proteus. It's still not his business as far as I'm concerned, and I don't want him asking about it.

"We're leaving in the morning." Before he can respond, I teletravel directly to Pearl's front door. I knock urgently, wanting this to be over and to move on to the next phase of our journey, and anxious to see where my mother lived.

Opal opens the door after thirty seconds or so, although to me it's an eternity.

"Ember? What can I do for you?"

"I'm looking for Pearl."

The woman in question walks up seconds later. "Ember? What are you doing here? I thought you were on your date with Proteus."

I pull her outside with me, not wanting to have this conversation in front of Opal. She gets the hint and closes the door behind her.

"Alexei and I are leaving tomorrow. I just wanted to let you know."

"Leaving? Already? What happened?"

"I mean, nothing really." I fill her in. "As much as I love being here with you, I'm ready to move on to the next territory, Pearl."

She nods sadly. "I knew it wouldn't take you long to master our powers. I'll miss you though. Any idea when you'll be home?"

"I have no idea. We have a lot of territories we're traveling to, and I'm going to be training in most of them, so it might be a while. It all depends on how much progress I make."

"Well, I'll miss you." She leans over and gives me a warm hug.

"I'll miss you too. Watch out for my dad when you get back, okay?"

"I will. I promise."

I teletravel back to my room and pack everything up. I don't shrink it quite yet since I'll need to pack some last-minute things tomorrow morning, but for the most part everything is done. Excitement builds in my chest that I'll get to see where both of my moms were from tomorrow. I don't know what I'll find there, but I think there's something important waiting for me.

Before I go to bed, there's one more thing I have to do. I need to let Coralia know I'm leaving. I haven't seen her since our little incident, and I need to put her in her place so she doesn't think I'm running scared.

The shirt that I'm wearing shows off my arm and back, and I'm grateful. I want her to see that I healed myself after she fucked me over.

I waltz into her receiving room to find her just coming out of the water. She seems surprised to see me, but she recovers quickly, despite the fact that she's naked.

"Your Highness. What can I do for you?"

"I wanted to let you know that we will be leaving tomorrow. I've gotten everything I need here. No thanks to you."

A snooty expression crosses her face, and I have the urge to show my hand and make her grovel. I resist, barely.

"Good riddance," she sneers, and my control snaps.

I hit her with a blast of wind, pinning her to the wall. She lets out her allure, her beautiful voice filling the space. "Leave," she orders.

"Oh, I will, but not yet."

Her eyes widen in disbelief. I laugh at the fact that she thought she was more powerful than me. "I will not be telling the king what you did to me." It's then that her eyes find my arm where I should have a vicious-looking bite that still hasn't quite healed but is perfectly smooth with the exception of the scar. Her eyes widen impossibly further, and she visibly pales. "I want to deal with you *myself*. And believe me, I will. Next time we meet I expect you to show me the respect I deserve. And if you *ever* attack me like that again, I will fucking end you. Do you understand me?"

She nods, and my inner savage delights at the terror in her eyes. "Tell me you understand."

"I understand, Your Highness."

"Good. Now bow to me and wish me safe travels."

She follows my orders, even without me using any sort of allure on her. I nod, and turn my scarred back on her, showing her that even after what she did last time, I'm not afraid of her.

I wake early, the sun having barely risen. My anticipation over today makes it impossible to sleep longer. I take a long bath, attempting to relax as I pull out all the stops—salts, bubbles, and candles. When I'm done, I try to take my time in getting ready.

I have to keep in mind that I need to tone my look down now that we're leaving Mermacovia. I no longer have to have elaborate hair and makeup and be dressed to the nines. I apply my makeup with a subtle natural look. I do my typical straight back dutch braid for my hair, which I have to admit I've missed. Then I pick my go-to outfit choice: a long black skirt, the front hem pulled up a bit so my brown boots and stockings are visible; a belt with my daggers strapped to it; and a loose, long-sleeved, white undershirt with a dark brown corset over the top.

I feel like a complete badass when I wear this outfit, and I don variations of it at every opportunity. I pack up the rest of my things and shrink my trunk, putting it neatly in my pocket. I check the room over to ensure I didn't forget anything, and when I'm satisfied, I walk across the hall to get Alexei. He answers the door almost immediately.

"Ready?"

I nod and walk to the front door. I know he's following me, and he might be curious as to why I didn't just teletravel from inside the house, but I don't want the last thing I see of this territory to be Coralia's fucking house.

The view outside is gorgeous, the morning sun shining over the water, with an abundance of birds flying overhead and diving into the ocean. I sigh. *This* is what I want to remember from this trip. Alexei comes up to stand next to me, and I hold out my hand to him. When our flesh meets, I swear my mate mark tingles in relief at being in contact with my mate instead of another man. He briefly runs his thumb over the mark, the tingling intensifying it before I feel the sensation of him pulling me with him to a new destination.

15

Ember

The first thing I notice is the heat. While Mermacovia felt tropical, the Mortal Sanctum is arid. I squint my eyes against the brightness. Experiencing the sun in the Mortal Sanctum is much harsher than what we just soaked up in Mermacovia.

When I can finally stand it, I look around and am not impressed by what I see. This land looks desolate, and reminds me of Tatooine from *Star Wars*. Even though I've barely seen any of the territory, I wonder if when they came here, the humans were given the section of the realm that was the worst, the land that nobody wanted. The thought makes my heart heavy, especially after seeing all the beauty this realm has to offer.

Alexei squeezes my hand, bringing me back to the here and now. I meet his eyes and see the same devastation written across his features. I drop his hand and inspect the building in front of us. It has a Moroccan vibe to it, which fits. I've always felt that the Moroccan aesthetic exudes sensuality, because of the natural materials and colorful elements of the architecture. The absence of right angles humanizes the form, which is an idea I've been intrigued with my whole career in studying past civilizations.

We enter the building, which is dark aside from penetrations in the exterior walls that allow the sun to shine through, masked with different color fabrics. There are beautiful lanterns all over the facility, and the air in here smells heavily of incense, but there's also the underlying smell of sex and sweat.

There's a woman at the front who I can tell immediately is human. She looks to be in her early twenties, and pastes a fake smile on her face upon seeing us.

"Welcome to the Sacred Rite and the Abandoned Bliss. I take it you two will want to be on the Abandoned side today? I'm assuming you're just here for fun and aren't in need of a conduit?"

Oh, great. She's mistaken us for a couple who wants to have a threesome. "Actually, I'm just here to…look around? My mother used to live here, or work here. I was hoping to look at her old quarters."

"We don't really do that, ma'am."

Alexei cuts in, saving the day as usual. "I know you don't normally do that, but you'll want to make an exception this time. This is Ember Solis, the king's daughter."

Her eyes widen almost comically. She quickly stands up and bows to me. "Oh, Your Highness, I'm so sorry. Let me go get the madam to show you around. Would you like anything to drink while you wait?"

"Just water for me, please."

"Same," Alexei says.

She bows again before rushing off. I am tempted to sit on the cushions on the floor, but think better of it. I don't know how and or why those are used. The girl soon comes back with two ice waters with little lemon slices in them. I take one gratefully, and the liquid refreshes me from the stifling heat.

"I'll be back with Madam in just a moment." She scurries off again.

Alexei and I stand there awkwardly waiting. Normally things between us aren't uneasy, but after yesterday's events with Proteus, and the fact that we're in a literal brothel and can hear faint noises coming from all over the establishment, things aren't as comfortable as they normally are.

Fortunately, it doesn't take long for "Madam" to show up. She's almost as beautiful as Coralia, and I'm shocked to see that she's a mermaid. I didn't realize that there was anyone living here besides the humans. There's something different about her from the mermaids in Mermacovia, and I try to put my finger on what it is.

After a moment of taking her in, I figure it out. Even though she's breathtaking, she looks worn. Her bloodred hair isn't shiny and glowing, and her turquoise eyes seem to lack the same vibrancy. Her voluptuous body sways as she makes her way toward us. A smile lights up her face, but I can't tell if it's genuine or not.

"Your Highness," she addresses me, bowing when she gets close enough. I wonder if I'll ever get used to that.

"Madam. Sorry to come here out of nowhere, but we were passing through, and I wanted to see where my mother lived."

"Antonia mentioned something like that. Are you sure your mother lived *here*?"

"Yes. Her name was Catalina. My father told me that they met here."

"Oh yes. Catalina. She was a lovely girl. I remember when your father came here."

"Yet, you did not realize Catalina was my mother?"

"I thought you died in childbirth."

"I did not. Eve brought me to Earth to protect me. Apparently I was in danger."

A strange look crosses her face, but it's gone before I can place it. "Well, let me take you to her chambers. They're currently empty."

She leads the way, and we're soon out of the lavish entrance and fancy corridor and into what is clearly the servants' quarters. It's small, run-down, and hot. My mother's room is at the end of the hall, and as soon as we enter it, I experience a strange sensation, almost as if I've been here before.

"I'll leave you here. Let me know if you need anything at all, Your Highness."

The madam bows again and walks out, closing the door behind her. My necklace that I inherited from my mother flares brightly, and I gasp in surprise. The stone hasn't done that since I fell into the portal. Alexei's shocked breath behind me tells me he can see it glowing as well.

I walk around the room, seeing if it gives me a clue like it did in Oregon. Sure enough, the necklace brightens and dims depending on where I go, and I follow the guidance to her closet. What is it with my mothers and closets?

I walk through the opening, the space almost too small to stand in, and look around for anything unusual. I knock on the walls, thinking that maybe she pulled a similar trick to Eve, but everything sounds normal. I get on my hands and knees, running my palms over the flooring, and I let out a cry of triumph when I discover a loose floorboard. I pry it up and find a skinny box stuffed into it. I pull it out and huff in frustration.

"Fuck. It needs a key."

"You didn't see anything else down there? Maybe she hid it here somewhere."

I double-check the floor, but don't see anything in there, not that I was expecting to. It would be pretty stupid to hide the key for something right next to it. Alexei starts combing the rest of the room, and I try to pry it open with my hands, but something tingles in my memory, like I'm forgetting something. I close my eyes and try to concentrate on it. Moments later, it finally comes to me. When I first found all of my mother's possessions in the closet at Eve's house, there was one thing that I had no idea what it was for but I brought it with me anyway. *A key.*

I grab my trunk out of my pocket, almost dropping it in my excitement before enlarging it. I find my purse within and rummage through it until I find what I'm looking for. Alexei has stopped his search, and his face lights up upon seeing what I'm holding. I insert the ancient-looking key into the box and take a deep breath before I turn it. I have no idea what's in here, but I know it's important. Alexei kneels down next to me and grabs my hand in his, showing me he's here with me, whatever I find. I don't want to appreciate the gesture, but I do all the same.

I open the box, and all I see at first is a stack of papers. I have a brief sense of disappointment because it's a bit anticlimactic. I thought there would be something really out of the ordinary here, but then I see my name written on an envelope in the same handwriting that I found on the notes in the box with her possessions. I drop Alexei's hand and open it as carefully and quickly as I can. My eyes are already brimming with tears, but I blink them back so that I can read.

Ember, my darling daughter,

I know you will find this. Penelope told me she has seen it. I left you what I've found regarding your heritage on my side. Madam Vita keeps a thorough record of all of the women in the Sacred Rite. It took me a while to track down, and she has no idea that I stole the records, but I wanted you to see where you came from.

I also wanted to tell you that I wish I could know you so much. I know how strong you will be, and more than anything I want to be next to you to witness it all. I will do everything within my power to be there with you every step of the way, even if you don't know it.

I love you so much, and know your father does too. I'm sorry that you didn't get a chance to know him when you were younger, but it was for your safety. If Eve didn't get you out, you would've died before you had the opportunity to change the realm. And the realm needs *you, Ember.*

So, give 'em hell, kid. And know that I'm here cheering you on.

All my love,

Your mother, Catalina

Tears are streaming down my face as I trace her handwriting gently with my fingers. I suck in a sharp breath as I'm suddenly plunged into a different time, but the same space.

I see my mother writing the very same letter I just read, her eyes red and swollen from crying, one hand on her giant belly. She puts the letter in the envelope and kisses the outside of it.

In the next breath, I'm forced into another vision.

This one, her belly isn't as large, so I know it must be earlier. There's a woman with her, and I can tell that she's not human. She has a strange look to her, almost frazzled. And even though she's young, she has an older quality to her, her pale-as-snow skin looking wrinkled around her eyes, but her eyes themselves are sharp, like her gaze can cut right through you. Her curly white-blond hair is frizzy and sticks out in every direction, but is held down slightly by a purple headband.

In the next moment, it is clear that she is a witch because she tells my mother a prophecy about me. I wonder if it's the same one that Mordecai heard, but have no idea how he would've heard it here of all places. Especially since it looks like it's just the two of them here.

"The child you bear

Won't be yours to care

For though her blood will be the call

You won't be there to see her fall

She will be an Ember in the dark

She will bring the spark

Through her pain

She will end the fae reign"

The witch does some scrying with my mother, tossing small bones into the air, and while I have no idea what she's doing, I can't wait to learn. She tells my mother that she won't survive the childbirth.

"Will my daughter survive the birth?" Penelope tosses the bones again. All the symbols are face-up.

"Yes."

"Will she be in danger?" Another toss. Face-up.

"Yes." My mother pales, visibly swallowing. "I want to do one more divination." Penelope places the bowl of water in front of Catalina, and gives her the burning candle that's sitting on the table. "Pour the candle wax into the water." She does. When she's finished, the witch leans over the bowl. "It's a hat. A change of location is indicated. Although, I don't know if it's for you or the baby."

"I need to talk to Eve." I draw in a sharp breath. This must've been when my mother asked Eve to take me to Earth.

"I'll get her in a moment. I need to tell you the rest of the prophecy.

When her life is truly at stake

Will then her powers fully awake

For far down below

A darkness has begun to grow

When fire and water meet

There will be only one who can defeat."

I'm reeling from finally hearing the prophecy. And this must've been the one that Mordecai heard because she mentions that my pain will end the fae reign. Before I can think too hard about that, Penelope gets Eve, and my eyes fill with tears upon seeing her. She looked so healthy here, and I wonder if being on Earth and not in a magical realm took a toll on her. I also wonder if it took a toll on me, now that I've learned that I have magic in my blood. Lots of it. I make a mental note to ask about it later.

I watch as the two women embrace, and I'm struck by how pivotal of a moment this is, and how lucky I am to be able to witness it. I can tell just by how they interact with each other that they were close.

"Catalina! Is everything okay? Is something wrong with the baby? Penelope just told me to come right away."

"Everything is okay for right now, but it's not going to be for long. I need you to do me a huge favor."

"You know I would do anything for you. What is it?"

My mother takes a deep breath and closes her eyes. Eve squeezes her hand, nervously waiting for her answer.

"Eve, I'm not going to survive the birth."

My mom gasps, clearly not expecting that answer. "Oh, Catalina."

"It's okay. But my daughter is going to be in danger."

"You're having a girl?" Even in the midst of this awful scenario, both women were so excited to learn what I was.

My mother smiles softly at her. "Yes. Her name is Ember," she says fondly, rubbing her belly. "But, I need you to take her. Take her far from here. Eve, I hate to ask you this, but I need you to bring her to Earth. Bring her to the Mortal Realm where no one will be able to find her."

Eve stares at her for a few moments, her eyes darting between Catalina's face and her stomach before she nods. "Okay. I'll do it."

Catalina exhales loudly in relief, her eyes tearing up. "Make sure she's loved and taken care of, Evelynn. It kills me that I won't be the one to watch her grow up."

"I know. I'll love her as much as I love you. She won't want for anything."

"Thank you."

I'm yanked away again by another vision, and I wonder vaguely if Alexei can tell if anything is wrong. I've never been in a vision for this amount of time before and have no idea how it looks on the outside, but for now I'm just along for the ride.

I immediately know that I'm witnessing my birth. The only people in the room are Catalina, Eve, and Penelope. My mother is on her bed, huffing, puffing, and sweating profusely. It breaks my heart because I'm pretty sure that I'm going to witness my mother's death at the end of this.

"Come on, Catalina. One more push and you'll get to meet your daughter."

Catalina fists the sheets in both hands before pushing and grunting with all her might. I slip free of her body, and let out a soft cry. She collapses back on the bed, completely spent, and Penelope wraps me in a soft blanket before setting me on Catalina's chest. From here I can see that blood is steadily flowing out of her, much more than is normal, and know that these are her last moments. I take comfort in the fact that she was able to hold me at least once, and that I was with her when she took her last breath.

"Ember. Ember Solis. You are the most beautiful creature I've ever seen, and the best thing I have ever done. You are going to bring peace to the realm. I will be with you. Always, my love." Her voice is getting weaker by the second, but she plants a soft kiss on my head.

Eve comes up next to her, kneeling beside her before she puts an arm underneath Catalina's, helping her to support me, knowing she won't be able to for much longer. Catalina meets her eyes.

"Take care of her, Eve. I left a box for you to take on the table."

Eve nods. "I will. I promise."

"Oh, and Eve? I'll be forever grateful to you."

They put their foreheads together, soaking in this last moment of true friendship before Catalina looks back down at me. "I love you, my sweet girl."

I'm ripped away before I see her die, and I'm relieved. This time, I'm not taken into another vision, but am back in the same room, holding the letter from my birth mother. There are tears on my cheeks, and Alexei is crouched in front of me, hands on my shoulders.

"Alexei?"

"Oh, thank the Gods. I was getting really worried."

"I was stuck in visions of the past. What happened?"

"Your eyes went unfocused before turning opaque, like you were looking through a pane of milky glass. I figured you were having a vision, but it went on for a while, and I started to get worried. I called out your name and shook you, but you weren't registering anything I said, but you kept crying."

I squeeze his arm to comfort him. "I'm okay."

"I know. What did you see?"

I relay everything to him, including the prophecy, which I'm surprised I remember with perfect clarity. I start sobbing when I tell him about my mother and seeing her last moments. He wraps me in his arms and sits me in his lap, gently rocking me while I mourn my mother. I shouldn't be letting him comfort me like this, but I can't help it. What I just saw shook my world, and I need to fall apart for a minute. And as much as I don't want to admit it, I need support.

After a few minutes, my tears dry up. I take a deep breath, slowly pulling myself together and away from Alexei.

"Okay?" he asks.

I nod, getting off of his lap. "Yes. Thank you. I wasn't prepared to see that. I'm glad I did though. It was a wonderful gift."

He nods, giving me a tight smile. His expression shutters, and I can tell he's feeling something after our little interaction, but I can't tell what. I'm tempted to read his emotions, but it wouldn't be right. He clearly doesn't want me to use my abilities on him. "Have you looked at what else was in the box yet?"

"No, but in the letter she said it was a record of my lineage that she stole from Madam Vita," I whisper, just in case anyone is listening in. It's a definite possibility considering that the prophecy was overheard in this very room and somehow got to Mordecai.

"Hey, before I forget, I had a thought when I was in the visions and I want to ask you about it."

His brows furrow in confusion, but he gestures for me to continue.

"If we possess magic but are on Earth for an extended period of time, does it affect us? My adoptive mother looked so much healthier when she was here than she ever did on Earth, even considering she was living in much worse conditions."

"I don't think there's a way for us to know. There have been no people who have gone to Earth like you and your mother did, but it would make sense."

His eyes travel over me, assessing. It's different from the way he normally looks at me, and I can tell he's thought of something.

"What are you thinking?"

"Your strip of white hair. Did you always have it?"

I shake my head. "It started out barely noticeable when I went through puberty. As I got older it became more pronounced."

He nods as if that doesn't surprise him. "Has it progressed at all since you came here?"

I'm taken aback. I haven't thought about it before now. "No." I look into the small mirror in the room. "It hasn't at all actually. In fact, it might've even lessened."

"As I thought. I think it did take a toll on you. Your magic was suppressed, and this is one of the ways that it manifested." He reaches out and strokes my strip of white.

I'm reeling slightly. I don't know why. It's not that big of a revelation, but the fact that my time on Earth visibly changed my appearance is shocking.

I don't have time to delve into all of that. And realistically, it doesn't change anything, or really even make a difference in my life. I move past it for now.

I sit back at the table and set aside the letter and instead look at the small stack of papers that was also in the box. Records. Thorough records that were kept by Madam Vita. Obviously I know that my first two direct lineages are human and fae, and are not included in the box. The one on the top of the stack looks like it's from one to two generations before my mother, and is a mermaid. Her name is Calliope, and I make note because she has to be the descendant from Surseiha, whether she knew it or not. I'm guessing not since she was never able to take another form. I also realize that besides fae and human, mermaid is my closest ancestor that's another species. It would explain why I had an easier time with those abilities.

I set that paper aside. The record directly beneath it is my connection to my elf ancestor. It looks like my mother only included the records where the species had changed. Witch is underneath that one, followed by vampire and finally mimic. The witch name catches my eye. Morgana Faellia. Why does that last name sound familiar? I tuck the name away in my brain for now.

If I'm going with the theory about my mermaid abilities, then it would make sense here too. I haven't been able to shift into my owl form since that first night, and it's always felt so far away for me. I finger the feather and beads in my hair, trying to find the pull toward these other women who made such an impact on who I am today. Did they have any idea what they were giving me? These human women were used for their ability to pass along powers to future children, but there's no way they could've known that all of their powers would manifest in *me.*

When I run my thumb over the feather again, I have a revelation that I never thought of before. The mimics are my furthest ancestor, and this hairpiece was passed down from generation to generation. Is it possible that this feather actually belonged to my ancestor in their shifted form? It would make sense that I would have the same form as they did. Alexei did say that it was common for the same animal to be passed down through the family.

It's then that I remember where I know that last name from. The journal. The teenage witch who lived in the caves. *Zenobia Faellia. Fuck.* Am I related to her? Is that why I had that vision and was able to communicate with her? I guess I'll never know for sure, but it seems possible at this point.

None of this information looping through my head is ground-breaking, but it makes a world of difference. I know more about my ancestry and where I came from now than I ever have before.

"Thank you, Mother," I whisper, running my hands over this precious gift. I swear her hand brushes my shoulder for a brief moment.

Alexei just sits patiently beside me, a support if I need or want. I finally turn to him, something else popping into my head that I need to address.

"There's one person I might be able to talk to about my mothers who knows even more than I was able to see in my visions."

His brows scrunch up in confusion. "Who?"

"The witch, Penelope. Do you think she's still here?"

Realization dawns on his face. "She might be. If she was sold to the madam then she would be obligated to be here for the remainder of her life."

"Let's go find out." I gently put the contents of the box in my trunk before shrinking it again and putting it in my pocket. I return everything to how it was when we entered the room and walk out.

Alexei and I make our way back to the front entrance. Madam Vita is waiting for us at the desk.

"Did you find what you were looking for?" she asks. I can tell she really wants to know *what* we found but is smart enough not to ask me outright.

I ignore her question completely. "Do you have a witch here named Penelope?"

Her eyes widen in surprise. "Y-yes. Do you have need of her?"

"I do."

I deliberately don't elaborate. It's none of her business, and I have a feeling that Vita knows more than she is letting on, and has some sort of agenda of her own.

"Antonia, go and fetch Penelope for the princess," she orders.

"Actually, would you mind escorting me to her rooms?"

Instead of answering me, Antonia looks to her mistress. Vita nods to her, albeit begrudgingly. I smile at them both before following Antonia up the hall. It's the hall next to my mother's.

"It's this one," Antonia says, gesturing to the door to our right.

"Thank you, Antonia, that will be all," I dismiss her. She looks uncomfortable, like she knows Vita would want her to stay, but doesn't want to go against my orders. Finally she nods before heading back the way she came. Smart girl.

"Alexei, can you wait out here? I already know this is going to be an important conversation, and I don't want to be overheard."

His mouth tightens, and I know he's not pleased, but he nods once.

I take a deep breath before holding my hand up to knock. The door opens before I get the opportunity. Penelope stands there, looking slightly older and more worn than she did in my visions, but she's smiling softly at me.

"Ember. I've been waiting for you." She opens her arms, and without a second thought, I walk into her embrace.

She's the closest thing to answers and my mother that I've come across in a long time, and the fact that we've both had visions of one another also makes me feel like we already know each other on some level.

She gives me a mother's hug, and I swallow hard, trying with all my might not to break down again.

"Would you like to come in?"

I nod, following her in. Alexei, as promised, stays in the hall. His reluctance bleeds toward me, but I ignore it. Maybe I shouldn't, but I trust Penelope.

"Please, sit. I had some fresh tea brought up. Would you like some?"

I nod, smiling gratefully at her. She pours us each a cup, mixing mine just how I like it, and I wonder how much she's seen.

"You found the box?"

"I did. I also saw visions of the past. I heard the prophecy and saw my mother giving birth to me."

She squeezes my hand sympathetically. "She loved you so much."

"I know," I say, squeezing back. "Do you know what's going to happen? Or what darkness is growing?"

She shakes her head sadly. "No. All I know is that you have the opportunity to bring peace to the realm. I don't know what the darkness is, but I know that you are the only one with the ability to stop it. But be careful, because it also has the ability to be your downfall as well."

Well, that's all super vague, and is no help. I don't tell her that though. "Do you know anything about Madam Vita?"

A twinkle lights her eyes. "Ah. There I can be a bit more helpful. You're wondering if she is the reason the prophecy got out. She is."

"Do you know who she told?"

"I never met him, but I know his name is Mordecai."

I suck in a sharp breath. Vita must be the one who Mordecai was in league with who he couldn't speak of because of the magical pact they made with one another.

"What's her motive?"

"That I don't know. I've never let on to her that I know anything. If I did, I would no longer be of service to her."

"I could make her tell me. She can't refuse an order from her princess."

"You're absolutely right. She would know I mentioned it to you."

"Well, that's an easy fix. I will release you."

Her eyes widen. "You'll *what*?"

"You heard me correctly. I'll release you. Whatever you want to do from here on out is fine. You can go back to Wickshire if you'd like to be among the witches, or you would be more than welcome to come to the palace. You could be my own personal seer if that is what you wish."

Tears gather in her eyes. "I don't have to stay here anymore?"

I smile softly at her. "No, Penelope, you don't. I'm so sorry you were never given the choice."

"I don't regret my time here. It was how I met your mother. Well, both of your mothers. They were like sisters to me. But since they've been gone, I've been so lonely. Knowing that you would come here and I would get to see you has kept me going for all of these long years." Tears spill over as she squeezes my hand. "If it's acceptable, I would very much like to go to the palace with you."

I exhale in relief. I was hoping she would choose that option. "I would love that. I really wanted you to, but I didn't want to take another decision from you, and I thought you might want to be with your own kind after all this time."

Her lip curls in distaste. "My own kind sold me into this life long ago, and I've been away from them for so long that I wouldn't feel welcome in Wickshire. It would be a different life and I'm sure I would be judged by them."

"Well, you never know. I'm going to be going there at some point in the future. If you would like to come with me, I'm sure that could be arranged."

"I'll think about it."

"Well, for right now, would you like to start packing? We shouldn't be here too much longer. Would you be comfortable traveling alone? We're going to be teletraveling to the Everchanging Glades after this, otherwise I would have you accompany us."

"I can travel alone. I learned to defend myself long ago."

I nod in understanding. I can only imagine the horrors she's seen while living here. "Well, in that case, why don't you start collecting your stuff, and I'll go talk to Vita."

"Thank you." We both stand and she wraps me in her arms, squeezing tight.

"You don't need to thank me. I'm honored that you're with me. We're going to have fun, aren't we?"

She laughs, the sound rough, making me wonder when the last time she laughed was. The thought makes me sad, but I don't let any of that intrude on this special moment with her. "Yes, we will."

I release her, and she immediately starts gathering her things. "I'll be back up in a bit to tell you how it went."

She nods, and I head back out into the hall. Alexei is right where I left him.

"So, Penelope is heading back to the castle?" he asks.

"Yes. And it's time I have a sit-down with Vita."

"I like this scary side of you," he whispers to me. "It's hot. Anytime you want to boss me around, feel free."

I flush and just keep walking, and he chuckles behind me. I do keep in mind what he just said though. Maybe I'll take the opportunity to boss him around in a way I know he won't like.

Vita is waiting right where I left her when we get back downstairs. She forces a smile to her lips, even though I can tell she doesn't really want to be polite to me. I'm guessing she'll be even more upset in a minute.

"Do you need anything else, Your Highness?" I know she's hoping I'll say no and leave her in peace. Sucks for her.

"I actually need to chat with you for a moment."

I take the opportunity now that I'm back in her vicinity to burst through her mental barriers. Well, maybe *burst* isn't the best word, seeing as she has no idea that I've gotten through them. More like

I've ninja'd my way in. She's nervous and reluctant, but she nods and smiles.

"Of course. We can talk in my office." She leads the way, and I follow behind her.

I take in the space when I enter, and I notice that she's made it feel as much like Mermacovia as possible. Mermaid paraphernalia is everywhere, and I almost have pity for her here in this dry desert climate with basically no water. That has to be horrible for a mermaid.

"What can I help you with?"

We take seats at her desk, and I realize that this is her power space. Her chair is intentionally much more elevated than mine, and I sit up as straight as I can, not letting her make me feel inferior. Alexei stands behind my chair in support of me, with more than a little bit of intimidation directed her way, I'm guessing.

Before I start talking, I push honesty and openness toward her and let out just a bit of my allure, not enough for her to notice, but hopefully enough for her to cooperate with me.

"Why did you tell Mordecai the prophecy about me?" Not wanting to beat around the bush, I go for bluntness.

"What?" She looks somewhat stricken, and I calm her down with my powers. She'll never tell me anything if she's distressed.

"It's a perfectly simple question."

"Well...I...how do you know that?"

"That doesn't matter. What does matter is why you did it. I need to know everything you can tell me about Mordecai. It would be a great service to your princess. I won't punish you, if you're worried about that."

She audibly swallows before taking a deep breath. "I had to. I didn't have a choice."

"If he didn't know about it before you told him, then why would you be forced to tell him?"

She sighs dejectedly. "I had a magical pact with him. It made it impossible for me to keep secrets like that from him."

"Why did you enter into a pact with him?"

"It's complicated."

I don't reply, I simply wait for her to answer me. She fidgets uncomfortably before finally speaking again.

"Long ago, I was banished from Mermacovia. I was forced to live here where there is no water, except on the southern border of the territory. A miserable existence for my kind. I came here and took over this establishment because I knew it would be something I would thrive at. I've come to be quite powerful here, as powerful as one can be in the Mortal Sanctum. I'm respected in my position, feared. When your father showed up, he brought Mordecai with him."

Disdain seeps through our connection, and I know that whatever deal she had with him, she did not like him.

"While the king was very respectful and gracious, not only with me, but with the girls, Mordecai was exactly the opposite. He pushed all my rules to the limits, even breaking one or two, but I couldn't do much since he was with the crowned prince at the time. Of course, he never did anything in front of your father, but he was blatantly disrespectful to me, even slapping me across the face once when I denied him something."

My eyes widen. Mordecai was an asshole to me, but hearing how he was with others is a shock. I thought it was only because he hated me since I was the king's daughter.

"I retaliated against him in the only way I could. I sent a girl up to his room. He, of course, did exactly what I wanted; slept with her and sent her on her way. He thought she was from the Abandoned Bliss, but she was actually from the Sacred Rite, a vampire conduit, to be specific."

Alexei sucks in a sharp breath behind me. This is clearly the story of how he was conceived that he never properly heard.

"Why did you do that?" I ask.

"It's forbidden for the fae to procreate with another species. I knew that if he had a half-breed child that he would be punished and removed from his position. Unfortunately, that plan backfired on me.

"When he found out that she became pregnant, and that she was actually a vampire conduit, he threatened me and the girl. He told me that if I didn't enter into a magical contract with him that he would kill the girl and tell your father what I did."

"Is that all? You don't seem like the type of woman to agree to something that you don't gain anything from," I nudge.

"Well," she says uncomfortably. "I did tell him he needed to offer me something in return. He promised me that when he was in a position of power that he would make me the Grand Mistress of Mermacovia."

"How would he offer you that?"

"He told me his plan to become king and how I could help. He needed me to supply him with the contraception preventative that I use with the women in the Abandoned Bliss. He snuck it into the late queen's food and beverages after she married Stavros so that they were never able to conceive."

"Why didn't he prevent anything in regards to my mother?"

"I'm guessing he didn't realize that Stavros would jeopardize his own future by sleeping with her. I think he was also under the impression that since she was under my employ then she was already on the preventative. I didn't know your mother was pregnant until I heard the prophecy. The pact forced me to tell Mordecai what Penelope said, but he was going to wait to do something about it until after the birth since we knew your mother was going to die. Penelope came to me after and told me that Catalina didn't survive and that you died in her belly with her. I told him that as well, and we didn't think anything of it after that."

I was curious how my mothers and Penelope pulled that off if they knew about me and the prophecy, but that made sense.

"And he made you enter a magical pact with him? Why did you agree?"

"Because I also wanted to make sure that he would keep his word to me. A lot of good it did. He died before he could fulfill his end of the bargain," she sneers.

"You know he's dead?"

"I felt the pact sever as soon as he died. That would've been the only way to break it."

I nod, appearing unfazed by everything, but inside I'm reeling. I'm sure Alexei is having the same reaction behind me and can only imagine how he's feeling about all of this. I open my senses to him for a moment and can almost taste his disgust and disbelief, but they are being completely overpowered by his overwhelming *anger*.

"Okay, so here's what's going to happen. I am taking Penelope with me."

"What? *No.* I bought her. She is *mine.*"

"Excuse me?" I stand, reminding her exactly who I am. I wish I was wearing my crown to push the point home further, but I don't need it.

She blanches, her face going pale.

"I mean, with all due respect, Your Highness, wouldn't you want your own seer to be more qualified? Penelope is nothing special."

My brows rise. "Oh really? Then why are you so upset at the thought of me taking her from you?"

"Because I've known her so long she knows what to look for in my future."

"Nice try. You have no say in the matter. She will be leaving today, and Alexei is going to teletravel to the king and tell him everything you just told us."

If possible, she goes even paler, and her overwhelming panic swamps me. "But you said you wouldn't punish me."

"I said *I* never would. The king can do whatever he pleases with you. For now, stay here. And I will be here until Alexei returns, so don't attempt to leave. That *will* earn my punishment. And you don't want that."

We walk out of her office and I turn to Alexei. "I need you to head back to my father immediately and let him know exactly what happened. Tell him about Penelope as well."

"I'm not leaving you here with her."

"You said you wanted me to boss you around. Now be my good little vampire bitch and do as I say," I tease, patting his cheek patronizingly.

He growls softly at me, and I can tell he wants to put me in my place. I can also sense his arousal coating the air between us. "Fine. But make sure Penelope is with you and have your daggers on you at all times. Do you understand me?"

"I thought I was the one giving orders."

"If you want me to leave then you need to agree to those conditions."

"Fine. Now go."

He's gone before I blink. Penelope takes that moment to show up.

"Wow. He's an intense one, isn't he?" she asks.

I chuckle. "He sure is. I take it you heard the conditions?"

"I did. Before he even said them. I will gladly sit with you until he returns."

We sit on the cushions in the foyer, Penelope having assured me that nothing sexual happens on them. Antonia brings us more beverages, and I tell her to keep her eyes on Vita's office door. We're watching it too, but you can never have too many eyes on a prisoner. I also keep my senses open to Vita. She's panicking, but angry too, and I wonder if she's going to do something. Sure enough, minutes later, her door flies open.

Her skin is glowing, and I know she's going to try to lure me in to do her bidding. Unluckily for her, she's just going to succeed in pissing me off.

"*Let me go*," she commands. Her allure is at full blast right now, and while she's decently powerful, she's no match for me.

I smile viciously at her. She just tried to use her allure on the king's daughter to go against her direct orders. Big mistake.

"I said, *let me go*," she orders again.

This time I laugh like a crazy woman, and her brows shoot halfway up her head.

"Nice try, bitch." I release my own allure. I don't even have to break through her mental shields since I already did that upon entering her office. I turn it up to full blast, as it's more difficult to use allure on other mermaids. "Get on your knees," I order her. She immediately obeys. "Now bow to me and beg me for forgiveness for disobeying my orders."

She folds her torso over her legs. "I'm sorry, Your Highness."

"You're not forgiven," I respond coldly. I feel nothing but hatred toward this woman. I hope my father punishes her accordingly. "Now, get out of my sight and stay in your office until I come to get you, or I will not be as gracious a second time."

She stands and does what I told her to. When the door is closed, Penelope whistles.

"That was impressive. I knew you were strong, but that didn't look like it took you any effort."

"It didn't. She's somewhat powerful, but not a match for me." I know I sound cocky right now, but it's the truth.

She smirks knowingly at me. The two of us chat for a while, mostly about the palace, her new role with me, and the time she spent with my mothers.

Two hours later, Alexei shows up with another man in tow. He must be a vampire because Alexei wouldn't have been able to bring him otherwise. I also know he must've had to take a break to let his magic refill since it took so long for him to come back.

"Devon here is going to take Vita to the king, and escort Penelope to the palace," Alexei tells me.

"Perfect. Does he have strong mental shields? Because Vita tried to use allure on me to escape."

"I'm not surprised in the least. Yes, he does."

"I would like to test it before we leave her with him. No offense, Devon."

"None taken, Your Highness," he says, bowing.

I stand up and head to her office, beckoning Devon with me. Vita is pacing the length of the room when I enter.

"You should have her try it on me too, just in case," Penelope chimes in.

I nod, gesturing her into the room as well. I bring my allure to the surface again. "Use your allure on them," I order her.

She complies instantly. "*Let me go*," she says, attempting the same command on them.

He scoffs. "I don't think so. Time to go," he tells her, pulling her out of the office. I smile at him, glad he can handle himself.

"I'm good too," Penelope says, and I'm relieved to hear it.

"Penelope, are you ready to leave? You have everything packed?"

"I do."

"I'll show you how to shrink and enlarge your trunk so that you don't have to lug it with you."

I go to her room and demonstrate the best little trick, making sure she can do it before giving her a big hug.

"Thank you so much for the information you gave me. I can't wait to work with you," I tell her genuinely.

"Thank *you*. I have been waiting for this day since your mother passed. It will be my honor to serve you, Your Highness."

"Please, call me Ember. And I'm sorry you have to travel to the palace with that bitch. But I am relieved you'll have an escort. I know how dangerous this realm can be."

"That it can. I look forward to your return to the palace. In the meantime, travel safely, Ember."

"You too, Penelope."

We see them off, and I turn to Alexei. "Are you ready?"

"No. Your good little vampire bitch needs to rest."

I bust out laughing at the unexpected statement, and chuckle even harder at the displeased look on his face.

"Hey, you said you wanted me to boss you around," I point out.

"That wasn't exactly what I had in mind," Alexei replies.

"Then maybe you should've been more specific. How long do you need to rest for?"

"At least a couple hours. I could use some food too."

"Antonia, we are going to take over Vita's room for the time being. Can you show me where it is and have some food brought up?"

"Of c-course, Your Highness." She seems extra jumpy after what happened to her madam.

"Also, is there anyone else here who has any power besides Vita? A human?"

"No, Your Highness. Madam Vita did not trust anyone else."

"Well, how long have you been here?"

"Me, Your Highness?"

"Yes. Is there someone here that you think would be capable of taking over?" I hate having this facility open still, but I'm not sure how to go about it. At the moment finding a decent replacement seems appropriate. "Also, do the women here get paid?"

"Not much, Your Highness. It's mostly room and board. As for someone to run it, I would suggest Greta. She's been here a long time, and is very well respected."

"Very well. Thank you, Antonia. Will you send her to Vita's office after you show us Vita's room?"

"Of course. Right this way."

Next to Vita's office is her room. It's fairly large, and like I would expect has a ginormous tub. The bed is also huge, but I don't know how promiscuous she was. I have no desire to be on that bedding.

"Antonia, could you also please have someone bring a fresh set of sheets?"

"Right away," she says, bowing as she leaves.

"Thank you, Antonia."

She looks astonished, and it makes me sad that these women aren't even thanked.

"Of course, Your Highness."

She closes the door and I blow out a breath, facing Alexei as I try to sort through all the emotions coursing through me. This was not at all how I anticipated this visit going.

Alexei looks at me sympathetically. "This has been a lot to deal with."

"Yes it has. For you too. I'm sorry you had to find out about your conception that way. And about all the things with your father."

"Thank you. It was pretty shocking. I wonder what happened to my mother."

My brows rise. I didn't even think of that. How stupid of me. I should've asked Vita. "Oh, Alexei, I'm sorry. I could've made her tell me."

"It's okay. I'm not even sure I want to know. At least not right now."

"I understand that."

A knock sounds at the door. I open it to find Antonia holding fresh sheets. "I brought these for you. Do you need me to change the bedding for you?"

"That won't be necessary, Antonia. We can manage."

"If you're sure, Your Highness. Also, I sent an order in to the kitchen for you both, and Greta is waiting in the office for you."

"Thank you so much, Antonia," I tell her, taking the sheets from her. She looks just as surprised as when I told her the first time.

I hand the sheets off to Alexei and tell him I'm going to go speak with Greta. He nods and starts stripping the bed.

I enter Vita's office, and find a woman who looks to be in her forties sitting where I was not long ago. I go around to the other side of the desk, taking Vita's usual spot. Greta stands and bows to me, her long honey-blond hair falling around her face as she does so.

"Your Highness. Antonia said you wanted to speak with me?"

"I did. Please sit, Greta. I don't know if she filled you in, but Madam Vita will not be coming back. Antonia told me she thought you would be a good replacement."

Her eyes widen. "Me?"

"Yes. She would know better than I who would be best for the position, and she recommended you. I want you to know that things will be run differently from here on out, and I will be checking in on this establishment often to make sure that things are running smoothly."

"Of course, Your Highness. What kind of changes?" She grabs parchment and a quill from the desk, getting ready to take notes. I like her already.

"First off, there will be a price increase for the Abandoned Bliss. It is far too low as of right now. And speaking of price, most of the money this establishment makes will go directly to the women working here. I've been made aware that they hardly make any of it, and that is unacceptable. Those who do not wish to work here will not be required to, even if they are a conduit. You will make a decent amount of money, but besides that and the cost to run the establishment, I would like the rest to go directly to the girls." She nods as she quickly jots everything down. "Now, did Vita have a healer here?"

"Yes, Your Highness. She has an elf employed here. She delivers the babies and makes sure the mothers are healthy. The madam wanted to protect her investments. Mainly the conduits," she says with disdain.

I wrinkle my nose in disgust. I mean, I'm glad they were protected, but of course that was her only motivation. "What about any type of security? Someone to deal with individuals who get out of hand?"

"She never had anyone like that. She normally just handled them herself since she could use her allure on them. But she usually only ever cared about the conduits. She didn't really give a shit about those of us at the Abandoned Bliss."

I resist the urge to growl. Horrid woman. "Okay. I will have Alexei send a vampire down here for security purposes in the next few days. Come up with a list of all actions and behaviors that are unacceptable. Make sure to pass it around to all the women who would like to stay, and they can add whatever they would like to the list. When it's completed you can give it to the bouncer, and he will make sure to take action against those who don't abide by those guidelines."

She nods, and when she's finished writing, she looks up at me, tears gathering in her eyes. "Thank you, Your Highness."

I reach over and squeeze her hand. "Greta, there's no need to thank me. These are things that should've been done from the very beginning. Rights that you were all denied, and I'm going to do everything in my power to make things better for all of you. It might take some time, but just know that I *am* working on it. This is just the start. I thought about closing the establishment, but I'm assuming that would end with the girls continuing to sell themselves in an unsafe environment. At least this way I can assure that you are all safe and well compensated."

The tears in her eyes spill over and roll down her cheeks.

"Now, is there anything else we need to discuss before I leave?" I ask her.

"I can't think of anything, Your Highness."

"Very well. Alexei and I are going to be staying for a few more hours in Vita's old room, but as soon as we're gone, please take the space and make it your own. This office too. They both belong to you now."

She looks around, taking in the space with new eyes. I wonder what she'll do with it.

I take my leave of her, heading back into Vita's old room. Alexei has the bedding changed and is lounging back waiting for me. No sign of food yet, but it will probably arrive any minute.

"How did it go?" he asks.

"Really well. We went over everything, and I think she's going to do great in her new position. I also talked to her about getting a security man in here within the next few days. I was hoping we could get a vampire?"

"Of course. I can send word to Twin Fangs and have someone teletravel down here."

I nod as there's a knock on the door. Antonia brings in a tray of food and some wine. I grab it from her, thanking her again before closing the door. I set it on the bed and we dig in, both starving from the events of the morning. When we're finished, we collapse back onto the bed and pass out for a few hours.

16

Ember

Hours later, we finally have the energy to make the trip to the Everchanging Glades. Everyone at the establishment gives us a kind farewell, and I promise I'll check in on them soon. I tell Greta to write to me if there's anything she needs, and she gives me a warm hug, thanking me again.

"Ready?" Alexei asks, holding his hand out for me.

I nod, grasping his hand. "And you've been there before? We won't get lost?" I remember him telling me about how most people other than mimics don't typically go into the Everchanging Glades because of how much the land changes.

"First off, yes, I've been to their capital before. Second, it doesn't matter if we get lost. We can just teletravel back out if we need to."

As soon as he says it, it's so obvious, but it's something I had been anxious about.

"Okay. Let's do it."

The familiar tingle of us leaving sweeps through me, along with the sensation of being pulled with him. We teletravel to a sprawling city. The capitol building is in the center, with water on all sides, and a gorgeous wooden bridge at the entrance. The building itself is stone and domed, like I was expecting, but it looks much more ancient. There are holes in parts of the structure where nature has carved its way through. There are multiple trees coming out of the top of the dome, and it gives the building a green tint and bathes it in shadow.

When I look out over the city itself, the best word I can think of to describe it is *wild*. Most of the structures seem like they're made from the earth, or that they're part of it. I'm sure there are a ton that I'm not even seeing because they're camouflaged with the land.

Then I see the Mutable Meadows. It's currently in a valley below the city, and it's picturesque. The sun is coming up over the land, and there are so many flowers I want to cry. A gentle breeze rolls through, bringing with it the smell of lavender. Birds fly overhead, deer run through the meadow, and fish splash in the river running through it. I wonder how many are actual animals, and how many are mimics in their shifted form.

Alexei gives me a moment to take it all in. I'm excited to see what the landscape looks like when it changes, and I imagine it has to be fun for the inhabitants to never know what their land is going to look like.

Finally having looked my fill for now, I turn toward the capitol. I take a deep breath, lift my head high, and start forward. It's always intimidating meeting one of the grand masters. I just hope this one is more helpful and friendly than Coralia. I guess I was technically introduced to all of the grand masters and mistresses at the ball, but I met so many people that night that I feel like it's the first time. Not to mention the fact that the events that followed basically overshadowed anything else that happened the entire night.

We head inside, Alexei a step behind and next to me, like a shadow. We enter the building, and I'm surprised to find there aren't many people here. Alexei knows where we're headed, and gives me directions as we go. The structure is even more wild inside. There's natural light coming in from the holes in the building where nature has grown through, blurring the lines between indoor and outdoor space. It's a strange juxtaposition that I've never experienced before. We finally arrive at what Alexei tells me is the grand master's chamber. He's housed in this building, and while his private rooms are in the same area, this is where he conducts business with others on a more personal level.

I lift my hand and knock. Nerves flutter in my belly, but I don't let it show. Just when I think there's no one here, the door opens. A man who looks to be in his fifties, but I know has to be much older, is standing on the other side. He has darker skin, almost Middle Eastern. His shaggy jet-black hair is wavy and peppered with specks of gray, which also matches his beard.

"Can I help you?" His dark brown, almost black eyes narrow on us.

"Are you Joseph?" I ask. Alexei told me about him before we arrived.

"Yes. Who are you?"

"My name is Ember Solis. I'm the king's daughter."

"Ahh yes, Your Highness. I recognize you now," he says reverently, bowing to me. "How can I be of service?"

I like him immediately. He's very respectful and seems kind. "I'm sorry not to have notified you that we were coming sooner, but we weren't sure of our timeline. I recently discovered that I have mimic powers, and I was hoping you would be willing to train me."

I can sense his surprise. "You have mimic powers? How is this possible?"

"It's a bit of a long story, but my powers awakened recently. Apparently, I have the blood of every species in this realm, and I have no idea how to handle all of them. I'm going around to the best in Queridian and hoping you will all assist me."

He smiles fully at me. "Well, that is a wonderful gift you've been given! I would be honored to help you, Your Highness. Please, come in."

Alexei and I step into his space. It's tidier than the rest of the building from what I can see, and it makes sense since this is where he meets with people.

He gestures to the seats by the window. "Take a seat. I'll have tea brought up."

He leaves for a moment, and Alexei and I are left alone looking out over the territory. "Well, he seems great," I tell him.

"He is, as far as I know. I've interacted with him a few times, and he's always been very polite."

He returns moments later with a tray of tea for us. I sigh contentedly. I love tea. It always comforts me. When we're all settled and have had sips of our drinks, Joseph addresses me.

"So, tell me about what exactly you need help with."

"Well, when my powers awakened, I was able to shift into my owl form, but I haven't been able to since that night. I've also never tried taking on someone's form before. I did find out yesterday that as far as my powers are concerned, my furthest ancestor is mimic, so I'm thinking that's why I've been struggling with it."

"That would make sense. You said you have all the powers?"

"I do."

"So, you have mermaid blood as well?"

I think I know where he's going with this. "Yes."

"Are you able to shift into your mermaid form?

"I am. That was actually a surprise, and something that I haven't struggled with since it happened. I've tried applying the same method with my owl form, but I can't seem to reach her."

He nods, thinking to himself. "Okay, well, I have some things to finish today, but we can start training tomorrow. You are both welcome to stay in the guest rooms here, and as for today, feel free to explore."

"We really appreciate that, Grand Master. I look forward to working with you."

"Please, call me Joseph."

"Only if you call me Ember."

He smiles at me, a twinkle in his eye, and I can tell we're going to have fun working together. "Deal, Ember. Now, let me show you to your rooms."

He leads us to a section of the building that's not too far from his. There are two guest bedrooms right next to each other, and he asks us to join him for dinner in a few hours before leaving us to it.

We each head to our respective rooms to settle in and clean up. The wildness of the territory is seeping into the dwellings, giving it a natural vibe. The bed is massive and takes up the center of the room with its large wooden and rustic frame. There are furs draped on the bed and flooring, protecting against the cold that I'm sure seeps into the stone building. I go into the bathroom and find that instead of an actual tub, one has been carved into the stone structure, and it reminds me of the cave pools. I feel a little gross after the events of the morning and spending so much time in the brothel that I want to wash off. I get my trunk out of my pocket and enlarge it. I take my robe out and set it on the bed before stripping. The tub fills quickly, and I groan as the hot water releases all of my tension.

I don't take as long as I normally would, only because I would like to explore a little bit of the territory before dinner. It's colder here than the last two territories we visited, so I dress accordingly and wear lots of layers. When I'm finished getting ready, I knock on Alexei's door.

He soon answers, not wearing a shirt. It's been some time since I've seen him in this state, and my traitorous eyes latch on to his chest and abdomen. Heat builds between my thighs quickly, and I struggle to meet his eyes.

"Want to go explore before dinner?" I ask, deflecting.

I can hear amusement in his voice. "Sure. Let me just find a shirt."

I wait in the hall, and by the time he's ready, I have composed myself. We wander back outside, and I'm not positive, but it appears as if the valley isn't quite as deep as it was when we arrived. We start walking, and I'm able to see the homes more clearly. They're built into the side of a hill, not like a hobbit hole, but like an elongated extension. Wood comes down on the outsides, but grass and leaves cover the top of the structures.

I also see some homes built high up into the trees, like nests. The only way to access them is to fly there, or climb the trees, I would suppose. I'm amazed at how spacious they are, and wonder if it supports them in their animal forms and their "human" forms.

We see quite a few people as we're walking, and all of them look very different. Their facial features and skin colors are all over the spectrum, and I wonder if that has anything to do with the fact that they can change appearance, or because they all are tied to different animals.

We head down into the valley, which now I'm positive isn't as deep as it was earlier, and I delight in the smell of all the lavender. It calms me instantly, and as the sun starts to set, I take a seat right there in the midst of it all and enjoy the moment.

Alexei joins me, and a moment later, his hand is covering mine. I know I should pull away, but I enjoy the comforting sensation. I've been having this problem far too often lately. We sit there in comfortable silence until the sun is fully down, and then finally make our way back to the capitol.

By the time we return, dinner is almost ready. We sit at the table and chat with Joseph while the wine is poured. The food is brought out minutes later, and I wonder what this territory will have in store for us in terms of cuisine. Meat. Lots of meat. They also bring out some nuts, berries, and cheese, but their specialty is varieties of meat. Thankfully I'm not a vegetarian.

"So, Joseph, do you mind me asking what your shifted form is?" I ask. I've been so curious, and unsure whether it's rude or not to ask.

"Not at all. It's a wolf."

I could see that from his personality. He's got that lovable way about him, but also a rough edge that I wouldn't want to fuck with. "Do you have a pack?"

"I pretty much view the territory as my pack. I protect them, keep them in line, and can count on them for help when I need it."

"That's a wonderful way to look at it," I tell him. From watching the inhabitants and hearing his comments, I can already tell how tight-knit this territory is with each other, and I love that. "I'm sure they love having you as their fearless leader."

He squirms, seeming uncomfortable with the admiration, and it's adorable. "Well, I don't know about that, but thank you for the compliment, Ember."

Soon after, we turn in for the night, and I'm looking forward to getting a solid night of rest. Today was so hectic with all the traveling, and the revelations in Sapien City, that hopefully I'll sleep like a rock.

I'm grateful to discover that there's a roaring fire going in my quarters when I enter, and I can't help but think how cozy this room is. I change and snuggle into the covers, delighting in the warmth that seeps into my exhausted body. I'm out within minutes.

Nerves flutter in my stomach the next day. I always get nervous when training for something new, but today seems worse, and I think it's because I haven't been able to shift into my owl since my powers awakened. I already know I'm going to struggle with this power, and I hate not being good at something, especially in front of people I don't know. Or anyone for that matter.

I get ready, attempting to distract my brain and just get going. I dress in my normal training clothes, not needing anything fancy here, for which I'm extremely grateful. I had enough extravagant clothing and posturing in Mermacovia to last me a lifetime.

I meet Joseph in his rooms, figuring this area is big enough for us to practice in, but he looks thoroughly put out by that notion.

"Mimics shift best outside, surrounded by nature. It's where we can truly become one with our animal natures."

We make our way outside, and I'm stunned to see that the valley from the previous day is now a massive hill. I knew the land changed, but seeing it in person is another thing entirely. We walk up the hill until we're at the very top. The land sprawls out beneath us, and I breathe in the wild magic of this city.

Joseph doesn't waste any time diving into training. "The shift comes from deep inside you. I think of it as a string I can follow. Once I reach the end, I pull on it, and the shift comes about."

It sounds similar to how I shift into my mermaid form. I think a big difference is that being in the water also helps to pull her closer to the surface. Either way, I close my eyes and try to find where my owl is located. I feel the string that's connected to my mermaid, but I can't find the string connected to my owl. I search and search, but she's just so distant.

Joseph is patient, letting me try to figure it out on my own. After minutes or maybe hours of me looking inside myself for that elusive owl, to no avail, I open my eyes, dejected.

"It's okay, Ember. Sometimes our animals are shy. They're part of us, but they're also their own beings. It might take a while to acquaint yourself with her, just like it would with a wild animal."

"Can I see you shift? Maybe that will help me see what I need to do."

One minute I'm looking at a man, and the next, a wolf the size of a lion. He's jet black with little bits of gray, just like how his human hair looks. I hold up a hand and reach out tentatively, having the urge to pet him. I hold my hand out though, giving him the opportunity to accept or deny it. He eyes my hand with amusement, but indulges me, pressing his head into my hand. I marvel at his fur, wiry, but soft at the same time.

Another moment passes, and he backs up, shifting back into a man. I'm grateful that his clothes are still intact, and that he didn't need to be naked in front of me.

"Your form is massive. Are all the wolves that big?"

"The more powerful the wolf is, the larger they will be. It's not true for all of the animals though, more so the predators."

He continues coaching me through what he can, but it's difficult since I can't access my owl. I try the whole time to locate her, being as gentle as I can. It seems like she pokes her head out at me for the briefest of moments, but then she's gone again before I can do anything about it.

We continue our training for several more days, Joseph always finding us a place high up to "train," even though nothing much is happening. If nothing else, it has been a good opportunity for us to get to know each other.

A few days into training, my owl makes herself known to me. I'm still not able to access her form, but she shows me where she's hiding in my body. I can just barely detect the string connected to her when it manifests, although I'm not able to pull on it quite yet. It's much too fragile for that.

After a week of being there and still not being able to shift, I'm ready to scream in frustration. Joseph tells me he has an idea. We make our way to the top of the capitol building.

"Do you trust me?" he asks.

I want to tell him yes, but the fact that he's asking makes me nervous. "I do, even though I feel like I should tell you I don't."

He chuckles, and in the next moment, he shoves me off the top of the building. A scream rips from my throat, but before I can curse him, however, the string connecting me to my owl flares brightly, solidifying fully. I yank hard on the string, and wings burst from my back, and I shrink in size. I shriek in joy, making a few laps around the building. Now that I've found her and have made our connection tangible, I don't feel so separate from her. She feels more like an extension of myself, just with more animalistic instincts as opposed to before when she was hiding from me. I soar high before landing gingerly on Joseph's shoulder.

"Well done, Ember! I knew that would work. I would've tried it sooner, but wanted to make sure you had established a good connection with your owl before doing so, just in case."

I nip his ear in anger. Even though it worked, I'm pretty pissed at him for that nasty trick.

He chuckles, and I realize he's got to be pretty good at nonverbal communication. "I know you're mad at me, and that's fine. For now, you've earned a break. Why don't you take a flight around the territory, and the rest of the afternoon off. We'll start back up tomorrow. Now that you've accomplished shifting into your animal form, we can start working on shifting into other people."

I hoot happily, and take off back into the sky. I circle around the city, delighting in the sight of it from this angle. At one point I come across a group of birds all flying together in the sky, and by the mix of the types, I know it's a flock of mimics. I join them, and they all welcome me into the group. I hoot happily, following them as they make their way around the area. It's marvelous seeing more of the territory but not having to worry about getting lost.

A dove flies next to me for most of the flight, and I'm not sure how, but I'm positive she's a female. She coos softly at me, gesturing with her head for me to follow her. Did I make a friend?

We split off from the flock and land gently on a hillside. She shifts and I do the same. The woman next to me is breathtaking. She looks to be about my age but has gray hair just like her bird form. Her eyes are the same shade, but there's a warmth in them.

"Hello, Your Highness. My name is Frida. I heard you arrived in town and I've been dying to meet you."

I smile at her, and we sit down to chat and get to know each other. It's wonderful meeting another female, and my neglected awkward teenage self rejoices that I'm making more girlfriends.

We make plans to meet up again while we're still here, and then take off to continue our flight. This time, the transition from woman to bird is seamless. I marvel at the simplicity of it.

After an hour or so of flying, we're once again in the Mutable Meadows. I spy Alexei down below, combat training by himself, and I dive out of the sky at a breakneck speed. Right before I reach him, I shriek loudly. He looks up in alarm, and I sweep by him, brushing his cheek with my wing. I shift in the next moment, standing across from him as I burst out laughing.

He narrows his eyes at me. "That was not very nice."

"But it was priceless. I don't think I've ever been able to startle you before."

He rolls his eyes at me, a fond smile on his face, before his eyes widen in surprise as if he just realized something. "You were finally able to shift?"

"Yes! Joseph had to push me off the capitol in order to make it happen, but it worked."

"He did *what?*"

"Oh, calm down. I'm fine. He knew what he was doing. Besides, if I needed to I could've just teletraveled if I wasn't able to shift. Or used my air magic to slow my landing. I was perfectly safe." I realized that while I was flying around, and it made me slightly less upset with Joseph.

"I guess you're right. It still could've ended badly though."

"But it didn't. Everything is fine. But, on the plus side, I have the afternoon off."

"Want to train with me?" he asks, gesturing to the weapons.

"For a little bit, but then I would like to go down and see the coast. It's been too long since I've had a swim, and I want to see the ocean here."

His eyes light up at the idea of doing something new. We train for a little bit, and I relish the feel of my muscles burning with the familiarity. It's a good reminder that I need to keep up with what I've learned so that I don't get rusty.

When we finish, I debate about going back to my room to change and shower, but figure that since I'm about to go for a swim, it doesn't matter much. Alexei and I sheath our weapons, him with a sword on his back, me with my daggers, and grasp hands.

"Do you know where we're going?" I ask.

He shakes his head. "I've never been to the coast here, but I've seen pictures. It'll have to do for now."

I smile at the challenge in his eyes. He likes not knowing exactly. "Let's go, then."

He pulls me along, and in the next moment, we're on a huge coastline, right on the beach. Instead of the white sand in Mermacovia, this area is a black sand beach, and I wonder if even the color of the sand can change here. When I ask Alexei about it, he says he picked this beach in particular because it's the defining characteristic of this area. It's how we didn't get lost. Apparently, this area of the territory is directly south of the Mutable Meadows.

It's quite a bit warmer here, which I'm grateful for since we're going for a swim. Before Alexei can say anything else, I start stripping my clothes off. He stares at me for a few moments, and I tease him about it.

"Are you just going to watch? Or are you planning on joining me?"

He smirks at me, removing his sword before taking off his shirt in that manly way, reaching behind and pulling it off from his back. My own eyes take him in, and at the moment I have a hard time remembering why I shouldn't be with him. When we're both fully naked, and doing nothing except staring at each other, I finally break eye contact and run into the water. He's right behind me, and I push harder.

I dive in, and once I'm fully submerged, I shift. My mermaid rejoices in being set free again. It's been too long since I've gone for a swim, and the salt water feels fantastic. I look behind me to see Alexei staring at me like I'm an angel that's fallen from heaven. I wave one of my tentacles at him, and it seems to break the spell a little bit.

He swims up to me and holds his hand out, reaching for my tentacle. I realize then that he's never touched me in this form before. I nod at him in permission, and in the next moment his hand is gliding up it. I revel in the sensation of having my mate touch something so sensitive. Before I can hope he does more, he stops and swims to the surface. I follow him.

"Sorry. I forgot you can't breathe underwater like I can," I tell him.

"It's okay. I wish I could. It would be nice to explore with you." His words give me an idea, but it would be too intimate, so I don't say anything. "Your tentacles are beautiful," he tells me, making me blush a bit.

"I don't think they're pretty. I think normal mermaid tails are much more pleasant to look at. These are practical, but I wouldn't call them beautiful by any means."

"I disagree. They're slender and sleek, and the colors are magnificent. Not to mention that the way you move with them is mesmerizing."

"Well, thank you."

We keep swimming around, and I let my water nature take over, releasing my speed and propelling out of the ocean a few times. It gives me an idea now that I can access my owl. I swim down far so I can build up my speed, swimming faster and faster until I burst out of the water, and then I shift into my mimic form, my wings bursting from my back, and I give an almighty cry. I take a few laps around, enjoying the sea breeze. Then I dive back down to the sea and shift the moment I touch the water again. I burst back out of the water next to Alexei, and see his mouth hanging open as he stares at me.

"What?"

"I've literally never seen anything like that before. That was incredible."

"I just wanted to see if it could be done. Apparently it can."

He shakes his head in incredulity. "I think that's a good note to end this swim on, don't you?" he asks.

I nod. My mermaid is satisfied. We make our way out of the water, and I quickly dry us with my air magic. As we start dressing, however, my stomach sinks like a rock.

"Alexei, I have a bad feeling."

"What do you mean?"

"I think something is about to happen." Goosebumps rise on my skin, and the hair on the back of my neck tingles.

Seconds later, a group bursts through the trees along the beach. There are fifteen of them, all armed and masked. I can't tell what species they are, but I grab my daggers and stand next to Alexei in solidarity.

"What do you want?" I shout at them.

Instead of answering me verbally, they shoot an arrow at me. At the last moment I blast it away with a burst of air magic.

"Nothing good, then? Wonderful," I remark sarcastically.

"Remember your training. All of it. Now is the time to put it to use, Ember," Alexei says seriously next to me.

I nod and ready myself, not knowing what magic they have, but prepare for anything. They run at us at once and surround us on all sides. Alexei looks at me and gives me a nod before vanishing. I love that he trusts me to take care of myself.

He reappears behind one of them, swiping his sword through his neck. He's gone again before anyone knows what happened. I follow his lead, teletraveling behind one and driving my dagger through his throat. Alexei and I take a few down that way before they pick up on what we're doing. The next time I reappear, they're ready for me, blocking my attack. I switch it up, blasting them with wind to throw them off as I swing my foot out, taking one down before driving my dagger into their chest. I know later I will probably worry about how I am killing all of these people without a second thought, but for now there's too much at risk.

I see Alexei out of the corner of my eye taking multiple down with his earth magic, binding them in vines and choking them out, while engaging another with his sword. I don't have time to marvel about the fact that his combat skills are phenomenal, because another one takes that moment to rush me, a sword pointed straight at my chest. I dodge the blow while I rip into his mind. His determination and his malice hit me, and I briefly wonder why he hates me so much before I throw fear at him. All the fear I can.

I see when it hits him, because he shrinks away from me before I scent something acrid. I look to see that he's pissed his pants. I delight in my power and the fact that I can reduce a man to that without even touching him. I put him out of his misery before he can start begging me. I look around to see only four left, Alexei engaging all of them.

I'm about to take one of them off his hands when I hear something in back of me. I turn, only to see one of them has snuck up behind me. Before I can engage him, I'm knocked down and he's plunging his sword toward my heart. I panic as I realize there's no time to deflect this. Suddenly Alexei is in front of me, and I scream in horror as I watch the blade pierce through his body.

17

Ember

Alexei falls to the ground in front of me, and time seems to stop all together. My powers flare stronger than I've ever felt them, even more than when they awakened, and I send out a blast of air magic all around us, blowing our enemies off their feet. I shriek in terror and fury. My mermaid is itching to come out of my skin, and my teeth sharpen to razors, my nails turning to claws before my eyes.

My mate mark flares on my wrist, demanding I take revenge for my mate who's lying in the sand in front of me. The man closest to me who plunged his blade into Alexei is my first target, and it's not going to be pretty. I teletravel right in front of him, and before he can react I rip his throat out with my teeth as I plunge my claws into his chest and twist menacingly, tearing his fucking heart out with my bare hand. I can feel the others coming at me from behind, some even firing arrows. I deflect them all easily with air as I turn to them and finally release my fire. I delight in their screams as I burn the rest of them alive. In my anger I engulf the entire area in my air and fire, laying waste to the scum that attacked us. I don't want anything left of them.

With our enemies taken care of, I rush to Alexei. I sob in horror, seeing the sword still sticking out of him, underneath his ribs since it was intended for my heart. He smiles sadly at me as I kneel down next to him.

"Why did you do that?"

"I had to save you," he says on a ragged inhale. "Nothing else matters, only you, my love." With that, his eyes shut, and I scream in panic.

"Alexei! No! Stay with me!" I pull the sword out from him and have no idea what I'm doing as I reach my hands for his chest. I cry out in relief when my magic takes over immediately and starts healing him. I give him everything I have, hoping and praying to whatever god is listening that it's enough.

His wounds close, but I don't see any sort of response from him. In my desperation, I kiss him, my tears coating both of our faces. I latch on to him and hold him as close as humanly possible.

"Do *not* leave me. Do you hear me, you stubborn asshole? I love you too much, and we have endured too much for you to fucking leave me now. *Fight.* Fight for me. Fight for us." I slap his face, trying to get him to come around. I sob harder when he still doesn't respond. "*Please,*" I whisper as I gently kiss his lips again.

Finally I feel the barest hint of movement from him. Just a twitch of his lips against mine. I press my lips harder to his, and this time his mouth moves fully, kissing me back. I break away and look down at him. His eyes are miraculously open, and he has a smirk on his beautiful mouth.

"All I had to do was die for you to forgive me?" he asks. "If I would've known that I would've done it a long time ago."

I laugh-sob as I smack him on the arm. "Don't ever do that to me again."

"I would do it again in a heartbeat, little doe. I will always save you. I love you more than life itself."

I fling myself into his arms. "I love you too, Alexei. I never want to be without you again."

He pulls back slightly, his eyes wide and vulnerable. "You really forgive me, Ember?"

"Alexei, you died for me. How could I not? Besides, I understand why you did what you did. Even if I was upset about it, I didn't blame you exactly. It was your father who killed me, not you."

Instead of responding verbally, he pulls me into his arms, kissing me deeply, flipping me as he goes so I'm underneath him. Our reunion is intense, rough, and overwhelming. I latch on to him like he's going to disappear, and he seems to be doing the same to me. Our mouths move against one another's like we're starving for oxygen, and only the other can supply it. His hands move to my breasts over my shirt, and I moan in response, having wanted this for as long as I've known him.

I'm about to start ripping his clothes off, when I remember hearing horror stories about having sex on a beach. I cringe at the thought of where sand might end up.

Alexei seems to be on the same page, because in the next minute he breaks our kiss and looks down at me. He pulls me along, and I teletravel with him without a second thought, my trust in him fully restored. Moments later, we're on my bed back in the capitol.

"I've been waiting for this moment with you for too long. Our first time isn't going to be on the beach like some horny teenagers. I want to worship you, and I'll need a proper bed to do that."

Before I can respond, he's tearing my clothes off, his mouth back to working against mine. I follow suit, and we're finally lying there in nothing but our skin. The star on my arm hums pleasantly, and I delight in the contented feeling of rightness in this moment.

Alexei breaks away from my mouth and kisses a trail down my neck. He pauses and sucks longingly on my vein, and I know he must be wanting to feed after he was so severely injured.

"You can feed." I tilt my head to the side, giving him better access.

He keeps sucking, and I'm going to have a hickey. I don't mind in the slightest, and I know that he must be marking me as his. The thought sends a thrill through my blood, and I want him to mark me in every way possible.

"Bite me, Alexei."

He groans against my throat, but I don't feel his teeth. "Not yet."

He moves on, traveling down to my breasts. He showers them with attention until I'm squirming and aching for more. He finally drags his fangs over me, but they don't pierce my skin, and heat floods my pussy at the thought of him biting me somewhere more intimate than my neck.

"Alexei, please. I need more. *More*." I know I'm begging at this point, and I don't care. We've been working up to this for months and months, and I can't stand it anymore.

He obliges me and brings his fingers to my stomach. He caresses it lightly while his mouth still works wonders on my nipples. His touch drags lower at a glacial pace, but he finally reaches my clit. I cry out, clutching his head to my breast as I shamelessly grind myself against his hand. His fingers move in circles against me, bringing me higher and higher, but before I can topple over, he shifts and moves them toward my opening.

I inhale sharply at the change in sensation before he suddenly plunges them into my wet heat. He pulls his mouth away from my chest, and his lips latch on to my clit as he sucks it into his mouth. It's so intense I have to hold back a scream, and then he's alternating between sucking and licking me as his fingers continue to plunder into me. I'm building so high that I fear I'll never come back down.

Right when I think I can't take any more, his fangs pierce my skin as his tongue continues to lap at me, drinking from me in multiple different ways. I explode into a thousand pieces. I can vaguely sense

Alexei growling against me, and it only adds to my pleasure. It takes minutes to come down, and only then does my mate pull back. He gently licks the puncture marks he left behind, and it stirs my pleasure again.

"Alexei, I need you."

He makes his way up my body, licking, sucking, and kissing as he goes. When he reaches my lips, he takes me up in a fierce kiss, his tongue thrusting into my mouth at the same time he slowly pushes into me. Alexei swallows my gasp of pleasure as he buries himself to the hilt. When he's fully seated inside me, he pauses and looks down lovingly at me.

"Ember, you are my heaven. I've always believed that heaven and hell are right here with us. That we experience both throughout our lives. You are my heaven. I don't know what I did to deserve you, but I am going to spend the rest of our lives showing you how honored I am to be your mate."

Tears gather in my eyes. I've never felt as close to anyone else as I do at this moment. Without another word he starts moving inside of me as he licks the tears from my cheeks that have spilled over. It starts out slow, him making love to me for the first time, and while I'm reveling in it, I want more from him.

I dig my heels into his ass, propelling him farther into me. He groans deep in his throat, his restraint seeming to snap. He powers into me, forcing my legs wider, giving himself more room to move. I'm building again, especially with every rub of his pelvis on the healed bite that he left me.

"I want something that I'm not sure you would like," he tells me huskily. "I have a feeling you will, but you can tell me no."

"What is it?" I'm pretty sure I would give him anything he wanted at this point.

"I want you to drink from me as I drink from you."

My eyes widen. I did not think that's what he was going to say, but now that he's mentioned it, tasting his blood is something I really want to try. I don't know if it's because I'm part vampire, or if it's just because it's Alexei, but the thought makes my heart pound. I nod to him.

He brings his wrist to his mouth, slicing open his skin with his fangs. I grab his wrist and latch my lips to his skin. For a moment I'm stunned by the taste of his blood. It's nothing like I expected and, at the same time, tastes exactly like I would imagine. He's smokey and sweet, almost like a honeyed whiskey, and his blood heats my throat as I swallow. It's then that his own teeth pierce the skin above my breast. We feed from each other as our movements become more frantic. Our combined blood heats between us, raising us higher and higher, until it finally fractures. Stars erupt behind my eyelids, and for a moment I swear Alexei and I are one person. He's inside me on every possible level, and I revel in it.

Alexei stills above me, and we do nothing for a moment except look into each other's eyes as our bodies come down. He's still twitching inside of me, and unbelievably, I still want more. I shift my hips slightly, and he sucks in a sharp breath.

"My need for you is nowhere *near* sated, little doe. Get ready for a sleepless night."

My blood heats at his words and the look in his eyes. I push him up, wanting to take charge. He obliges me, intrigue and curiosity flooding from him. He slips out of my body as I make him sit with his back against the headboard. His seed spills from my body, and I fight back a moan at the feeling and the knowledge that a part of him is still inside of me.

I straddle his hips, dragging his length through my folds, coating him in both of our release. I tease him for a minute, circling my hips, but never allowing him to enter. I smile when he growls and grasps my hips tightly, trying to finally bring us together.

I take pity on him, and impale myself on his length in the next breath. I don't give him any time to recover as I immediately lift myself back up and slam myself down upon him. It's rough, unleashing, and wild. With Alexei's hands free, they roam all over my body before he settles his thumb on my hotspot. I moan as I grind against it, wanting more, but knowing it will be too much.

Just as I have the thought, Alexei's finger on his opposite hand snakes around to my backside. I can feel him touching underneath where we're joined, gathering the wetness there and bringing it to my asshole. I inhale sharply as he pushes his finger inside. I've never had this before, and I love that I'm experiencing it for the first time with Alexei. He moves his finger in and out opposite my thrusts, and I whimper at the pleasure coursing through my body.

"Are you going to come for me again?" he asks, a cocky look on his face. I have the urge to be a smart ass, but I can't find the motivation or the words. Instead I just whimper again, bringing an even bigger smile to his face. "I told you this pussy was mine. I know you've never felt like this before."

"If this pussy is yours, then this cock is *mine*," I tell him, squeezing him tightly with my inner muscles. I return his cocky smile as he curses under his breath.

"You own it, little doe. It's yours. Now come for me. I want you strangling my dick again."

My body instantly follows his command, and I spasm around his length. He groans and joins me in oblivion moments later.

We collapse on the bed completely spent. He's still inside me, but it seems neither of us have the energy or motivation to separate our bodies. It's then as we're lying there in each other's arms, something flares on my wrist. I look down only to see the mate mark has changed slightly. My star is darker, and slightly above and next to it is the faintest outline of Alexei's own mark. I show him and his brows furrow. He lifts his own wrist to see the same thing, only opposite.

"This must be from us finally coupling. We made it official," he says as he grabs my wrist, giving our mark a soft kiss. It tingles in approval, and I smile softly at him.

"When did you know you were in love with me?" I ask.

"I knew for sure when you were attacked and poisoned and I had to take you to the healing springs. I've never been more terrified in my life. It dawned on me while I was holding you in that pool that I wouldn't be so scared if I felt anything for you less than love. When did you know?"

I give him a soft smile and run my hand over his bearded cheek. "It wasn't one exact moment for me, but I could feel it building and building as we traveled. You training me was a huge part of it. You not only wanted to protect me, but you also made sure that I could protect myself. But I was overwhelmed with it when we danced in the cave castle together. There was no doubt in my mind then."

His eyes sparkle with the memory. "I'm sorry it took me so long to act on it. And I was almost too late. And then I almost fucked everything up and made you hate me."

"I still loved you, even when I hated you. I couldn't stay away from you, no matter how hard I tried. My dreams were the only place I could be with you."

His eyes light up at the mention of our shared dreams. He hardens inside of me again. "You mean the dreams where I made you come your brains out?"

I roll my eyes and swat him on the arm. "I believe I made *you* come *your* brains out."

"Well, you certainly did that."

I smile at that. With our talk about the dreams, we start moving again. We have a lot of time to make up for, and I know neither of us is getting any sleep tonight.

The next morning, I'm dragging ass, literally not having gotten one wink of sleep, but I'm so happy I couldn't care in the slightest. Alexei joined me in the bath this morning to "help" me wash off. Which he did, after he made me thoroughly dirty...again. He was reluctant to let me out of the bedroom, but I really want to keep up with my training. I also need to talk to Joseph about the attack yesterday, and Alexei wants to be part of that conversation too.

We trust Joseph, but we have no idea what species it was that attacked us. It did happen in his territory, but that could've been purposeful to make us suspect the mimics.

We decide to meet up with him for breakfast and talk to him about it then, before I start my training. We walk hand in hand to Joseph's quarters. He likes eating best there, and we don't mind it either. It's more intimate and private, which is perfect for the conversation we're about to have.

We knock on his door, and he beckons us in. When we enter, he stares at our joined hands before cracking a smile. "It's about time the two of you got together."

My brows rise in surprise. "You knew?"

"Of course. I could smell your mate bond. Obviously it's *much* more pronounced now, but I could also sense the connection between you. It's a wolf thing."

I guess that makes sense. "Why didn't you say anything?"

"There was clearly a reason why you two were keeping it secret. It's none of my business. Congratulations, though, you two."

I blush slightly, and Alexei puffs his chest out in male pride. "Thank you, sir," he says.

"Joseph, there's something we actually need to talk to you about."

He gestures for us to sit while he pours us each a cup of tea.

"We were attacked yesterday. We don't know who they were. There were fifteen of them, and they had masks on so we couldn't see any of their features to tell where they came from."

His face pales in shock. "I'm so relieved you're both all right. I'm assuming they're all dead?"

I nod in confirmation.

"Did you not take their masks off after you killed them?"

I hum uncomfortably. "Well, it's actually quite the story. Alexei teletraveled in front of me to save me from a fatal blow, taking it himself, and in my vengeful anger, I sort of burned them all. I didn't think about how we wouldn't be able to identify them until later."

I can see so many emotions running across his face, and when I open my senses to him, they're all genuine. He has no mask up. There's anger, relief, astonishment, and pride.

"Did you save your mate, Ember?"

"I did."

"That's impressive. Have you done your healing training yet?"

"Not yet. The elves are my next stop after you," I say, giving him a wink.

His brows are halfway up his forehead. "Yet you were able to save him from the brink of death?"

"It would seem that the threat of losing your mate is a very good incentive to accomplish something. Although, I have done some minor healing on my own as well."

"Well, in reference to the attack, I can't say for sure, but I'm almost positive it wasn't my people. Everyone I've encountered is very excited you're here, and love that there is someone with our blood in the palace. All the same, I will do some digging and see if I can find anything within my territory." I can tell he's being sincere, and I'm reassured.

"Thank you, Joseph. I don't think they were mimics either, but I wanted to bring it up to you since it did happen in your territory."

"May I ask where you were when it happened?"

"We were on the Savage Sands," Alexei tells him. I didn't know the name of it, but with the black sand, it's fitting.

"You were on the coast? Where did they come from?"

"They came out of the trees," I respond this time.

"Have you considered the mermaids since you were close to the ocean?"

"I have. And there would definitely be a reason for them to. Coralia doesn't like me much. And I may have threatened her before we left."

Alexei turns to me with a question in his gaze. I cringe. I forgot to tell him about that.

"But, her son, Proteus, and I have a good friendship,"

Alexei's eyes darken even more at the mention of the mermaid who I went out on a date with before we made up.

I ignore him. "And he has more sway among his people, so I also have reason to think it wouldn't be them."

"Well, the witches I think would be too far away. They tend to keep to themselves anyway. I doubt the vampires or fae would be the culprit either. I've heard they have great respect for Alexei, and the fae love you, Ember. So that basically just leaves the elves, mermaids, humans, and, even though I don't think it was, mimics."

"You think it could be humans?"

"Their territory is right next to ours."

"But we just helped those at the brothel."

"What about the others? They could have heard you were in the territory and maybe were upset you didn't help them out before you left?"

My heart sinks. I hate the thought that the humans I want to help so badly would hate me and want to get rid of me. Now that I'm thinking about it, the attackers didn't use any magic. I originally thought that they didn't want to give themselves away, but what if they didn't *have* any?

My stomach churns at the thought, and Alexei squeezes my hand in sympathy.

"But we'll figure it out, Ember. For the time being just be on your guard. I can guarantee you will be safe in the Mutable Meadows. If you go outside this area, though, keep your wits about you."

We eat after that, although my appetite is funky after our discussion. When we finish, Joseph has me come with him to train. I can tell Alexei doesn't want to leave me, and I understand his reluctance. After all the events of yesterday, it will be strange and worrisome to be parted from him.

"Go whack the shit out of some stuff with a sword. It'll cheer you up, and I'll join you soon," I tell him.

He smiles half-heartedly at me. "I'll be where I was yesterday when you're done. Then I'll kick your ass in the ring." He winks at me and gives me a heated kiss before I can dispute that. In the next moment he's teletraveled, not letting me get the last word in. Asshole. He loves to do that.

When I turn, I see Joseph watching me with a kind smile on his face. "Ready?"

"As I'll ever be. What are we training on today?"

"Well, first, shift into your owl."

I do so without difficulty. She seems to be within reach now, and I know we've crossed into friendly territory.

"Very good. I'm glad you're able to access her on command. You can shift back now." I do. "Today I want you to start working on shifting into others. I think Alexei would be a good place to start. I'm sure you've touched him without his shields up, and you know his form better than anyone else here."

"So, what do I need to do?"

"This one is more complicated than your owl. You carry your shifted form with you at all times, but this is someone else's form. Close your eyes and picture Alexei's face in your mind."

I do, his handsome face behind my eyelids immediately.

"To start, let's just focus on one feature at a time. Start with his hair. Now, picture that on your own head. Not just the color and the length, but think about the texture of it, the thickness."

I focus all of my energy, willing my hair to change to the honey-wheat blond waves. I open my eyes, and disappointment shoots through me when I see my dark hair is still exactly the same as it was.

We continue on like that for the rest of our training session, me trying to change different features of my own, all to no avail. We go our separate ways for the day, and I teletravel to the training yard, eager to see Alexei and get out some of this frustration.

His face lights up upon seeing me, and he teletravels directly in front of me, kissing me fiercely and leaving me breathless.

"Ready to train?" he asks.

"After that? I'm thinking maybe our energy would be best spent elsewhere."

"If you want that, then you're going to have to earn it," he tells me, smacking my ass with the flat side of his training sword.

I narrow my eyes at him, a growl building in my throat. "Earn it, huh?"

"Yep." He puts his sword down and takes a defensive posture. "Are you going to get me on my back?"

"You would like that, wouldn't you?" Before he can respond, I teletravel behind him, planning to kick the backs of his knees in.

Unfortunately, he's ready for me, and grabs my foot before I can connect with anything. I try to rip it out of his grasp, but he holds on tight. Fine. If that's the way he wants to play it. I pull my leg back one more time to let him think I'm still struggling against him, but in the next second, I'm pushing his shoulders with both hands as I jump onto him, wrapping my other leg around him. He grunts as I connect with him, not anticipating me coming into his personal space like that. He goes down hard with me on top of him, and I delight in the fact that I already took him down.

"Want to talk about my reward now?"

I know he's going to try to flip me so I'm underneath him, so I lean down and kiss him senseless first. Only when he hardens between my legs do I pull back.

"I win," I whisper against his lips and nip playfully at his nose.

He tries reconnecting our mouths, but I pull back, standing and dancing away from him. He narrows his eyes at me, and I smile innocently. I've never quite played with him like *this* before, and let me just tell you, I *like* it. He tries to teletravel to me, but I anticipate his move and teletravel across the training yard.

I delight in the way his eyes darken and follow me like a predator hunting its prey. The comparison is actually fairly accurate, except for the fact that I am no prey.

This time, when he teletravels to me, I let him. I don't know if it's a mate thing or a witch thing, but I'm positive he's going to travel behind me this time. Instead, I spin, drawing my dagger. When he materializes, I have my knife positioned right at his throat. His eyes twinkle in a mixture of excitement, pride, and frustration.

"I'm just utterly kicking your ass today," I tell him teasingly. "How does it feel?"

He growls at me, grasping my wrist and trapping it against my lower back, and pulling me firmly against his erection that's pressed to my belly.

"I know what you're up to, little doe."

"And what's that?" I ask innocently, batting my eyelashes at him, biting my lip.

With his other hand he reaches up and pulls my lip free of my teeth. In the next moment his mouth is on mine, biting the same lip I was only seconds ago. A moan breaks free, and when he finally pulls back, his grin is triumphant.

"I won," he tells me.

I guffaw in his face. "Nice try, but not even close," I tell him, poking him just in the slightest with the other dagger that I pulled and is now resting against his low back.

His brows fly up his forehead in surprise. "Little doe, how are you doing this?"

"Apparently it's pretty easy now that I've got you so distracted."

"Well, since you thoroughly earned your reward and I seem to have only one thing on my mind, want to head to the room and cut training short for today?"

"Excuse me? I'm in the mood to train now. I'm on a roll." With that, I teletravel to the weapons table and pick up my bow and arrow.

He groans in frustration but follows me, making me smile in triumph. I load an arrow and take aim, but hold back a gasp when Alexei presses himself against me from behind. He's still hard, and I know he's trying to distract me in the same way I was with him, but I'm not going to let him.

I take a deep breath, making sure to push my ass out as I do so, rubbing it against his length. I hear him curse softly as I release the arrow, and am delighted when it hits the bull's-eye. I nock another arrow and back up even farther to make it more challenging for myself. Alexei follows, this time resting his hand on the front of my hip. I close my eyes, ignoring the heat from his hand spreading through my pelvis. I take another deep breath as I take aim. I am determined. I will *not* let him distract me. The arrow once again hits the middle of the target, and I resist the urge to whoop in excitement. Even with my mate distracting me I still managed to stay focused.

I guess this is probably one of the best forms of training. After all, if I can maintain my composure now, I know I'll be able to anytime. We continue on like that for a while, him attempting to screw me up, and me sticking to my guns.

When I can't stand any more, though, I toss my bow on the table and grab his hand. I teletravel to my room, pulling him along with me. He smirks in triumph when he sees where we are, and I attack his mouth with my own, ripping his clothes off like the feral bitch I am in the process.

He returns the favor, and before I know it, we're both standing there fully naked. I push him onto the bed, straddling him immediately. I sink down on his length, moaning into his mouth as I do so. Our coupling is hard, dirty, and fast. The bed knocks against the wall with every shift of my hips, but I can't bring myself to care. His fingers grasp my thighs in a punishing grip, and I delight in the roughness. It takes me no time at all to reach my climax, and I bring Alexei with me, relishing the sound of him coming apart beneath me.

I collapse on the bed next to him, and he wraps me in his arms. Our night of no rest finally catches up with us, and we pass out.

The next couple weeks pass much the same way. Training with Joseph, but struggling hardcore, and then combat training with Alexei. We've been so wrapped up in each other though, that training, sex, and eating are basically the only activities I have time for. I have never been more exhausted or more content.

I do meet with Frida a few times when I can. We mainly go on flights together to decompress when it all becomes too much for me.

She's as sweet as her mimic form, and I really enjoy having a calm female friend to keep me company. As much as I love Pearl, sometimes her intense energy can be a tad much for me.

Frida is like a bubbling brook, serene, go with the flow, quiet. I've enjoyed getting to know her, and I make sure she knows she can come to visit me in the castle anytime she wants. It will be easy to stay in contact considering I'm able to teletravel and she's able to fly.

I have been making some progress with Joseph, but it's very slow going. At this point, I've managed to copy all of Alexei's features separately, and now we're finally at the stage where I can mimic his entire form at once.

"Now that you've mimicked all of his traits, you should be able to bring them together like a puzzle. Just close your eyes and unite all of those separate pieces."

I do as he says; copying others' forms is slowly getting easier for me, but all the traits at once are difficult.

"Focus on your connection with him. Most of us do that through the touch we've had with them with their shields down. Let that guide you. Take a deep breath and follow that same thread. It's different from your owl. It's in another part of you."

"I think I found it," I tell him.

"Good. Chase that connection. When you reach the end, surrender to the change."

I follow his instructions, and when I find the end, I see every single feature of Alexei's. I will myself to take on all of it, falling into the shift. When I open my eyes, I'm eye level with Joseph, and he's smiling broadly at me.

"I did it?" I ask. Even my voice sounds like his.

He nods in confirmation, and I do a happy dance, so relieved that I finally accomplished it. His face scrunches up in confused amusement. I laugh at the fact that I'm doing a happy dance in Alexei's body.

"Well done, Ember. The first one is the hardest. The rest should come easy to you now. Why don't you take a break. You've earned it."

I give him a hug, and he returns it whole-heartedly. I was curious if he would feel strange about it, since I'm in Alexei's body, but I guess being a mimic, they're used to being around people who don't always look like themselves.

I teletravel to the training ring to meet with Alexei still in his form. He shouts in surprise when I arrive, and I give him his most infuriating smirk.

"Ember?"

Instead of responding verbally, I shift into my normal form and kiss him. He gives as good as he gets, and we're breathless when we break apart.

"That was a little weird, seeing myself, I mean."

"I figured. I don't think I've ever gotten that reaction out of you before."

He chuckles, but moves on quickly. "Today, I want to test something out. If it works, it will be immensely beneficial for you if you're ever in battle. I want you to load up on weapons."

I do so, strapping my dagger onto my thighs, my sword on my back, and then my bow with an arrow nocked in my hands.

"Now, I want you to shift into your owl form."

I raise my brows at him in question, but do as he says. The weapons are still with my human form, and I fly around happily, landing on

Alexei's shoulder with a soft hoot. He pets me lovingly, and I nip at his ear softly, making him growl at me. I take off from his shoulder, awaiting his next instructions.

"Now, fly high and shift into your regular form while in the air, and try to shoot the target with your bow and arrow."

Oh shit. This is going to be difficult.

"Don't forget to shift back into your owl if you start getting too close to the ground."

I flap my wings hard, propelling myself into the sky. I make a circle, trying to get a better angle of the target, and give myself a better shot. When I'm finally ready, I shift. I immediately start falling, but I try to focus on the bow in my hands. I take a shot at the target, but it's extremely difficult since I'm moving so quickly, the air trying to rip it out of my hands. My shot lands in the general vicinity of the target, but I don't hit it by any means. I shift back into my owl before I hit the ground.

"Want to try again? Or want to try something else, like daggers?" Alexei asks me.

I shift back into my human form. I set the bow down and palm my daggers, shifting back into my owl form. I fly high again, but this time I have a different strategy. I dive toward the target, already visually aiming at it. Even though I'm not in my human form, I can feel myself holding the blades. I grip them tighter and get ready to throw them.

When I get close enough, I shift, and in the next breath I'm launching them toward the bull's-eye. One hits the target on the outer edge, but the other misses it completely. This time, instead of shifting again, I use my air magic to slow my descent. I land softly in front of Alexei, and he looks at me with amazement.

"Should I go again?" I ask.

He nods, but doesn't seem able to say more than that. I smile at the fact that I'm stunning him speechless.

I already know this will be our new form of training, and I like that I not only am learning a new skill—that's incredibly badass, I might add—but I'm also getting more acquainted with my owl form.

We keep practicing for a while, sticking with the daggers for now since they seem to be a bit easier for me.

The next few days continue on much the same. I've had a breakthrough in my training with Joseph now, and I've been able to shift into anyone. At first it would take me a few minutes to follow the thread, but after days of practice, it takes me only seconds.

"Well, I think our time together is officially at an end, my young apprentice," Joseph tells me after watching me shift from person to person with barely a thought.

I knew this was coming, but tears well behind my eyes regardless. We've spent a lot of time together, and he's become a kind of father figure to me. I'm going to miss him.

"I know, Joseph. Thank you. For everything."

"You're very welcome, Your Highness."

I make one last visit to Frida. We chat and go on one last flight together. I give her a hug, pushing the tears back and telling her to visit and write when she can.

Alexei and I gather our belongings, and get ready to head into the Healing Springs. I almost groan at the thought of spending the next however long with the elves and their unpleasant attitudes.

"Don't worry, little doe. You'll get used to them quickly. And I don't think we'll need to be there long with all the healing that you've already done."

I nod as I shrink my trunk and stick it in my pocket. Even though I'm not looking forward to leaving the Everchanging Glades, I am excited to see what the elf territory looks like. The only part that I've actually seen is the caves.

When we're all packed and ready, we knock on Joseph's door. He invites us in for one more meal, and we enjoy our time together. Joseph hugs us both once we're finished, and when I pull back, tears are running down my face.

He wipes them from my cheeks and smiles fondly at me. "I will see you again. And if you ever need anything at all, you send for me. Understand?"

"Same goes for you."

He looks at Alexei. "You take care of her, you hear me?"

"With my life, sir."

When there's nothing left to say, Alexei and I grasp each other's hands and he tugs me with him to the Healing Springs.

18

Ember

Trees. *Everywhere.* Not only are they everywhere, but there are people inhabiting them. There are an abundance of twinkly lights, and this whole place just looks magical, there's no other way to describe it. My eyes are drawn up, up, up. Houses line the ancient, huge trees, all the way up. There are ramps that wrap around the trunks, making it possible to get all the way to the top, and bridges that connect some of them.

In front of us is the largest tree of them all, and it's centered in the forest. The trunk of it looks completely hollowed out, and has a door on the front of it. I realize that this is the capitol building of the Healing Springs.

"What city are we in again?" I ask. We've been traveling so much lately that it's easy to forget.

"Nylaluna. It's close to the healing cave pools I took you to, as well as Thunder Peak."

"What's Thunder Peak?"

"The volcano here."

"They have a volcano?" I ask, slightly terrified. I've never been this close to one before.

"Yes. They use the volcanic soil and ash in a lot of their remedies and tonics. They can heal basically anything themselves, but they make a lot of salves and things like that for people in other territories. They made the solution I've used on you to make sure you don't get an infection."

"How does the volcano help with that?"

"The land here is like the rest of the realm, the magic is imbued in the territory itself. There are healing qualities in certain things here, like the volcano and the cave pools. They've found a way to incorporate them into some of their remedies."

Before we can continue our conversation, a woman comes out of the tree in front of us.

"Who are you, and what do you want?" She's as stern looking as Agatha, the palace healer, but she's much more beautiful. She has skin as pale as the moon, hair and eyes the color of the tree trunks she's surrounded by, and russet lips. Her hair is braided back in a fishtail braid that makes her look like a warrior, and shows off her heavily pointed ears.

"Hello, Serena. How lovely to see you again," Alexei says to the grand mistress.

She scoffs, and I internally chuckle at the way he always attempts to charm the elves. It really is a futile effort.

"Oh, hello Alexei. What brings you here?" Even though she's not exactly *friendly*, she seems more pleasant than most elves.

"I'm sure you remember Ember Solis, the king's daughter. You met her at the ball a few months ago." He gestures to me, and she looks back at me.

Her face is set in a bit of a scowl, but I think I see a splash of surprise across her features.

"Of course, Your Highness." She bows slightly to me, not much, but I'm guessing she never bows lower than that to anyone, even my father. "How can I be of service?"

"Can we talk privately?"

She nods, turning and walking back into the tree. We follow her a little more slowly. When I enter, I'm literally stunned into silence. The room is absolutely massive, and the glowing lights that seem to be all over this realm continue up the entire tree. It's split into different levels, and there's a spiral staircase that goes right up the middle, and looks like it's made out of the tree itself. Obviously there's no fire, since we're in a literal tree. That sounds like a disaster waiting to happen. Instead, little fireflies surround the space, giving off a gentle heat.

An earthy scent clings to the walls, along with the smell of lavender and rosemary. I have a feeling I'll be smelling lots of different pleasant herbs whilst here, and am looking forward to it.

Serena gestures to two seats across from her, and Alexei and I take them. She pours us each a cup of tea that was already prepared, and I breathe in the scents of spearmint and honey. I take a grateful sip before setting it down and addressing her.

I go through a similar explanation as I did with Joseph. She doesn't give any sort of inclination as to what she's thinking, and I try to sense her emotions. I can feel a little bit of surprise, but not much of anything else, and I wonder if that's why their race is so prickly.

"I've already had multiple instances where I've had to heal either myself or another, so I'm hoping it won't take me long to learn. It comes pretty naturally to me."

"We'll see about that. I would be willing to teach you. I will also make sure you know how to make our ointments and tonics. Only elves can make them, and even though you'll need ingredients that we only have here, it is still a useful skill that every elf should know."

While her words are polite enough, there's that undercurrent of disdain in her voice that it seems only elves can manage.

"Thank you. I greatly appreciate it."

"We will start now. Alexei, get your things settled in the guest houses. You're welcome to use the training yard if you wish, but make sure you stay out of the way of any training. Including hers."

He fights a smile as he responds, "Yes, ma'am."

"You do realize that we will have to injure you, I'm assuming? Elf training isn't an enjoyable experience."

Alexei and I exchange a glance. It seems neither of us had thought of that.

"She can practice on me," Alexei volunteers, and I like that idea even less.

"No. Not yet she won't. She needs to practice on herself first. It's the easiest way to start, because she will have the motivation of no longer being in pain. When she's ready to start practicing on others, I will notify you. Now, go on so we can begin," she says, effectively dismissing him.

He looks at me, and I know he's struggling to follow her orders.

"It's okay, Alexei. I'll be fine. Go." I give him a reassuring smile.

He nods reluctantly. "Come find me if you need anything." With that, he teletravels to what I'm assuming is the guest house.

"All right, let's get started. Want to do the honors of cutting open your hand, or would you prefer me to do it?" Serena asks, like she's talking about the weather.

I grab the dagger from its holster and hold it up to my palm. I have a brief moment of hesitation, as I think most people would.

"Oh for the Gods' sake, just do it already," she snaps at me.

I resist the urge to be a smartass, and with a deep breath, I drag it across my palm. Blood wells under the sharpness of my blade, and I hiss at the pain that blossoms.

She hands me a rag. "Don't bleed on anything," she warns me, just like Agatha. Must be another elf trait. "Now, picture healing it, but from the inside out. You want to make sure to heal the tissue underneath, not just the skin on the surface. If it's not done correctly, it will still be sore and, depending on what it is, won't ever fully heal."

I look at the cut on my hand and imagine the tissue stitching itself together. Nothing happens, but I don't give up.

"You can use your other hand if you need to. Sometimes you won't be able to use your hands, and you'll need to do it through pure force of will, but for now when you're just starting, gently and slowly move your thumb up the cut, still picturing it healing in your mind."

I do as she says, and am amazed when the skin left in the wake of my thumb is healed and pink. There's a mark, but I'm sure we will get to the point when she teaches me to do so without leaving a scar, and hopefully how to heal scars themselves.

"Well done," she praises in her monotone voice, but I don't care if she's not as excited as I am. I learned how to properly heal, and it wasn't too difficult.

When I did this in Mermacovia, I was basically only healing it on the surface, only picturing it closing, and that's why it was still sore after I was done.

I tell her as much, showing her my scars. She gently runs her hands over them, and hums in disapproval.

"These weren't healed correctly, you're right. There is a bit of scar tissue under both. I'll fix those for now. I was also going to ask if you wanted me to heal your other scars?"

"I like having them. Is there a way you can heal the tissue under-neath, but keep the scar visible?"

She frowns at me, looking puzzled, but nods all the same. Her hands make a sweep over my body, healing all the damaged tissue, but leaving them the same on the surface like I asked.

"I'll teach you how to do that, but you're not quite ready for that yet."

After that, we get back to our training.

We continue on with me cutting and healing myself for an hour or so, and while it's not fun slicing myself open again and again, I will admit I'm already getting better and faster. I do end up needing to take a potion to replenish my blood multiple times since I'm losing so much.

When we're finished for the day, Serena surprises me.

"You did well today. You were correct, and our training should be relatively quick. Only a few days on actually healing itself, and then one or two to teach you how to make the ointments."

"Perfect. Thank you so much for your help. I know this probably isn't how you want to be spending your time."

"I don't mind," she says, surprising me again. "My days are usually fairly boring. It's enjoyable to do something different."

"Don't you have a lot to do since you're the grand mistress?"

"Not really. Occasionally there will be something I have to deal with, but our territory is pretty smooth."

I let that sink in, and figure I should try to think of ways the grand masters and mistresses can be more involved in the realm.

"Well, I appreciate it all the same."

"I'll see you tomorrow, Ember. And bring Alexei with you. You'll need him for training." I gulp, not liking the idea of my mate in pain, but maybe that will be even more of a motivation for me.

I leave for the day, Serena having pointed me in the direction of the guest houses. I head to the tree that she indicated and make the climb up the ramp. Weeks of training with my owl has knocked my fear of heights right out of me. It's not so scary when you can just shift and fly off. The guest house is at the very top, Serena told me, and while it's a bit of a hike, it gives me an opportunity to look out over the territory.

There's some light here from the sun, but there are so many trees that it isn't nearly as bright as the other territories. There's also quite a bit of water (which makes sense with all the trees here), rivers, ponds, and it looks like a lake in the distance. Everyone seems to be housed up in the trees instead of on the ground, which I find interesting. It's almost mimic-like.

I finally reach the top, and Alexei opens the door upon my arrival, like he's just been sitting here waiting for me. He pulls me into the guest house, and immediately starts examining me.

"Are you okay? How did it go?"

"Calm down, I'm fine. Training went really well. She said I get to start practicing on you tomorrow and that we should only be here for a little less than a week."

He looks relieved that I won't have to injure myself anymore. I'm finally able to look around the space, and it's similar to the building I was just in with Serena. Lots of twinkle lights, very earthy, with a cozy round bed in the center. What really catches my eye, though, is the patio on the other side of the room. It's huge, and overlooks the area, and surprise, surprise, more twinkle lights.

I head out there with Alexei on my heels to find cozy-looking chairs, and I have the urge to sink into them with a cup of tea and a good book. Alexei plops down on one of them, pulling me with him. I end up in his lap, and he snuggles into me, burrowing his face in my neck and breathing in my scent. A contented sigh escapes us both, and I bask in finally being able to have intimate moments like this with my mate.

If it weren't for all the training I've been doing, it would almost be like we're on an extended vacation together. We settle in, unpacking some of our things, but not much since we shouldn't be here for very long. When that's done, and there's not much else to do, Alexei suggests a walk. The idea is pleasant. I would like to see more of Nylaluna, and we usually teletravel since it's the quickest.

We head back down the tree and start walking. There are so many inhabited trees, but within probably fifteen minutes of walking, it starts to thin out a bit. We don't see anyone around, and Alexei grabs my hand. At this point, we've openly accepted our bond, but I don't want to flaunt it for the realm to see before we've told Stavros.

Alexei tells me there's a waterfall close by, and we head in that direction. It's probably my mermaid blood, but I've always been a sucker for the water. After about a half hour of walking, we finally come across it. It's like a secluded little oasis of perfection. There is indeed a waterfall that flows into a decent-sized lake. There are cliffs that line three sides of the lake, giving it an air of privacy.

I strip quickly, wanting to swim. It's once again been too long. Alexei follows me, and as soon as the water's deep enough, I shift, lifting my tentacles out of the water, and flopping them down again, splashing him in the process. I can hear his outraged shout from underneath the surface, and giggle to myself. He dives in after me, and I swim away before he can reach me and retaliate. He narrows his eyes at me, and teletravels directly in front of me, and his fingers are digging into my ribs and tickling me before I can pull back. I squeal, even though it sounds more musical since I'm in my mermaid form and underwater.

We continue to play for a while, me dragging him with me while I swim at speed through the water. It's then that I have an idea, and we break the surface so I can tell Alexei.

"I want to go up to where the waterfall drops down."

He teletravels up there immediately, but instead of following his lead, I jump out of the water and shift into my owl. I fly up to meet him, and he smiles at me, looking just as in awe of me as he was the first time I did it. I land gently on his shoulder, nipping his ear playfully. He gives me a soft pet, and with that, I leap off his shoulder, giving a shriek before I dive toward the water again. A few feet above the lake, I shift back into my mermaid. She's a little reluctant to come out since I'm not in the water yet, but my training with Joseph taught me how to pull her free. I land in the water with a giant splash, and I come up just in time I see Alexei leap from the cliff. But instead of coming straight down, he teletravels to the spot above the middle of the lake, I'm guessing to avoid any potential rocks too close to the cliffs. He cannon balls about ten feet from me, drenching me in the process.

We do the same thing a few more times since we're enjoying it so much. On the last jump, I follow the waterfall in my owl form, brushing my wings through the falling water before sweeping out over the surface of the lake, and then flying back up and flipping upside down to dive back toward the water. I shift the second I hit the water.

After we've had our jumping fun, I remember the idea that I had when we were swimming in the ocean before we were attacked in the Everchanging Glades.

"Alexei, I want to try something. Meet me below."

He does as I ask, and I swim up to him and press my lips to his. I breathe into his mouth, and when I pull back, his eyes widen in surprise. I point to the surface, and he meets me there.

"Did it work?"

"Yeah. It felt like breathing above water, actually."

I smile broadly at him. "Perfect. Now you can come exploring with me underwater. I'll hold on to your hand, and just give me a squeeze whenever you need a breath."

We're able to explore underwater for about fifteen minutes. There isn't too much in this lake to look at beneath the surface, but it's good practice for us. It makes me want to bring him to the underwater community in Mermacovia.

After our fun and adventurous day, we teletravel back to our room, having tired ourselves out. When we get back, we're absolutely starving. Alexei tells me that he'll go grab us some food before he teletravels out. While he's doing that, I take a bath to wash off the lake water. I add lots of bubble bath and good-smelling stuff to get rid of the lake smell still clinging to me.

Alexei returns with a tray of food as I'm washing my hair, and the scent makes my mouth water. His eyes find me immediately, and his gaze heats when he discovers that I'm wet, naked, and covered in bubbles.

"I know that look, mister, and you are not getting any until I am fed."

His eyes light at the challenge. "Well, how about we eat in the bath, then?"

My brows rise at the idea. I don't think I've ever done that before. I rinse my hair quickly as he brings over a bath tray I didn't see earlier. He positions it across the tub before setting the food on top of it. I pour myself a glass of wine, but it almost overflows as my mate starts stripping in front of me. I'm still not used to the sight of his glorious body naked, and all mine.

He smirks, and I forget about the food for a moment when his pants come off. He's getting excited already by my attention, but he doesn't pay his body any mind as he climbs into the tub on the opposite side of me. I hand him the bottle of wine so he can pour himself a glass while I take the lid off the food. It smells good, but I'm slightly disappointed when I don't see any meat.

"Oh, by the way, elves are vegetarians."

I groan in frustration. Of course they are. What I find on the plate is eggplant parmesan, salad, and bread. At least there's a lot to eat, and it'll go well with the wine. And thank the Gods for the bread, 'cause I love me some carbs. I dig in. At first it's a little strange eating in the tub, but with the warm water relaxing me and the act of one of my favorite activities, eating, I get over it quickly.

Alexei jumps in with the same gusto, surprising me since he usually doesn't eat like I do, but I suppose since we're eating in the tub, manners have kind of gone out the window.

"I think I'm wearing off on you," I comment after I take a drink of my wine.

"What do you mean?"

"You rarely eat this quickly."

"You wore me out today. It's your fault."

"You'll be even more worn out in a bit." I wink at him.

"Promise?"

"Of course. I'm going to make you work for it tonight."

"I look forward to it, little doe."

I blush at the sex coating his words, and if possible, I start eating faster, wanting to get down to business. He chuckles, but follows my lead.

When we're finished eating, instead of getting out like I think we're going to, Alexei takes the tray off the tub and sets it on the floor next to us, and then yanks me into his lap a moment later. I gasp at his hardness pressing against me. In one move, he impales me on his length.

"I thought I said you were going to have to work for it tonight?" I reprimand, but the moan takes the sting out of it.

"I'll worship you after this. I need you too much right now." He grasps my hips and starts moving me up and down in his lap. Water sloshes around us, some spilling over the edge of the tub, but I don't give a shit, too lost in the pleasure rolling through my body.

His thumb presses against the bundle of nerves between my legs, making tingles shoot through me. We reach our peaks quickly with how fast we're moving.

"I want your blood coating my tongue," he growls against my throat as we build even higher.

"Yes," I moan, tilting my head to the side to give him access.

His fangs pierce my skin seconds later, and my pleasure breaks. I clench around my mate in time to the pulls of blood that leave my body. Alexei finds his release shortly after, and finally pulls his teeth free from my neck.

He seals the wound, and then picks me up in his arms. He steps out of the tub and I dry us with my air magic before he sets me on the bed.

He sticks to his word and thoroughly *worships* me for the duration of the night.

Training goes by quickly that week, and I am grasping everything really well. I practice on Alexei, and after I have that down, we move on to healing scar tissue, and more fatal injuries. I check his abdomen again to make sure that everything healed correctly after his fatal attack. He hasn't complained about it at all since I healed him, but now that I know what I'm doing, I want to make sure. I'm amazed to find that aside from a little bit of internal scar tissue, I did a damn good job. I guess having my mate's life hanging in the balance is an excellent motivator.

When we finish all of that, Serena teaches me how to make the tonics she was telling me about. While she still isn't *pleasant* exactly, I've actually come to really like her no-nonsense attitude, and I think she likes me as much as she's capable of as an elf.

She tells me we have only one day left of training, and then she won't have anything left to teach me. Excitement bubbles up inside of me. After this I'll have only one of my powers left to train. As fun and exciting as this whole experience has been, it will be a relief to head back to the castle. I miss Stavros and Pearl too.

Alexei and I spend our night exploring more. We've been doing this every day, and it's been a really special time for us. We've been discovering neat areas of the territory, as well as getting to know each other better and having some quality time to ourselves. We usually go in the afternoons, but training went a little later today, and I'm excited to see the territory at night.

We usually teletravel to the area where we left off the day before. We do the same thing tonight, and end up closer to Thunder Peak. I can see it through the trees, but there aren't many people out this way, and the forest we're in is extremely dark.

We start walking toward the edge of the forest, heading for the volcano. I told Alexei that I wanted to see it up close after finding out about its properties from Serena. Plus, she mentioned that she was needing more of the volcanic soil, so I wanted to bring some back to her for all of her help. Before we can get to the edge, however, I swear I hear something rustling in the trees.

"Alexei," I whisper. "Do you hear that?"

He nods, grabbing my hand and tugging me along as quietly as possible. I look to my right, thinking I see something, but there's nothing there. My breathing accelerates. Maybe this was a dumb idea, but at this point I've already told Serena I would get the soil for her. I clutch on to Alexei's hand, my heart beating so fast it's like it's going to pound out of my chest. The full moon is shining high above us, feeling like an omen, but it is shedding some light so we're able to see a little bit better.

Alexei squeezes my hand as we break through the trees. I breathe a sigh of relief as we do, hoping we just left whatever that was behind us. Alexei is doing the same thing, and we relax a bit as we get closer to the volcano. By the time we get to the base, I've chalked it up to there having been a harmless animal in the forest.

"Okay, I think this should be a good area to collect the soil," Alexei says.

I nod and take out the jar Serena gave me. I kneel down, scooping the dirt in. I notice it's darker than normal, almost black from the volcano. It smells different too, less earthy and more burnt.

Just as I'm scooping the last of the soil in the jar, I hear a howl close by. My skin erupts in goosebumps and I freeze. Is it the same thing we heard in the forest?

"You finish with that, I'll go over and check if whatever that is is close," Alexei tells me. I want to tell him no, but he knows what he's doing more than I do.

"Be careful."

He nods, teletraveling to the tree line, and my hands shake slightly as I screw the lid back on the jar. I shrink it, putting it back in my pocket just as I hear a growl coming from the trees, followed by a startled shout from Alexei. Without further thought or prompting, I teletravel to where I saw him last, trying not to flip the fuck out. I remind myself that he can handle himself.

I hear scuffling a little farther in and follow. All the feelings from before are back, heart pounding, goosebumps, hair standing on end. I hear a twig snap off to my right and it takes all I have in me not to jump three feet in the air. I hold my hands out, ready to blast them away with air if necessary.

I keep heading toward where I think Alexei is, shaking off the sensation of being chased. All that matters is getting to my mate.

For a brief moment, I think I'm about to have a vision, but I push it away. Now is *not* the time. I need to find Alexei and shake whatever the fuck is following me. I go faster, still hearing rustling behind me, but figuring Alexei and I can either deal with it together, or I will handle it on my own whenever I reach him. I just don't like not knowing if he's okay. We never should have separated.

Finally, I'm sure I'm getting closer. I can hear him just through the next set of trees. He comes into view and I have to hold back my terrified yell, not wanting to distract him. Alexei is fighting an abyss hound. I recognize it from when we saw one at the black market. I remember Alexei telling me that if they bite or scratch you, you need a team of elves to heal you basically immediately. I also remember that they are native to this territory. I had forgotten that. We've been doing so much exploring through Nylaluna that I got comfortable and didn't think to be on my guard. Rookie mistake.

Fortunately, my mate is strong and fast, and he's moving around its large green body with relative ease. I'm about to teletravel to him to help when I hear a growl come from my left, right before a blur shoots in front of me. Another abyss hound towers over me, howling threateningly. I pull my daggers free as it locks black eyes on me and opens its hideous mouth, its sharklike teeth dripping venom.

I ready myself, knowing Alexei is still fighting the other and can't help me right now. I throw a huge gust of wind at it, knocking it off balance before throwing my dagger, aiming for the neck. It lets out a blood-curdling screech as my knife connects with its shoulder instead, and I curse as I realize that instead of legitimately injuring it, I just pissed it off.

It roars in my face, its venomous spittle flying toward me. I throw up a blast of air just in time, and the ground sizzles when it lands. I fling fire at its face and it hisses and shrieks, backing away from me. At least I know it doesn't like fire. I bring more of my elements, surrounding it. With it trapped, I'm able to throw my other dagger. This time it hits true and embeds itself in its heart. I give myself a mental high-five as the wretched thing goes down. Alexei finishes his off at the same time, and I sigh in relief as I walk up to it and grab my daggers. I cringe upon seeing the black blood covering the blades.

Alexei smiles proudly at me, and I return it. We move closer to each other, getting ready to head back. Before we can disappear however, another abyss hound pops out of the trees to our left. I turn, daggers in hand, but it's too quick and its claws sink into my abdomen. I scream as its venom pierces my skin. It's ten times worse than the áspro vrykólakas. Alexei is already moving, roaring in outrage as he slices its head clean from its body. I collapse on the ground in a heap, curling in on myself. I try to heal myself like I've done with Serena so many times, but to no avail.

"Ember, are you okay?"

I can't answer him. All I can do is moan in pain.

"*Fuck.* Little doe, I need you to listen to me. We need to travel back to Serena. She and the other elves can fix this, but I need you to teletravel with me. I can't do it alone."

He squeezes my hand as he tries to pull me with him. I'm trying to follow, but I've never been in this much pain before.

"Come on, little doe. *Please.* It's almost too late." The sound of Alexei pleading with me finally breaks through just enough. I teletravel with everything I have left. I barely feel myself land before unconsciousness slips in.

19

Alexei

I thank whatever Gods are listening that Ember was able to teletravel. If she hadn't managed it, she would've died there, and I would've lost my mate. The thought alone makes my mate mark burn to high heaven. Although, it's felt like that since she was injured.

We land in Serena's quarters. Luckily, I find her right away. The longer Ember waits for the healers, the more danger she's in.

Serena sucks in a sharp breath as soon as she sees Ember. "Alexei, go to the hall and bring healers with you. As many as you can find."

I look down at my mate, literally not able to leave her. She's extremely pale and has blood pooling underneath her from the vicious slash to her abdomen.

"Alexei! *Now!*"

I go against every base nature that calls me to stay with her. I'm the only one who can travel fast enough. I teletravel to the hall just a minute away from the building. I yell at the ten or so people in here that there's been an emergency and they need to go to Serena's immediately. I stick around just long enough to see that they're following my orders, and I instantly teletravel back to Ember.

"They're coming," I tell her.

She nods but doesn't respond. She already has multiple jars out and has poured numerous things into the wound. I'm hoping something she has can at least slow the process of that venom. Even though the mess hall is only a minute away, it feels like it takes everyone days to arrive.

They finally all file in and gather around Ember without another word having been spoken. They all recognize abyss hound wounds, and each one finds a place to put their hands on her. My animal nature is really struggling to let them touch her, and I bite my own lip to keep the growl that's building from ripping free.

Minutes later, I finally start to see the wound stitch close. I breathe a sigh of relief and almost collapse from how strong it is. The venom pushes to the outside of the closing wound, and someone reaches over with a rag to gently wipe it off. The rag is then tossed into the fire, the venom making the flame spit. Her breathing, which had been very shallow before, deepens, as if she can take a full breath without pain. The mate mark on my arm finally stops burning, and that's when I know she's actually going to be okay.

I fall to the floor as tears build behind my eyes with the knowledge that she's going to make it. I vaguely notice the others leaving, until the only people who remain in the room are me, Ember, and Serena.

Serena continues to work, and I watch her, anxiously waiting for my mate to wake up. Ember looks so pale and helpless. I *hate* it. I'm the reason she was injured. Again. The guilt is eating me alive, and I worry that if she doesn't wake up, it will consume me.

Serena seems to know where my thoughts are headed. "She might take a day or two to become conscious. That's normal. You just need to be patient. I'm fairly positive that we were able to get to her in time."

I want to snap at her that "fairly positive" is not the outlook I'm wanting or needing right now, but just as I open my mouth, Ember abruptly sits up, her eyes popping open, black and unfocused. She's not herself, and she snarls at us. When her mouth opens, I can see that fangs have descended, and immediately know what's happening. I didn't expect this since she has such a small amount of vampire genetics, but apparently it's enough when she's been injured like this and lost so much blood.

"It's okay, little doe. You can feed from me," I tell her soothingly. I know she's too far gone to register what I'm telling her, but I try to comfort her all the same.

I pull her into my lap and direct her mouth to my neck. She needs no further prompting, and her fangs pierce my skin. She's not conscious enough to make it painless, and I bite back a hiss. I've never been bitten by another vampire before, and although it's painful, I'm ecstatic that it's my mate, even though the circumstances are horrid.

She drinks and drinks from me, and I let her, giving her everything she needs. Serena looks concerned, but doesn't stop her.

When she's finally taken enough, she collapses in my arms, unconscious once more. I gently set her where she was lying before, covering her with a blanket Serena brought over.

"You need a blood replenishing potion. She took way too much from you," she reprimands.

"I'll be fine," I argue, standing. I wobble slightly, and my foot is immediately lodged in my mouth.

"Sit down." She pushes me back down and forces something into my hand. "Drink all of this. That's an order." She also heals the somewhat savage bite on my neck for me.

I begrudgingly obey. The potion tastes vile, but I swallow it all the same. Within moments, the lightheadedness passes, and I admit to myself that Serena knows best. I don't tell her though.

She comes to check that I followed her orders, and then leaves Ember and me alone on the floor of her living room. I lie down next to her, pulling her close to me and listening to the sound of her steady breathing. My heart rate calms for the first time since we heard that howl, and I fall asleep within minutes.

Sometime later, I'm woken by Serena checking on my mate. I raise my eyebrows at her in question.

"Everything looks good. The wound is healed, but I need to give her a potion to cleanse anything out that we weren't able to get. Hold her mouth open for me."

I do as she instructs, and Serena pours a tiny vial of the brightest silver liquid between her open lips. She then holds her palm over her throat, her magic coaxing Ember to swallow.

"I need to monitor her for the next few hours, but after that I think you'll be able to bring her to the guest house if you'd like. For now would you like to move her to my spare room?" By the look in her eyes, I can tell that she knows what Ember and I are to each other, but neither of us comment on it. There are more important things to worry about than Serena knowing our secret.

I nod, picking my mate up in my arms. When she's like this, she feels so fragile, even though she's the fiercest person I've ever met. Serena leads me to a room one floor up; it's plain, but it has everything we need for the moment. I set Ember down gently on the bed, climbing in next to her. After what we experienced, I have no desire to be parted from her.

Ember continues to sleep, but I'm fully awake, seeing the attack replay over and over in my head. It slowly drives me insane, but at the moment there's nothing I can do. Serena comes in a few times to check on her, but leaves shortly after. I just wish she would wake up. Despite Serena's reassurances that she should be fine, my anxiety is increasing with every moment she stays asleep.

After a few more hours, Serena declares she's doing well enough that I can take her back to our quarters. "It usually takes a day or two for victims of the abyss hounds to wake. Even though their bodies have been healed by us, it's a traumatic experience, and they take time to recover on their own. Just be patient. She'll come around eventually."

I know her words should calm me, but they don't. I'm still worried she'll take a turn for the worse, and I'll lose her.

Serena must sense my distress. "Alexei, if she were going to die, it would've happened already. The fact that I'm letting you leave my sight means that I have every confidence she will be her normal, feisty self in the next couple of days. Now leave. I'm tired, and I would like to rest."

The smallest amount of relief finally trickles into me, and I nod. Before I forget, I reach into Ember's pocket, taking out the soil she had stashed there. Somehow, with everything that happened, it's miraculously still intact. I reverse the shrinking spell, and hand Serena the full jar of volcanic soil Ember promised her.

"Even with all that, she still managed to bring this?"

I smile sadly at her. "Yes. She was quite determined."

She has the closest thing to a fond look on her face an elf can have as she glances down at Ember. "Well." She clears her throat, the moment over. "I'll come and check on her in the morning. Now, go and get some sleep. And don't worry. She'll be fine."

I pick my mate up and walk us back to our quarters. I wish I could just teletravel us there. Now that my panic is abating, I'm exhausted. I set her down on the bed, stripping her filthy clothes before grabbing a rag and a bowl of warm water. I tenderly wipe her down, not wanting her to wake up covered in blood and dirt. The bowl of water is filthy minutes later, and I swap it out with fresh water.

When I've cleaned her whole body, I dress her in the warmest, most comfortable clothes I can find, including one of my shirts. I tell myself that she will be comforted by the smell, but in reality, I just want her to wear my clothing. I tuck her in, and quickly wash myself before crawling into bed with her.

I listen to her steady heartbeat and even breathing, the sounds lulling me to sleep.

20

Ember

The first thing I'm aware of is that I'm lying on something soft, and am extremely comfortable. I stretch and moan, and I can tell I'm well rested. With my arms overhead there's a slight twinge in my belly, but I can't figure out why I feel the discomfort.

When I finally get around to opening my eyes, I see that Alexei is wrapped around me like a vine. His brow is furrowed like he's in pain, and his breathing is accelerated. I swipe my thumb up his third eye, attempting to help him relax.

"Everything's okay, Alexei. I'm here," I murmur softly to him.

Hearing my voice seems to soothe him, and then his eyes open and our gazes lock. Tears build and start rolling down his cheeks as we stare at each other, and I don't know why.

"What's wrong, my love?" I ask him.

"Oh, Ember. I was so scared I was going to lose you, little doe."

"Lose me?"

"Do you not remember? The abyss hound attack by Thunder Peak?"

I close my eyes, searching for the memory. I vaguely sense what he's talking about, and my hand makes its way to my belly. His own covers mine and squeezes as if in confirmation.

Alexei tells me exactly what happened, and things slowly start to come back. I don't remember anything after the searing pain in my abdomen though; not Alexei killing it, not teletraveling back to Nylaluna, not biting Alexei in my desperation for blood, nothing.

I'm horrified when he tells me I basically ripped into his neck with my new fangs. Not that he said it like that, but I hate the thought that I hurt him how those vampires in the caves hurt me. I tongue my new elongated teeth, marveling at how they appeared when I needed them.

"Serena is coming to check on you soon, and then you might want to take a bath. I washed you last night, but I wasn't able to clean your hair, and I don't know how well I was able to get your back."

I look at the bath longingly, wishing I could hop in now. I don't want Serena to walk in on me naked either. Enough of the kingdom has seen me without clothes. My stomach growls loudly, and I realize just how hungry I am.

Alexei smiles at me. "I'll go get us something to eat and tell Serena you're awake." He kisses me and then disappears.

I lift my shirt up so I can look at my stomach. The wound is healed, but there's still a scar. I wonder if because of the severity, they weren't able to get rid of it. Maybe eventually. I'll have to ask Serena.

Alexei appears with food a few minutes later and tells me that Serena is on her way up. I scarf the food, hungrier than normal. Serena comes up just as I'm finishing. She checks me over quickly, telling me that I need to rest here for a few days, and then I should be able to leave.

I'm grateful and ready to move on to Wickshire. I have a sense something is waiting for me there. What exactly, I'm not sure, but I feel it in my witchy bones.

Alexei and I spend the next two days relaxing in bed. He gives me massages and gets me all the food I could want. He's coddling me, and I'm not complaining about it. Except when I go to be intimate with him, and he gently tells me that he's worried my body isn't ready for that yet. I pout and sulk, knowing I'm being childish, but the rejection stings, and brings back memories from when we couldn't be together.

He tries to console me, but I tell him to stay here and that I need to finish my training with Serena. I don't know if she'll let me, but I need to get out of the guest house. He nods sadly, and lets me go.

I teletravel directly to Serena's quarters. She isn't expecting me and startles when I appear, dropping a jar. It shatters at her feet and I curse softly.

"Sorry, Serena," I tell her as I repair the jar with a spell I learned in the Immortal City.

"Ember. I wasn't expecting you." She regains her composure quickly. "What can I help you with?"

"I'm much better today. I was hoping to finish our training? I know there were just a few more tonics you needed to teach me to make."

She narrows her eyes at me and comes to stand in front of me. She examines my eyes and does a sweep over my body with her hand. She gives a single nod.

"Yes. You are well enough now. We will finish your training today, and you will be able to leave tomorrow."

"Serena, before we start I have a question for you."

She waits expectantly, eyebrows raised in my direction.

I blush, embarrassed, but I plow through it. "I wanted to ask if my body is healed enough for, uh...physical activities?"

She doesn't even look fazed. "More intense activities like combat training should be done slowly, and make sure to pay special attention to how your body reacts. Sexual activities are fine as well, but same thing, just take it slow to make sure everything is back to normal."

"Okay. Thank you. I also wanted to tell you that I know you're aware of my relationship with Alexei. We haven't gotten the chance to tell my father yet, and I was hoping you'd be willing to keep that information to yourself. I just don't want the king hearing about it from someone else."

"I understand. I know how to be discreet, Princess." Even though her tone is as stern as ever, there's a twinkle in her eye. "Now, let's get started."

We spend the rest of the day concocting different remedies, and I make sure to write everything down for reference. I delight in the fact that I'll be able to put these together on my own, and even though we don't have the ingredients in the Immortal City, Serena is sending me home with some for right now, and if I need more, it won't be hard to teletravel here.

We finish for the day, and Serena has officially declared that I'm fully trained, healed (with the exception of my scar, which Serena tells me I'll always have), and ready to move on. I tell her Alexei and I will leave first thing in the morning so I can get a good night's rest before our travels.

"It was a pleasure working with you, Princess." It's the most sincere and kind I've ever heard her, and I smile warmly at her.

"Thank you, Serena. I've learned so much from you. I don't know how I can ever repay you. Especially after you saved my life."

"I'm sure I'll think of something you can do for me in the future," she says seriously.

I laugh as I touch her gently on the shoulder. I know she won't be one for hugs. "You got it. Write to me if you ever need anything."

I teletravel back to our room and find Alexei pacing anxiously when I return. He comes up and kisses me softly and pulls back before I'm ready. I'm tired of him treating me like I'm made of glass.

"How did it go?"

"I'm all done with training. She also said that sexual activity was perfectly acceptable as long as everything feels normal." I try not to sound too smug, but I don't think I succeed. It's difficult not to gloat when we women know better and the men who didn't believe us are proven wrong.

"Oh, did she now?" Alexei prowls toward me like the predator he is, and my heart rate increases in excitement and a pinch of adrenaline.

I nod as I back up with every step he takes. When the backs of my legs hit the bed, and I have nowhere to go, he crowds my space. I expect him to kiss me, but instead, he grips my hair and tilts my head to the side, exposing my neck. He runs his nose along it, and my body clenches in anticipation. I want him to sink his fangs into me as he slides into my cunt.

He growls against my skin, and I wonder if he's going to give in and give us what we both want. Instead, he places a gentle kiss against my pounding pulse.

"Alexei, please."

He chuckles darkly as he spins me faster than I'm able to anticipate. In the next breath, he's pushing my torso so I'm bent over, my hands resting on the bed. My pants are yanked down next, and I'm incredibly exposed to him. My breathing accelerates as I wait to see what he's going to do next. His palm strokes my backside, and I push myself into his hand. He chuckles at my eagerness, and before I know what's happening, his touch disappears, and then a stinging slap heats my backside, making me suck in a sharp breath.

I wasn't expecting that, but wetness gathers even more between my legs. Apparently my body likes it. His tongue licks clean through my center, and I moan at the first touch. He takes his time, exploring me thoroughly, building me up slowly and painfully. We've never gone this slow before, and I know he's still being careful with me, but I can't say I hate the change of pace. I kind of like being driven out of my mind with pleasure.

His hands touch any part of my body they can reach, my ass, my breasts, my legs. He leaves no area out, and I'm thoroughly sensitized, my skin buzzing with all the attention. When I'm completely incoherent with need, he plunges his fingers inside of me, sinking his fangs into my ass cheek at the same time. I explode around him, sobbing with my release, which goes on and on with every pull of my blood from his mouth.

He finally removes his teeth, sealing my wound as he goes. Before I'm fully recovered, he spins me again and pushes me down on the bed, grabbing my legs and spreading them wide. I don't know when he took his clothes off, but he's gloriously naked, standing at the edge of the bed like a Greek god. He positions himself at my entrance and sinks into me with exquisite languidness. I gasp at the fullness and try to move my hips to increase the pace, but his hands still me.

"Patience, little doe."

I growl at him. I don't want slow anymore. I try to rip my legs out of his grasp so I can wrap them around his body and control his movements, but he holds firm, smirking. He's toying with me. Fine. Two can play this game. I reach up and tweak my nipples, giving him a show as I clench around him. The smirk disappears immediately, and he groans as he tracks my hands with his eyes.

"You don't play fair," he complains as he thrusts forward a little harder and faster than before.

I smile in triumph. "Neither do you." I pinch my buds tightly in both hands, hissing through my teeth at the pleasure that shoots through me.

Alexei growls as he roughly grabs my hands and pins them above my head, freeing my legs from his grasp. I immediately take advantage and wrap them around his waist, squeezing tightly and forcing him deeply inside of me. We both groan, and I know I've got him. He starts moving in earnest then, and even though I just came minutes ago, I'm building already.

He brings his mouth to mine, and we lose ourselves in a savage kiss. I'm not used to my new fangs yet and they nick his lip. I can taste his blood in my mouth, and I suck greedily on the cut. I pull back, meeting his gaze.

"I want to feed from you," I tell him, more heat building between my legs just thinking about it.

My words cause him to shiver, and he hardens further inside me as he thrusts deeper. He nods, bringing his hand under my head to support me and guides it to his neck.

"How do I make it good for you?" I whisper against his skin, kissing his racing pulse.

"Just pour all of the pleasure from my blood back into me."

Sounds simple enough, especially when we're in the height of ecstasy. I slide my fangs into his vein as gently as I can, and as soon as the euphoria from his blood hits me, I ricochet it back to him. I know I'm doing it right when he moans above me, clutching my head tighter against him.

"Ember, I'm going to come. I can't stop it. Follow me. Come for me."

With one more thrust and one more pull from my mouth, we both explode. He fills me in more ways than one, and I delight in having all of his essence in me. I pull back and tell my brain I need to seal the bite. When I go to lick it, it heals automatically, and I'm proud that I didn't need anyone to teach me that. We collapse onto the bed, breathing heavy.

"I never knew a bite could feel like that. I mean, technically I *did* know, but I've never experienced that before."

"I know. It's intense."

We lie there in silence for a while before he breaks it. "So we're leaving tomorrow?"

"Yes. Wickshire here we come."

"This is going to be the biggest jump you've ever done. I, myself, have only made a jump that big twice. It was a big stretch, but I think we'll be able to manage it. Just be prepared for the exhaustion. We're probably going to need to rest all day tomorrow and put off training for a day until we recover."

"Oh, we'll need to *rest*, huh?" I ask suggestively, trailing my fingernail down his chest.

"Behave," he growls at me, making me laugh.

I keep my hands relatively to myself for the duration of the night, so that we are in fact well rested enough to make the insanely large jump.

The next morning, I dress in my warmest set of clothes, the gray wool dress I bought in the Immortal City along with the fur cloak. It's way too warm for where we currently are, but based on what Alexei has told me, I know I'll be glad I put it on when we get there.

When it's time to say our goodbyes, I'm a tad more emotional than I thought I would be. Definitely not as much as when we left the Everchanging Glades, but I wasn't expecting to make significant connections here.

Serena goes to grasp my forearm, but I pull her in for a hug instead. She tenses, but relaxes into my embrace a moment later, patting my back somewhat awkwardly.

"Thank you so much for everything, Serena. And please write to me if you need anything at all."

"You as well, Your Highness. It was an honor."

A crowd has gathered to watch us depart, and Serena addresses them all. "Bow to the Princess of Queridian," she says loudly.

I'm overcome with emotion as they all dip low, offering me respect they somehow feel I deserve. I hold my hand to my heart upon seeing it. I never expected the residents of this realm to welcome me so openly, especially the elves, who don't seem to like anybody. I'm moved beyond words. I reach over and squeeze Serena's hand as she rises, trying to convey my appreciation and respect. She smiles softly at me, receiving the message loud and clear.

"Serena, a pleasure as always," Alexei says in his charming voice.

She narrows her eyes at him, but there's a slight lift to her lips, and I know that she secretly enjoys his teasing.

I grab Alexei's hand, and he tugs me with him, and the elves and their forest fades. This time is different. I'm pulled taut, stretching myself thin. I would scream if I could. Just when I think I'm going to snap in half, we materialize.

21

Ember

My body doesn't quite know how to handle the extreme temperature difference, but my attention is too fixed on our surroundings to notice. We're at the very entrance to Black Moon City, and the most imposing figure sits at the gate, looming over us. She's glorious and intimidating all at once. She's built out of the ice itself, and is easily the size of a four-story building. She stands there, judging us as we pass, a knowing look on her face.

"That's their goddess, Revena. They say those with ill intent are unable to pass through the gates because she watches over it," Alexei tells me as we step over the threshold. I guess we passed her test because we enter with no issues.

The landscape before me is an icy wonderland. There are jagged mountains in the distance that are completely frozen and look beautiful and treacherous all at once. In the immediate area, there are cabins in the square, smoke pouring from all of them. I'm sure they have to have fires going constantly in order to stay warm.

A woman comes into the main courtyard from one of the cabins. Her features are similar to Penelope's, but she doesn't look as withered or tired. I wonder if that's because Penelope wasn't among her people or the magic of her land. She appraises us, her ice blue eyes not missing a single thing.

"We've been expecting you, Your Highness."

Surprise makes my heart stutter for a moment, although I don't know why I didn't expect this. They are witches after all. I'm sure they saw us coming.

"I am Raven, the Grand Mistress of Wickshire, and it will be my honor to train you. Although, most of your time here will be spent in a way you will not expect."

Well, that sounds cryptic as fuck. My heart starts beating a little faster with anxiety, and Alexei squeezes my hand in support and comfort, no doubt hearing my reaction with his vampire senses.

"I know you are weary from your travels. We will start your training tomorrow. For now, let me show you to your quarters."

I follow her, dazed. Alexei and I still haven't said a single word, but it seems unnecessary at this point. I also want to be out of the cold as quickly as possible.

She leads us to a cozy-looking cottage, similar to the others, but on the outer edges of the town. There's smoke already billowing from the chimney, and at the moment, I'm grateful she knew we were coming.

"Thank you, Raven. I look forward to working with you," I tell her, speaking for the first time. It's then that I realize how exhausted I am. And hungry. My stomach takes that moment to growl.

She chuckles, the snow pale skin of her friendly face crinkling as she does so, even as her unnerving eyes zero in on me. "You too, Princess. I'll have some food brought for you this time around, but typically we all dine together in the main hall. It would be good for you both to join us. You can get to know the others here during your short visit."

I smile gratefully at her. That's a wonderful idea, and I wish I could have done that in the other territories. I mean, I had gotten to know a few people here and there, but dining with a large group of people is the perfect opportunity.

"We look forward to it. Thank you, Grand Mistress."

"Just call me Raven." She smiles kindly at us and leaves.

Food arrives shortly after, and we scarf it down. As soon as we're finished, we pass out for the rest of the day.

When we wake, I'm shocked to realize that it's the next day. We slept for just short of twenty-four hours. We spend a little longer in bed, having a special kind of fun with each other before we venture out in search of food.

The main hall is located in the middle of the square, and it seems like everyone is congregating there for breakfast. I was too tired yesterday to actually register what we were eating, and I'm interested to see what type of food they have here.

We walk into the main hall and it immediately reminds me of a cafeteria. There's a long table set up on one side with loads of food covering it, a roaring fire on the other side that heats up the entire room, and then smaller tables situated throughout the rest of the room.

We get in line, and when it's our turn, we load our plates up with potatoes and cheese, sausage, and eggs. I grab myself some tea, and we park our asses right in front of the fire, the warmest place here. I still haven't warmed up.

A lot of curious looks are thrown our way, and I have to wonder if we actually will end up meeting any of the citizens here, or if they're just going to gawk at us for every meal. As soon as the thought crosses my mind, a couple about our age comes up to our table.

"Hello. I'm Esmeralda, Mera for short, and this is Jinx. Would you mind if we sat with you?" the woman, Mera, asks. She's gorgeous, with light skin, honey eyes, and smooth, long, white hair.

"Please," Alexei says, gesturing to the open chairs.

I smile warmly at them. It's kind of them to include us. The man,

Jinx, returns it. His skin is slightly darker than hers, and he has green eyes that seem to see everything, and shaggy blond hair. I can't help but think that everyone here looks like they belong in the Malfoy family, and I inwardly chuckle.

"I'm Ember and this is Alexei."

"We know who you are, Your Highness," Jinx remarks teasingly, but not disrespectfully.

"Ember is fine," I tell them. If I'm going to make friends with them, I don't want them addressing me so formally.

"So, are you enjoying your time here so far?" Mera asks.

"Well, we haven't explored at all. We were so tired from traveling that we slept all day yesterday. I'm also *freezing*."

She laughs. "You'll get used to it soon. It looks like you brought sensible clothing with you, at least."

"I don't know if I'll ever be able to get used to it."

"You better if you end up going to Familiar Forest," Jinx chimes in.

"What's that?" Alexei asks. I'm surprised he doesn't know of it.

"You'll only know about it if you get a vision." Mera glares at Jinx as if he's said something he shouldn't. I open my mouth, but Mera cuts that glare to me. "Don't ask. We can't tell you anything. He shouldn't have even said anything."

I nod, relenting, even though my curiosity is piqued. We continue chatting and eating. We all actually really get along, and it's fun to meet another couple who we could potentially spend more time with. Yes, they're in another territory, but with us being able to teletravel, that won't be an issue.

Mera volunteers to show me around after breakfast, and Jinx tells Alexei that he needs to see their training yard. Of course, after he hears that, that's all he's interested in. The four of us go there together, and Alexei and I marvel at their facility. It's as large as the one at the palace, but the floor is coated with ice. They also have blindfolds on the tables, and I assume that because they have the gift of premonition, they know when they're going to get attacked, so the blindfolds help them hone that ability.

Alexei asks about it, and Jinx confirms my theory. Then they start talking about different training methods, and Mera and I give each other a bored look.

"Care to see more and leave these two?"

I nod eagerly, wanting to explore. We take off, leaving the guys to it. We wander around and she shows me the living quarters, the temple honoring Revena, and the building they have for scrying and channeling visions, which she calls the House of Intuition.

It's that building that I'm most interested in, and when I run into Raven there, she informs me that she'll show me around before we start my training. Mera waves as she leaves me with the grand mistress, and I thank her for the tour.

Raven guides me to the vision room first. It's essentially a sensory deprivation room, completely dark, no sound, and the only things in here are meditation pillows on the ground.

"We receive visions easiest when there are no distractions around us. This room is used to hone our concentration. That is the only thing you can do to trigger a vision on your own. Occasionally an object or location will also cause them, but those are random, and most of the time we have no way of knowing when that will happen. But when we come here, clear our minds, and focus inside, the visions will come more naturally. The most important thing to remember is not to force anything. If something comes to you, let it happen naturally, and without pressure."

The next room she leads me to is for scrying. There are apparently many different ways to tell the future, and all of these tools will help me. I see the bones that Penelope used with my mother, along with candles and bowls, mirrors and crystal balls, cards, semiprecious stones hanging from chains, and much more. Raven also informs me that they have a courtyard designated for divinations that need to be done outside, like fire or star gazing.

"Before I train you on any of this though, you need to visit Vision Lake."

"Why?"

"Every witch goes to Vision Lake when her powers awaken. It's tradition to go there before any sort of training because it will give us a better idea of how powerful you will be and what type of training you should receive. All witches get visions, but since there are so many different types of scrying, each witch has different modalities that they are more prone to and feel more of a pull toward. This will give us those answers. Among other things."

The "among other things" comment has me intrigued, but I figure I'll find out soon enough.

We leave the building, and Raven points out far into the distance. "Vision Lake is about fifty miles northeast of where we are now. Normally I would need to take you, but since you have the ability to teletravel, I can show you a picture, and it will be much quicker for all of us. All you need to do once you get there is to sit on the frozen lake in the center, and touch the pointer finger of your right hand to your third eye. Visions will come to you. When you return, you'll be able to vision-share with me, and we can figure out where to go from there."

"Vision-share?" I ask. I've never heard that term before.

"Witches have the ability to share what they *see* with fellow witches through touch. I can show you how to do that when you return. It's very useful when you need another opinion on something you *saw*."

That does sound handy. I wonder if Penelope knows about it, and I look forward to discussing it with her.

"Can I bring Alexei with me?"

She looks at me thoughtfully for a moment. "Normally, I would say no, but since you're going to teletravel there and won't be able to have one of us with you, I think that would be fine. Just make sure he knows he can not disturb you while you're there. That is *essential*."

"Understood. I will go let him know."

She shows me a picture of Vision Lake before I leave, telling me Alexei and I should travel there immediately. I teletravel to our quarters and change into a set of training clothes, figuring it will be more practical. I also strap my daggers on, just in case. If there's anything I've learned in Queridian, it's to never be unprepared, which makes me feel like a Boy Scout.

I find Alexei still in the training yard with Jinx. I smile to myself that he made himself a new little boyfriend. Jinx is demonstrating the use of the blindfolds and the ice, and Alexei is *riveted*.

"Alexei, I'm sorry to interrupt, but I need you for something."

He looks toward me, concern lining his features. "What is it?"

"Everything is fine, but before I can begin training, we need to make a little trip to Vision Lake."

Out of the corner of my eye, I see Jinx smirk to himself. I wonder what's in store for me there. Everyone's reactions are making me a little nervous. I ignore him for now and concentrate on what Alexei and I have to do.

"Raven wants us to go now. Are you ready?"

His brows rise in surprise. "Yes. Do you know where we're going?"

I hold out my hand to him in answer. I picture the image of the lake in my head and pull Alexei along with me. It's easy since our destination is much closer than any place we've gone recently. We jump right to the edge of the lake. The landscape is harsh and open, with the exception of the frozen mountains to the north of us. The wind slaps us hard with nothing to block it, and it's so overcast that not even the sun can warm us.

"What do you need to do?" Alexei rests his hand on my lower back.

"Raven just said I need to walk to the middle of the lake and sit, and the visions would come to me. You should stay here. And she said it's extremely important for you to stay silent. I can't be distracted in the least."

"I'll be here keeping watch."

I kiss him in gratitude and take a deep breath attempting to calm my nerves. When I'm ready, I walk out onto the ice. My third eye is already burning, waiting for me to be ready to receive the visions. I resist the urge to touch it, knowing I need to wait until the right time.

The lake is fairly large, and it takes me a few minutes to reach the center. I was worried I wouldn't know where exactly the middle was, but I know the second my feet touch it. I carefully sink down and sit my ass down on the ice. Despite the fact that I'm on something that's supposed to be cold, when my body connects with it, a slow heat spreads. I don't worry that the ice will melt because it's only an energetic warmth.

When I'm settled and ready, I bring my finger to my face and press it to my third eye just as Raven instructed. I can feel myself gasp even as I'm sucked into the most intense visions I've ever experienced, even more than the ones I had in my mother's room.

I see the mountains here, and I'm alone at the base, with a pack on my back. Determination lines every feature of my face and I press forward. I climb. Up, up, and up I go. In the conscious part of my brain, I wonder why I don't just teletravel. It takes me all day to get over the mountain and onto the other side. When I reach it, I come to a forest filled with dead trees. I stop in the middle, an opening in between the trees. Before I can see what I'm doing there, I'm sucked away into another vision.

I see myself back in the House of Intuition, using the same bones Penelope had, staring into a fire, and gazing up at the stars. These must be the modalities that I will do best with.

I figure that's going to be all I see, but for a moment, there's a dark presence with me. I immediately think of "the dark ones" that Zenobia talked about, but instead of multiple, there's only one. I think it's female, but I'm not positive. I can't see clearly, but catch glimpses of black hair, red eyes, horns, and arms as dark as night that fade into white.

"Who are you?" I ask into the void.

"I'm you..." a whisper floats back as a shiver racks my body.

I'm thrown back into reality, cold penetrating every inch of me, and I know it's not just from sitting on the ice. I stand, slightly woozy, and make my way to Alexei. By the time I arrive, I'm trembling all over.

"Ember? Are you okay, little doe?"

"I sensed a dark presence. She said she was me," I whisper to him, needing to get it out, but also terrified of voicing it.

His face scrunches up in confusion. "That's not possible, Ember. You're the furthest thing from dark. You are my light. You are this kingdom's light."

I nod, not quite believing him after that, but needing to.

"Let's get you back to our quarters. You need to warm up." He pulls me with him, and we're in our rooms.

He wraps a blanket around me and runs the bath while I start the fire with a flick of my fingers. I sigh as the heat slowly pushes away the relentless cold. I could never live here. I don't mind cooler weather, but this is miserable.

Alexei guides me over to the bath and undresses me and himself. Then we're both in the bath and he's wrapping his arms around me. My body finally relaxes and heats under his attention.

"What else did you see?" he asks, no doubt trying to distract me.

I tell him about the little trip I'm going to take and the types of scrying I think I'll be doing.

"You were alone?"

I knew this was coming. "Yes."

"I don't like that."

"I know. I don't either. But we don't even know what it is or why yet. Let's talk to Raven first, and see what she has to say."

He sighs dramatically, but nods all the same. When we're thoroughly warmed through, we get out, dress in the same clothes, and find Raven.

She's in the mess hall with almost everyone else, and I realize that it must be lunchtime. We both load our plates with potatoes, carrots, beets, bread, and more sausage. Their food reminds me of Russian cuisine, which would make sense with the cold climate.

We sit next to Raven, who's talking to a man who appears to be in his fourth decade, but I know he must be much older.

"Your Highness, welcome back. How did it go?" Raven asks, turning to me.

I eye the man, not wanting to give her details in front of him. "Fine. I'm curious to hear what you think about what I *saw*."

I can tell she notices that I don't elaborate. I have no idea if I can prevent her from seeing parts of the vision, and I'm hoping I can because I don't want her to see the dark presence at the end. It feels like a secret, and one I don't want to share with anyone besides Alexei and my father.

Her eyes assess me and seem to see through me, but she only nods. "The three of us will go to the House of Intuition after our meal and discuss it."

I smile gratefully at her. I make myself eat, even though my stomach is churning. All I can hear is "I'm you..." over and over in my head, those red eyes burned into my brain.

Alexei notices my uneasiness and takes over talking, rubbing soothing circles on my low back. After what seems like forever, we stand and make our way to the House of Intuition.

"So, to vision-share, all you need to do is grasp my right forearm with yours, and then concentrate on what you saw while you touch the thumb of your left hand to my third eye."

I grab her forearm and take a deep breath, focusing on the visions. From the sounds of it, I should be able to concentrate on showing her just what I want to and not let my mind slip to the last vision I had. Easier said than done.

I touch my thumb to the space between her eyebrows, and she sucks into a sharp breath as she's pulled into what I *saw*. I show her my trek up the mountain, the forest, and the magic I learn from her before I pull back, breaking our connection before my mind automatically goes to what it saw next.

When the glazed look in her eyes clears, she smiles at me. "I see you *saw* Familiar Forest."

My eyes widen. I didn't think I would hear more about that after Jinx mentioned it this morning and got chastised. I don't want to get anyone in trouble for saying something they shouldn't have, so I just wait for her to continue.

"Not everyone *sees* Familiar Forest. It is very special, and a great honor that's been bestowed upon you."

"What is it?" I ask impatiently. I've hardly been here any time, and I'm already sick of the witches' cryptic bullshit.

"You are destined to have a familiar."

I guess I shouldn't be surprised by that, considering the name, but I am. A familiar? I wonder if it's the same thing I'm thinking. "Like an animal that I'm bonded to?"

"Yes. Although, they're more than an animal. They're past spirits of our world that have come back to help and guide us on our paths. We have a tradition here. You go to Vision Lake, and if you see yourself going to Familiar Forest that's a sign that your familiar is calling to you."

"Why didn't I see myself meeting them?"

"You never know what they are until they present themselves to you in person."

"I take it from my vision that I can't teletravel there?"

"No. There are wards around it that prevent that sort of thing. You must test your mettle and *earn* your familiar. Now, once you get there, your familiar will bond to you, a mark will appear on your body, and they will fade into your skin, with you at all times. If you ever want them physically present, you only need to call on them. That being said, the wards that prevent you from teletraveling *into* the forest will not prevent you from teletraveling *out*."

I take all that in. So, I only need to get there and bond with my familiar and then I can come straight back. "How long does it take to get there?"

"Usually it's a three-day trip for witches, there and back, but seeing as you can teletravel to the base of the mountains—the White Heights—and then back afterward, it should only take you about a day, I would imagine."

"I didn't see Alexei come with me in the vision."

"That's right. You are the only one who can go on this journey. It's the same reason that you cannot teletravel there. You need to prove your worth to your familiar. On your own."

"I don't like it," Alexei finally speaks up next to me. "I can't protect you if I'm not with you. And we don't know how dangerous this trip is going to be."

"Alexei, you taught me well. I'll be fine. She's waiting for me. I need to find her."

I don't know how I know my familiar is female, I just do. And now that I know everything, I'm itching to go find her. It's a pull I can't and won't deny.

He growls softly under his breath, his frustration and protective nature getting the better of him. I know this won't be easy on him. He'll likely spend the whole day pacing, waiting for me to return.

"The land will guide her," Raven speaks up next to me, laying a comforting hand on his arm. "Her premonition powers will be severely heightened on the mountain. Besides the lake, that's the area where our powers are strongest. She will know if trouble is coming for her in plenty of time. But rarely do witches come across danger on their journey."

He seems to relax just a fraction. "I still don't like it."

"Neither do I. But I need to find her, Alexei. I don't have a choice."

He gives me a resigned sigh. "Fine. But wait 'til tomorrow. I want you to travel while it's light as much as possible."

"Deal." I smile at him, even though my heart is pulling me to go immediately. I know he's right and that's the smart decision. Besides, then I can get a good night's rest and have a filling breakfast before I go.

We spend the rest of the day together, and I try to calm his fears as much as I can. Raven lets us take our dinner in our rooms under the circumstances, and I'm grateful. It's been quite the day, and I don't want to be around anyone besides my mate.

We go to bed early. Not only am I exhausted from the events of the day, but I also need to make sure I'm well rested for my trip tomorrow. Still, even as I lie there drifting off, I see red eyes and hear the words "I'm you…" echo in my thoughts.

I wake early as my familiar calls me to her, more insistent than yesterday. She's as impatient as I am. That could be a dangerous combination. Alexei is still asleep, but I quietly get up and pack a bag full of anything I think I might need. I'll also need to grab snacks in the mess hall, but I fill it with warm clothes and a full water bottle for now. I take a warm bath, getting my blood as hot as I can before I leave and am in the freezing elements for a day.

Alexei wakes while I'm bathing, and he thoroughly distracts me, no doubt trying to get me to stay. I let him for a while, but when I can no longer ignore the call in my blood, I make my way to the mess hall. I fill my plate to the brim in preparation for my day, also grabbing things to snack on for later.

When I'm all packed, fed, and ready, I kiss Alexei and take a deep breath as I teletravel to the base of the White Heights. The frozen mountains seem so much larger and intimidating this close, but like I saw in my vision, I'm determined. I lift my foot and begin the long journey to the other side.

It's a hard climb. The ice makes it difficult to traverse, but Raven gave me some special shoes. I have to take breaks more frequently than I normally would have because of the freezing air, but my fire magic keeps me warm.

I realize that I have an extreme advantage over the other witches who make this trip. I'm able to teletravel for one, so I don't have nearly as long of a journey. I also am able to keep myself warmer with my elemental magic. I keep that in mind when I feel myself lagging and wishing for a fire and a bath.

Fleurie serenades me in my head about how soldiers keep on marching on, spurring me on. It's like the theme song of my journey, and I sing along with her when I get bored.

Halfway up the mountain, I get a vision of a bear wandering into this area. It looks hungry, and with all the food in my pack, I don't want to draw its attention to me. I hide behind a rocky section that overlooks where the bear will be coming into view. I wait for it, and five minutes later, he stomps into the open section. I blow my scent and the smell of the food away from him with my air magic, and after a few minutes of him searching for something to eat, he moves on in the opposite direction I'm traveling.

"Raven was right," I say, talking to myself. It's comforting to know that the land and my power can give me such a long heads-up if danger is coming so that I have time to prepare myself.

I continue on, stopping only for lunch when I reach the summit. I wrap up in the small blanket I brought with me as I sit on a rock and look out over the territory, munching on cheese, bread, and nuts. I drink from my skein of water slowly; I brought only one with me and I need to make it last.

This whole territory is so different from anywhere I've been before. It's a frozen wonderland, and as cold and harsh as it is, there's a beauty to it, a purity that I've never seen anywhere else.

When I'm finished eating, I relieve myself, literally freezing my ass off as I go, and once all of my needs are met, I start making the trek down the other side of the mountain. I've always hated going down more than up. I always worry more about slipping, and considering everything is covered in snow and ice, it takes me twice as long as going up.

I make it to the base right as the sun sets. I'm exhausted, freezing, and my legs are made of jelly. But I'm here. I walk into the forest, the dead trees ominous, like I'm in some creepy horror movie. I push past my fear and head for the clearing, where I saw myself waiting for my familiar.

Nerves build in my stomach, and I wonder what animal she will be. It would be neat if she was another bird and we could fly together, but I don't think that will be the case. I sit on the ground while I wait for her, trying to call out energetically to her. Watch her be a sloth or something. The thought would make me laugh if I wasn't wound so tight just waiting.

Half an hour later, I hear a twig breaking among the trees. I stand up, tempted to grab my dagger, but then a calming presence, like a balm soothing over frayed nerves, makes itself known. My shoulders relax, and I know this is her.

She's hard to see at first, but once I spot her, I inhale in awe. She emerges from the trees as majestic as she is terrifying. A large black panther. Her eyes glow yellow in the night, and she prowls toward me with intent. If I wasn't positive she wasn't going to hurt me, I would be shitting my pants right about now.

I dip my head to her in acknowledgment, and she reciprocates. I should be surprised to see that she has a higher intelligence than a regular animal, but I'm not. All of this is right.

"I've traveled a ways to find you."

I know. I gasp upon hearing her silky voice in my head, similar to how I can hear other mermaids underwater. *I've been waiting for you.*

"Do you have a name?"

She cocks her head at me in a purely animal way. *Ebony. This is the only time I'll be able to speak with you. The forest allows us this only while we're here.*

My heart sinks a little that I won't hear her voice again, but I'm glad I'm able to experience it now. Her name is fitting, and I wonder where she got it from.

"It's a pleasure to meet you, Ebony. My name is Ember." I walk closer to her, and she to me.

When we're facing each other, I kneel down before her, so we're at eye level. Her eyes are full of intelligence, and I marvel at the creature in front of me. I have a strong temptation to pet her, but I don't know if she will let me.

I slowly lift my hand up, making my intent very clear. She lowers her head, giving me permission. My palm connects with the warm fur of her head, and I'm shocked to find how soft she is. I scratch behind her ear, and I'm pleased when a purr vibrates through her chest. *She's definitely at least part animal, then*, I think to myself with a smile.

It's then, as we're touching, that a mark burns onto my body, similar to that of my mate mark with Alexei. A scorching heat like a brand on my chest, just under my collarbone on my right side. I look down to see four claw marks, like she literally just scratched her claim on me. I already know that she won't have one. The mark I have is so I can carry her with me at all times.

"Are you ready to head back with me?"

Instead of responding verbally, she blinks her yellow eyes at me and gives me a single nod. In the next second, she disappears, but her presence is inside of me. It's subtle, but I can tell she's there.

"Here we go, Ebony."

In the next moment, we're gone and back in the room I share with Alexei. He's pacing in front of the fire, just like I knew he would be. His eyes immediately latch on me, and relief floods them and pours toward me.

"Little doe, thank the Gods."

"Alexei, calm down. I'm fine. Everything went great." I drift as close to the fire as I can get.

His shoulders relax and he smiles at me. That is, until he sees the claw marks on my chest. "What the fuck is *this*? I thought you said everything went great? Why do you have scratch marks on you? What attacked you?" He's talking so fast that I don't even have time to set his mind at ease.

"Alexei, *stop*. It's my bonding mark with Ebony. It appeared when I touched her, just like with me and you."

He relaxes again. "Ebony?"

I nod. "Want to meet her?"

He smiles. "What do you think?"

I coax her out in my head. She seems a little shy now that Alexei is in the picture, and I think it's adorable.

After a minute or so, I finally get her to come out. She appears in the middle of the room, looking even larger than she did in the forest. I stand next to her, my hand resting on her back. Her eyes lock on to Alexei, and they size each other up like the two predators they are.

A few moments later, Alexei slowly holds his hand out in front of her as a peace offering. "Nice to meet you, Ebony. Are you going to keep my mate safe?"

She stares at him, blinking and nodding once like she did with me before sniffing his hand and giving it a tentative lick. He smiles genuinely at her and reaches up to pet her head. Within moments, she's purring, soaking up the attention from him. Uh–oh. Looks like I've got some competition. I expect jealousy to flare within me, with both of them if I'm being honest, but all I feel is a deep contentment that the two of them are bonding.

I chuckle and leave them to it as I run the bath. Ebony curls up in front of the fire, finding a cozy spot on the floor, and promptly falls asleep, her head on her enormous paws. Alexei comes in to keep me company, squeezing into the bath behind me, and diligently washing every inch of me. I love having him take care of me after the long trip I had on my own today. I can tell this is just as much for his benefit as it is for mine. He's reassuring himself that I'm safe.

When I'm clean, and the water is filthy, he picks me up, dries me off before wrapping me in my robe, and carries me to bed.

"Stay here. I'm going to grab us some dinner."

I smile at him. Eating alone in our room like this is one of my favorite things. It reminds me of the old days when it was just the two of us on the road to the palace. The weight of the day catches up with me, and before I know it, I'm drifting off. I wake when Alexei returns with a tray of food and wine for us, but barely. I'm eating while half asleep, and when I've finished, I pass out again. I vaguely notice Alexei moving the tray off of the bed before lying down next to me and pulling me into his arms.

22

Ember

The next day, I make my way to Raven. She'll want to know how everything went, and we'll need to start training soon. Hopefully it will be quick. I'm eager to get home.

Home. That definition has changed for me, and I realize that this is the first time I've thought of the palace in that context. In the past, home meant Earth. It no longer does. My life isn't there anymore. It's here. With my mate, familiar, father, and friends. The thought is a little jarring, even though it's pleasant.

I have the urge to go back to Earth and collect all my things, and just close that chapter of my life. Maybe after we get back, I can take Pearl and Alexei on that field trip that I promised them. Hell, Stavros might even want to come, and I smile to myself, thinking of showing him my world and where and how I grew up.

I ask Ebony if she wants to come with me or stay here with Alexei. She opts to come with me but not to reveal herself. I have a feeling this feline is going to be very selective who she shows herself to. I can appreciate that. Alexei watches in fascination as she disappears from the room, fading into my skin, and I feel her take up residence in the mark I bare for her. I rub it, soothingly and reassuring. It's a comfort to me, knowing that she's always with me when I need her.

I find Raven in the House of Intuition. Her back is to me when I enter, but she greets me all the same. "Good morning, Ember. Glad to see you made it back in one piece."

"Good morning, Raven. I would like to start training."

"I know. I've got everything set up."

It's unnerving how much she knows. Maybe it shouldn't be, but I definitely find the witches set me on edge more than most of the other species, with maybe the exception of the mermaids. In a different way though.

The mermaids are very vain and don't have a problem throwing you under the bus for their own gain. The witches just seem to see *through* me, knowing things before they should. I know that's just their magic, but it sets me on edge.

"Your training will not take you long. We will focus the majority of your training on the forms of scrying and future telling that we saw in your vision. Today you will learn astragalomancy, divination from bones, tomorrow pyromancy, divination by fire and flames, and the day after aeromancy, divination by watching the skies, and astrology, divination from stars and planets. Astrology and aeromancy essentially go hand in hand so you will learn both. The fourth day, I will teach you the basics of the others."

I hold in a sigh of relief. Less than a week. I can do that. Although I've really enjoyed learning all I have, it's exhausting, and I'm glad that it's almost at an end.

She teaches me the basics of astragalomancy, which is fairly simple. I need to ask yes or no questions, shake the bones, and the answer will be in front of me. If the symbols on the bones are face-up, that means the answer is yes. If they're all down, no. Straightforward.

"What are the symbols on them?" I ask.

"They're called 'runes.' Each one means something different, and will bring a specific element to your scrying. For instance, this one means 'intuition.'" She shows me the rune that's etched on her set. "And this one means 'wisdom.'

"You will need your own set of bones. I will bring you to our collection, and you will need to feel for the ones that call out to you."

She brings me to what she calls "the graveyard." It's not actually a graveyard, just a collection of animal bones they have. They're mostly all from rodents, the bones needing to be small enough to handle. I'm slightly disgusted about the fact that I'll be touching parts of a dead animal, but I'm sure I'll get over that quickly.

"Hold your hand out over the bones and move slowly along. You'll know when you find the right pieces for your set."

"How many are in a set?"

"Seven."

How appropriate, I think to myself. I do as she says. It takes a fair amount of time since there are so many bones here, but after about ten minutes, right as I'm about to tell her that I don't think it's working, there's a small tingle in my hand. I move in the direction that feels right, the sensation growing stronger. A few minutes later, my hand is hovering over the first piece in my set. It's from a squirrel. I don't know how I know that, but I do all the same. I pick it up reverently, and energy seems to flow from the bone all the way up my arm. I know I'm gaping at it, but it's impossible not to.

When I'm ready to move on, I put it in a pouch Raven gave me, similar to the one I saw Penelope using in my vision. It takes me an hour to complete my set, and when I do, Raven has me carve the runes into each piece myself. It's not as pretty as someone with a practiced hand, but the magic will be stronger if I do it. When I'm finished, I have the urge to send just the smallest amount of fire into the symbols, not enough to do any damage to the bones, but enough to char them just the slightest bit.

Raven and I test them, asking simple questions that we already know the answer to to make sure they're accurate. They are. In fact, Raven tells me she's never seen any respond so quickly.

After training, Alexei and I have dinner with Mera and Jinx. Alexei and Jinx have been getting pretty close while I spend all my time with Raven. Alexei is learning more and more about how the witches train in combat, and he's fascinated to say the least. They talk animatedly at dinner about new techniques, and while I'm somewhat interested, combat is more his deal than mine.

"What are you training on tomorrow, Ember?" Mera asks. She must not want to talk about fighting either.

"Pyromancy."

"Ooh, that one is my favorite! Mind if I tag along?"

My brows fly up in surprise. "You would want to?"

"Of course! Raven is a great teacher, and I like to see how new witches learn, especially in areas I'm really interested in."

"That's fine with me, as long as Raven is okay with it."

She beams at me.

"Are there types of divination you don't like?" I ask.

"I can't stand anthropomancy. It grosses me out. But there aren't very many witches that do it anymore. It's inhumane."

"What is that one?"

"Reading entrails."

I almost gag on my food.

"I also have found that I'm not as efficient with the water divinations—hydromancy and lecanomancy—but I think that's because I do better with fire."

I nod. That makes sense to me. And since it looks like I'm going to do well with fire, I bet it will be the same for me.

The next day, Mera and I meet up at the House of Intuition with Raven. She brings us outside where the firepit is located. She carries the wood out, piles it on the firepit, and then looks at me expectantly.

"A little help, Ember?"

I smile at her, extending my hand in front of me and lighting the wood with a flick of my fingers. I fan it with my air magic, and it quickly grows into a roaring fire, letting off enough heat to warm us through.

Mera gasps at the magic I've wielded, and I realize they probably don't see many other magics here. Not only is the kingdom segregated, but I don't think a lot of people travel here with the weather being as cold as it is.

"So, pyromancy is pretty straightforward. You should see images and shapes in the flames. The tough part is figuring out what you're seeing. The symbols used in almost all forms of divination are the same, so you don't need to learn new ones for every type."

"If two witches are looking at the same fire, will the same image present itself?"

"Yes. Although, one might see more than the other if they have more talent. That's why it's good that all three of us are here, because we can start out telling you what the shapes are so you can see what everything looks like before you try interpreting what you think it is."

"That makes sense."

Raven gives me a book so I can study what all the images mean. It's thicker than I would expect, and I know it's going to take a long time for me to remember them all.

We all stare at the fire, and images start emerging. Raven and Mera tell me what they are. At first it's difficult to see the same thing, but after a while, my eyes adjust and pick up on the forms.

After about an hour or so, they let me start guessing on my own, and they confirm or deny if I'm correct. By the next hour, I'm right most of the time. Raven assures me that with practice it will get easier and easier. She sends me off with my new book to study, telling me that I can keep it. I study it throughout the night, trying to remember as many things as I can. That night I dream about seeing images in the fire. I don't think it's a premonition though. More just my brain trying to process everything and retain all the information I learned. When I wake, I'm just as exhausted as I was the night before.

It turns out that aeromancy is more complicated than any of the other forms of divination I've learned so far. There are a lot of subcategories. Images in the cloud formations is one of them. Luckily, in that arena, it's the same concept as yesterday. Unluckily, we don't spend much time on that part because of what I've already learned. There's also wind divination, observing thunder and lightning, and finally, meteors and shooting stars.

We spend all day on that. We were really only able to bring the wind divination into practice today. It was a clear day so there were no storms. We continue training into the night, learning more about meteors, and we also dive into astrology.

It's fascinating to me, because the stars here are the same as on Earth, but they have different names for their constellations. Some of which aren't even ones we have on Earth, using completely different stars. The concept is similar to back home though, and I'm grateful that I'm not as in the dark with this as I was with the other forms.

When I get back to our quarters, I'm thoroughly wiped out, and I collapse into bed. Ebony can tell how worn out I am, and shifts out of my skin and cuddles up next to me. I'm situated between her and Alexei, and it's so comfortable and warm that I'm asleep within minutes.

My final day of training is spent learning the basic concepts of the other forms of divination. Raven teaches me about the ones that Mera mentioned to me, and I have to agree that dealing with entrails is definitely *not* my thing. She also teaches me about catoptromancy, the use of mirrors and crystal balls, chiromancy, the art of palm reading, and finally cartomancy, card reading. She tells me there are more, but these are the most common, and therefore the most useful. She doubts that I'll need to use any except my main three, but the more a witch knows, the better.

Our final night, the witches host a great feast in the mess hall. They make their signature dish, meat pies, and we all toast with our warm meads.

"To our fearless Princess Ember!" Raven yells out.

I smile warmly at her, and after I finish eating, I make my rounds, trying to get to know as many people in this territory as possible before heading back. I've met so many great friends on this journey, and I'm lucky that I have connections and relationships all over the realm. I feel a burning behind my eyes, and I know tears are threatening at the thought that my training trip is almost over. I'm relieved too, but it's definitely bittersweet.

The evening eventually comes to an end, and Alexei and I decide to head back to the Immortal City tonight, ready to be in our own bed. Well, technically *my* bed. Nerves flutter in my stomach with the thought of telling Stavros that Alexei and I are mated. I'm hoping he'll be thrilled. I mean, he loves Alexei, so I don't see why he wouldn't be, but it's such a big deal, and I am his only daughter, so there is a chance that he'll be upset. Only one way to find out.

Once we're packed, we join hands.

"Ready?" Alexei asks, looking just as nervous.

I nod, and we disappear. I sigh in relief as the temperature increases. Stavros made sure to change the wards before we left, ensuring that the two of us would be able to teletravel back into the territory, which I am extremely grateful for. I would not want to travel on foot or by horse to return here. Been there, done that, don't want to do it again.

We teletravel to right outside the castle, startling the guards, but they quickly get over it, bowing to me before embracing Alexei. I let him bro-talk with them and make my way inside to find my father. I've missed him, and am excited to catch up with him.

I knock on the doors to his wing of the palace, and moments later, the door opens, and his warm face is staring at me in pleasant surprise. I launch myself into his arms before either of us can say anything. His arms wrap around me, squeezing me tight to him in a dad hug. I squeeze back equally hard.

"I missed you, Dad." It feels like I haven't seen him in forever.

"I missed you too, daughter. Come in and tell me everything."

We sit by the roaring fire, and he pours us each a cup of tea. I start with the easy stuff and tell him all about my training. He tells me how proud he is of me, and that he can't wait to see all I've learned. I take a deep breath. Now is the time to tell him about Alexei.

"So, Dad, there's something else I need to tell you. Something wonderful."

"Well, what is it?" His eyes are welcoming and accepting, giving me the courage I need.

"Alexei and I are mates."

I watch as shock overtakes his features. He just stares at me for what feels like minutes, but in all actuality is probably only seconds. "Are you sure?"

I hold out my wrist, showing him my mate mark. He grabs my arm gently, running his thumb over the star and moon branded there.

"When did this happen?"

I still can't read his reaction, and it's driving me insane, but I answer him all the same. "Well, erm, it actually happened a while ago. The night my powers awakened. Something happened that night between us, and I was really upset with him. I wasn't ready to accept that he was my mate. But then when we were in the Everchanging Glades, we were attacked. He took a killing blow for me. I was able to save him with my healing powers, and that's when I forgave him and claimed him for my own."

He stares at me, and I can tell he wants to ask what happened the night my powers awoke, but he refrains, for which I'm extremely grateful.

"Does he make you happy?" It's such a dad question that a laughing sob leaves my throat.

"Happier than I've ever been in my entire life."

He smiles brightly at me then. "Then I am ecstatic for you, my darling daughter. He's a good man, and I look forward to calling him my son." He wraps me in a warm hug, and a surge of relief and happiness hits me.

When he breaks away though, there's a dangerous look on his face. "You were attacked?"

Fuck. "Yes. We still don't know who did it. I told Joseph about it, and he's convinced it's not the mimics, but he's looking into it all the same."

"You couldn't tell what species they were?"

"They were completely covered, including their faces. And they didn't use any powers. There were fifteen of them against the two of us."

"So, it was the last one that almost killed Alexei?"

"Erm, no." I don't know why, but I'm slightly uncomfortable telling him this next detail. I'm nervous he's going to think poorly of me. "After Alexei was stabbed, I sort of freaked out. I killed the rest of them and burned them all to ash. We weren't able to see who any of them were. I was so angry about my mate that I wasn't thinking clearly."

"You're even more powerful than I realized."

I'm shocked at the pride I hear in his voice. "You don't think I did the wrong thing?"

"Ember," he says gently. "The mate bond is one of the strongest things in our world. Of course you did what you did. Any mate would have done the exact same thing in your position. It's nothing to be ashamed of."

I breathe a sigh of relief. Truthfully, I've been a little frightened of myself since that moment.

"I will have my own people look into the matter, but is there anyone you suspect?"

"Coralia did not take well to me, but Proteus and the other mermaids seemed to like me just fine."

"Ahh yes. Coralia is an interesting one indeed. I will find out who did this to you, Ember. And they *will* be punished. You have my word."

I smile at him. I don't need people to take care of me, but it's nice all the same. "Thanks, Dad. Okay, now there's one other thing I would like to show you. It's just as wonderful as my mating bond."

His eyes widen in shock. I close my eyes, and talk to Ebony through our bond. She once again takes a few moments to coax out, but eventually she materializes next to us, standing proud and fierce next to me. Stavros lets out a shocked yell, almost falling out of his chair.

"This is my familiar. Her name is Ebony."

Ebony dips her head, clearly sensing his power and realizing that he deserves respect.

It takes him a few moments to gather himself, but eventually he says, "An honor to meet you, Ebony. Are you going to keep my daughter safe?"

I smile. Alexei asked her the same thing when he first met her. I can feel how badly she wants to roll her eyes, but she nods her head all the same.

"Can I pet you?" he asks her.

I love that he talks directly to her and not me. She pushes her head toward him in invitation. He slowly raises his hand, so as not to spook her, and gently strokes her big head. She immediately starts purring, and I laugh. She loves pets. Stavros finally looks back at me.

"How did this happen?"

"It happened in Wickshire. I had a vision that led me to Familiar Forest. She was there waiting for me." I pull the collar of my shirt down a bit so he can see the mark that I bear for her.

"Incredible. I didn't know that the witches had familiars."

The king didn't know that? It's a little shocking, but not at the same time. "Well, it did seem to be a pretty heavily kept secret. I think only the witches that get the visions and have familiars know about it. I don't even think the witches that don't have familiars know."

He nods in understanding. "Well, then I shall keep it a secret as well." For his part, he looks completely smitten with Ebony. Her head is now in his lap, eyes closed.

I smile fondly at them both, so happy to be home.

"So, listen. I know we discussed this a while back, but I want to make sure you're still on board. I would like to announce to the kingdom that you are my heir and next in line for the throne, if that's okay with you." Stavros looks at me questioningly.

I take a deep breath, calming my nerves. "Yes. I would like that. I'm ready."

His smile lights up his face, and I can tell that he's excited that he officially has an heir.

"Excellent!" His face turns serious for a moment, and I fight off a flinch at the abrupt change. "After we officially announce it, there are some things I need to tell you, Ember."

"What sort of things?"

"Things that are the utmost secrecy. The reason that all the species must remain segregated."

"Why can't you tell me now?"

"We need to wait until it's official. You still have time to change your mind, and I want to make sure to give you that chance. I can't tell you this if there's the slightest doubt in your mind that you want to take over. It's been a secret kept in the royal line for thousands of years."

I blanch. Thousands of years? Still. "Dad, I'm not going to change my mind."

He relaxes a bit and smiles at me, the easygoing expression back on his face. "Just as well, we should wait."

I don't quite understand why, but I nod all the same. "Okay. On a separate note, I was thinking that now that I'm back, Alexei and Pearl wanted to go on a little field trip to Earth with me sometime. I'm not planning on going for a few weeks since we just got back, but I was wondering if you would want to come with us?"

"You would want me to go with you?"

"Of course. Why wouldn't I?"

"I don't know. Maybe because I'm the old dad."

"I would love for you to come with us. I thought you might like to see my house and the area that I grew up in?" It comes out like a question because I'm not sure if that's actually the case.

His eyes soften. "Ember, I would be honored for you to show those things to me. I'll see when would be the best time to go and make arrangements. I won't be able to be gone long though. Only a few days at the most."

"Do we have to travel back to the northwest portal?"

"No. We have a portal here."

My eyebrows rise. I had no idea. "Perfect. I wonder where it will spit us out on Earth."

"The two realms mirror each other, so I would guess somewhere in the middle of your country."

I think about that. It will probably end up being pretty close to where we're trying to go. I tell him as much.

"Will there be a way for us to easily get to where we need to go after we travel through the portal?"

"Yes. Means of travel are much easier there. With the exception of teletraveling."

"I'm interested to see it all."

"It's definitely convenient. I'll show you as much as I can while we're there. I don't know if you'll want to come to the club with us though, considering your reaction to us dancing. Although, maybe this will be my chance to prove to you that I wasn't lying," I tease.

He looks traumatized at the thought of coming with us. "No, there's no need for that. I believe you." His blush makes me laugh loudly. I love flustering Stavros.

"So, I meant to ask you, did Penelope and Vita show up?"

His eyes darken. "Yes, they did. I really appreciate you finding that information out for me. I would have never known."

"Of course. I could sense there was something off about her. What happened to her?"

"She's locked up in a holding cell."

I nod. Seems like a fair punishment. "And Penelope?"

"I have her set up in your old rooms. She's very happy to be here. We've been occasionally getting together. It's nostalgic being able to reminisce with her about your mother."

My eyebrows rise. I didn't anticipate that at all. I wonder to myself if this "reminiscing" will turn into something more, but keep that to myself. "Yeah, I bet she has some fun stories for you. They knew each other really well. I bet she has some stories for me about my adoptive mother too."

"I'm sure you're right. I'll invite her to breakfast tomorrow, and you can catch up with her."

"That sounds perfect. I'm glad she's happy here. She had it pretty rough in the Mortal Sanctum."

"I'm aware. Vita will be locked up for a long time." Something dark inside me relishes that he's punishing her, and I wonder what that says about me. Nothing good, I'm sure, but I can't bring myself to care. Vita's a bitch, and she caused a lot of people more grief than anyone deserves, including me and my parents.

"Well, I'm sure you're exhausted from your journey and all of your training. Would you like food sent to your rooms?"

"No, we ate before we left. It'll be so wonderful to sleep in my own bed again. And have more than a trunk full of clothes to choose from."

"I can imagine," he says, chuckling. "You've been gone for a while. We missed you around here."

"I've missed you too, Dad."

He smiles fondly at me. "Off to bed now. You need your rest."

The fact that he's dad-ing me would probably have pissed me off right after we met, but now it just makes my heart squeeze. We have a lot of lost time to make up for.

"Okay. Good night. I'll see you in the morning."

"I look forward to it. And bring that mate of yours along."

"Will do." I head to my set of rooms next to his, Ebony following behind me.

I'm delighted to see that Alexei is already in our rooms. He is putting away a few sets of clothes, and I like that he's getting comfortable in my space.

"Hey there, good lookin'."

He turns at my cheesy come-on. "Hey yourself. Did you and your dad have a nice catch-up?"

I nod. "He wants us to come to breakfast with him and Penelope tomorrow."

"Did you tell him?"

"Yes. He took it very well. He's happy for us, but he's probably going to give you the stern dad-talk, so prepare yourself."

"Consider me warned."

Instead of continuing our conversation, I start stripping, dropping my clothes on the floor as I head for the bathroom. I hear him growling behind me, and know he will follow me sooner rather than later. Ebony lies on the bed, thoroughly ignoring us, and dozes off.

I start the shower up, excited to be able to finally take one again. As I lean in to check the water temperature, Alexei's hands wander up my naked back. I purr, basking in his touch. I step into the shower, soaking my body and hair. When I'm thoroughly drenched, I open my eyes to find Alexei's on fire. He's stripping quickly, fully intending on following me in. I turn from him to fill my hands with shampoo, lathering my hair. Suds slip down my body, and I inhale the calming scents of jasmine and vanilla.

Alexei's hands are suddenly in my hair, taking over washing for me. I moan as his strong fingers massage my scalp. When he's finished with my head, he moves on to my neck and shoulders. I love being taken care of. I haven't had a lot of it in my life, and it makes me feel cherished. I let him for a few minutes before I turn in his arms, rinsing the shampoo out of my hair. When that's done, I open my eyes and stare into his. There's heat in his gaze, but more predominantly I see his overwhelming love for me. I wrap my arms around his neck and he pulls me close to him.

"I love you," I tell him.

"And I love you, little doe."

I stand on my tiptoes and press my lips to his. He takes me slowly and tenderly in the shower, making me come more times than I can count, before finally following me. By the time we're finished, the water has cooled significantly, but I'm able to heat it with my fire magic so we can finish cleaning ourselves.

I dry us both with air, and we collapse into bed next to Ebony, and are asleep within minutes.

23

Ember

The next day is extremely hectic. We meet Penelope and my father for breakfast, and I'm pleased to hear that Penelope is settling in so well. She deserves it after all the time she spent at Vita's. It seems like she and my dad are becoming good friends. Apparently he gave her a tour when she arrived, something that he totally could've passed onto Humphrey, and they share most meals together.

It's nice to see my dad with a companion. I have no idea if they have any romantic interest in each other, but I think they've both been pretty lonely after they lost my mother.

After breakfast, I meet up with Pearl and Xanto. They're so smitten with each other it's adorable.

"I knew you two were going to make up!" Pearl yells at me when she sees us holding hands.

"Well, he did take a killing blow for me. I figured that was worth forgiving him for."

Her brows rise in surprise before she turns to Xanto. "You've never taken a killing blow for me," she accuses with a glint in her eyes.

"I would gladly lay down my life for you, my love." The seriousness in his voice is more than any of us expected, and Pearl gets slightly teary and gives him a meaningful kiss.

"Hey, do you guys want to go for a swim?" I ask, wanting to spend some quality time with them.

"Yes! Let's go!" Pearl grabs my hand and tugs me along, leaving the guys to wander behind us. I can feel Alexei's gaze on my ass, and put a little sway in my step to taunt him. I hear his faint growl behind me and smirk to myself.

"When we're alone, you need to give me all the dirty details," Pearl whispers in my ear.

"Same goes for you, bitch," I reply, giving her a wink.

We make it down to the lake, and we all start stripping. Alexei looks reluctant to take off all of his clothes, and I give him an encouraging nod. We're all naked anyway, and Pearl and Xanto are so used to nudity with their respective species. Technically, Xanto doesn't have to undress. His clothes would still be there when he shifted back, but he always undresses so he doesn't get his clothes wet.

Alexei reluctantly removes his undergarments, and all of us dive into the water. It's kind of a fun little excursion to have all of us friends skinny dipping together. We shift when the water becomes deep enough, and Alexei holds on to my hand so I can help him breathe when he needs it.

We explore the lake since Alexei hasn't really been able to, and it's fun watching Pearl and Xanto swimming together. They're like magnets, drawn together and dancing with each other.

When we're done exploring, we head up to the surface so that I can swim freely. Pearl and I do some tricks, and I'm proud to say that I've gotten much better. She's impressed by the new things I've learned, and the fluidity with which I've started swimming.

I show them my owl form, and do my water to air trick. They're both thoroughly impressed, and I preen at their attention.

"Ember, your owl form is gorgeous," Pearl exclaims. "Can you just perch on my shoulder as I stroll through the streets? You would be the perfect accessory."

I scoff. "Sure. Just let me know when you need me to be your ornament."

We head back up to the palace, and Pearl and I make plans to meet up after dinner to have some quality girl time. I join back up with Stavros to talk about how we're going to announce the fact that I'm next in line for the throne.

Alexei gives me a kiss and says he has business to attend to. Apparently a new batch of guards just showed up, and he's going to be busy training them now that we're back home. I like that he'll be occupied again and not just waiting around for me to finish my own training.

I meet Stavros in his office, and he greets me with a smile. I let Ebony out so she can get some love from him while we talk.

"So, I wanted to ask you what you'd like to do for your announcement. We could do another ball if you want?"

I tense up at the mention of a ball. I have some bad memories attached to that event, and I don't think I want to have another one anytime soon. "Do we have to?" I ask.

His eyes soften in understanding. "No, of course not. Our other option is to do a balcony announcement. The Immortal City and probably others from across Mystic Mountain will gather in front of the palace, and we will announce it to them, as well as send out paper notices across the kingdom."

I exhale in relief. "Yes. I like that idea much more."

"Perfect. Let's do it in a week. The sooner the better. I want to tell you everything you need to know, and I can't do that until we announce it."

"That sounds good to me. Is there anything I need to do?"

"Just make sure you have an outfit fit for a queen, because the whole territory will be seeing you as such."

I nod. I think I have a few options to choose from. There's also a chance that Imelda has made more for me since we've been gone. I'll have to go through my closet and see what I have to work with.

We talk and hang out for a bit after that, and it's so enjoyable to just have some quality time alone with him. We chat about his time while we were away. He was busy, as usual, and there were also more disappearances. He's been working harder at trying to find out who's behind it, but coming up empty at every turn.

I can tell he's frustrated and worried for his citizens. I don't blame him. I am too. I think back on my time spent away, trying to remember any details that might be of help, but nothing comes to me.

We go our separate ways until dinner, where we have the perfect group. Me and Alexei, Pearl and Xanto, and then my dad and Penelope. We drink, eat, and just generally have loads of fun together. When we finish up for the night, Pearl comes back to my suite for some girl time, and Alexei goes to his old rooms to pack up his things.

"I need your help picking out an outfit fit for a queen," I tell Pearl as we head in that direction.

"Ooh, my favorite."

We walk into my huge closet, and sure enough, there are more pieces here than when I left. I peruse the options. There are many, and I'm glad Pearl is here to help me sort through them. We narrow it down to two different gowns.

The first is fairly simple. It's floor-length, and has somewhat of a corset style torso, with a sweetheart neckline and spaghetti straps. The skirt is mostly tulle, but with so many layers, she was able to do a deep purple on the top that fades to a lighter purple with a bluish tint at the bottom. It has little silver stars, constellations, and moons on it.

The second one is a huge emerald green ball gown. The top is mostly all lace, with swirly little straps coming up to rest on the shoulders, and cutting down to a deep V-neck, the swirls continuing down. It's also covered in sequins and embroidery, which continues into the extremely full skirts in sections.

I pick the second one. The green will go beautifully with my crown, and is just extravagant and elegant enough for the announcement. I set it aside so I can make sure to have it pressed and ready.

Pearl insists on getting us wine and snacks, even though we just ate dinner. "It's not a girls' night without food and booze."

Once we open the bottle, Pearl starts in. "So, is Alexei fantastic in bed? I've been dying for you to tell me."

I blush a little bit, not used to having sex talk with girlfriends. Mainly because I never had any besides my mom. "The sex is earth-shattering."

She fans herself. "Is the blood play superhot too? I've never been with a vampire before, but I always thought that would be fun."

"Fun is one way to put it," I say, blushing more deeply. "Enough about me though. What about you and Xanto?"

"Bitch, it's so good. Like literally the best I've ever had. He's the perfect combination of dominating and submissive."

"How does that work?"

"I'm usually the dominant in my relationships, so he lets me take control when I need to, but I never realized how much I like him taking control too. I don't let go of it easily though, and the fight for it is always really hot."

That does sound hot, I think to myself as I take a drink of my wine. The more we drink, the more detail we go into about our love lives. Pearl gives me her signature makeover, exclaiming the whole time about what a mess I am. With anyone else I'd be offended, but mermaids have such a high standard of beauty that I just laugh and let her make me look like a queen.

Alexei comes in with loads of his stuff when we're thoroughly trashed, laughing at us fondly. He disappears and returns minutes later with Xanto.

"Come to bed, my love," Xanto says, scooping Pearl up into his arms.

"Ooh, I like the sound of that," Pearl purrs, stroking his face before leaning in to suck on his neck.

Xanto clears his throat awkwardly before heading for the door. "Thanks for getting me, Alexei. Have a good night, you two."

When Alexei and I are alone, he comes into bed with me. "Well, don't you look beautiful. Although, you're *always* stunning."

I thank him by pulling him down for a heated kiss.

The day of the announcement has arrived, and nerves flutter restlessly in my belly. I put my dress on, and Pearl does my hair and makeup. Not that people will be able to see me that well up on the balcony, but it makes me feel like a queen all the same. I have a regal-looking braid, and Pearl sets my crown gently in my hair as the finishing touch.

Ebony can sense the nerves building inside me, and I know she's itching to get out, wanting to take on some threat that doesn't exist. I mentally talk her down, and she settles a bit.

Stavros meets me outside the balcony doors that overlook the territory. He looks kingly in a black pants and jacket combo that's lined with gold, a cape, and his crown. He looks at me approvingly and gives me a fond smile and a warm hug.

"You look lovely, Ember. Are you ready?"

"As I'll ever be."

He extends his arm out to me. I grasp it tightly, and then the doors are opening, light flooding in from the afternoon sun. The crowd below is *massive*. They erupt into cheers the moment they spot us, and I stop myself from wincing at the volume, not wanting anyone to see me grimacing. I wave at everyone and smile warmly. This is their first impression of me, and I want it to be a good one.

Stavros holds up a hand, quieting everyone. "My good people! It is my honor to introduce to you my daughter, Princess Ember Solis!"

The crowd is even louder than they were the first time, and I'm surprised by the reception.

"I am ecstatic that the Gods have finally brought my heir home to me, and that she has accepted her position. She will be next in line for the throne, and the Solis line will continue to rule this wonderful realm."

I wave and smile some more. Stavros told me that I didn't need to say anything. Me making an appearance and letting everyone see their next queen would be enough.

Unfortunately, in the next moment, the peace is broken, and the people that I knew wouldn't be happy about me finally make themselves known. There's shouting from down below, and I'm able to pinpoint the general location. I see Stavros frowning and think that he's going to do something about them when something flies at me from their direction. It looks like an egg, and before it connects with me, I hold up my hands and stop it with my air magic, launching it back in the direction it came from. The crowd collectively gasps at the reveal of my magic. Before I can think better of it, I'm shifting into my owl form. I give an enraged screech and take off over the crowd, heading for the group attempting to make a fool out of me. They try to bomb me with more eggs, but I shift back into my normal form so I can access my air magic, and once again stop all of them and reverse the trajectory before shifting back into my owl.

The rest of the crowd cheers for me and laughs at the group that now has egg all over themselves. I give them another shriek before heading back to the balcony where my father waits. I shift in a flash, and am back before them, not a hair out of place, making the fae below go even more wild for me. Stavros gives me a proud look, and I'm relieved. I'm not sure if I should've revealed my powers to everyone, but from the looks of it, he's pleased.

He holds up his hand again to silence them. It takes a little longer than the first time, but they eventually quiet.

"As you all can see, the princess has multiple gifts. She has every power in our lands."

The crowd increases the volume again, cries of shock, some of outrage, some of joy. Stavros quiets them again before they get too rowdy.

"It is a great gift given to our kingdom by the Gods. She is honing her skills, and using this opportunity to make connections with all of our grand masters and mistresses. She will bring peace to our realm. Bow to your future queen!" His voice rings out loud and clear across the territory, and every single person in attendance does as he says.

With my gifts I can sense so many different emotions that I'm temporarily overwhelmed. The most prominent is joy and excitement. I do feel some anger and hostility, but not nearly as much as I would've expected. There does however seem to be an undercurrent of nervousness running through everyone. It makes sense. I'm different from anything they've come across before, and they can see how powerful I am, and I haven't even revealed the full extent of my gifts yet.

"All hail Princess Ember!" someone in the crowd surprises me by yelling out.

The rest of the group echoes it, and I'm stunned that they've accepted me so readily. I wonder if the people are more ready for unity than we've realized. I smile and wave to them, and before any more drama can break out, we head back inside.

"You did so well, Ember," Stavros tells me.

"You don't think it was a bad idea that I revealed my powers to everyone?"

"Not at all. They were going to find out sooner or later. Better to let them know now so they have time to get used to it."

I nod. "I'm sorry I acted without thinking. I didn't want them to think that I would be a leader that would be easily cowed. I won't tolerate that kind of disrespect."

He smiles proudly at me. "As you shouldn't. I think you reacted perfectly."

"Thank you." I lean in to give him a hug. I appreciate how he handled this whole situation. "Now, do I get to hear the big secret?"

The smile vanishes from his face, but he gives me a solemn nod. "Not here though. Why don't you go change and meet me in my quarters when you're finished?"

Nerves flutter in my stomach. I can tell what he has to tell me is not going to be good. But I need to know. It's like it's already at the tip of my brain but I can't quite grasp it. Like it's tied to me in some intrinsic way.

I teletravel back to my room, impatient to learn whatever it is. I change in record time, going with my usual multiple layers look. Alexei gives me a kiss before telling me how wonderful I did and promising to worship me like a queen when I return, making me even more impatient.

I walk across the hall to Stavros's quarters, and he leads me to the fire like always, tea waiting per our routine. After I sit, Stavros mumbles a few words I can't understand, making motions with his hands.

"What spell did you cast?" I ask.

"A privacy spell. No one will be able to hear us or disturb us until I reverse it.”

I knew this was a big secret, but each measure he's taking to ensure no one else hears us, the more apprehensive I become. I take a deep breath, trying to calm myself.

“The fae didn't always rule,” he starts out, surprising me.

“I know. The mermaids used to rule, right?”

He flinches in shock. “Yes. How did you know that?”

“I found out in the library. I was looking into the history of Queridian, and I saw that the mermaids used to rule and then the fae took over, although I couldn't figure out how that happened.”

“It's a messy history. The greatest and most well-known mermaid queen was named Surseiha.”

“The one I take after with my tentacles?” I clarify.

“Yes. Because of how powerful she was, any who had her blood always became the ruler. For a while, they had thought that her line had died out, but one woman came forward about three thousand years ago, having discovered that she was a descendant of Surseiha.”

“She was a mermaid? Wouldn't she have known as soon as she could shift into her water form?”

“She wasn't just a mermaid.”

My brows crease in confusion. “Humans weren't here three thousand years ago though, right?”

“Right. There was another species that used to live here, Ember. One that's been erased from all of our records and history. They were conduits like the humans.”

My heart is racing. “What were they?”

“Demons.”

24

Ember

"Demons?" I echo.

"Yes. They were how the races were mixed before the humans arrived. They were treated much the same way, and weren't respected by the other species."

"So, this woman was a demon?"

"Yes. Her name was Demonica."

"Okay, so this demon figured out she was a descendant of Surseiha and wanted to take over the throne?"

"Yes. And she did. Before that happened, though, she was approached by a fae male named Theon."

That name is ringing bells in my head, but I can't place where it's from.

"He wanted to form an alliance between the mermaids and the fae. He proposed to Demonica. She wanted to court him during the time before she took over the kingdom to see if they would make a suitable couple. She wasn't born into royalty, so she wanted to marry for love. She agreed to marry him during her coronation, and they were married and crowned at the same time. Theon woke up to her dead hours later. Someone had snuck in and slit her throat."

I gasp in horror. "How awful."

"Yes. But there's more to the story." I raise my eyebrows for him to continue. "Demonica didn't actually die. Well, she technically did, but it was the same thing that happened to you."

I cry out in surprise. "You mean she had all of the species in her blood too?"

"Yes. Except instead of human she was demon. She brought herself back to life and her powers were awakened. You see, demons have the power to feed off emotions. It's similar to a human, except they can literally feed off them. It powers them. Most didn't do that, or if they did, they would take the negative emotions from people, but they also had the ability to take the good ones, and if they fed too much, it could cause the victim's soul to leave them. And if they fed off of too many negative emotions it could taint the demon's soul. When Demonica awakened, she was so enraged by what happened to her that her demon nature took over and she fed off every negative emotion she could, and it changed her irrevocably. She started a chain reaction, and somehow pulled all the other demons into her madness."

My eyes are wide, and I have no idea how to even respond. An entire race just suddenly turned evil because of one person?

"At that point, she was too powerful to remain here, so King Theon made a deal with her. She no longer wanted to be among the other species here, so he gave her her own kingdom in another realm."

"Another *realm*?" I shouldn't be that surprised since I'm from a different realm, but for some reason I thought that there was only Earth and Queridian.

"Yes. It's underneath this one. It's called Domonia. It also used to be known as the Domain of the Dead, only because those who reside there are as good as dead with how evil they are."

"So, Demonica left and took all the demons with her?"

"She also took all of the slaves."

"Queridian doesn't have slaves," I say, confused.

"Not anymore. That was part of the negotiation. She wanted people to feed off of so that she could live forever."

"Live forever?" I know I'm parroting everything he says back to him, but I can't help it. Every word out of his mouth shocks me even more than the last.

"Unfortunately, yes. Remember how I said the demons could feed off of their victims? They take part of their life force when they do that. It enables them to live much longer. And if they have access to an essentially unlimited number of victims, then they could live forever."

"So, she's still alive?"

"There's no way for us to know. She definitely could be."

Something occurs to me then. "So, is there any chance that Demonica is behind the disappearances around the realm?"

"Ah. I thought you would ask that. No. Firstly, I have all of the portals heavily guarded. Secondly, when Demonica left, the entire realm was warded against all demons. No one from Domonia would be able to travel here, even if they wanted to."

His reasoning makes sense, and I deflate a bit. I was so sure I had figured it out, but of course that would've been the first thing he thought of.

"So, you mentioned that all this had to do with why all the races are so segregated?" I'm dying to know how that's all connected. Maybe I can find a way around it.

"Yes. One of Demonica's stipulations was that the races stayed separate. She didn't want her kingdom being taken over, and she knew that if the races mixed they could potentially be strong enough to defeat her. Especially if we found another race that could be a conduit and therefore have someone else who contained all the powers, just like her. The wards around Queridian are tailored with that in mind. If all of the races are together for an extended period of time, especially a large group, the wards will start to fail, starting with where that group is located. That's what happened to the individuals in the caves. They started getting larger and larger until the wards were buckling. The demons were going to come for them, and that's why they had to leave."

"The demons are 'the dark ones'?"

"As far as I've been able to tell. I read through the journal after you told me about it."

"Wow. And no one else knows about all of this?"

"No. At the time, everyone in the realm had the demons wiped from their memories, and then they were erased from all and any records in our land. The only ones to ever know about it were the kings and queens, so that they could keep the realm safe. I've pushed the boundaries a bit where I could, but keeping the species apart is literally the only thing preventing the demons from coming through to our lands."

My heart sinks at the realization that things may never change here. Although, I wonder to myself if there's still a chance that things could be different. This all happened three thousand years ago. We don't know for sure that Demonica is still alive. And if she's not, does that mean that the other demons were freed from the corruption her mind had on all of them? There's no way of knowing right now, and that frustrates me to no end.

"Well, thank you for telling me," I say lamely.

"You're welcome. You're bound to secrecy now though, Ember. You can't tell anyone this. Not even Alexei. That is, until he becomes king, since the two of you are mates."

Fuck. I didn't think about that, but I nod anyway. Alexei won't like it, but he'll understand. Especially since it's for the betterment of the kingdom. If there's one thing he loves as much as me, it's Queridian.

"Okay. I understand."

He exhales. "Honestly, it's a relief to share this with someone. I've been the only one who's known since Queen Amira died."

"That had to be hard. And I'm sure I didn't make it any easier with my constant questioning and pressure."

He chuckles. "No, but I would've done the same thing in your position."

"Well, now that I know, you can always talk to me about any of it if you need to. We can also brainstorm solutions or tactics. I don't know if there's anything we *can* do, but it doesn't hurt to talk about other options."

"Thanks, Ember. I don't think there's anything else we can do right now, but if I need your opinion on any of it, I will definitely come to you. You can also approach me with more questions or concerns if you think of anything else after everything sinks in. I know it's a lot to digest."

"It is." We stand and I give him a hug. "I know this hasn't been easy for you. I'm here now to share the burden."

He squeezes me harder. "Thanks, daughter." He disbands that privacy spell around us, and I head back to my room.

Alexei is showering when I enter, and I'm momentarily distracted by his hard, wet, naked body. He catches me ogling him, and smirks at me in that cocky way I used to hate, but love now. I strip my clothes off and join him, wanting to get the events of the last hour off of me. Crazy to think of how quickly things can change. My whole world has been flipped on its head.

His hands find my shoulders as soon as I'm in, and I moan as he works out the tension that's building there.

"How did it go?"

"Not good, Alexei. I can't tell you any of it, but it's *bad*."

His brows furrow in confusion and concern. "Is there anything we can do?"

"I don't know. I can't think of a solution that doesn't include the possibility of war."

"War?"

I nod solemnly. Fuck. My vision comes back to me from Vision Lake. The horns and the red eyes. "I'm you…" echoes in my head, and I finally understand it. I saw Demonica. She's not *actually* me, but she is my mirror. We're essentially the same person. Neither of us knew we were royal, we're both descendants of Surseiha, and we both have the blood of all the races of the realm. I suck in a sharp breath.

"What is it?"

"I understand the vision I had in Wickshire," I say quietly.

"I take it you can't tell me?"

I shake my head, giving him an apologetic look over my shoulder. "I wish I could, but I can't until you become king. Or maybe just when we get married. I'm not sure."

He nods. "Well, whatever happens, I'm here. We can handle anything together." He wraps his arms tightly around me from behind, and I sigh into his embrace.

I don't know if we can handle this or not. Not if we want to make things better for the people living here. I want to change things, and today I felt like my dreams of seeing that come true were completely wrecked.

"Hey. It will be okay. I promise, little doe."

I nod, turning in his arms and hugging him back. He holds me for as long as I need him to, and then we finish showering. He temporarily makes me forget everything by licking my pussy until I don't even remember my own name. I clutch his head and ride his mouth until I'm screaming my climax out for him. He growls, and as soon as I've come down, he rises, lifts me into his arms and plunges roughly inside of me.

I hang on for dear life as his fangs find my neck. He holds his wrist in front of my mouth, and his teeth pierces my skin at the same time mine sink into his vein. We collectively moan as we're joined in more ways than one. We circle our pleasure back and forth between us until it's built higher than it's ever been before. We break apart within moments, and for a second I fear we'll pass out in the shower. I think I black out for a brief time, but when I come back, we're in the same position as before.

"You're amazing," he tells me in awe.

"You are. I didn't do much."

He chuckles. "You did *everything*, little doe."

We clamor out of the shower and collapse into bed, snuggling against each other.

The next few weeks pass by fairly uneventfully, which has been strange for me. Ever since Stavros told me about Demonica, it's as if the world is about to be ripped out from under my feet. I'm grateful for every day that passes where nothing has happened, but I keep waiting for the other shoe to drop, especially after I realized I saw Demonica in my vision.

I still haven't told Stavros about it. I don't know what it means. I have a theory that I was seeing her because he was about to tell me about her, but the sinking pit in my stomach tells me differently.

Needing a distraction, and wanting to escape for a while, if I'm being honest, I bring up to Stavros that I want us to go to Earth together soon. He's surprisingly receptive, and we plan to leave a week later. Pearl is extremely excited, and I smile every time I think of what she will be like when we get to Earth.

Alexei is excited too, but I think he's more looking forward to seeing what my life was like before I moved here. He wants to see every part of me, and that warms me to my core.

I plan on having us stay at my house, although since I've been gone so long I hope that they haven't sold it and gotten rid of all of my things. I have a feeling that won't happen though. It's been only a few months, and there would be no one back on Earth to notice that I was missing. If that's not the case though, I have enough money for us to be able to stay at a really nice hotel.

I look through everyone's wardrobes and try to pick out items that would work for them on Earth. There's not much to choose from, and I finally throw in the towel, realizing I will have to take them shopping when we get there. Luckily, they all have at least one outfit that will suffice for now, and they all change as we prepare to leave.

The portal is only half a day's journey on horseback, and I'm really glad that we don't need to travel all the way back to Twin Fangs. I'm curious where we'll end up, and I would guess with Mystic Mountain being central in Queridian, that we will end up fairly central in the US as well. Only one way to find out.

When everyone is ready and I make sure I have my purse, wallet, and all of my electronic devices, we head toward the central portal. Alexei and I share Ash again, wanting a bit of nostalgia on our trip, and both Pearl and Stavros mount their beautiful horses as well. Stavros's is a jet-black stallion. He is the picture of majestic. Pearl doesn't have her own horse, but is borrowing a snow-white mare who seems just as feisty as Pearl.

We slowly but steadily make our way down the mountain. I delight in having Ash under me and Alexei behind me. It feels just like the old days, and I lean contentedly against my mate. I'm excited to just be able to relax and spend some quality time with my favorite people. It will be like a little vacation for all of us.

It strikes me as odd then that the idea of going back to my old life will be like a vacation. Not because I don't love my life now and where I live, but because it's different, and I will be able to enjoy the luxuries on Earth that we don't have here. I'm really excited to be able to show my companions different aspects of my old life, and things they've never experienced before.

We reach the bottom of the mountain on the southwest side, and the portal is there. I can feel the energy pouring from it, even from here, and sure enough, the horses start shifting nervously. We leave our horses with the guard, and he promises to take good care of them while we're away.

The motion sickness hits me first, and my necklace starts flaring brightly, just as it did the first time. Nerves build in my stomach at the thought of this next part. I know what to expect from last time, and I'm not looking forward to it. Alexei senses my trepidation and squeezes my hand in support.

"Everyone ready?" my father asks.

We all nod, and he leans into the portal as if he's free-falling. Pearl follows next, and Alexei and I step up to the portal.

"I've got you, little doe."

I nod. "See you on the other side."

We fall in, and it's just as disorienting this time around, even though I know what's happening.

We tumble out, and if not for Alexei, I would've ended up on my ass once again. He grips my hand tightly and steadies my back with his other hand. I smile gratefully at him before I look around. I gasp at the heat, and the setting we're now in. We're surrounded by cacti, huge rock formations, and desert sand. *Earth.*

25

Ember

The place itself looks pretty touristy, and it's a miracle that no one seemed to notice four random people sprouting up out of the ground like weeds.

"Where are we?" my father asks.

"The desert somewhere. I'm not positive which city yet." I spot a sign ahead of us, and we make our way in that direction.

Cathedral Rock Vortex

Templeton Trail

Sedona, AZ

"Oh cool, we're in Arizona."

"Is that far from where we need to be?" Pearl asks, staring around in wonder.

"I mean, yes, but we can take a flight. It won't be a big deal."

We start hiking down Templeton Trail to get to the parking lot, and when we arrive, I take out my phone and turn it on. I'm surprised to see that it's pretty early in the day here, only 10 a.m., and I remember last time I traveled through the portal, the time didn't seem to be exactly the same.

I open my Uber app, but no cars are available. It could be because I barely have service, but I am able to see that there's a car rental place close by. I figure that's a good enough option.

Luckily there is a picture so I won't have any trouble teletraveling. I thank my past self for putting all my bills on autopayments because I still have full access to my phone. I tell my entourage to wait and not move, and I teletravel there. I'm able to get a car for us with my debit card (which thankfully still has money on it), and drive back to them. It takes only a half an hour total, and then we're moving again. They all marvel at the vehicles, which move much faster than anything they're used to.

It's strange to drive considering I haven't done it in about six months, and combine that with the fact that I'm in an area I've never been to before, and it's a bit messy at first. We acquire a map from a gas station nearby, and learn from the clerk that the closest airport is forty-five minutes away in Flagstaff. I drive us straight there and return the car about an hour after renting it in the first place.

We head inside, and I buy us four tickets to Denver, Colorado. Our flight is scheduled for an hour and a half later, and I thank the Gods that we don't have to wait a long time.

The clerk asks us all for identification, and I almost freak out before remembering that I can use my allure on her. It's a little more difficult for me to do here versus back in Queridian, but I manage. I show her mine, and then tell her that she's already seen everyone else's. She nods a little dazedly before directing us to security. I tell them what they'll need to do to get through, and I pull the same thing on the TSA agent. We make it to our gate and still have an hour before our flight.

"Are you guys hungry?"

They all nod, and I find a restaurant where we can get some food and drinks. I order us some nachos, mozzarella sticks, and hot wings, as well as a round of Bloody Marys. It's always my preflight drink, and I've been craving one for a while. They don't really have anything like it in Queridian. Alexei looks at me funny when I order them, and I chuckle.

"It's tomato juice with other stuff in it."

"Oh. I thought it was blood from someone named Mary."

I laugh loudly as I plug my phone into a nearby outlet, along with my portable charger and speaker. I have all three chargers with me so I can load up before we go.

Our drinks are brought out soon after, and I take a healthy swig. The flavor hits my tongue, and while the quality isn't as good as anything in Queridian, I enjoy the taste of it, especially since I haven't had one in months. The rest of them try it, and they all have looks on their faces like they can't tell if they like it or not. I chuckle. I remember being the same way the first time I tried a Bloody too.

"Don't worry, it'll grow on you," I assure them.

Our food comes out in the next moment, and the smell of greasy Earthy food makes me smile. It's fun to be here with them and watch as they experience it all for the first time. They all look so out of place, and I can't tell if that's just because I've only ever seen them in Queridian, or if they're just uncomfortable. Either way, it's amusing.

I dig into the bar food, and while it's not great, it's nostalgic, and I enjoy it. They all have that same look on their faces, but they keep eating it anyway.

"I can't tell whether I love this food or hate it," Pearl says, making me laugh.

"Bar food is like that most of the time."

We finish eating and find our gate. I laugh at the way my companions look so uncomfortable and out of place. They stand at the window and gaze out, watching the employees getting the flights ready and marveling at the size of the planes.

"So, we're really going to fly on one of those things?" my dad asks.

"Yes."

"It flies like a bird?"

"Well, the wings don't flap. And it's much faster than a bird."

We load onto the plane and find our seats. I got us first class since I have a shit ton of money that I won't end up being able to spend anyway. Pearl looks around nervously as we sit down. "Are we going to have to sit here the whole time?"

"Yes, but it will be fine. The bathrooms are up there if you need them, but you have to wait to get up until they turn off the seat belt sign. Do you want me to push some calm onto you?"

She eyes me reluctantly for a minute before finally nodding. I smile at her reassuringly. I realize then that I've never done this for her before. I create a cloud of calming lavender in front of her, and she lowers her mental shields for me. I push the emotion onto her, and I watch as her shoulders deflate and she relaxes into her seat.

The plane takes off, and Alexei whoops in excitement. I feel like he would be the type to love rollercoasters. I've always hated them, same with plane takeoffs. I settle back in my seat, closing my eyes and concentrating on the music playing through my headphones. I occasionally look at my traveling companions and smile to myself as they look out the window at my world. Our cities are so different from theirs, and I look forward to showing them all I can in the time that we're here.

I order another drink from the flight attendant as she comes by, and everyone else gets one too. It's not a long flight, only about an hour and a half, and we're all enjoying ourselves by the time we touch down in Denver. I marvel at how much construction they've done since I was last here a few months ago.

Alexei looks on edge being around so many people, and I can relate. It's been a long time since I was in this crowded of an area, and honestly, I've never been fond of crowds. They always make my anxiety increase, and it makes sense now because I'm picking up on so many different emotions.

We quickly make our way through the airport and get a cab. Half an hour later we're pulling up to my house. Tears build behind my eyes. Years of memories press in on me, and I take a deep breath, attempting to pull myself together. We get out of the car, and Alexei squeezes my hand as we walk up to the front door. I push the key into the lock and the house seems to sigh in greeting. I open the door wide, and am delighted to see that everything is exactly like I left it, albeit a little dustier.

I try the closest light switch and relief floods me when it immediately switches on. I'm glad my automatic payments kept everything going. I show them all around. Since I have only one guest room, Pearl has to sleep on the couch, but she doesn't seem to mind. It's comfortable enough. After traveling all day, I feel dirty, especially since we were in the desert, and turn the shower on in my master bathroom. Alexei joins me, and we take our time washing each other.

"I already like this trip much better than my last one. I love seeing your home and your life from before."

I smile at him. "I'm excited to show you everything I can. I think we're going to have fun."

We finish our shower and head back out to the living room. My dad and Pearl are sitting on the couch looking around my house with interest.

"Do you guys want to go out to dinner and see a movie? I think that will be a good introduction into our world," I suggest.

They all nod eagerly. I look at them before realizing that we'll need to go to the store first. Pearl could get away with wearing my clothes, but I don't have anything for the men. "Okay. First things first, we need to go shopping."

Pearl claps excitedly, and we all pile into my car, still in my garage since I had originally taken an Uber to the airport when I went to

Oregon. I have to use my self-charging jumper cables to get it to start, but it does eventually. I drive us to Target, figuring it will be the safest option.

They marvel at how one store has so many different things and are overwhelmed by the enormity of the place. I know I'm going to have to help each of them pick out clothing because they don't know the styles here and will likely end up in something ridiculous.

We start with the men, figuring they will be quickest. I pick out some jeans for each of them as well as a pair of slacks just in case we end up going anywhere a little fancier. I also grab them some T-shirts, button-up shirts, and then some comfier clothes for them to sleep in. They both look a little horrified at my selections, and it makes me laugh. I look forward to seeing them actually wear them.

Pearl is next, and she just seems excited to be able to wear something different. She's actually much better at picking out items than I thought she would be, and I guess her fashion sense transferred to Earth too. We pick out a lot more clothing for her, jeans, shirts, dresses, and then of course a clubbing outfit. I get one for myself too because I don't think I have one. I've always been antisocial after all.

I also get them all a toothbrush, as well as some shower stuff for the guest bathroom. While I'm at it, I pick up some food for the house. We don't have anything since I haven't been home in months. I cleaned out my fridge before I left for Oregon so I don't really have much that was going bad. I figure I should also buy some extra portable chargers and load those up so I have plenty of electricity to bring back with me.

We head back home after checking out, and I have them dress in a new outfit while I unload the groceries. As I'm putting the last of the food away, they come out. They're all dressed casually in jeans and different shirts. Pearl is wearing a cute pink lace shirt that matches her eyes, Alexei is in a blue flannel shirt, and Stavros is wearing a plain button-up gray shirt. They all look slightly uncomfortable in their clothes, and I have to admit it's weird to see.

"Why are these so tight?" Pearl complains about her skinny jeans, and I laugh.

"That's the style. They look great on you."

"Well, I know that. I just wish they weren't so uncomfortable."

"You'll get used to them. Is everyone ready?"

They nod and we head to dinner. I take them to my favorite Italian restaurant, in the mood for wine and pasta. They're playing Frank Sinatra as we enter, and I soak up the familiarity.

"Mom and I used to come here a lot. It was our favorite Italian place."

Alexei squeezes my hand and Stavros smiles sadly at me. "I'm glad we could come here to see it," my dad says.

I order us a bottle of Seven Deadly Zins as well as some bruschetta and calamari. Soon, we're all chatting and relaxing as we eat and drink. I open my phone to check what movies are playing, hoping we can see something classic.

I get really excited when I see what's available, and I don't know how I'm going to pick between them. They're playing *Back to the Future*, *The Princess Bride*, and *Titanic*. We should go with *Back to the Future*. It's fitting even if it's not the same kind of situation. Plus, I've always wanted to see it in theaters.

We finish our dinner and head to the movies. We wait in line, and even though we just ate, I make sure to get us all the things: popcorn, candy, and slushies. If they're going to experience this, it needs to be the whole nine yards, even with Stavros complaining in my ear that he's too full to eat anything else.

"You'll want snacks for the movie. Trust me."

We get seats in the back, and once again, my dad has a comment. "Won't we be too far away all the way back here?"

I roll my eyes, nearly growling at him. "Dad. You want the Earth experience. You have to let me show it to you. These are the seats people want the most. You will be able to see and hear everything perfectly fine. Promise."

He holds up his hands in surrender. "Okay, okay. I'm sorry for questioning you."

On the other side of me, Alexei chuckles in my ear as he squeezes my thigh. "Parents always have to question everything we do, don't they?"

I give him a fond smile. I realize then that this is one of the first times I've been frustrated with my dad in the typical "parent" sense, and the thought brings an even bigger smile to my face. I don't think anyone *wants* to be frustrated with their parents, but I'm glad we've reached this point in our relationship. I want to experience all the things with him, and I'm grateful that I have the opportunity.

The lights dim, and I settle into my seat for one of my comfort movies. The previews play, and I take the chance to look around at my group. All of their gazes are riveted on the screen. They wince at the volume, and I grimace in regret. I should've warned them. They've probably never heard anything at this decibel before.

When the actual movie starts, my excitement builds. It's been so long since I've seen a movie, and this is one of my favorites. I don't realize how many of the jokes they wouldn't get because they're not from here, and they look at me strangely a few times when I laugh out loud.

We power through our snacks, just like I knew we would, and I smirk to myself when I realize my dad is eating more than any of us. He looks at me as he eats the last of the popcorn, and I raise my eyebrows at him. If it weren't so dark in the theater, I'm pretty sure I would see him blushing.

We finish the movie, and they all have that glazed look in their eyes when the lights come back up.

"What happens next? Why is the movie over but the story isn't?"

Pearl asks, clearly freaking out about the fact that Doc is taking Marty and Jennifer back to the future with him.

"I have the movies at my house. We can watch the next ones before we head back home," I tell her reassuringly.

"Well, what happens?"

"You'll have to wait and see."

She growls at me in frustration, and I laugh at the fact that she's never really had to deal with this problem before. It's one we all know well. At least those of us who love stories. I've always had a love/hate relationship with cliffhangers, and it's torturous having to wait to find out what happens next. Sometimes I think writers enjoy making us suffer.

We head home, and we're all so exhausted from the long day that we go to bed immediately.

When we wake the next morning, it's much later than when we normally get up. I guess we did have quite the day yesterday.

"Do you guys want to go out to brunch?"

"What's brunch?" Alexei asks.

"It's breakfast and lunch all mixed into one. Usually with liquor too."

"Oh no. We're going to be drinking this whole trip, aren't we?" Stavros shakes his head, looking exhausted already.

"Of course. We're on vacation. You have to drink on vacation. It's like a cardinal rule."

We dress for the day, Pearl and I wearing cute sundresses, and Dad and Alexei dress casually in jeans and T-shirts. I drive us to my favorite brunch spot, the one that I came to on my birthday. I order us a carafe of peach mimosas and point stuff out on the menu for everyone that I think they will like. Pearl says she wants whatever I'm eating, and I order us the huevos rancheros and the blueberry French toast to share. I always used to get this exact thing when Mom and I would come here, and it's special to share it with another woman who I care for.

We scarf down our breakfast, and when we're finished, we walk around the city for a bit. They marvel at how large our buildings are, and how busy the streets are. We walk along 16th Street Mall and stop to watch or listen to all of the street performers. As we work off our breakfast, I try to think of other things I could show them while we're here. I definitely want to take Alexei and Pearl to the club. I don't think Stavros would enjoy that though, and obviously it's way too early in the day for that right now. I think Pearl would like to come to a yoga class with me. Ooh, I bet they would have fun at an arcade! Or maybe Skate City. It has skating and an arcade. I think maybe we'll do that tonight and yoga and clubbing tomorrow.

We head back to my house and relax for a bit. Pearl requests that we watch the next *Back to the Future*, so we all load up on the couch and I turn the second one on. This one was always my favorite, but it was definitely a disappointment when we got to the year 2015 and we didn't have flying cars. They seem to get the humor a bit more in this one, just slightly more familiar, and I'm glad I can share this with them.

We finish the movie and get ready for the next exciting night of our trip. Pearl and I change since it wouldn't be the best idea to go skating in dresses, and when we're ready, we head to Skate City. I don't even remember the last time I was here. Middle school maybe? We walk in, and the sights and smells bring a wave of instant nostalgia. I get us all a pair of skates, and soon we're rolling out onto the floor. Everyone is wheeling their arms around, trying to stay upright, including me. It's been a long time since I've done this. I get the hang of it quicker than they do, but soon all of us are gliding along the rink, cheesy music playing and encouraging us on.

Alexei and I hold hands, keeping each other upright. My heart swells. I always saw other people doing things like this in my old life, and

I yearned for it, even though I told myself I was content on my own. Being here now with all the people I love most, and experiencing these things that I always envisioned myself doing with others makes me happier than I ever could've guessed.

After a handful of songs, we take a break and head over to the arcade. To start, I show them the best arcade game ever, *Pacman.* I show them how all the controls work first, and then I start. They watch me, shouting at me when things get more intense. I play a few times, letting them get used to how I move, and before long, they're begging for a turn.

I let Alexei go first, and his turn is fairly short, but that's expected since it's his first try. Stavros goes next, followed by Pearl. I'm thrilled when my best friend has the longest run out of any of them, almost doubling their times. I high-five her, and Alexei insists on another turn. I leave him to it, and guide Pearl over to the dancing game. We do the partner one, and after a few songs she really starts getting the hang of it.

We make our rounds of the arcade, playing a driving game, *Centipede*, and of course some air hockey. We collect multiple tickets and bring them up to the counter. Everyone spends theirs on different things, Pearl getting a little stuffed animal, Stavros a light-up frisbee, and Alexei a toy gun.

We go back out on the rink when we're ready, and it's more crowded now. We get pulled into the tide of people, the press of bodies moving us forward. We skate until we're breathless, a little sweaty, and have huge smiles gracing our faces.

"You guys ready to head home?" I ask.

They all nod, and we return our skates before climbing into the car. We had gotten some junk food there, but it isn't until we get back that I realize how hungry I am. I order us some pizza, figuring this will be a new experience for them too. Stavros eats his and then heads to bed.

I ask if Pearl and Alexei want to watch *Dirty Dancing* with me so they can finally understand my reference from their dancing lessons. They nod eagerly, excited to see another movie. I'm a little grateful Stavros went to bed so we can watch this together. It's not a movie I would ever watch with him around.

I consider letting Ebony out, figuring she might enjoy lounging with us while we're here too, and then realize I haven't introduced her to Pearl yet. In fact, Pearl doesn't even know about her, since it's been such a big secret.

"Pearl, I have something to tell you, but you have to promise to keep it a secret."

Her eyes light up with the prospect of gossip. She loves being in the know. "I promise. What is it?"

Alexei looks at me with confusion, but he'll find out in a moment.

"I have a familiar."

"A familiar?"

"Yes. A spirit animal that's bonded to me. That's what these marks on my chest are. Want to meet her?"

"Bitch, of course I do."

"Good, 'cause I want her to roam around a little with us. At least at home here."

I coax Ebony out, and as always, she's a little reluctant with someone new, but seeing as we've been around Pearl a bit lately, it doesn't take as long as normal. Her huge paws hit the ground a moment later, and Pearl sucks in a sharp breath in shock and awe.

"Gods, she's *gorgeous*," she breathes in wonder.

Ebony sticks her head up a bit in pride, and I can tell Pearl has immediately won her over. As if Pearl knows this, she reaches out without hesitation and scratches her behind her ear. Ebony purrs loudly and plops down on the couch next to her, her head in Pearl's lap.

I sit on Ebony's other side and rest my hand on her. I like having her out with us. I need to remember to let her out more often. Sometimes I forget just because she's a part of me. I also have to be careful not to let others see her since the whole "familiar" thing is supposed to be kept secret. There are even some witches who don't know about them.

Alexei sits next to me, and I curl up against his side as I start the movie. I'm once again struck by the feeling of getting something I've always wanted. This sense of normalcy with people I care about.

Pearl swoons as Patrick Swayze comes on screen, and I don't blame her. I think every woman who's ever seen this movie has had a thing for him. They both laugh when the dance training scenes come on screen, finally getting my joke after all these months.

When the movie ends, Alexei and I head to bed, leaving Ebony on the couch cuddled up with Pearl. We finally have enough energy to make love, but make sure to keep quiet since we don't have privacy, and that kind of makes the whole thing more exciting. We fall asleep satisfied in as many ways as possible.

The next morning, I make us all some breakfast and rummage through my closet to find the family pictures. I especially want to show them to Stavros so he can see me growing up, and see how well my adoptive mother took care of me.

We spend the morning eating and going through them. I tell them about the memories attached to the photos, and they learn more about my past. After my dad sees a picture of Eve, he remembers her. He didn't interact with her much, but she does look familiar to him. I don't know why it matters to me, but the fact that he knew her warms my heart.

"So, I was going to take Pearl to a yoga class with me. I don't know if either of you would enjoy it though."

"Is there anything you think we would enjoy while you're doing that?"

"Would you guys want to go on a hike? Explore a little?"

"Yeah, that sounds great," Stavros chimes in.

"Perfect. I can take you guys to a trail, and then Pearl and I can pick you back up after our class."

We all get changed into some workout gear, and I get us all some reusable water bottles from my cupboard. Luckily, I'm a water bottle whore. I drive the guys to my favorite hiking trail, Chautauqua Park. It's in Boulder, and quite the drive, but it will take them longer to hike than it will for us to do the class. Plus, Boulder will be a fun place for them to see after. We can grab lunch and maybe walk around Pearl Street a bit.

When we drop them off, they look up in wonder at the Flatirons. I wave goodbye and tell them I'll see them soon. I roll down the windows and blast some fun dancing music. Pearl and I jam out, and I sing my lungs out as we drive back to Denver for yoga. We probably could've gone somewhere in Boulder, but there's an instructor whose classes I really like going to while I'm here.

We walk into the studio and are immediately greeted by the scents of sage and palo santo. I breathe in deeply, letting it settle my soul, and go up to greet the instructor, Lauren. I always thought she was adorable with her brown and pink hair, tattoos, and sweet personality.

"Ember! How nice to see you! It's been a long time."

"I know, I moved out of town, but I still have my house here so I came back for a visit and brought some people with me. This is my best friend, Pearl. She's never done yoga before."

"Well, I'm so glad I got to see you while you're here, then. And, such a pleasure to meet you, Pearl. I'll be demonstrating most of the moves throughout the class up front, but if you need anything just raise your hand and I'll come around to help." I can see she's a little dazzled by Pearl, just like everyone always is, but she stays professional.

We head into the studio and grab some spots in the back. I figure that it'll be better not being up front that way Pearl can see what everyone else is doing. We set up and I start stretching on my mat. Pearl watches me, and I demonstrate some poses that we are sure to get into.

Lauren comes in soon after, and the class starts. I move and breathe and get into the groove. It's refreshing to have a bit of normalcy after the craziness of the last few months. When we get back to Queridian I should really start doing this on my own. I've always really enjoyed it, and it helps to keep me calm.

I glance over at Pearl, and she's a natural. It's probably because she's a mermaid and the movements of a vinyasa class are so fluid. By the end of the class, she looks like she's been doing this for years.

"Wow, Pearl, you did great!" Lauren tells her after class. "I can't believe that was your first time."

"I'm a natural at most things that require movement," she states like a cocky bitch, winking at her for added effect.

I roll my eyes as Lauren blushes a bit. "Ignore her. We don't let her out in public very often for this very reason."

Lauren chuckles. "It's fine. My best friend Anna is the same way. I find it endearing."

"That name sounds familiar. Does she work at a tattoo shop?" I ask.

"Yes! She's blonde and has just as big of a personality as this one. My other friend Savannah works there too."

"No way! Savannah tattooed me before I left." I show her my arm with the snake and apple. "I loved them. Can you tell them that they made my birthday very special for me?"

She smiles kindly at me. "I will. And good luck, Ember. I hope to see you again soon."

We leave and head back to Boulder to pick up the guys. They're waiting for us when we return. They hop into the car, and I drive us to Pearl Street. We walk around a bit before stopping at a restaurant. It's Boulder so it's a fairly "hippie" meal, but it's fitting since we all just got good workouts in.

When we're finished, we go back to my house and get ready for our night of clubbing. As I suspected, Stavros has no interest in going, and is more than content to stay at my house with a good dinner, along with either a book or a movie. I recommend he watch *The Matrix* if he's in the mood for another movie, but tell him he is absolutely not allowed to watch the third *Back to the Future* until we're able to watch it with him.

Pearl and I shut ourselves in my room to get ready for the evening. Alexei chuckles fondly before plopping down on the couch next to my dad as they turn on the movie. I smile, knowing they're going to love *The Matrix*. What man doesn't?

I get out my curler, excited to show Pearl. While it's heating up, we do our makeup and get dressed. I pick out a short green velvet dress with little gold stars on it. Pearl found a slinky silver sequin creation. It makes her look even more like a mermaid than she already does, and everyone at the club will surely be flocking toward her.

When the curler is ready, I do both of our hair. She's impressed at the result. "I've never seen anything like this before. We have ways of curling our hair at home, but nothing like this. It's amazing."

"I wish we could bring it back with us, but it needs electricity. Ooh! Unless we found one that was solar powered! I don't know if they have those, but we could check." I feel like it's something that exists. I could see that for camping or something. If they don't have it, someone should invent it.

When we're both ready, glimmering, and smelling fantastic, we waltz out into the living room. The guys are utterly invested in the movie, just like I knew they would be. I didn't realize how long it took us to get ready, but apparently a while, because they're at the part where Neo goes to see the oracle.

"Alexei, are you ready?" I ask.

"Hell no. I need to see what happens."

I chuckle, and Pearl and I sit down to finish the movie with them. I feel bad for Pearl since she missed the beginning and is thoroughly confused. I mean, it's not like you can properly describe the start of the movie to someone, especially someone from a different realm that doesn't have electricity, but I try my best.

When it ends, the guys freak out and gush about how good it was. I think to myself that I might've created some monsters by showing them TV. I make Alexei quickly change so we can go, and I grab a book for my dad to read if he wants to while we're gone. I give him *Harry Potter*, figuring he'll enjoy the magic aspect of it, but I think he'll end up watching another movie.

Alexei emerges minutes later in dark jeans and a gray button-up shirt that matches his eyes. We check each other out, and my dad grimaces.

"Get out of here. I don't need to see you ogling each other. Be safe."

I smirk but turn toward the door. "Oh, Dad. Do you want Ebony to keep you company? I don't think she'll enjoy being out in a loud and crowded place." I don't like the idea of leaving him here by himself, even though I know he'll be fine.

"Sure. I would love that."

I smile and let Ebony out. She immediately cuddles up next to him on the couch.

"See you kids tomorrow."

"Night, Dad."

I take us to the Church Nightclub. As you've probably guessed from the name, it's a renovated church. There's a long line out front, but I lead us to the doors. I'm not typically the person to do this kind of thing, but I don't want to wait, and what's the point when I can get us in in two seconds? I use my allure on the bouncer, and we're in. The lights are dim and even though they basically just opened, the place already smells like sweat and booze. We find a table and I go get us some drinks.

I chuckle to myself as a plan forms. I order us the girliest drinks I can think of. They're pink and have fruit and umbrellas in them. I can't wait to see Alexei drink this fuckin' thing. I bring them back to the table, and my mate eyes the glasses with a look of revulsion.

I hand the drinks out, and hold mine in the air between us. "Cheers!"

They clink their glasses with mine, and we all drink. Alexei's eyes widen as he takes in the flavors and the sweetness of it. "This is delicious," he states, although somewhat reluctantly.

"Well, of course. When are you going to learn to trust me? Now drink up. We're going to need some liquid courage for all the dancing we're going to do."

We finish our drinks and then make our way to the dance floor. It's already packed with bodies, and I drag them into the middle, wanting them to have the full experience. "Me Too" by Meghan Trainor comes on and I freak out. This is my *jam*. Alexei and I grind up against each other, and I see Pearl making her way around the crowd and dancing with multiple partners. As expected, everyone is completely smitten with her, and they look thoroughly disappointed when she inevitably moves on to someone else.

We dance for hours, occasionally going back to the table and having more drinks, and by the time the night is over, I'm exhausted and a hot mess. I'm sure half my makeup melted off from the sweat and humidity. I'm sore from yoga earlier, and I'm ready to collapse on my feet. It's too bad that we have Pearl with us, otherwise Alexei and I could just teletravel back to my house, I think longingly. When we finally get home, I collapse into bed, thoroughly spent.

When I wake the next morning, I think to myself that I'm going to need to rest for a week straight after this. I down tons of water and make us a hangover breakfast. Stavros is much too chipper for me this morning, and I take my tea into the bath so I can have some peace and quiet to recover.

It's our last full day here. Tomorrow will be spent traveling back home, and while I'm sad that we're leaving, I'm excited to be going back to Queridian. And I remind myself that we can come back anytime we want. It's convenient that I have this place for us to stay. Almost like a vacation home. I'll just need to remember to bring the important things with me back to the palace.

I want to bring all of my pictures and childhood mementos, along with some of my favorite clothing. When I'm human again, I go out into the living room and we turn on the final *Back to the Future*. The last thing I think I'm going to have us do tonight is go bowling. That's pretty low-key, and it will be fun for them to experience. We take our time since we have all day. We just relax, watch more movies and TV, have a late lunch, and then finally start getting ready. I know there are some fancier places you can go to bowl, but I want them to experience the really run-down, grungy bowling alleys. That's half the fun, right?

I'm delighted to see when we get there that they have the neon lights on and the overhead lights off. I get us a lane, and they cringe when they have to put on the bowling shoes. I show them how it's done, relatively speaking. I've never been a great bowler, but they get the concept.

"This thing is so *heavy*," Pearl complains as she picks up her ball.

"I know. You'll get used to it though."

She lines up like I did, and I smile in anticipation. I know this is going to be ridiculous. Maybe I should've gotten bumpers for them at first. Oh well, too late now. She swings her arm and the ball back then forward, but she releases the ball too late. It flies up and forward before bouncing loudly on the lane. It starts moving toward the pins at a snail's pace, and when it finally gets there, one pin barely topples over.

"I hit one!" she yells in celebration.

I smile at her enthusiasm. "Well done! Now this time, release it a bit sooner."

She nods seriously before grabbing her ball when it makes its way back around. This time, she seems to have a bit better of a grasp on it. She still releases it just a bit too late, but it's much better than the first time, and she knocks down two pins on the opposite side.

We all cheer for her and she blushes in her typical mermaid fashion before taking a bow. Alexei is next and I already know that with his excellent hand-eye coordination and all his weapons training that he's going to do great. He grabs his ball, and swings it back before taking a step forward. When he goes to bring it forward, however, his feet come out from under him. I gasp in shock before rushing up to see if he's all right.

He groans from his place on the floor, but seems fine. I set my hands on him and sweep my healing magic through him just to be sure, and when I find nothing, I laugh a little bit even though I'm trying to hold it in.

"Are you okay?" I ask, even though I know he is.

"Yeah. What happened?"

"You stepped onto the lane. They apply something to make it slippery so the ball glides down it easier."

He starts laughing loudly then, and we all join in. "Well, that bit me in the ass, didn't it?" He stands and takes up his position again. He somehow held on to his ball, and he's able to try it again.

This time he does much better, making sure to stay well away from the slippery flooring. The ball sweeps down the lane, and he takes out three pins on the right side. I knew he'd do well. With the exception of the fall, that is.

His second time around, he's more in the middle and gets all except two on the left side. I fucking *knew* he would kill it. It's his first time bowling and he's already got a better score than I do.

Stavros is next, and nothing of consequence happens. He does well too, although not as good as Alexei.

We continue to play, and I get us a pitcher of beer. We play two games, and everyone gets better. Pearl is easily the worst in the group, but she gets so excited every time she hits a pin that she makes it ten times more fun.

The first game Alexei and I are pretty close together in our score, but the second game he smokes us all. I roll my eyes at the fact that he beat me at a game he just started playing. We turn our shoes in and head back to the house.

"Well, that was really fun. Thank you for taking us and giving us all a wonderful Earth experience," my father says on the drive back.

"Thank you all for coming with me. It was really special sharing this with all of you."

When we get back, I start collecting the things I want to take with me. I grab my favorite sets of clothes, all of my pictures and special mementos, and the multiple portable chargers. Also, I wasn't able to find a solar-powered curler, but I did find one that's cordless and comes with a cartridge. I don't know how long it will last, but I got Pearl and I both one. I figure when we come back I can buy us more cartridges.

I look at my bookcase longingly. I wish I could take them all with me. Maybe I can just take a few every time we come here so I can build up my library back home. For now, I grab my paperback copies of Harry Potter and Throne of Glass. My two favorite series.

When I'm all packed and ready to go, I collapse into bed with Alexei. The next morning I make sure to toss all of the leftover food. Our flight back to Flagstaff is at noon, so we get an Uber to the airport at 9:30.

We're just getting through airport security when I hear my name being called by a familiar voice.

"Miss Ember?"

I turn. I don't recognize him at first, but then I'm shocked. "Chaplain Jenkins?"

He smiles kindly at me. "What did I tell you about calling me that?"

"Sorry, Frank." I give him a hug. "It's so good to see you."

He squeezes me tight. "It's great to see you too, Miss Ember. You look much happier than when I last saw you."

Alexei lets out a growl so low that I know Frank can't hear it. He doesn't understand though. He saw me after my mom died, but not like Chaplain Jenkins did.

"These people behind me would be the reason for that. Frank, this is my father, Stavros, my...boyfriend, Alexei," I say, not having a better term for him at the moment. I don't think he would know what to do with the term "mate." "And my best friend, Pearl."

Frank's eyes widen in shock when he takes in my dad. "You're her father?"

I laugh. Stavros definitely does not look old enough to have a daughter my age. I take pity on him. "Yes. It's a long story, Frank."

"I can see that. I just need to know one thing, Ember. Did you get the answers you were looking for?"

I smile. "I did. And all I can tell you is that we were right."

Excitement and wonder dances behind his eyes. I think back on our meeting at the coffee shop so long ago. When we talked about the possibility of me being from "somewhere else."

"I don't know if I'll see you again, Frank, but I just want to thank you for everything you did for me. It means more than you know."

"You're so welcome, Miss Ember."

I give him another hug, and we go our separate ways.

Now that everyone knows what to expect with flying, the process is a bit smoother and we don't have any problems getting to our destination. Once we reach Flagstaff, I get another Uber. I tell him that we want to go to the Cathedral Rock Vortex. He eyes my bag but doesn't comment as he takes us there.

We hike the Templeton Trail to get to the portal, and I hold tightly to my Queridian necklace. I remember roughly where we came in, but I know that my necklace will guide us once we get closer. The others also have their gems with the Queridian rune carving that allows them to pass through the portal, but mine is the only one that is a piece of jewelry, allowing me to let it hang and guide us.

We reach a section of the trail that looks familiar and the motion sickness hits me. "We're close."

Stavros nods. "I think it's straight ahead, off the trail."

We get closer and my stone flares brightly. "We're here."

26

Ember

Alexei grabs my hand, and we tip into the portal. It's just as disori-enting, but by some miracle I stay on my feet with no help. Pearl and Stavros appear moments later, and we head to the watch station. The guard sees us and runs forward to greet us.

"Your Majesty, welcome back," he says, bowing low.

"Thank you. Rise. If you would prepare our horses, we will be on our way."

"Of course, Your Majesty."

"Thank you," I tell him as he walks away. I sense his surprise, and I wonder how often royalty thanks people for doing their jobs.

He brings our horses out shortly after, and I pet Ash lovingly. "Hi, my pretty girl. Did you miss us?"

She neighs into my hand, and I smile fondly at her. This horse. She has my heart. Alexei comes up and pets her too, making me fall even more in love with him.

Stavros and Pearl give us strange looks, but don't comment. I remember what Alexei told me when I first met her, that people in Queridian don't treat animals like this, or even name them. It makes me sad. I think with Ebony it's different because they know she's a spirit animal, and therefore has more intelligence than regular animals, but that doesn't make them any less special.

We mount and make the trek back to the palace. The trip catches up with me, and before I know it, I'm drifting off against my mate.

It's dark when we reach the Immortal City, but the market is in full swing. The streets are loaded with people, and I'm relieved that we're on the horse and have a little bit of distance from them.

We slowly but surely make our way up to the palace, and we dismount when we see the stables. The stable boy looks up at all of us before zeroing in on Pearl. She gets off her horse and the stable boy holds out a hand to help her. She doesn't need help, but she accepts his hand to be polite, giving him a winning smile. He smiles back, but I'm surprised he isn't beet red. He takes all of the horses from us and leads them into the stables, bowing as he goes.

We head into the palace and are greeted by many, and Humphrey hurries forward to take my bag from me. I thank him and we head to our rooms, thoroughly worn out.

"Ember, a moment before you go to bed?" my dad asks.

I nod and Alexei heads inside to give us some privacy.

"I just want to say thank you. That was a really wonderful trip, and I want you to know that I cherished every moment of it. I'm so lucky to have found you, daughter."

Emotion clogs my throat, making it difficult to respond. "You too, Dad. I'm really glad I got to share all of that with you. I love you."

"I love you too." He gives me a hug and a few tears slip free of my eyes.

We part ways for the night, and I go to sleep with a happy smile on my face. I never thought I would get this again after my mom passed. But it's so special having the love of a parent.

The next day, Alexei and I start my combat training back up. It's refreshing to get my muscles moving and get back into the groove of training. I've been so focused on my ability training that I've been neglecting my combat skills a bit. But now that I'm finished with that, I can put more effort into fighting as well as incorporating my powers with combat. It's an interesting dynamic, and one I'm excited to explore.

Alexei is already talking to the king about expanding the facility and bringing in some of the better ideas from the other territories, particularly Wickshire. He loved their training yard, and really wants to make something similar here as well. It will only improve the guards' skills. Even though they don't have premonition like the witches do, they could still benefit from that type of training, arguably even *more* than the witches.

We spend the next day getting back into our groove, and I like having a routine again. The king is busy catching up on everything he missed while we were gone. I help him a bit, considering I might have to do this stuff eventually. Most of it is boring admin stuff, but I help however I can.

"Thanks for the help, daughter. See you tomorrow."

"Night, Dad."

I head back to our room, and as I'm drifting off for the night I have a sinking feeling in the pit of my stomach. Something is about to go terribly wrong.

27

Stavros

I watch my daughter go with a smile on my face. I don't know what I did to deserve her, but I thank the Gods every day that they brought her to me. She looks just like her mother, especially when her feistiness kicks in.

That was always one of my favorite things about Catalina, and I'm so glad she passed it down to our daughter. I miss her every day, and even more so since Ember came into my life. It would've been so special for us to watch her grow together, and I know Catalina would've absolutely loved how strong she is. What a force she's become.

There's a lightness in my chest that hasn't been there in years. Partly from her presence, and another part from finally being able to talk to someone else about Demonica. I didn't realize how much that secret was weighing on me until I was able to share it with her.

Something about that whole situation has nagged at me since the day I was told about it. I can't put my finger on what exactly. I mean, obviously the whole situation is ludicrous, but it's more than that. Like a word that's on the tip of my tongue that I can never think of. Anytime it crosses my mind, I'm almost driven to insanity.

I push it away for now. Honestly, there's not much we can do about it, or anything, really. I just have to keep doing what's best for the realm, and right now, that's keeping the demons *out*.

I still have a lot of work to catch up on from being gone for a few days, so I burn the midnight oil long after Ember leaves. This has always been my least favorite part of ruling. Unfortunately, it's also the thing I do the most. I have advisors and assistants, of course, but ruling the realm is *my* job. It's also hard to trust anyone else after Mordecai. He was my man. Little did I know, he was *his* man. No one else's. The only person he had any sort of loyalty to was himself.

Every betrayal from him has stung worse. And things have piled on, even after he died. I was shocked when Alexei came to tell me what happened with Vita. Speaking of which, I still have her in the dungeons. I'm not sure what to do with her. I thought about having her executed, but that's never been my style of ruling. For now she's out of the way and not harming anyone. And suffering. Which is fine by me. She caused the girls there more than enough suffering.

Alexei told me that too. I was more than ready for her to be brought here. Of course I had to wait for them to travel here, but my anger only heightened during that time, and when she finally arrived I had her thrown in a cell, unable to look at her.

That was also when Penelope was brought to me. I smile thinking of her. She's the first woman since Catalina who I've been remotely interested in.

Guilt slices through me at the thought. While I was married to Queen Amira, and I respected her deeply, I wasn't in love with her. She was a smart match, but she knew it could never be that way between us. I discussed it with her before we were married, and she understood that I had given my heart to another. We were very close friends though, and it was a good union in that sense. I was lucky to have her.

Nothing's happened between Penelope and me yet, but there's interest there on both sides. It simmers just beneath the surface whenever we spend time together. I've really enjoyed having someone to be with. Someone to curb the loneliness that I've battled for years.

Maybe tomorrow I will finally act on the budding feelings between us. I'll go to her in the morning. With that in mind, I go to bed, eager for the start of a new day.

She comes to my room in the morning for tea. It's become something of a tradition for us, and I enjoy starting my day with her. Today she looks different though, distracted.

"Are you all right, Penelope?"

"I'm not sure. I have a feeling. But every time I try to bring my focus to it, it slips from me. I tried doing some divinations this morning, but it was all gibberish. It has me on edge."

I reach over and squeeze her hand, trying to offer some comfort. "I'm sure everything will be fine."

She meets my gaze and gives me a grateful smile.

"There was something I wanted to discuss with you," I say as nerves spring to life in my stomach. I swallow hard. I don't remember the last time I felt like this. Well, technically I do. Ember's mother, although it was quite a bit stronger. "As I'm sure you've realized, I think I'm falling in love with you. I know that since we aren't the same species it's going to not be looked on kindly, but if you enjoy my company as much as I enjoy yours, I was thinking we could give this thing between us a shot." I don't typically struggle with being articulate, but that was a mess, and I mentally shake my head at myself.

She smiles fondly at me before standing up. I can't tell what she's thinking, but she sits down in my lap, and I tell myself that's a good sign.

"It's about time, Stavros," she says, wrapping her arms around my neck and pulling me in for a kiss.

I'm so shocked that I don't move for a few seconds. She wants this too. It's the first time I've chosen something for *myself* since Catalina.

It feels wonderful. I wrap my arms around her and pull her in closer. Her lips are soft and warm against mine, and I lose myself in the kiss.

After a few moments, I pull back. I trail my thumb along her cheekbone, delighting in the fact that I can touch her like this. "Before we do anything else, I should tell Ember."

She nods in agreement. "Yes. She will likely have an opinion on it. You know where to find me after you've met with her."

I smirk at her before giving her another gentle kiss as my heart flutters in my chest. A giddy smile lights my face for the first time in a long time. We finish breakfast, talking about nothing and everything all at once, and I enjoy the comfortability that's already between us.

When we're finished, I head to the receiving room where I first met Ember. I don't know why I don't go to her rooms, but this is something special. And maybe part of myself wants to remind her of the fact that I'm the king, just in case she's upset with me. I know that sounds petty, but it makes me a little bit more comfortable.

I have Humphrey call for her, and while I wait, I sit in my chair and admire the room. It's all purely decorative, but it's beautiful all the same. As I'm sitting there thinking about what exactly I'm going to say to my daughter, Pearl walks in from the door behind me. I scrunch my face in confusion.

"Pearl. Is there something I can do for you? I was just about to have a meeting with Ember."

Ember walks in at the same moment from the front door. She looks from me to Pearl with a smile on her face.

"Humphrey said you wanted to see me?" she asks.

"Yes. I have some exciting news I wanted to share with you, but it can wait until I hear what Pearl needs." As much as I like the girl, I don't want to have this conversation with my daughter's best friend present.

I look at her in question, but my brain doesn't quite make sense of what I'm seeing. Pearl pulls a knife and, before I can react, flings it at my daughter. I yell in horror, but it cuts off in a gurgle as she swipes a sword across my throat, and everything goes dark.

359

28

Ember

The knife imbeds itself in my stomach and I hunch over in pain. What in the actual *fuck*?! Pearl? Why would she do this? It just doesn't make sense. There's a roaring in my ears, and my heart pounds furiously as I rip the knife out of myself. My healing magic springs to life inside me, sealing over the hole that's penetrated my body, although it can't heal the emotional wound that's been left on my soul. She was my best friend. How could she do this?

When my body is no longer pouring blood onto the floor, I look up, intending to blast her to kingdom come with my magic, but she's fleeing out the side door. It's then that my eyes are drawn to the center of the platform where Stavros was standing moments ago. My body is frozen for what feels like minutes, but I know it's only seconds. Blood. Everywhere.

My mind finally reconnects with my body, and I run to my father. He's collapsed onto the ground, his throat slit so deep that I'm surprised he wasn't decapitated. My magic responds before I do, rushing to my fingertips. I hold them against his neck, my fingers trembling uncontrollably as my anxiety reaches new heights. I can save him. I saved myself and Alexei. I have to have at least *one* parent left.

I pour all of my magic into him, giving him everything I can. Minutes go by that feel like hours, and he still doesn't stir.

"Dad, don't go. Stay with me." Tears finally rush to my eyes, I know what I haven't accepted yet. He's not coming back. "We were just getting to know each other. We have so much more to learn."

My breaths start hiccuping in my body as his lifeless eyes stare back up at me, holding none of the warmth that I've come to know from him. I pour more magic into him, my hands lighting up from the force of it, but it makes no difference. I scream in frustration and grief as my heart shreds. I thought I'd have so much more time with him. Fae are supposed to live hundreds of years. I got only *months* with him.

Pearl's face flashes in my mind, smiling in malicious glee as she threw that knife at me. That fucking *bitch*. I am going to absolutely annihilate her when I get my hands on her. My next scream is a promise to her. That I will find her and make her pay for taking him from me.

Eventually my screams alert the guards, my mate included. They come rushing into the room, taking in the scene with wide shocked eyes. They try to take his body from me, but I'm in full animal mode as I growl at them, covering his body with my own. No one will touch him. I release Ebony from my body, and she immediately guards Stavros and me, not letting anyone near. They back up in fear, raising their hands in a gesture of surrender.

Through the haze of anger, grief, and all-consuming rage, I hear my mate call out to me. He is literally the only thing that could pull me from this.

"Little doe. Let me through. I need to get to you. I need to see what happened to the king."

Ebony looks back at me, her entire loyalty with me, and I know that if I didn't want him to, she wouldn't let Alexei close. I nod, and she lets him pass. He kneels down next to me, his hand rubbing soothing circles on my back. He looks me over, making sure I'm okay. His eyes latch on to the blood on my torso. I have Stavros's blood all over my hands, but I know he can tell that what's on my stomach is from me.

"I healed myself."

He finally looks down at my father. His king. Tears pool in his eyes. "What happened?" he asks me quietly.

I hear a note of darkness and revenge in his voice. That same need rises up in me, and my power hums with the force of it.

"Pearl."

His gaze snaps to mine. "What?!"

"Stavros asked to see me and she was here when I showed up. She threw a knife at me, and once I was down and healing myself, she slit his throat."

The guards all gasp in horror, some of them denying it.

"*You dare to question me?*" my voice rings out through the room, loud and clear.

"No, Your Highness." They bow their heads in respect and fear.

"Not 'Your Highness.' It's now 'Your Majesty,'" Alexei reminds us all.

I suck in a sharp breath. It stabs me in the chest, much like the knife that pierced my skin not long ago. Something occurs to me then. The prophecy was right. Mordecai was right. I'm the end of the fae reign. I'm not just fae. I'm *everything*.

"My first command as your queen: find Pearl and bring her to me."

Author Note

Thank you all for reading! I hope you're enjoying the story. Demonica's story, *A Demon in the Dawn,* will be coming soon, followed by the third and final novel, *A Queen in the Ashes,* so stay tuned! Please remember to leave me a review if you liked it. We indie authors really rely on the support of our readers. Find me on my website at Ljburkhart.com and join my newsletter below!

http://eepurl.com/hRZzz5

Thanks again!

Acknowledgment

Here we go. Another book done. I'll try to come up with something new in this section, but honestly, it'll probably end up the same as my others.

To my husband, thank you for always supporting me in my writing journey. I love you more than words can express.

To my family, thank you for always having my back. I got lucky when the universe gave you to me, and I'm grateful for every one of you. Big shout-out to my sister, Becky. Once again, you have helped me polish this book and make it what it is. I couldn't have done it without you.

To Iris, I love you, bitch. My writing journey would be much harder and more lonely without you.

To my llama ladies, I'm so grateful to have found you all. Having our community is so special to me, and I love all of our get-togethers and fuzzes. Extra shout out to Tracey for giving me the term "my vampire bitch" in reference to Alexei.

To Beth, my editor. Thank you again for your marvelous work. I always look forward to your comments and how you transform my books.

To Les, my graphic designer, thank you again for a beautiful cover. I'm always impressed by your work.

Finally, to you, dear reader. Thank you for joining me on this adventure. I hope you love Ember and Alexei's story as much as I do.

About the Author

L.J. Burkhart is the author of the new novel *An Ember in the Dark.* She writes Contemporary Romance and Fantasy Romance. She has two series; The Fire Series, which includes *Fire & Ink*, *Light Me Up* and *The Fire Inside Me,* and the Realm of Queridian series, which includes *An Ember in the Dark,* and coming soon, *A Blaze in the Shadows.* L.J. has been a lifelong writer, starting with songs and poetry in the third grade, before eventually moving on to novels in her early twenties. When she isn't coming up with dramatic plot twists and steamy sex scenes, you can find her doing yoga, hanging out with her best bitches, baking, or reading, curled up on the couch with her husband and dog with a big glass of red wine.

You can connect with me on:

🌐 https://www.ljburkhart.com

Subscribe to my newsletter:

✉ http://eepurl.com/hRZzz5

366